FRIENDS OF THE
SACRAMENTO
PUBLIC LIBRARY

THIS BOOK WAS DONATED BY
FRIENDS OF THE
CARMICHAEL LIBRARY

The Sacramento Public Library gratefully acknowledges this
contribution to support and improve Library services in the community.

SACRAMENTO PUBLIC LIBRARY

RIDE or DIE

GAIL-AGNES MUSIKAVANHU

Published in the United States by Soho Teen
an imprint of Soho Press, Inc.
227 W 17th Street
New York, NY 10011

Library of Congress Cataloging-in-Publication Data

Musikavanhu, Gail-Agnes, author.
Ride or die / Gail-Agnes Musikavanhu.

1. Risk-taking—Fiction. 2. Best friends—Fiction.
3. Friendship—Fiction. 4. High schools—Fiction. 5. Schools—Fiction.
6. African Americans—Fiction. I. Titles
Classification: LCC PZ7.1.M89345 Ri 2023 | DDC [Fic]—dc23
LC record available at https://lccn.loc.gov/2022050962

ISBN 978-1-64129-420-1
eISBN 978-1-64129-421-8

Interior design: Janine Agro

Printed in the United States of America

10 9 8 7 6 5 4 3 2 1

For the Crystal Angels –
Michal, Bongani, Chloé, and Mutsa
My original ride or dies

CHAPTER

1

TRACK:

SECOND DEMO

It started because I threw the biggest party Woolridge High had ever seen—just to steal a necklace.

"A party?" Cairo asked, collapsing next to me with her lunch tray.

She didn't quite know about the second part yet.

I smiled. "You got my text."

"Text?" Cairo furrowed a brow, crinkling the scatter of dark freckles on her forehead. Our cafeteria's natural lighting did wonders for us all but, like all other lighting, it was especially good to her. "What text? I heard the news from Connor."

I shot her a tired look. As much as I admired Cai's ability to detach from social media and exist apart from her phone, it really messed with the flow of things. I opened my mouth to say this for the thousandth time but was stopped short by a brush on my side and a low voice in my ear.

"The Golden Eagle has been snagged. I repeat, The Golden Eagle has been—"

"Ryan," I interrupted, holding a hand up in his direction without looking at him. "I swear. If you call him by that name one more time, I will force these highly processed Double Stuf Oreos down your throat."

Ryan eased onto the bench next to me, tousling his blond hair as he did. Like any good best friend, he knew just the way to get on my nerves. "Hey, you're the one who dated him," he said with a smug smile.

I winced. There was nothing smart I could say about that, because it was true and I would never live it down.

Tristan Mattaliano was disgustingly wealthy, very good-looking, and the captain of the football team, but I cared for none of these things. I only really dated him because everyone at school kept saying we'd be the ultimate dream Couple of Color, and I loved that powerful image; it made sense to have the most popular guy go out with the most popular girl, right? But you see, Mattaliano was popular for normal things, like his attractiveness and his ability to play sports, whereas I was popular for slightly less conventional things, like cutting Ms. Davenport's hair in her sleep and kidnapping all the animals on my block to stage a Pet Rapture.

We had our wires crossed from the start.

I ripped open my yogurt. "Let's just call him Mattaliano, okay?"

I hated the way everyone at Woolridge said his name; *Tristan Mattaliano,* spoken slowly and with admiration, like it was something to be savored or revered. It was never just "Tristan." It was *Tristan Mattaliano,* or "The Golden Eagle" if you wanted to really show off that you were close with him.

I think the simple knowledge that the latter was a thing was half the reason I broke up with him.

"There are a lot of people who just call him Mattaliano, Lo," Cai said, when I voiced my thoughts aloud.

I scowled. "That's beside the point."

"Either way," Ryan said, looking between us both. "He's been snagged. The venue is secure."

Cairo raised her eyebrows. "Venue? For the party?"

"Wow, Cairo didn't get the text?" Ryan teased. "What a shocking twist of events."

Cai stretched a long, tan arm out to flick Ryan's head, but he dodged out of the way just in time.

"Hey don't hit me, I'm trying to help you!"

He whipped his phone out and spun it across the table to her. She stopped it with impressive agility and squinted at the screen.

Emergency party.
Tonight. At Mattaliano's.
Let everybody know
they're not invited.

Cairo slid the phone back to Ryan. "Well that barely clarified anything."

"We're throwing a party," I explained, yet again. "And thanks to Ryan, the venue has been secured."

"It was actually pretty easy," Ryan said, pulling out his re-usable plastic utensils and his blue lunch container. "All I did was 'accidentally' bump into Mattaliano in the hallway and casually bring up the big party that was happening at his house tonight, making sure to emphasize how lucky he is that you'd planned for it to be at his house before the breakup because, well, we all know you would never have let him anywhere near the party if it wasn't."

I nodded, impressed by his guile. Across the cafeteria, a girl with a custom Perigold lunch box handed out overly priced iced coffees to her friends and pointed in our direction. I smiled at her and waved politely. Looked like news of our party was spreading nicely.

"Mattaliano was completely dumbfounded at first," Ryan continued, "but he played along immediately. Turns out his mother is out of town this weekend."

"She's out of town every weekend," I said. "Most days of the week too."

Cairo grimaced. "Ouch."

Mattaliano's parents were divorced and his mother—a successful businesswoman, NAACP board member, and high-profile motivational speaker—was almost always out of town. Sure, it was sad to know he was alone at home again, but I only allowed myself to pity him for a second. He was the reason I was in this mess in the first place.

"Wait. Hold on . . ." Cairo squinted at me. "You want to throw a last-minute party at your *ex-boyfriend's* house?"

Crap.

I'd been praying the excitement of a potential party would distract them from that part. My hope was to keep them in the dark for as long as I could. Forever, if possible. Ryan especially.

I shrugged, willing myself to look relaxed. "Well. Yeah . . . he lives in a mansion. Didn't we always say he had the best space for a party?"

Cairo scoffed and shook her head. "This is so classically Loli Crawford," she said, dipping her fry into ketchup with more force than necessary. "You can't just do stuff like this, you know. What's that saying? About eating cake? You can't have your cake and eat it too."

I grinned sweetly. "You can if you have two cakes."

Water sputtered out of Ryan's mouth and Cairo smirked.

"I'm gonna ignore that," she said, placing both elbows on the table. "So. What's the plan?"

I relaxed. That's what I loved about Cai. No matter how many questions she needed to ask to get there, she was always down for anything I threw at her.

"I'm gonna get all my usual contacts: my mom's go-to catering company, that party decorator who did my sixteenth birthday, and—you know that kid we usually call for fake ID's and fireworks? Wolf? I'm sure he has college contacts to get us drinks. Which means all you have to do is get the people. A lot of people."

"And you plan on doing that by telling everyone that they're not invited?" Cairo asked skeptically.

"Oh, Dahmani." I rested my face in my palm. "Sweet, sweet, Diamond Dahmani. How do you think the news reached you so fast? I told just three girls about an exclusive super-secret pool party this morning, and the news reached you before my text message could."

Cairo leaned back, impressed. "Touché." Behind her, one of the Dani twins jumped up and scuttled to the other side of the cafeteria. "By that rhetoric, all we really have to do is invite Nate Wilde, Sarah Plaxton, and the theater kids, and by the end of the day the entire school will be buzzing."

"Genius." I smiled and clapped my hands together. "Clean and concise. Perfect."

We had great food, a luxurious venue, pending guests, and the target all lined up. If everything went according to plan, I would have the necklace back in my rightful possession and yet another feat for the history books—all before the start of the weekend.

Ryan turned to face me. "Obviously I'm on music for tonight."

"Obviously," I repeated. "We wouldn't trust anybody else."

He stretched an arm above his head, smiling the most genuinely blissful smile at the prospect of creating a fresh playlist. Ryan lived and breathed music. It was his truest passion, right above staying in trouble and taking care of his car, affectionately named Baby. I glanced at his lunch: an apple, a bottle of water, and a beautifully made chicken salad. Eating healthy was also somewhere up there on his list.

"Gee, *red* onions today?" I commented. "You've been going absolutely crazy with these salads lately."

Ryan rolled his eyes and ignored me, stabbing his fork into a cucumber.

Cairo grabbed my packet of Oreos off the table. "Proximity of carbs," she explained. "I'm not trying to kill you, Ry. I know how deathly allergic you are."

"Ha-ha-ha," Ryan sarcastically droned. "I get it, okay? You guys make fun of my nutritious lunch—which is, by the way, much more delicious than the cardboard our school calls pizza—I shoot out a comeback, we all have a good laugh etc. But can we skip all that today? Can we talk about something else? Like for example, Lo, why the emergency party?"

I stilled.

Ryan took a bite of his salad and looked back at me, waiting for an answer, and as soon as his eyes landed on mine, I knew I couldn't tell him the truth. There was no point in getting him upset when I was on the cusp of getting it all fixed anyway. My plan was falling perfectly into place—ideally, it included him not finding out.

"Really?" I asked, feigning indifference by licking the back of my yogurt lid. "When do I ever need a reason for anything I do?"

There was a second of silence as my friends exchanged a look.

I sighed. "I'm bored!"

"We know, we know," Cairo cut in. "It's the constant state of Loli Crawford; the reason for all your dangerous and impulsive actions." She reached into my packet of Oreos and stuffed a whole one in her mouth. "At least this time we're getting a party out of it and not a court summoning."

Ryan raised an eyebrow and lifted his fork. "Yet."

In retrospect, I think a court summoning would have been easier to deal with.

CHAPTER
2

TRACK:
SHE'S MY COLLAR
Gorillaz (feat. Kali Uchis)

The plan was simple. First, I was going to be a fantastic host. I'd pour drinks to the brim, offer finger foods, laugh at bad jokes, and dance with everyone I could—until Kathy Summers arrived.

Then, when she did, I would welcome her as if she were any other guest, get her whatever she wanted and eventually encourage her to change and get in the pool, sans necklace. I'd take the necklace—*my* necklace—as soon as she was distracted enough.

See? Simple.

I ran the plan over and over again in my mind as I walked around Mattaliano's house with Cairo, topping up everyone's drinks, sprinkling jokes into boring conversations, and stopping to pose for the occasional snap between gentle pushes toward the dance floor, all while keeping my eye out for the high ponytail I'd grown to recognize as a harbinger of Kathy Summers's nauseating presence.

As expected, Ryan used his music magic to mix together a playlist that appealed to everyone in the diverse crowd of retro-snobs, pop junkies, and amateur rap enthusiasts. The dance floor extended all the way from the living room to the foyer—people were pushing to get to it as soon as they walked in.

"Dude." Cai nudged me with her elbow. I turned my attention from a selfie with Deola Merck and watched as another stream of kids poured through the front door.

"That's a loooot of people," Cai muttered.

In the throng, I spotted Jalissa, Brianna, and the rest of what we liked to call our "second-tier" friends: a mixture of popular athletic and performing arts kids. They were all cool enough to hang with in the cafeteria and at parties, but none of them permeated our trio. None of them passed my test.

I clapped hands with a few of them as they passed by and watched as dozens of other kids I didn't recognize trickled in between them. A giddiness bubbled in me as I took it all in, spinning round in wonder. I'd expected a ton of people, sure—some Woolridge upperclassmen and a few brave underclassmen maybe—but I hadn't expected *this*.

"Bro . . ." Cairo leaned against a very expensive-looking table and held her soda out toward the crowd. "This party—"

"I know," I replied.

Someone ran past us with a broomstick and a blond wig.

"Lo, there are college kids here."

"I know."

"Some people are claiming they saw Mr.—" Cairo paused, her eyes flicking above my head. "Uh oh. Your replacement is here. Kathy. Ten o'clock."

I tore my eyes away from the newly blond chandelier. Sure enough, Kathy Summers had entered the room, her springy pony-tail flicking high above the crowd.

Game time.

It took all the self-control I could muster to appear calm and composed as I approached the foyer, when all I really wanted to do was scream. It wasn't that Kathy was Mattaliano's new girlfriend; I couldn't have cared less about that. It was that he *knew* how special that necklace was to me, and he very purposefully gave it to the most difficult person at Woolridge High.

"Kathy," I said, as pleasantly as I could muster. "Come on in."

She narrowed her eyes, scanning the room. "Where's Tristan Mattaliano?"

I counted to five in my head, choosing to overlook the fact that she'd ignored my greeting.

"Uh, I'm not sure," I said. "But can I take your coat? It's pretty hot in here—"

"Ugh, it's boiling," Kathy interrupted.

She shrugged her coat off and folded it over her arm, flicking her hair over her shoulder. As she did, my eyes froze on the glimmering object at her neck. My locket, brilliant and gold and radiant against her skin, on site, just as I'd planned.

The light reflected off the *L*-engraved oval pendant, which was slightly misshapen from decades of wear and tear. I knew because some of those years were mine.

I gritted my teeth, willing myself to look back up at her face. "Well, it is a pool party. So . . . you're in luck."

"Wait, a pool party?" a nearby voice cut in. "I thought this was a costume party."

"Someone told me it was formal."

I cut my eyes at two inappropriately dressed kids lingering awkwardly by the door. "It really doesn't matter," I said. "The point is there's a pool and a hot tub if any of you want to use it. Which you are more than free to do."

Kathy peered beyond me to the window outside. I didn't have to turn around to know what she was seeing: her boyfriend stretching and readying himself for yet another swimming race. She smiled, confirming my suspicion.

"I think I just might," she said. "Where can I get dressed?"

I smiled back, the bass of an electro beat pulsing triumphantly around me. I knew I wouldn't need to tell Ryan; my plan was coming together perfectly.

Scheming was my specialty, after all.

Five minutes later, I stood by the staircase, waiting impatiently for Kathy to get in the pool. She'd gotten dressed in Mattaliano's bedroom and was now walking downstairs with a towel on one arm, the necklace still on her neck. I watched from across the house as she ducked into the coat closet and emerged necklace free.

Her coat. It had to be in her coat pocket.

"—will tell you it's so hard, right, Loli?"

I snapped back to the conversation happening around me, surprised to find six girls watching me expectantly. I'd only latched on to them to look like I wasn't spying on Kathy Summers, but now I was slowly realizing I knew a couple of them from my art class.

"I'm sorry, what did you say?" I said. "I got distracted by the guys outside screaming that last Nicki verse."

"I was just talking about shading and how hard it is," one girl said. "But you're, like, the best in our drawing class."

"Aw." I smiled. *Gina.* Her name was Gina. "Thanks, Gina. I think you're really good too."

In the distance, Kathy tossed her towel over her shoulder and headed outside with a group of her friends, sliding the door to the backyard closed behind her. I watched as they drew nearer to the pool.

Time to move.

"Excuse me," I said to the group. "I have to get a refill."

I cut through the next room, ditching my cup on the way. When I reached the dance floor foyer, I discovered dozens more had arrived. The house was packed to the brim.

I rolled my shoulders back. I could do packed. Packed was good. It meant less chance of being spotted. All that was standing between me and victory was a busy dance floor.

Of course, it was at that exact moment that Ryan decided to play a popular Drake track.

Screams pierced the room as the opening chords announced the song, and the house went wild. People from every corner of the house ran to the dance floor, adding themselves to the expansive sea of bodies between me and the closet. I glanced back at the sliding door across the house—and sucked in my breath.

Kathy was climbing out of the pool with her arms folded, looking very upset. She yanked her towel off the ground, and I watched in horror as she reached for the glass door.

If Kathy decided to wrap up, there was no chance I was getting the necklace back tonight. And if I didn't get it back tonight, who knew when I'd ever have another chance to get it back. My promise would be broken and the necklace gone, forever.

Panicked, I looked toward Ryan at the DJ booth and briefly considered confessing it all. If anyone could fix this mess more efficiently, he could. My missions were always accomplished faster with him. Albeit with a little less flare.

"Loooliii!"

An arm stuck out from the crowded dance floor and grabbed mine, pulling me deep into the hot and sweaty mire. Through the flashes of blue and red light, I caught a glimpse of brown braids and a nose ring.

"Bri?"

Brianna smiled and spun around. "You're a genius! This is the best party I've been to in my entire life!"

"Thanks . . ." I glanced back over my shoulder, searching for Kathy. Through the scatter of raised arms, I was relieved to see her and Mattaliano holding hands, heading back toward the hot tub. Looked like Mattaliano had miraculously calmed his girlfriend.

"Come on, girl!" Bri yelled, grabbing my hand. "Dance!"

On a normal day, she wouldn't have had to ask me twice. Usually, if I wasn't dive-bombing from the roof to the pool or holding a blindfolded truth-or-dare competition in the kitchen, I was making my rounds on the dance floor.

I skimmed an eye over the mass of swaying bodies and realized I might have to do my rounds after all. If I wanted to make it to the other side in this chaos, I was going to have to dance through it.

Falling into step with Brianna, I tactfully grabbed hands with Kyara Vitelli, who twirled me into the middle of the dance circle. One calculated move put me right behind Nate Wilde, who grinned when he saw me and pulled me into his circle at the center of the room. I grimaced, surveying my sticky surroundings. It was just as hot, heavy, and dense as you'd expect the middle of a dance floor to be.

Nate cupped his hands to holler out that line about loving your bed and your mom. I glowered at him, suddenly jealous of his six foot five inches. Not only could he see the closet from where he was, he probably had fresher air up there too. Then I had an idea.

"Hey!" I shouted, inching closer toward him. "Lift me up!"

"What?" Nate asked.

"Up!" I repeated, raising my arms in the air.

Nate grinned. "Ahh. Like at Raycher's?"

"Yes," I said. "Exactly like at Raycher's."

Nate handed me his solo cup and lifted me onto his shoulders, giving me a full view of the closet door over the bouncing heads and waving hands. I wasn't far at all—just a little over halfway there.

I leaned backward, counting on Nate to remember what to do. Sure enough, he shifted me on his shoulder until I felt a different pair of hands grab my back, and then another. Someone rushed to prop my shoulder up as soon as they saw what we were doing, and I wobbled, trying to keep Nate's cup upright as I was lifted higher in the air.

Looking up from the stabilizing cup, I caught Ryan's eye at the DJ booth. He laughed, shaking his head at the sight of me, and I raised my cup in his direction, letting punch slosh over the sides.

I knew what he was thinking. *Typical Lo, soaking in all the attention she can get, as usual.* Well, good. As long as he didn't see through it all and figure out what I was actually doing, he could think whatever he wanted to think.

When I reached the edge of the room, someone delicately lowered me to my feet, right in front of the closet door.

Perfect.

I fixed my dress and cast a sharp look around before slipping into the closet.

Like much of Mattaliano's house, the closet was huge. And it was *dark*. Shades of blue and black swirled all around me, contrasting sharply with the strobe lights outside. I held an arm out to the left and stumbled forward, feeling for the texture of obnoxious fur, leather, and polyester. I pushed aside a cotton sweater and a raincoat, scrambling until my hands landed in a thick plush fluff.

Excited, I brushed my hands down to the pockets, wriggling my fingers in the empty spaces before I made my way to the inner pockets. Almost as soon as my hands slipped through the silky interior, my fingers touched a chain. I gasped, bringing it out on my palm.

The necklace.

My necklace.

I breathed a sigh of relief and held it to my chest before collapsing to the ground. Mission accomplished.

Then: another sigh.

Not mine.

I blinked into the dark. "Hello?"

A sharp exhale, the ruffle of a few coats. "Hi."

I sat up straight, alert and searching in the dark. "What the hell?"

"What?"

"Who's that?"

"I was here first." The voice paused. "Who are you?"

"Who am I?" I repeated, incredulous. "What the hell are you doing sitting in a closet? At a party?"

"I could ask you the same thing," the mysterious voice shot back. "Actually, I can do you one better: what the hell are you doing stealing from someone's jacket at a party?"

I gripped the necklace tighter and opened my mouth to retaliate but then I closed it. They had a point, whoever they were. I squinted, trying to make out who they could be, but all I saw was darkness.

"Sometimes," I started, "to see is to be deceived."

"So . . . I didn't just see the shadow of your hand steal something from someone's jacket?"

"You only see that which you interpret yourself to have seen."

Silence. Then a laugh. "Touché."

I relaxed—slightly. The person belonging to the voice leaned against some especially noisy jackets. I was considering making my escape when, in a completely disinterested tone, the voice said, "Whether you're stealing or not doesn't matter to me at all."

"Oh, really?" I asked.

"Sure. I'm an amenable guy. I'm more interested in why."

"Well," I said, straining to pull myself to my feet in the pitch black. Who knew how much time I had left before Kathy and Mattaliano's next argument sent her straight to the closet. "That should be something interesting for you to ponder as you continue to sit alone in this closet by yourself, like a creep."

I would've left right then if he hadn't said what he said next.

"Probably for the best," he said. "I'm guessing the story I've made up in my head is far more entertaining than the truth."

I stopped and turned around to face the deep end of the closet. "You think?"

"I know," he replied. "Almost all fictional stories are better than real ones."

"Well that's just not true at all," I retaliated. "It's the real-life stories that are the most interesting. They're the only ones that give you any reason to be shocked or entertained, because they happened. And that's a weight no made-up thing could ever achieve."

Silence.

"We'll agree to disagree," he said.

I shifted on my feet and glanced at the door, squeezing the necklace in my palm. I could leave now, victorious, with plenty of time left to enjoy the party . . .

But a few seconds couldn't hurt, right?

I sat myself back down on the ground.

"Okay then," I began. "Let's hear your hypothesis."

The mystery voice cleared its throat. "I would guess that you're stealing someone's car keys?"

"Really . . ." I said.

"Either that," he continued quickly, "or a flash drive with top secret government information that you know your best friend has been harboring because you recently discovered she's not really a teenager but a spy, and you caught her slipping a drive labeled Top Secret: Woolridge UFO Landing Investigation in her coat before you arrived at this party."

I laughed. "That one's interesting, I'll give you that."

And then, maybe because he was intriguing—a rarity for someone in Woolridge Grove—or maybe because I wanted somebody to know about the feat I'd managed to pull, I decided to tell him the truth.

I pushed a pair of Valentino boots out of the way (patent leather gloss with a VLogo is easy to spot, even in the dark) and stretched my legs out in front of me.

"Getting comfortable?" he asked. "You sure you want to sit in a closet at a party?"

I leaned back. "If there's anything you need to know about me, Mysterious Voice, it's that I stay wherever the fun is. And I've found that people—especially the ones out there—are often more boring than not."

"Huh," he said, his voicing piquing with interest. "Well. I'm glad you seem to think I'm fun."

"Don't flatter yourself," I replied, flatly. "I'm only staying because of the mystery. Who are you anyway?" I shifted uncomfortably. "And why were you sitting alone in this stuffy closet?"

"If the answers to those two questions are the only things keeping me interesting, I'm not telling you."

I smiled. "Good point, Mysterious Voice in the Closet. Is it okay if I call you MV for short?"

"Yes, please. Mysterious Voice in the Closet was my father."

I chuckled and then stopped. Gross. We were just one flirtation short of turning into an overplayed cliché (teens hooking up in a closet? Shocking), and there's absolutely nothing I hate more than a cliché.

"Okay," I started, changing the tone of the conversation. "Do you want to know the real story behind why I'm stealing this necklace?"

Mysterious Voice was silent as he considered my question. Contemplation. Yet another rarity in Woolridge.

"No," he decided. "I'm happy with my story. Don't want you ruining it with the boring details."

"I guarantee the truth is at least on the same level of excitement as your story," I said.

"That's a hard thing to guarantee," he replied. "Especially considering the fact that as soon as you disclosed that the stolen object was a necklace, about half of my interest fell away. The magic of the mystery is gone."

I brushed off the insult. "I'll tell you the story and then you can be the judge."

"Okay," he said, breathing out. "I'm all ears."

I paused, soaking in the feeling you get the moment before you tell a good story. My favorite feeling in the world. Then, I took a deep breath and said the truth out loud for the first time.

"I made this party up this morning so I could attend it and steal back my stolen necklace."

There was a rustle of coats. "Wait . . . what? You threw this party? To steal a piece of jewelry?"

"Not to steal it," I clarified, "to take it back. I made the mistake of leaving it at my ex's house the day I broke up with him."

"And what, you couldn't just ask for it back?"

"Ask for it back?" I laughed. "Where's the fun in that?"

Somewhere in the dark there was a puff of air. Amused? Disgusted? I couldn't tell.

"It was revenge," I continued. "My ex knows I love this necklace more than anything in the entire world. He also knows that the person he gave it to wouldn't let go of it without a fight."

"Why? If the necklace was yours to begin with?"

I paused. I wasn't about to explain the long and complicated Crawford-Summers history to a stranger. Partly because it was boring and partly because it was a history in which I was often in the wrong, no matter how much Kathy deserved it.

"She . . ." I started carefully, "isn't exactly known for her ability to listen to fairness, reason, and logic."

This was true.

If I'd confronted her the moment I'd noticed my necklace glimmering on her neck earlier that morning, not only would she have refused to give it back, but she would have doubled down on ensuring that it never left her sight. She would finally have had something over me that I actually cared about, and I wasn't about to give her that. So, that morning, as she sauntered into my English class with a bright smile and a sleeveless low-cut shirt, I forced myself to say nothing.

I endured her friends "ohh"ing and "ahh"ing as she showed it off; I kept quiet as she told them she'd never take it off ("unless I had to, like, swim or go in a hot tub"); I refrained from laughing when she told them how sweet Tristan was; and I didn't even snort when she claimed the custom engraved *L* stood for love. But when Emma Hall lifted the pendant from Kathy's neckline, thumbing her nail along its edge as she questioned whether the locket opened or not, I finally cracked.

First of all, the *L* did *not* stand for love; it stood for Loli. I'd had it personalized right after Ryan gave it to me as a symbol of our friendship in the fourth grade. The necklace was a Pope family heirloom that had been handed to Ryan after his grandmother had had no luck with having any daughters or granddaughters. When it came into his possession, he gave it to me—his best friend. But he made me promise two things: one, to never ever lose it and two, to never ever try to open the locket. At least, not until he said I could. I knew the key was somewhere up in the Pope's attic, but I liked the mystery of it. It was like another gift waiting to be unwrapped. I agreed and we wrapped pinkies on it: *"friends for life, ride or die"* as we used to say.

And Ryan and I never broke our pinky promises.

"So . . ." Mysterious Voice interrupted.

I snapped back to reality and cleared my throat.

"Right," I continued. "So I came up with a last-minute plan.

This girl had mentioned that she'd only ever take the necklace off if she ever had to swim or soak, so I used this information to my advantage. I stormed up to her, pretending to be furious because I'd heard her talking about swimming, and the pool party that was happening at her boyfriend's house that evening was supposed to be exclusive . . ."

I shrugged. "Jealousy and insecurity did the rest. She didn't want to seem clueless about the party in front of her friends, so she played along."

"Man," the voice said. "That necklace must be quite something—can I see it?"

I blinked, slightly taken aback. People didn't typically just go along with my antics. They were almost always either in awe, shock, or complete disapproval. Yet here the Voice was treating the situation like it was completely normal.

I raised my fist and reached out for his hand in the darkness. When I found it, warm, fingers outspread, I placed my free hand under his and lowered the necklace onto the center of his palm. He laughed.

"I didn't think that one out too carefully," he said. "No good asking to see something in the dark."

I laughed quietly. "Well it's not much to look at. Just a small necklace from a friend."

Of course, it was much bigger than that, but again, I wasn't about to tell my life's story to a stranger in a closet.

"So why a party?" he asked.

"Didn't I just explain—"

"I mean you could've stolen it back any other way. It didn't have to be this complicated and extravagant. Why the drama?"

I laughed. "Do you go to Woolridge High?"

"Unfortunately," Mysterious Voice responded. "For almost a year now. Why do you ask?"

"Just . . . because if you knew me, you wouldn't bother asking that question."

"Why?" he asked. "Who are you?"

I hesitated. I knew he didn't mean my name. It was more a *what* are you, or a *why*. And it was weird: I'd never had to explain myself to someone who didn't know me before. Everyone just knew that this was how I was. Unstable. Unpredictable. Truant.

"Someone who lives for her next adrenaline fix, I guess."

The stranger laughed. "Really?" he asked.

"I have a deadly illness," I sighed. "This party is just one of my daily prescribed shots."

"Sounds dangerous."

"Boredom is more dangerous, believe me," I said. "I need peril and chaos just to get by."

He laughed again and I wished I was being funny.

Silence.

"You have a point," he said after a while. "Real stories take the cake. What fiction could possibly top the real-life story of a girl who threw a huge party all for a necklace?"

I smiled, flattered. "If we're being honest, it was really all for an important friendship—not so much a random necklace. But you know the saying: '*Oftentimes, symbols of love become its face.*'"

Mysterious Voice took a sharp breath in. "You read Edward North?"

I paused. "Who?"

"That quote," he said. "It's from *Perfect Resistance*."

"Oh, no," I said, laughing. "I only know that quote because I see it on the wall of my favorite coffee shop every Saturday morning."

There was a loud bang on the closet door. I straightened, suddenly alert. How long had I been sitting in the closet? The bang repeated, and I heard Frances Henry's voice on the other end. I had to get out of there. Frances was Kathy's best friend.

"I've got to go," I said, shuffling onto my feet. "Great meeting you, Mysterious Voice."

"And you, Necklace Thief."

"No, please. It's just Thief. Necklace Thief was my mother." I quickly straightened my outfit. "Good luck with your . . . shoe sniffing, or people spying or whatever the hell you're doing in here."

I found the door handle in the dark and cracked it open a smidge, darting back out into the party in one swift move. The party was raging on more than before: the dance floor was impossibly stacked, the chandelier now had a kid on it, and someone was doing a keg stand off the diving board outside. No sign of Kathy.

I breathed a sigh of relief, feeling pleased. I really was a genius, wasn't I? Now that my mission was accomplished, I could kick back and let loose—and what better way to let loose than to take my rightful place as the belle of the ball, dancing, flirting, singing, and posting stories to my heart's content? But first, I had to find Ryan and Cairo.

After elbowing my way through a dougie contest, I made it to the floor-length mirror in the entrance hall to give myself a quick once-over in case anything had fallen out of place in the closet. Everything looked good, of course—until my eyes fell onto my bare neck.

Bare.

I glanced down at my open hands in shock and patted my sides, then reached into my bra. Nothing.

The Mysterious Voice.

Heart pounding, I retraced my steps back to the closet and threw the door open, panting as I watched my shadow collapse against the door frame. The Mysterious Voice wasn't there. Neither was the necklace.

I touched a hand to my neck and leaned against the closet door.

There was no way I'd find him again. I'd lost the necklace, forever.

Great. I'd thrown the biggest, baddest party in Woolridge Grove history, and all for nothing, I thought, slamming the closet door closed.

It's kind of hilarious how wrong I was.

CHAPTER
3

TRACK:
PROMISES
Aly & AJ

It was impossible for me to enjoy myself at Mattaliano's after losing the necklace again, so I caught a ride home. I watched the rest of the wild happenings unfold through various snaps and stories as I wiped my makeup off and secured my hair in a silk wrap.

With one hand, I tapped through multiple POV shots of Robbie's soon-to-be-infamous double backflip off the roof. On his story, Nate zoomed in on a flash of white in the backyard with the caption *Adrian lost his clothes!*

At least some people had fun.

My phone buzzed and two texts came through in quick succession: the first from Ryan, the second from Cairo.

> Hey, you sure you're good? I had a whole lot of Megan queued up just for you.

R

> sorry about your headache. i'll let u know if anything spicy happens

C

I tossed my phone aside. I should've been there, celebrating the successful reunion of myself and my necklace by dancing on tables and instigating mischief with Ryan and Cairo.

How could I have left that closet without the one thing I went there for? It was so unlike me to be distracted by a boy—how had I messed up so dismally?

I played the scene in my head and the answer suddenly crystallized: the stranger must have done it on purpose. He'd wrangled the necklace into his grasp and distracted me with chatter before making a run for it the first chance he got. I felt a flash of anger, followed by a dull pang in my chest.

What on earth was I going to say to Ryan?

I shut my eyes, trying not to imagine the hurt-but-trying-not-to-be-hurt expression he would have on his face when I told him I'd lost the locket. Shockingly, trying not to imagine it only made it worse.

I sighed and reached for my phone in search of a distraction that was louder than my thoughts, and for the next few hours, I scrolled through an endless parade of party videos and internet content.

I must've fallen asleep at some point because the next thing I knew, I was awoken by the Saturday morning sound of my parents making breakfast. I didn't know which noise bothered me more: the metallic whir of the blender downstairs—my mother's breakfast smoothie—or the annoyingly chipper music my father insisted on playing every weekend morning as he cooked.

Today, instead of the usual soft jazz or the sweet and delicate sound of "Clair de Lune," an unnervingly current-sounding pop-synth melody floated up the stairs. I frowned, glancing at my phone, then groaned when the glowing notification confirmed my suspicions.

I'd been receiving a notification for Ryan's song of the day every morning since he'd discovered there was an app for that. He'd created a queue of 365 songs (subject to change upon new discoveries, obsessions, and changes of mood) every New Year's Day for the last three years, and the list was exclusively shared with Cairo and me.

At least I had *thought* it was exclusively shared with Cairo and me. Between this week and last, I was starting to think the merging of Dad's Saturday morning tunes and Ryan's song of the day weren't quite the coincidence I'd initially thought it was.

The smell of coffee and bacon wafted its way up the stairs, and I sighed as another kitchen appliance started to screech. I knew I wasn't going to get any more sleep, so I kicked my sheets off, rolled out of bed, and got dressed.

Downstairs, Dad was sitting at the table reading on his tablet, and Mom was just finishing up frying some egg white and spinach concoction. She'd retired from an acting career at thirty-six to start a home and lifestyle magazine, but she'd never retired from maintaining her figure. My father, a film industry executive, didn't care what he ate. But he did care about his hundreds of work emails and news roundups.

"And she lives!" my mother sang, scraping a perfectly white circle off the pan and plopping it on her plate.

Dad looked over his glasses. "Better yet, she exists!"

"Only barely," I mumbled. I slumped into my seat and took a swig of orange juice. "Do you always have to make so much noise?"

"Only on the days you come in at two A.M.," my mother answered. "Really, Loli? Two?"

I shrugged and took a bite out of my toast. "I texted you. Emergency party."

Mom brought the plate of eggs and a jar of green smoothie to the table. "An emergency party. I don't even want to know what that entails."

"Hey—you're lucky I actually tell you what I'm doing most of the time. Do you want me to be like other kids, lying about some project I have? Or about how I'm 'sleeping over at Becca's?'"

"The only reason you don't do that is because your 'Becca' is Ryan, and we've learned that if you're sleeping over at Ryan's last minute, it's very likely that something worrying has gone down. Or is about to."

I smirked.

We used to get away with it when we were younger. We'd coordinate which house was the "safest" (a.k.a. most parent-free) and then watch R-rated movies, or sneak off to high school parties in middle school, or do dares around the neighborhood. It worked perfectly—at least until the time we told our parents we were sleeping at each other's houses and managed to skip a full week of school to go to Disneyland. The Minnie Mouse figurine was still sitting proudly on my bedroom shelf.

"Hey," Dad said, "as much as the Popes are part of this family, and as much as I love Ryan, I think sleeping over there is a red flag, last minute or not."

He raised his eyebrows and placed his tablet on the table. I rolled my eyes.

"I'm not talking about this again." I scowled. Though we all knew that I was definitely talking about it again because I hated. *Hated.* Absolutely *loathed* when people questioned my friendship with Ryan. Not only did it make my blood boil to think that people still thought it wasn't possible for a girl and guy to be anything other than romantically involved, it also annoyed me that people would ever think that I, Loli Crawford, could ever lower myself to be so much of a teenage cliché. And, like I said before, there is nothing I hate more than a cliché.

"Dad, take a step outside sometime. Go on Twitter, stalk a few blogs. This is the twenty-first century, and I'm running out of examples and reasons for how a girl and guy could be friends and it could have nothing to do with romance at all."

My parents shared a look.

"Come on," I said, exasperated. "What's it going to take? Is it going to be like this forever until one of us gets married?"

I stood up and placed a peppered egg white circle on my buttered slice of toast.

"What?" my father exclaimed. "Is sh—where are you off to?"

"Westerns," my mother and I said simultaneously.

"You're not going to finish your breakfast?" he asked.

"I am," I said, heading toward the door. "I'm just going to do it on the way to Westerns."

I reached to grab my car keys from their hook, but as I did, the stabbing pain of remembrance shot through my chest. Images flashed of me handing over my keys and stomping upstairs. The phrase, "three months or else indefinitely" echoed in my ears.

I lowered my hand from the empty space on the wall, rearranged my face as I turned around and tried to smile as sweetly as possible. "Mom?"

"No."

"Dad—"

"No."

"If I promise to drive there by myself and be back in less than two hours?"

"No."

"Please? I'll—I'll." I hesitated. "I'll turn my location on?"

My mother raised her eyebrows. "Really?" she asked, impressed with where this was going. "Okay. But no friends."

I dropped my shoulders. "What, you think I'm going to uncontrollably jump on top of the vehicle as soon as someone else is in the car with me?"

They both stared at me blankly. No crack of a smile this time. They had forgiven the speeding tickets, the dents and the scratches, they had even forgiven me for driving donuts in the school parking lot last year. But as soon as they found out that I was the reason Noel Sang ended up in the hospital after our car-surfing race, they put the hammer down and took my keys. Ryan had been largely responsible too, but I took the blame for both of us to save him from being grounded before his band could perform at our annual "Battle of the Bands."

It was all a bit dramatic if you ask me. No one died. Noel just freaked out and curled up in the fetal position on top of Ryan's car, hyperventilating—the rest of us were perfectly fine.

My mother smoothed her already perfect never-out-of-place bob and fixed her gaze on me. "You know the drill," she said.

She left the kitchen and came back with my confiscated car keys, dangling them in the air until I made a point of turning my location on. Satisfied, she placed the keys in my hand. I grabbed my bag and went for the door. "I'll be two hours!" I shouted back at them.

"Yeah, right," my mom shouted. "We stopped counting on your idea of time frame a long time ago."

After the abject failure of the previous night, I desperately needed a Plan B for getting my necklace back. But as I drove the familiar route to Westerns, it dawned on me that I was perfectly screwed. There was no way I'd ever find my necklace without a lead, or a prospect or even the faintest clue for where to start looking. How was I supposed to find someone I didn't know?

I bit my lip. No. I wasn't going to think about that. I was going to enjoy my Saturday morning, the way I deserved, by distracting myself at Westerns. The answer would come to me eventually. In the end, it always did.

I had discovered Westerns, the perfect grungy hole-in-the-wall coffee shop, while driving back from my previous getaway spot, a tattoo parlor called Ink About It. I used to sit with Reese, the owner, and sketch as he inked people. It was fun for a while—he even let me get some pokes in on his employees—but the whole point of having a getaway space was to actually get away from everything. To sit alone, plug into Ryan's playlist of the week, and just sketch. I'd gone from diners to playgrounds and skate parks before the tattoo parlor, and now it was Westerns, the unconventionally tacky and earthy little café that was so far away and so un-Woolridge that I never had to worry that I'd bump into anyone.

I hopped out of my car, surveying the parking lot over my rose-tinted sunglasses. It wasn't the cutest café in the world—the pavement outside was disintegrating, and the crumbling alley walls were covered in graffiti—but to me, it was a breath of fresh air compared to the perfectly manicured, pruned, and trimmed suburbs of Woolridge. Most Woolridge kids wouldn't be caught dead at Westerns.

Inside, I ordered a cappuccino, sat down in my usual corner, and was just about to make the first stroke in my sketch pad when I felt a tap on my shoulder.

"Um . . . excuse me?"

I pulled an earphone out and glanced up, annoyed at having been disturbed. A girl I'd never seen before was holding a piece of blue paper and looking slightly uncomfortable. "Um . . . Are you Robyn?"

"Robyn?" I repeated, narrowing my eyes.

"Yes, Robyn," the girl said. A flicker of doubt crossed her face. "Although it sounded like he said Robber but . . . that can't be it. Do you know a Mr. Reeyus?" She paused and read from the envelope in her hand. "Mr. Reeyus Voyce—"

"Look," I cut in, trying to still my irritation at being disturbed. "I'm not Robyn, okay?"

"Are you sure?" she asked. "He said that a girl who would recognize that name would come in this morning. Said I should remind you that you met last night in—I don't remember . . . something about being in a dark place?

Something pricked in my chest. I took out my other earphone. "Mysterious Voice?" I asked in disbelief.

"Yeah!" The girl looked relieved. "That's him. You know him?"

I nodded slowly, incredulous.

"Then this is for you."

She handed the envelope to me. Wordlessly, I took it from her.

A thousand questions whirled around in my head as I turned the envelope over in my hands. It was ink blue, an unusual color for an envelope, and the thick cursive script across the back was beautiful, yet foreboding.

For: Robyn

I scanned the coffee shop in search of anyone who looked suspicious or like they were enjoying this at all, but no one was paying me any attention. How did he know where I was? My gaze drifted along the café walls, and my eyes caught on the words written in cursive toward the back:

Oftentimes, symbols of love become its face.

My mind flashed back to the closet, my near-parting words, someone hitting against the door.

Of course.

One of the last things I'd shared in the closet was that exact quote, which I'd told him was on the wall of my favorite coffee shop. The one I went to every Saturday morning.

Maybe Mom had a point about sharing personal information with strangers.

I ripped the envelope open and shook the contents onto my lap. A neatly folded piece of paper fell out, and on top of it, a sliver of something small and shiny. I gasped.

It was my necklace: shimmering in perfect gold.

I picked it up, relief flooding through me. I'd been spared hours of fruitless searching and, most importantly, the horrible heartache of disappointing Ryan. I hadn't broken my promise after all.

Then, curious about what else was in the envelope, I turned my attention to the paper.

Dearest Robber,

the letter began. The two words were beautifully calligraphed, but the rest were written in a normal and surprisingly neat hand.

I thought about what you said last night, and I think you're right: life does get a bit dull sometimes. So why don't we spice it up and play a game? It's a little rough around the edges since I've just made it up, but the rules are simple—

THE RULES:

1. <u>Set a mission for the other person to accomplish</u>. This could be a dare to complete, a code to crack, a riddle to solve. Something exciting and worthwhile.

2. <u>Leave a package to be collected on each mission</u>. Like this letter. Congratulations, you've just collected your first one.

3. <u>Do not, under any circumstances, give your identity away, or try to figure out who the other person is</u>. Because where's the fun in that? Let's resolve to just be two strangers on a mission to make life as not boring as possible.

Leave a response with the cashier so I know you're in.

(If you're really in, you won't ask her what I look like)

Yours anonymously,
Mysterious Voice

I lowered the letter and lifted the necklace between my fingers, running a thumb over the engraved *L* as I attempted to sort through my conflicting emotions. The Mysterious Voice had taken the thing that was the most precious from me, and now he wanted to play a *game*? I clipped the necklace around my neck, irritated by his gall. But when I lifted the letter to read through it a second time, my annoyance was overtaken by curiosity. Excitement even.

It was a mystery, some blurred lines, a whole world of possibilities that I could lose myself in. I reread the rules of the game. They weren't perfect—they needed higher stakes, and a touch more adventure—but I knew just how to fix it.

I ripped out a fresh sheet of paper from my sketchbook, dug out my best ink pen, and started to write.

Dear Mr. Voyce.

I'm in.

CHAPTER
4

TRACK:
CAPE COD KWASSA KWASSA
Vampire Weekend

"I just can't believe Thade Logan actually came to our party . . ."

"Hmm," I replied, scrolling on my phone. It was Ryan's third time saying this, so I didn't think it warranted a third reaction. The delicious smell of breakfast filled the air: turkey bacon, fresh coffee, and eggs. Real eggs. Not the stiff white stuff my mother always made.

After giving the barista my response to The Mysterious Voice's letter—or "MV" as I decided to call him—I had texted Ryan and Cairo to meet up at Ryan's for an urgent post-party catch-up. I couldn't stand to be alone with the mixture of excitement, relief, and slight element of ire fiercely bubbling within me. Now that I wasn't wallowing in defeat, I could tell them about the mysterious stranger, his letter, and the intriguing game he had proposed.

I sat in my usual spot in the Pope's kitchen: on the counter by the stove, swinging my legs in time to Ryan's music as he cooked. He nodded his sleep-disheveled blond head in time to the music, letting the beat of the song control his every movement as he grabbed the saltshaker. He looked like the classic ray of Pope light that he was, even in sweats and an old hoodie from the basketball team. Beams of sunlight danced across his golden hair from the skylight above, bending and leaping to the carefree sound of sunny indie pop.

There was never a time I was with Ryan and there wasn't music playing. Having music constantly playing in the background could be distracting at times, but at other times Ryan's playlist would align perfectly with our lives, like it was right now, and everything felt full of beauty and purpose.

The timer on the oven beeped and Ryan sighed. "Cody!" he yelled. "Your chicken nuggets have been done for like an hour!"

Cody, Ryan's ten-year-old brother, yelled something incoherent down the staircase and Ryan resumed his cooking, tapping the timer off.

"You know, I'm practically a celebrity," he continued, shoving his spatula underneath the omelet. "Thade vlogged me kicking Sam out of the party for smoking, and that guy gets views in the millions."

I laughed. "Nice. Now you'll be known as the guy who kicked someone out of a party on Thade Logan's vlog."

Ryan turned away from the stove. "I'm sorry—did *you* get Thade Logan's number last night?"

I stopped swinging my legs. "You got his number?"

"Yeah," he said, turning to scoop the omelet out of the pan. "He says he wants us to invite him when we throw another party."

"Okay, that is kinda cool," I admitted.

"Right? I think it'd be fun having the number of a guy like that for future exploits."

"Or for opportunities with your band," I pointed out.

Ryan pointed his spatula at me. "You're a genius. That guy posts thirst traps to a new video sound almost every day—Basilica's big break could be one video-sharing-app sound away."

I snorted. "Imagine Thade grinding to 'Don't You Cry.'"

Ryan grinned. "I think it's doable. Hell, I'll do it myself if it'll get us more plays."

He placed the omelet on a plate and handed it to me before grabbing his. My stomach growled. It was nearing midday already and Mom's breakfast seemed centuries away. Jumping off the countertop, I followed him to the kitchen table where Mrs. Pope had left orange place mats, silverware, and bulbous glasses filled with orange juice.

Things were always perfect in the Pope household. Even the sunshine seemed to bounce at an angle carefully calculated by Helen Pope, scattering golden specks around the kitchen.

Ryan reached for a fork. "By the way, have you heard about the crazy things that went down last night?"

I froze at the mention of last night, triggered by the all-too-fresh memory of having almost broken our promise. But when I glanced at him, Ryan seemed just as oblivious as he had been the day before.

"I mean, yeah," I said, grabbing a fork. "I think I saw a few videos last night . . ."

Ryan stopped cutting into his omelet and looked at me. "Oh man. You don't know."

"Don't know what?"

"That our party practically imploded all of Woolridge High?"

He dug his phone from his pocket. "Did you know that Robbie Cage almost died jumping into the pool from the rooftop? Or that Brianna found out that Audrey Han is her half sister?"

"What?" I started. "Wait, how—"

"They put the pieces together during a particularly thrilling round of truth or dare." Ryan slid his phone across the table. I grabbed it and scrolled through the tweets on his timeline.

"The way people are talking about the party . . ." Ryan struggled for words. "It's like no one walked out the same. It broke social boundaries, it ruined reputations, dissolved lifelong grudges . . ."

I frowned at a picture of Ellen Chase and Rick McCurdy dancing arm in arm—I hadn't seen those two in the same room since the leaked-number incident freshman year.

"These stories are wild, Loli," Ryan continued. "Some people claim to have seen Mr. Robinson duck in and out of the party with sunglasses and a carton of milk."

I looked up. "The physics teacher? You're kidding," I said, feeling a sick sense of glee.

Ryan shook his head. "Not one bit. I heard from a good number of credible witnesses."

"Credible witnesses like this?" I angled the phone so he could see the tweet I had tapped on. It was a tweet by Channing Adler, one of the senior lacrosse players at our school.

 Channing Adler
@Chadler

Yo speaking of that party at #Mattalianos . . . d d anyone else see Superman riding a UFO outside by the pool?

Ryan rolled his eyes. "I'm being serious. You can ask people yourself."

I turned the screen back around and scrolled further down the timeline of posts tagged #Mattalianos.

"It looks like it's become a running joke to post the most ridiculous thing you can imagine with that hashtag," I said.

"I know," Ryan said. "I'm not surprised that it's reached local, niche-meme stage."

I scrolled through dozens of tweets, reading a couple of the funny ones out loud, until I reached one that stopped me in my tracks. I looked back up at Ryan.

Somehow, he was already halfway through his plate of food. I watched as he downed a glass of OJ and reached to pour himself another.

"So . . ." I started, nonchalantly. I had to tread carefully if I wanted to get the full scoop. "Did you really hook up with Julia Flynn last night?"

Ryan stopped chewing and stared blankly. "What?"

"According to @Nicolacola there's a rumor that someone saw you two alone together at the party," I said, wiggling an eyebrow.

Ryan resumed his chewing. "Well there are about six million of those flying around right now."

Judging from the look on his face, I'd tried, and failed, to broach the topic lightly—again. Ryan was always skittish about his love life. Even way back in fifth grade when our friend group planned to give Valentine's Day gifts to our crushes, he tore his card up before anyone had a chance to see who it was for.

Ryan blinked a few times before looking up and then back down at his plate. "Julia Flynn?" he repeated.

He cut into his bacon, nodding slowly, and then he must've been hit with a new wave of distaste for this rumor because he dropped his knife and fork and looked back up at me, annoyed. "Really, Lo?" he said. "Julia Flynn?"

"What!" I exclaimed innocently. "I mean it makes sense. Didn't you have a crush on her one time?"

In fact, Julia was the one person Ryan had ever actually admitted to having a crush on. It made sense—he was particular about everything he cared deeply about, like music and food.

I could've used some of his romantic discretion.

"Well, I know she likes you," I continued. "And you're a good-looking young man . . ."

Ryan shuddered and I stifled a laugh.

"No," he said. "Absolutely not. There's nothing to say about Julia. And please never use that tone of voice again. You sound like an overly invested mother trying to catch a glimpse into her son's love life."

I shrugged. "Just—don't be afraid to talk to me about these things, okay?"

"Shut up."

I smiled sweetly and took a bite out of my omelet. There was something incredibly thrilling about teasing Ryan. He always presented such a perfect front—so smooth, confident, and cheerful. Getting under his skin felt like winning.

Of course, he let me have it just as often—we'd been playfully ragging on each other for so many years that I honestly couldn't imagine life without it, or him.

I know, people use that line all the time, and it's usually a really dumb exaggeration people use when they've known someone for, like, one semester, but when I say I can't imagine life without Ryan Pope, I really, genuinely mean it. He was my first ever real friend, which means a lot more than it probably sounds. Surprisingly, despite my current social status, finding friends was never easy for me.

I'd been on the playdate blacklist from the very beginning; sometime between the time I cut the Stewart twins' hair so that they didn't have to leave my playdate to get it done, and the time I told Hannah Wood she'd land softly from the tree to the ground if she flapped her fairy wings fast enough.

These two incidents, combined with a few lesser ones here and there, led to the beginning of my bad reputation in Woolridge. Parents had heard enough about me to be wary when they heard my name, and there was kind of an unspoken collective playdate ban in the neighborhood. Of course, this only made everyone want to hang with me more. I don't know whether kids were in awe of me, scared of me, or just wanted to rebel against their parents, but they flocked toward me, vying for my friendship and attention. But no one could handle it. Even if it weren't for their inability to hang out after school, they all failed the various tests of mischief and endurance—until Ryan.

We were in cahoots the moment he discreetly tapped me on the shoulder and forced a packet of Gushers onto my lap during snack time, his eyes trained pointedly on my packet of Mini Oreos. Snack swapping was completely forbidden in kindergarten due to deathly peanut allergies, but that didn't stop him from offering an exchange anyway, and it certainly didn't stop me from slapping the Oreos in his palm as soon as Ms. Williams's back was turned.

After that, our secret snack swapping became legend. Our method evolved, some other kids found out, and just like that we were snack dealers, facilitating illegal snack swapping under the bridge during recess at a fee of one bite of something good for both of us. It was all going fine until some kid went crying to a teacher after I took six of his M&M's instead of five. The principal told us we'd have monitored recess for the rest of the year, which was fine with us; by that point it wasn't about the treats anymore. Ryan pulled a face when the principal's back was turned, I laughed, he giggled, and the rest was history.

Ryan took a swig of orange juice and slammed it back on the table. "You know, Cairo called me this morning," he said.

I looked at him skeptically. "Our Cai? You sure? That doesn't sound like her."

Ryan grinned as he chewed his breakfast. "Right? I don't think she's called me since the eighth grade. I picked that phone up so fast, I doubt she'd even finished typing my number out."

"Wait—do you think this is about the party?" I laughed. "Imagine that! A party so wild that our calm, cool, and collected Cairo left with drama of her own. What did she say?"

"That she's got something major to tell us."

I raised an eyebrow. Of the three of us, Cai was the least dramatic. She never exaggerated for attention like I did. She never threw around over-the-top words and phrases like Ryan did. Even when our adventures got out of hand, Cairo always managed to keep her cool—it's why she was the second and only other person to pass my friendship test.

I knew I loved her the moment I saw her pick a snake up on our outdoor science field trip in sixth grade. Someone had noticed it slithering in the grass, and the whole class screamed and ran in different directions except for me and Cairo, who walked up to it, placed it on her arm, and stroked it.

I'd walked closer to her, slowly, and when she looked up I was surprised at her face. She looked like a Jackson Pollock painting: splashed with a thousand dark freckles from the top left of her forehead to the bottom right of her chin. I'd heard of the new girl from Morocco with the specks on her face but still I couldn't help staring at her. No one could help staring at Cai.

"It's a garden snake," she said when she saw me staring, then gently transferred it to her other hand. "Want to stroke it?"

"Aren't you scared?" I'd asked.

"No," she'd answered. "I'm not scared of anything, especially tiny little snakes."

Now, in the kitchen, I leaned back in my chair.

"Should we be worried?" I asked Ryan. "I mean, what could she possibly have to say to us that she couldn't just say in the group chat?"

Something moved outside the window. Sure enough, Cairo was stepping out of her mother's car.

"Well," Ryan said, standing up, "I guess we're about to find out."

Ten minutes later we were all sitting in our usual spots in Ryan's bedroom: Ryan in the blue swivel chair by his desk, me on his bed, and Cairo sprawled out on the beanbag to my right. She held a bag of assorted nuts, crunching them as she crafted an especially long text on her phone, an odd sight to see if you knew about Cairo and her allergy to cell phones and technology. She had no games on it, few social media accounts, and often refused to use the thing all together because she could "just speak to friends face-to-face" when she saw them.

Ryan and I watched the strange scene in amazement.

"Uh . . . Cai," Ryan started, breaking the silence.

"You can't tell us you have big news and then just sit there on your phone," I finished.

She held a finger up, typed for five more seconds, and then put her phone aside. "Okay." She smiled that small lazy smirk of hers, then leaned forward. "Sit back and relax because I have the wildest story from last night."

"So it is about the party!" I exclaimed. "I can't believe you left with a story too!"

"Didn't everyone?" Cairo asked. "Don't act like you two haven't got a story of your own to tell."

I thought about The Mysterious Voice and felt a flicker in my chest. "Maybe," I said slowly, looking between the two of them.

Cairo looked surprised. "And you've managed to keep quiet about it this long?"

I ignored the teasing quality in her voice and Ryan's snicker, crossing one leg over the other. "Hurry up and get on with your story. I've been keeping this to myself for so long I'm about to explode."

"Okay fine, I'll go first, then you, and then Ryan," Cairo said.

"What?" Ryan straightened. "I didn't say I had anything to sh—"

"So," Cairo started, interrupting Ryan. She leaned forward again, legs apart, elbows resting on her knees. "Just after that trap song about throwing money out the window or whatever, I went outside for a soda and a breath of fresh air. I overheard these guys arguing over who should take their shirt off first to get in the hot tub. The argument went on for a while, and it didn't seem like it was going anywhere, so I walked up to them and told them that you didn't necessarily have to take your clothes off to get in the hot tub, you could just get in. They just kind of stared at me with this dumb look on their faces, so to prove my point, I got into the hot tub fully clothed, soda can still in my hand."

"Is this your story?" I asked, my voice flat.

"No," Cairo said, narrowing her eyes. "Let me finish. The guys turned out to be Tyler Keene, Clay Killinger, and Sid Oakes."

"Who?"

"Just some photography and tech kids. They were really cool. We all ended up just chilling together with our clothes on in the hot tub, having a fun time. Anyway, just as I was about to get out, one of them said it was nice of me to sacrifice my clothes with them despite the fact that I was—and I'm quoting here—'basically a model.'"

"They're not wrong," I interjected.

"Then, suddenly, the Sid kid got all excited and started hitting Tyler, saying something about the girl his uncle was looking for, and then Tyler got excited and hopped out of the tub to get his phone so he could take my number. Long story short, Tyler's uncle is Michael Keene. Like, *the* Michael Keene: creative director of Superet—that brand of clothing everyone's wearing on IG these days? So Tyler sent his uncle my photo, and I got a text from him today saying he'd like to see me."

I sat up straight on the bed, my mouth wide open. "You're kidding!"

"Not at all," Cairo said, leaning back in her chair.

"I can't believe I'm friends with a model . . ." Ryan said.

"I can't even imagine you modeling . . ." I said. Cai had always been extremely disinterested in fashion. Her idea of *haute couture* was cutting her brother's hand-me-down clothes to wear as crop tops and ripped jeans.

"Hm. Neither can I, to be honest." Cairo reached into her bag for more nuts. "I'm more excited to go to a professional shoot and learn more about photography. I'm gonna worm my way into Keene's heart and get an internship. Mark my words."

Ryan shook his head in amazement. "A modeling job for Superet . . . that's incredible."

"Yeah," I agreed. "Good job on being so hot, Dahmani."

Cai rolled her eyes. "Shut up," she said, but she said it with a smile on her face. She nodded toward me. "Okay, your turn."

I smiled and leaned back on my arms, savoring their attention. "I met someone last night."

Cairo raised her eyebrows. "Met someone, met someone?"

"Met someone as in . . . I met someone," I said. "But the thing is, I have no idea who he is."

They both narrowed their eyes, confused.

"How do you meet someone and not know who they are?" Ryan asked.

"Well . . ."

I paused. I lived for moments like these; moments where I had everybody's undivided attention and a platform to deliver the perfectly crafted story in a way that was so unforgettable it would be repeated in classrooms, hallways, cars, and in people's heads for years to come.

I held out the silence and Ryan and Cairo leaned forward in curious anticipation.

"Yeah . . ." Ryan said.

"You see," I said, bringing my hands together, "I met him but we didn't actually see each other."

Cairo cocked her head.

"It was in the dark," I clarified. "I was . . ." I cut myself short. My chest tightened at the memory of having almost lost my necklace; it was all I could do to not touch the pendant at my neck for reassurance. "I was just looking for something in Mattaliano's coat closet, and there he was, sitting all alone in the dark."

Ryan nodded, dissolving the tension in my chest. At least it wasn't a lie.

"At a party?" Cairo asked. "He was sitting in a closet at a party?"

"That does not sound right," Ryan said. "In fact, that sounds anything but right. That's, like, serial killer behavior I'm pretty sure."

"Did something . . . happen in this closet?" Cairo asked with a suggestive eyebrow raise.

"Something did happen," I said. "But it's something you're never going to guess."

"Transmutation," Ryan quipped.

"The seven plagues," Cairo threw in.

"You found the secret chord that David played to please the Lord?"

"Shut up—can I just tell the story, please? We just sat and spoke for a while before I went back to the party, but during this conversation, he stole something of mine—and get this," I added quickly, "this morning at Westerns, I got a letter, along with the thing he stole, asking if I want to play a game with him."

I'd hooked them with that one.

"A game?" Ryan asked. "What sort of game?"

I pulled the letter out and let them read it over twice.

Cairo looked up at me first, excitement in her eyes. "A mystery," she said. "Oh, this is going to be fun."

Ryan was still holding the letter in his hands, an incredulous expression on his face. "This . . . is—" he started.

"The best thing to happen since the Cromwell Forest search two years ago?" I finished.

"Yes," he said, handing the letter back to me. "Exactly."

"Tell me you responded," Cairo said.

"Oh, I responded." I took my phone out to show them the photo of the letter I had written to our dearest Mr. Reeyus Voyce.

Dear Mr. Voyce,

I'm in. I love a good game—although yours could do with a few improvements.

First of all, we'll need a discreet mode of communication to leave the clues. Let's try AnonChat, tonight at 21:00. Use the common interest "Frozen Mudpies."

Second, I think we should raise the stakes by adding a time limit to these missions. If either one of us fails to retrieve their package within a given time frame, everything is off, there is no further contact, and that person loses.

Third, no flirting, no mushiness, and no sappy love confessions. I've got enough on my plate as it is and I'd really hate to turn into a predictable, letter-writing, love-struck teen cliché.

And lastly, don't you ever. Ever. Steal from me again. I sincerely promise that I will find you and ruin you if you do.

Yours Elusively,
Robyn Yubach

"Frozen Mudpies?"

Ryan's eyes flickered to me, questioning and slightly accusatory. Frozen Mudpies were our special childhood recipe of rolled-up balls of mud coated in snow. We'd made them up one particularly cold winter on a visit to Lake Tahoe; the recipe became our secret weapon for killer snowballs whenever snowball fights broke out between all the kids in the neighborhood. Our mothers were not happy when we all came back bruised and covered in mud.

I shrugged. "It's the first thing that came to mind."

Cairo sat back down on the beanbag. "AnonChat? Isn't that a chat room that links strangers with common interests?"

"Yep," I said, "and because no one else could possibly have Frozen Mudpies as a common interest, it'll match us and serve as a private chat room that won't reveal our identities."

Ryan nodded, impressed, and handed me my phone. "You know we're doing this mission with you, right?" he said, sliding back toward his desk.

"Mmmm," Cairo grunted through a handful of nuts. "I'm definitely in. I need to know who this guy is."

I looked between the two of them and smiled. Of course I knew they were in; their ears pricked up at the first sign of adventure. It's what I loved most about them.

"Okay, Ry," Cairo said, leaning further into her beanbag. "What you got for us?"

"Nothing," he said.

I narrowed my eyes. "*Nothing?*"

"Honestly," he insisted. "I just . . . played music, hit a few kegs, jumped in the pool . . . nothing groundbreaking."

"So . . . no modeling gig or mysterious closet meeting?" Cairo asked with a teasing smile.

"Nope," he said with a shrug.

I eyed him skeptically. Ryan always had something to share after a time like last night, whether it was actually interesting or he'd just discovered some weird new fact about an obscure band I hadn't heard of before. Then I remembered our conversation in the kitchen.

"Wait, what about Thade Logan?" I asked.

Ryan blinked, looking confused before it seemed to come back to him. "Oh, right! I got Thade Logan's number. Which was cool."

I raised an eyebrow. Weird of him to have forgotten something he wouldn't shut up about thirty minutes prior.

"Thade Logan?" Cairo asked. "How the hell did that happen?"

As Ryan retold the story of how he befriended Thade Logan, I wandered over to the mirror to reapply my lip gloss. Through the crook of my arm, I caught my friends' reflections in the mirror, so alive with excitement from the night before, and I found myself thinking about The Mysterious Voice again. How he hadn't shied away from my over-the-top story in the closet. How he'd created something exciting and surprising out of thin air.

What if my friends weren't the only interesting people in Woolridge? My chest fluttered at the possibility. In fact, my entire body fizzed with more and more excitement at the prospect of MV's game and the possibilities it brought with every minute that passed.

I just prayed he wouldn't disappoint me. I hoped he would pass my test.

CHAPTER
5

TRACK:
GENESIS
Grimes

I was acutely aware that my "just two hours" at Westerns had turned into a full day when I pulled into the gate to my home. I winced as I opened the front door and tiptoed inside, making sure to leave the keys on the kitchen counter in plain sight.

I was probably fine. Helen Pope had likely kept my parents up to date on our activities all day. And we lived just a couple of blocks down from the Popes. If they had wanted to get me, they would have.

Once I was safely in my room, I pulled my laptop out and sat on my bed.

The house was quiet. So much quieter than it ever was at Ryan's house. It felt strange. Uncomfortable. I connected my phone to the speaker and tapped on Ryan's updated playlist, letting the warm sound of synth trickle into my room. "Genesis," read the song's title.

I smiled to myself. How fitting. This was the start of something after all.

I typed "AnonChat" into my browser's search bar, and as soon as the website loaded, I put "Frozen Mudpies" in the common interests bar.

A confusing mix of emotions stirred in my chest as the website searched for someone to pair me with: excitement, nervousness, and residual annoyance at having been robbed.

And then:

AnonChat
— You are now connected with someone who likes Frozen Mudpies, just like you! —

I blinked at the white screen; the stranger was typing. This was happening. It had actually worked.

Stranger: Hello? Robb?

I stretched my fingers across the keyboard, ferociously typing what I'd wanted to say ever since the party.

You: You're the worst person I've ever met.

Stranger: Oh thank God, it's you.

Stranger: I'd recognize that loving tone of voice anywhere.

You: Shut up. You know how much trouble I went through to get that necklace and you took it anyway!

Stranger: Well you have it back now, don't you? I see no problem.

I gritted my teeth. He was right, of course. I was happily reunited with my necklace and only minimal, mostly psychological, damage had been done. Still, a line had been crossed. Part of me was tempted to disconnect the chat just to spite him, but no matter how momentarily satisfying it would have been to leave him hanging, I couldn't sever the line of our only direct mode of communication.

Stranger: Aren't you impressed that I was able to get the necklace back to you without knowing who you even are?

To tell the truth, I was ridiculously impressed. But I didn't want to give him that satisfaction.

You: I'm decidedly more freaked out than impressed. You go to Westerns??

Stranger: Yeah, I go there quite often.

You: Why? It's far away and it's so old it's falling apart

Stranger: Which is exactly why it's perfect. I go to avoid people and enjoy a change of scenery.

I paused, surprised at how his reasons mirrored my own. I'd never met anyone from Woolridge at Westerns, no one from our town would waste time traveling to a place as unimpressive as Westerns. The two places existed in entirely separate universes.

Stranger: Why do you go? If it's so decrepit and so far away.

I pulled my knees up to my chest, determined not to let him talk me into oversharing again. I wasn't about to start bonding with him so soon after suffering the consequences of doing exactly that.

You: You know, I didn't come up with this AnonChat idea so we could sit here and chat. Aren't you supposed to be giving me a clue or a riddle or something?

Stranger: I know.

Stranger: I was just trying to show you that, contrary to what you might believe, I can be sociable and polite.

You: You stole from me

You: And I met you in a closet.

You: It's going to take a lot more than one chat to convince me you're anything close to sociable and polite.

Stranger: Ha. Fair point. I'm not giving up though.

Stranger: Okay. Mission No. 1 is to pick up your package at 14 Chestnut Hill.

I copied the address in my search engine and dropped my shoulders. The first *daring mission* was just to go to a house that was just around the corner?

You: A house? Really?

Stranger: Yep.

You: It's not yours is it?

Stranger: Not mine. No idea whose house it is actually.

Stranger: I just spotted a house with no activity and no car in the driveway, snuck inside, and dropped the letter off— You'll have to figure out where.

I raised an eyebrow, pleasantly surprised. Sneaking into a stranger's house? He had guts. Luckily, I had guts too.

You: Alright. Hit me with the clue.

Stranger: I'll sound at three to one

Stranger: When everything is done

Stranger: No piece how old

Stranger: Will be too cold

Stranger: As long as I am on

Stranger: Report back to AnonChat when you retrieve the package. You have until 5:30pm on Monday. Good luck.

AnonChat
— Stranger has disconnected —

CHAPTER 6

TRACK:
HATE TO SAY I TOLD YOU SO
The Hives

There's a certain buzz that exists on the first day of school that lasts for about a week and never returns through the school year.

Because, let's be real, nobody is thinking realistically on that first day; everyone's forgotten how horrible things will get. They run around chatting excitedly with friends they haven't seen in months, fluttering around in new outfits while flaunting summer tans and freshly done braids. Every year without fail, people believe that this year will be like no other. That things will finally change. Only a three-month holiday could create such electric excitement and brazen hope in the air.

Or so I thought.

As soon as Ryan and I pulled up to the school parking lot, we noticed it. The buzz. Instead of the humdrum-book-lugging, hunched-back-feet-dragging we were used to seeing on a Monday morning so close to the end of the year, Wooldridge High was alive.

I gaped from Ryan's window, as he parked in our usual spot, staring through my sunglasses as the rhythmic strum of a garage rock song played through the car. "What—"

He pulled the hand brake and we both immediately stepped out to survey the crowd, ignoring the fact that the engine was still running and the music was still blaring. People were actually hanging out outside the front door in groups, like . . . talking to each other and smiling, and . . . *laughing*. At seven in the *morning*.

I spotted Ty Praino, robotics club president, standing in a huddle with the senior jocks. Not far away, about thirty random students sat in a circle on the lawn, holding hands. Incredulous, I slammed my door and caught Ryan's eye over my shades. He appeared to be just as bewildered as I felt.

As we started up the pavement to the building, a trio of freshman girls ran past us toward the boys' locker room, and a guy on a skateboard, who was holding a cup of coffee, cut in front of us, stopping a few feet away to give the cup to a tall girl with a springy ponytail. She grabbed his hand lovingly before taking a sip.

I knew that springy ponytail. I raised my sunglasses to make sure my eyes weren't playing tricks on me. "Is that Kathy Summers? And a *skateboarder*?"

"Yep," Ryan said, squinting his eyes and ruffling his hair. "Looks like she found herself a skater boy and said see you later to your ex."

"Did that happen because of our party?"

"My guess is yes," Ryan said. "Man . . . What have we created?"

I cast another look back at the new couple as we reached the front doors—only to open them to greater chaos.

Inside, the buzz was louder, warmer, and there was a strong undercurrent of gossip. Ryan and I stepped in cautiously, and the energy immediately turned toward us.

A few kids cheered as we walked in, and I smiled, nodding a greeting toward the parting crowd as we walked past. The people who didn't cheer, whispered and pointed, some with their phones out at suspicious angles. We were used to attention, sure, but not like this.

"This is weird, right?" Ryan muttered, looking around. "I mean— the whole vibe is completely off." He grabbed my arm, eyes suddenly wide. "Dude . . . I swear I just saw Rodney go up the back stairs."

"Rodney Yacko?"

"Yes, Rodney Yacko!" He blinked. "That was like seeing a ghost.

The kid hasn't been to class in months. I legit thought he switched schools."

As we neared our lockers, Scott Hayes and a group of guys from the football team banged their fists on the walls, whooping and cheering us on. I grinned semi-bashfully. "You guys really don't have to do all of this."

"Of course we do!" Scott bellowed, looking over my head. "We've gotta give the mega-party planner the welcome he deserves!"

"He?" I repeated.

I followed his gaze, spinning in place, and my mood instantly soured. "He" had been behind us all along. The last person I wanted to see on the entire planet Earth.

Tristan Mattaliano.

"Thanks, man," Mattaliano said, flashing his obscene dimples. He was very pointedly not looking in my direction.

I scoffed as the two embraced. "I'm sorry—Mattaliano had as much to do with that party as the French do with fries."

"Uh, I don't know about that," Mattaliano replied, furrowing his brow. "It was literally at my house."

Even though he was talking to me, he still refused to look me in the eye, focusing instead on bumping fists with some of Scott's friends.

"At your house?" I repeated, folding my arms. "Your house was just a venue."

Mattaliano ignored me, turning to Scott, and the two of them pushed past us and proceeded down the hall, followed closely by the rest of Scott's crew.

Heat rushed to my neck. I hadn't made Woolridge history to not be rightfully recognized for it. And I especially hadn't done so for the credit to go to *Mattaliano*, of all people.

"It was only at your house because *I* wanted it to be!" I shouted down the hall, but my words were swallowed by the persistent hallway buzz.

"Damn," Ryan said. "Who would have thought he could get worse?"

I wanted to go after him, guns blazing, but Ryan must have sensed my desire for blood because he placed a gentle hand on my arm and stepped into my line of vision.

"Don't," he cautioned. "He's seriously not worth it. I mean, who wants to waste extra energy on a guy like that?"

"I might." My eyes flickered to Mattaliano's shrinking frame. "If it means hurting him."

"But think about it—isn't this kind of a good thing? If we let Mattaliano take credit for the party, it makes it easier for you to stay anonymous with your whole . . . letter game. Don't you want to complete your first mission?"

I turned my attention back to Ryan's concerned, hazel eyes. He had a point. I had told The Mysterious Voice that I'd planned the party. If he ever caught wind that it had been thrown by a girl named Loli Crawford, he'd put two and two together and our game would end.

I sighed. Classic Ryan, wrapping something bitter up in something sweet.

"Dammit, Pope," I groaned. "You're right."

"I'm always right," Ryan said, grinning and rubbing an eye. "That's what this friendship is—me being right and you realizing a beat later."

He lowered his hand, and that's when I noticed the red patches of skin under both of his eyes. I frowned, leaning forward. "Wait . . . are you okay, Ry?"

He blinked. "Yeah. Why?"

"You seem . . . frazzled."

"I'm not frazzled," he argued.

I ran an eye over his excessively tousled hair, his reddened eyes, his fidgeting hand. There had been so much going on that morning that I hadn't noticed how off *he* had been. I opened my mouth to counter back, but the second bell cut me off.

"I gotta go," Ryan said. "See you at lunch?"

Before I could respond, he touched my shoulder and took off down the hallway toward his homeroom.

I frowned. A lot of strange things were going on that morning, but the fact that the chillest, most easy-breezy, carefree guy in the world was skittering down the hallway was the strangest of them all.

The rest of the school day was extremely weird—like we were living through a Woolridge-specific Purge or some bizarre apocalypse.

Only ten kids showed up to my first class, and my second class was canceled for reasons that were undisclosed in the email we received from Dr. Trader, our school principal. Teachers started to patrol the hallways, and underclassmen mingled with seniors in the cafeteria.

But the strangest thing of all was the creeping, impossible feeling of The Mysterious Voice's presence. He was all I could think about all day as I painstakingly counted the seconds for school to end so I could be free to complete my first mission.

Of course, I had no idea who he was—he could have been anyone, anywhere, peering from behind me in class, sitting right next to me, walking casually by my desk. In the hallways my eyes lingered on people a little longer than they usually did, scrutinizing every face, every movement, no matter how many times I told myself I shouldn't, let alone how pointless it was to even try.

School was like attending some weird sort of masquerade, only instead of having to look out for a familiar set of eyes, I had to keep an ear out for that familiar, dark voice.

At 3:59 P.M. that afternoon, I found myself stalking an elderly woman across the street from her house.

This was less than ideal, for more than the obvious reason. How was I supposed to break into an old woman's house while she was still around?

I was squinting through Ryan's binoculars, trying to make sense of her movements, when my phone pinged.

> Hey—you sure you don't need help?

> We could do the classic distraction method. You sneak round back to search the house for the package and I'll hold them up at door.

I looked down the street to where he had parked his car, Baby, just a few blocks down. No, I typed back. No helping—I'd told him that a thousand times on the way over. I knew that he wanted in on the action too, but having him help me on my first mission would be too easy, a cop-out, shameful almost. But he owed me for the confiscated car, plus, he made a perfect getaway driver.

> Okay. Send signal when you're ready.

I gave him a thumbs-up on the off chance he could see me, and then I muted and pocketed my phone. The old woman switched on her television. I stuffed the binoculars away and took a deep breath. I could handle old women. Old women were easy.

I smoothed my clothes out, rolled my shoulders back, and walked toward the front door without so much as a glimmer of a plan in my mind. Plans were more Ryan's and Cairo's speed. Action was mine.

As I rang the doorbell, I ran through a list of possible identities to assume: Survey Volunteer? Girl Scout? Jehovah's Witness? A brusque look down at my outfit disqualified the possibility of all of the above.

I tossed my hair back and was just pulling my skirt down to an appropriate length when the door rattled and heaved open, revealing a petite old woman with a wary expression on her face.

"Hello?" she asked, eying me up and down. "What can I do for you?"

I stretched my neck to sneak a look into her house, as if the package was going to be waiting for me just behind her, wrapped and sitting under a large sign with my name on it. Obviously that was not the case. Instead, MV had an extremely vague riddle for me to solve, which I'd now committed to memory:

I'll sound at three to one
When everything is done
No piece how old
Will be too cold
As long as I am on

"Baby?" The old woman asked. "Are you lost?"

Her concerned voice dragged my attention back to where we stood at the front door. I blinked a few times. Yes—lost! Lost was perfect. I was a professional at lost.

I gulped. "I think so. I, um—"

The woman shakily removed her glasses from her face, and I silently prayed that my ability to cry on command hadn't left me. My fake tears had gotten us out of all sorts of trouble back in the day, but old age had made me a little rusty.

"I—I thought—" I took a deep shaky breath, making sure it quivered on the way out, and then I let my face crumple.

"Oh, honey, no!" the old woman exclaimed. "Don't cry!"

Her round face blurred as a single tear trickled down my cheek. Like riding a bike.

"Come on, sweetie," she said, pulling me in. "Come inside and we'll figure this out together, all right?"

As she steered me through the door, I surreptitiously scanned the room for anything that might conceal a letter.

Her sitting room was quaint and filled with all the classic old-lady decorations: flower-patterned couches and chairs, crystal cutouts of cherubs and fairies on an aging mantelpiece, framed photos of

young faces on every surface, and doilies thrown on top of everything. I ran my hand underneath a doily and ruffled through the
letters on her side table, sniffing loudly to cover the sound. No
out-of-place letters. Nothing out of the ordinary at all.

"Why don't you sit down and I'll get you something to drink,
okay?"

I nodded, casting a quick, searching look over my shoulder.

"Here . . ." She gently angled me toward the couch and I sat
down. "Are you hurt?"

I shook my head.

"Well, I want you to know that you're absolutely safe here with
Aunt Mae, all right . . ."

I tried to look attentive as she began to detail her years of experience raising children and grandchildren.

I sound at three to one . . . No piece how old . . .

Old. I looked around. Everything in the room was old. What
could he mean? An antique? An old photograph? There was no
trace of the dark blue envelope he'd given me once before.

I lifted my eyes to the wall across the room, and that's when I
noticed the huge grandfather clock tucked between the curtains.

I sound at three to one when everything is done.

I sat up straighter, more alert. A clock. Of course. They made
sounds, had numbers, and this particular one did look very old.

"What you want, sweetie?" Aunt Mae asked. "A cup of tea?
Glass o' water?"

I blinked my wet lashes. The longer she was out of the room,
the more time I had. "Tea, please."

"All right," Aunt Mae said. "I'll be back in a jiffy."

As soon as I heard the faucet turn on in the next room, I jumped
up from the couch, wiped my tears away, and rushed toward the
grandfather clock, brushing a hand along either side before noticing the key in the glass door and tugging it open.

"Please, please, please," I whispered, tapping around the walls
for anything that felt out of place. A piece of tape, a slip of paper,
scratches in the wood, anything.

Nothing.

I felt along the sides again, reached up to the top, and peered around the back to see if there was anything there. Nothing still.

"You all right, sweetie?"

I froze. Caught in the act.

"The water's going to take a while to boil so I thought we might as well have a little chat."

I kept my hands on either side of the clock and didn't turn around. After years of snooping, I'd learned that nothing was weird or out of place until you made it appear that way; you're only guilty as soon as you act it. I turned to face her, keeping my hands still.

"Well!" the old woman exclaimed as she neared me. "Looks like you found my old grandpappy clock!" She laughed lightly. "You're just like my daughter, Nunu. She couldn't sit still if she was hardened in cement."

"I'm sorry," I replied, closing the door behind me. "It just looked so shiny . . ."

"Bee's Wax Polish," she replied. "Applied once a leap year."

I brought my hands to my lap. "I was supposed to catch the bus to my dad's an hour ago," I said softly. "But I got lost in the middle of nowhere—"

"You want to use my landline, sweetie? Give him a call?"

I shook my head. "It's fine. I called him when you left and he said he was going to share his location with me."

She looked confused. "Share his location . . . ?"

"On my phone," I clarified.

Aunt Mae looked troubled. "That sounds dangerous."

I smiled, wiping my eyes. "It's not, don't worry. I'm sorry I'm a mess."

"Don't worry about it, dear," Aunt Mae said with a smile. "Come, let's relax and let me show you my Nunu. You remind me of her, you know?"

She angled me toward the couch, and as she grabbed a lilac folder, I started sweating.

Grandmothers, photo albums, and couches were a terrible combination. I could be stuck for hours, and I only had one until I was supposed to meet Mysterious Voice on AnonChat. My stomach tightened. I would never survive the embarrassment of failing the very first mission.

I hovered by the coffee table, anxious to keep searching the house, and as I reluctantly lowered onto the flower cushion, I was saved by the whistle of the kettle.

"Oh!" Mae said, startled. "That'd be the hot water! Hang on a second while I fix us some tea."

"Wait," I sprang up from the couch, an idea forming in my mind. "I'll come with you."

"Sure, sweetie! Follow me."

We rounded the corner into her startlingly white kitchen, and as she poured hot water into flowery mugs, I discreetly peeked through her glass cabinets and into the diamond cubbyholes along the walls. The riddle said nothing about kitchen cabinets but looking somewhere was better than looking nowhere.

"Here, pop these brownies in the microwave, would you?" Aunt Mae handed me a plate of four square brownies. "Twenty seconds should do."

I absentmindedly placed the plate in the microwave and looked helplessly around the kitchen.

I sound at three to one . . .

"Nunu used to do ballet, you know," Mae started. "I'll show you the photos. She was the cutest little girl. Here, darling, take your tea. And keep an eye on those brownies."

She left the kitchen with her tray and I watched the digital timer count down: 3, 2, 1.

When the timer beeped, I stared at my reflection in the window. Three, two, one.

I could've kicked myself.

I flung the microwave door open and stuck a hand inside, feeling all around the sides and the back wall. Nothing. I felt along the outside and back. Still nothing.

"You good there, sweetie? Need some help?"

"I'm good!" I yelled back, trying to keep my voice cheery.

Desperate, I removed the clear glass tray, looking in and around it before I thought, to hell with it, and decided to lift the whole thing up.

There was nothing underneath the microwave, nothing on the surface below either, but as I placed the machine back down, my fingers touched a smooth square patch at the back that was nothing like the cold hard metal and plastic.

Instinctively, hungrily, I curled my fingers between the space between the paper and the metal, and pulled it off before bringing it round for inspection.

It was another dark blue envelope, slightly thick and glued closed, addressed to a Miss Yubach.

Relief flooded through me. I clutched the letter to my chest.

Package retrieved.

I'd made it with just under an hour to spare. Now all I had to do was get out of there, sign on to AnonChat, and prove to him that I had collected the package before the time ran out.

I considered leaving through the kitchen door and making a run for it but my mind went back to the old woman sitting alone in her sitting room, holding photos of children who were no longer around, waiting for a brownie. I may be selfish (as I've been told many times) but, unfortunately, I'm not cruel.

I grabbed the brownies, sent Ryan an emergency butterfly emoji, and made it back to the sitting room before my cell phone rang. I turned my back on Aunt Mae, who was just beginning to show me pictures from the day of Nunu's birth, when I answered the call.

"Hi, Dad."

"I'm outside," Ryan said—as if I needed him to tell me that. The thrashing music and sputtering engine had done well enough to alert the entire neighborhood. Aunt Mae frowned out the window, craning her neck to see who could possibly be making such an unnecessary racket.

"I know, dumbass," I hissed. "Turn it down."

Aunt Mae turned her troubled gaze from the window to me. I smiled meekly. "Yes, okay, I'll be right there. Love you." I hung the phone up and grabbed my bag. "Thanks for the tea and brownie, Aunt Mae, but I've got to go. My dad's here."

"Oh yes," she said, somewhat troubled. "I can see that."

I placed the brownie between my teeth, stuffed the letter into my bag, and mumbled a goodbye before rushing out the door and into the baby blue Mustang on the other side of the road.

When I sat down, Ryan looked amused. "Nice touch with the 'love you' right after the 'dumbass,'" he said. "I think you really sold your part."

I smirked. "Shut up," I said, reclining my seat. "And drive."

Dear Robyn,

As much as I love the dark and lustful mystery of our first interaction, I'm not sure it's worth it if you left with the impression that I'm the type of person who lurks in the shadows and corners at social events.

I'm not, I assure you. Not completely, anyway. I had my reasons, same as you, and maybe I'll figure out a way to explain them in a way that makes sense in a future letter.

Next, I need to make it clear to you that I did not set out to steal your necklace. You gave it to me, and then you got distracted during your melodramatic tirade on how life was so boring, and you never asked for it back. I wondered for a second if you'd forgotten, and I won't lie, it did occur to me that I could get up and leave with your necklace in order to pull some kind of sick joke on you, but I immediately dismissed the idea when I realized there was absolutely no way you would forget the belle of the ball, the pièce de résistance, the party's raison d'être. I mean, with all the energy you'd put into getting it back, how would I possibly get away without you realizing that I still had it?

So you can imagine my surprise when you voluntarily left me in the dark holding your precious necklace.

I could've run out after you or tracked you down after all the drama you went through to get it back, but it seemed to me that you like drama, so I thought—what better gift than prolonging the suspense?

So I left the closet and went back out into the party; I met with friends, listened to the surprisingly good music (amazingly good—I mean, Led Zeppelin? Who'd expect Led Zeppelin, the greatest band of all time, at a Woolridge party?) and all the time I thought about what I could do with this unique opportunity.

At first I thought about blackmailing you. I spent an hour coming up with this whole convoluted plan that's too boring to really go into detail, but while I was plotting, I realized how much it would suck for this to be a one-way thing and how much more it would suck to push away the only interesting thing I've come across in this town.

Anyway, I decided to leave the party sometime around midnight, and on my walk home I stopped and held your necklace up to a streetlight. Even in the harsh light, it was so beautiful and authentic, and so intricately made, unlike those reproduced pieces you often see in stores. It looked like it was cared for when it was made.

And it's funny because lately I've been thinking a lot about the old, and all the things we've lost because of what we've gained. Things we technically still have but no one bothers with anymore. Like quills or typewriters, or the lost art of letter writing.

There's something about communication that was always meant to be personal. It's the reason for the unique pitch and cadence of one's voice, the specific slant or crawl of one's handwriting. Electronics just don't do it justice.

I was thinking all of this that night as I walked home, and I thought about the peculiar way that we met, and how it was shrouded in mystery and distance and yet strangely personal in its lack of convention. And I thought why not extend the experience, revive a sleeping beauty, and create something for you to enjoy all in one.

So I'm not a monster. At least not for the reasons you stipulated.

I look forward to your first challenge.

Sincerely,
Mr. Revoyce

AnonChat
— You are now connected with someone who
likes Frozen Mudpies, just like you! —

You: The "letter writing is a lost art" part was a bit pretentious but I'll bite.

Stranger: Well hello to you too, Stranger.

Stranger: I see you found the letter—thank goodness.

You: Of course I found the letter! Failing the first mission was never an option.

Stranger: Of course not.

Stranger: Imagine how embarrassing that would've been— all that buildup only for the game to be over before it even started.

You: Careful not to jinx it before you've had your turn, MV.

Stranger: Don't worry about me, I'll find it. Hit me with the clue.

You: Ok, well riddles aren't really my style so I've put together a code for you to crack:

You: ISBN-10: _57230_ _4_

Stranger: An International Standard Book Number . . . the letter's in a book?

You: Look at you! Smart as a whip. Find the missing numbers then find the book with the matching ISBN. The package will be inside.

Stranger: And how exactly am I supposed to do that?

You: The numbers match the birth date of the late former Woolridge resident "Sarah Elizabeth Walsh."

You: You have until midnight on Friday. Good luck!

AnonChat
— Stranger has disconnected —

CHAPTER 7

TRACK:
SOUR TIMES
Portishead

I wouldn't have admitted it to anyone, but I read his letter five times that night.

I read it the first time just to read it, and when I got to the part about letters being a lost art, I scoffed and rolled my eyes. I read it the second time to really let it sink in, and when I got to the lost art part, I merely rolled my eyes. It was only around the third or fourth time that I kind of got what he meant.

As I held the papers in my hands, looking at the folds, crinkles, and slightly raised black ink, it hit me that somewhere out there, a living, breathing person had sat down to write to me. They'd touched that same piece of paper with a stable hand and the tip of their fountain pen, and they'd deliberately thought of what to say and how to say it before putting it down in black ink. I held something unique in my hands, and these folded pieces of paper—as gross as it was to say—were a piece of art. The original and only copy.

After that final read, I lowered the volume on my speakers so that the music was barely audible, switched off the light, and then I got into bed with my phone. Two unread messages flashed on my screen: one from Ryan and one from our joint group chat. I opened Ryan's first.

> Today was weird, right?

Weird was an understatement. I'd somehow managed to find someone entertaining who was almost as daring as I was within the halls of Woolridge High. I burrowed deep in my covers and typed out a response.

> So weird. It's trippy to be talking to someone and not know who they are

Ryan immediately started typing.

> Oh lol I was talking about the chaos at school

Right. Of course. I reminded myself that not everyone had been sucked into the world of MV and his letter-scouting game.

> Oh yeah that was crazy too

> It was like an extension of the chaos from Friday

> Ha. You mean the day Mattaliano threw the biggest party in Woolridge History?

> Hahaha, yeah that day

> Honestly we should be happy to let him bask in our glory. It's all the poor guy ever wanted

> That's actually sad. I can't believe I dated him

> Me neither

I glanced up from my phone as the sultry tone of an unfamiliar song began, and for a second, I was transfixed by the blue and purple lights under my speakers as the singer's lament droned over the instruments.

I'd decided to completely swear off boys after Mattaliano. All I'd ever wanted was to be with someone who was the complete package of looks, fearlessness, nerve, who understood me entirely. Someone who didn't make me explain myself or force me to shrink my ideas. Through the years, I'd only ever met two. And seeing as they were my friends, Ryan and Cairo weren't viable dating options.

But . . .

Life does get a bit dull sometimes. Why don't we spice it up and play a game . . .

The song slipped back from the chorus to the verse, and I went back to my phone, pushing away my nonsensical thoughts. I was *not* about to entertain romantic ideas about someone I hadn't even met, no matter how intriguing they were.

You gotta cut me some slack, I typed eventually. Clearly I wasn't in my right mind.

I've known you twelve years & I don't think I've seen this 'right mind' of yours

You know what I mean
It was like . . .

You know when you see someone extremely hot and all thought goes out the window?

• • •

Ryan was typing. And then he wasn't. And then he was. I turned onto my back and just as I was about to send a second question mark he replied:

Sure.

I frowned. Ryan rarely ever sent one-word answers. I watched the screen, waiting for him to type something else as the song faded, but he didn't. Instead, he sent a message to our Cake Tier group chat with Cairo, which I realized I hadn't checked since school ended. I left the conversation with Ryan and tapped on our group chat.

@loli, did u get the letter?

Yeah, thanks to a flawless getaway driver

Weird. Cai's message hadn't even been directed toward him. My thumbs scattered across the keyboard.

> It was a close call but yeah! I got it

Cairo replied uncharacteristically fast.

> C nice. what did it say?

I paused. Half of the letter had been about the necklace situation, which was something I didn't plan on revealing anytime soon, and even though I knew they'd die laughing at his pretentious tirade just like I had, it felt . . . wrong sharing it with them.

> Nothing much. He just introduced himself without giving anything away.

> C lmao good for him

> C clearly he knows that's the only thing keeping u interested

> R And he's made himself a blank canvas for you to project yourself onto

> C oooo! the person she loves most

I rolled my eyes at their back and forth, then responded:

> I'm going to sleep. Please save your insults for tomorrow

An Instagram notification popped up on the screen just as I was about to put my phone down. It was a message from a larger group chat featuring the three of us, Noel Sang, and a few other second-tier friends from our crowd. Ryan had sent a photo. I expected it to be to some dumb meme or video, but it was the poster for this year's Babble of the Bands concert.

CairoLikeEgypt:

> that looks sicckkkk ry

ThottyScotty48:

> OH MAN HERE IT COMES

I sat up abruptly. Until recently, I had been the resident artist for Ryan's band, Basilica, but they'd decided they wanted to "try something new" by commissioning work from one of Noel's favorite local artists. I was okay with the change, but it felt weird being on the outside of something so central to Ryan's life. I zoomed in on the artwork, scrutinizing the bubbly orange font and the retro '60s-movie-poster aesthetic. It felt a little off. In my opinion, Basilica was better suited to acidic colors with sharp, lightning-like font. I zoomed back out and blinked in surprise at the written date. Babble was less than three weeks away? My fingers flew across my keyboard.

LoliCrawford:

What? Babble's coming up already?? That was fast.

RyAlexPope:

It only feels fast bc you haven't been working on it

Noel_Never_Sang:

Ha. You can say that again. Hope you guys can all make it!

TheConnorSullivan1:

I'll be there, Sang.

CairoLikeEgypt:

okay guys im heading to bed, but let's meet @ lunch tomorrow? i have to introduce u to my hot-tub-story nerd friends.

Noel_Never_Sang:

What?

CairoLikeEgypt:

oh. this changing back and forth between platforms and chats confuses me. ignore that

CairoLikeEgypt:

> unless ur Ry or Lo bc then u shld meet me
> at lunch tomorrow so i can introduce u to
> my hot-tub-story nerd friends.

I tried to fall asleep after Cai's message, but after a few minutes of tossing and turning I gave in to the pull of my sketch pad. I started with a lightning bolt in the shape of the letter *B* for Basilica, the way it was supposed to look, and when I'd done the name right, I filled my poster with shades of black and green until I was satisfied.

CHAPTER
8

TRACK:
NO SURPRISES
Radiohead

Something was definitely up with Ryan.

To the untrained eye he seemed as he always did—carefree, laughing, and joking with everyone he passed in the halls. But I could see the truth: his usually loose smile was taut, his airy laugh was deflated, and instead of gliding smoothly through the halls, he was merely roaming, without a single sign of the usual bounce in his step. At first, I'd put it down to overexertion from the party. However, it had been four days and it was only getting worse. When I caught him trudging along the hallway and listening to a depressing Radiohead song instead of the usual hip-hop or Hendrix tune he kept in one ear during the school day, I knew it was bad.

I brought it up with Cairo during our poetry discussion group, but she just shrugged.

"Something definitely happened at the party though, right?" I probed.

"Of course something happened at the party," she responded matter-of-factly.

I opened my mouth to ask what she meant by that, but our randomly assigned group member, Emma Russell, who was sitting expectantly with a stack of highlighted notes and a blank notepad—forcefully cleared her throat and brought the conversation back to Whitman.

At lunch, I spotted Ryan at a table of a mixture of our second- and third-tier friends laughing and dapping them all up. Ryan was exceptional at hiding his feelings. In his view, there was no point in bringing everyone down just because he was, so he hid everything sad, sugar-coated everything unpleasant, and joked through everything devastating. Happiness was his brand.

As I neared the table, Ryan moved his leg and nodded for me to sit next to him. It was sweet but unnecessary—there was an unspoken rule that when one of the three of us sat down, there had to be two open seats nearby. Kind of like how there was an unspoken rule that half of the jocks now had to sit on the opposite side of the cafeteria (at jock table number two) since Mattaliano and I broke up.

"Look who it is!" Ryan announced. Nate, Connor, and Jalissa put their hands together.

"The party legend herself!" Nate grinned.

"Okay, okay, guys. Calm down," I said, lowering myself into my seat. It was nice to get credit for the party from the few people who knew the truth, but I was wary of being too loud about it with MV on the loose.

"If Mattaliano sees you being too friendly with me, you might get on his bad side," I reasoned.

"Mattaliano?" Nate asked. Nate—buzz cut, good-looking, rarely seen without his letterman jacket—was the most jocular of all our friends. "Oh, he's perfectly fine. I mean, after that party . . ." He looked over at Scott who snickered while Jalissa raised an eyebrow.

"I'm just saying," Nate continued, "he has to be over it by now—he's stacking clout."

"Hmmm," I said, distracted.

In a normal situation I might've dug deeper, but my attention was pulled toward Ryan. The skin around his eyes was tinged red, presumably from stress-rubbing his eyes, which was concerning.

He glanced up and caught me staring. I raised my eyebrows and gave him a "listen to these fools" look before turning back to my lunch as though nothing was wrong. That was a confrontation for a different time, and definitely a different table.

"Ay, Loli." Nate waved a bright orange paper in the air, edging it closer to my face. "What's the beef between you and Babble?"

Frowning, I grabbed the paper from his hands. It was the poster design that Ryan had sent last night over Instagram. I still wasn't sold on the typography.

"There's no beef," Ryan answered for me. "She's just taking a break from being Basilica's pet artist."

"And it seems to be biting me in the ass," I said, still frowning at the poster. I should've been relieved not to be a part of the chaos leading up to the big event and to be able to focus all my energy on winning the game with The Mysterious Voice, but I felt oddly wistful. "I can't believe you guys are already hanging signs up."

Ryan shrugged. "Must be nice to be a civilian for once." He smiled. "We've been stressing about this show for months."

I picked a meatball from my box. Maybe Ryan's stress was stemming from something as completely justifiable as preparing for the show. I made a mental note to write the date down in my calendar.

The Babble of the Bands was a big concert at The Ivory that featured a select group of local high school bands. Instead of having the bands battle (an archaic, non-constructive and super cringe concept), bands were invited to just play. It was supposed to be a conversation and compilation, rather than a competition, where bands sometimes mixed and collaborated improv-style. I always had to go to Babble because (a) it was one of the biggest events of the year and (b) both the event and the crowd favorite, Basilica, were fronted by Ryan. He and Noel had started Basilica at the beginning of freshman year, and by the end of the year they'd created Babble so they could play their songs with other bands in the area. It was a genius outlet for Ryan's creativity and Noel's incredible skill, but it was something I had to adjust to, even in its third consecutive year.

It was strange watching Ryan become a part of something that had nothing to do with me.

"Sup, losers." Cairo magically appeared on the opposite side of the table. She stood as though she had no intention of sitting down, with her tray resting on one hip and a trail of odd-looking boys hovering awkwardly right behind her. I appraised them, utterly confused, before I realized they must have been her nerdy hot tub friends from the party. The ones who'd hooked Cairo up with a potential modeling gig.

"Can I steal these two from you?" she asked the table.

Nate extended a welcoming hand. "Go ahead."

Ryan and I looked at each other. In all the mission planning and Ryan stressing, I'd forgotten about Cai and her hot tub friends, and judging from Ryan's expression, so had he. We gathered our things, said goodbye, and followed Cairo to an empty table.

"You know," I said, sidling up to her as we set our stuff down at the new table, "you could've just had them sit with us at the other table."

"I know," she said. "But they didn't seem to feel comfortable with that."

Ryan sat down opposite us and slid down to make room for Cai's friends, but they didn't sit down. I raised an eyebrow, amused at their awkwardness.

"Okay," Cairo said, clapping her hands together. "Let me introduce you guys. This is Tyler, Clay, Sid, and I'm sure you guys know Wolf."

I smiled tightly. I thought I knew almost everyone at this school but, bar Wolf, I had never heard of or seen these guys in my life. How was that even possible?

The two kids in front, Tyler and Sid, looked nervous as hell: Tyler, the more tanned of the awkward duo, waved slightly; Sid, the blond one with glasses, smiled weakly. The third one, Clay, was at least a foot taller than the two. Instead of looking terrified, he looked distracted, like he was attempting to feign disinterest. Later, Ryan and I joked that his square glasses and rigid air made him look like a Frankensteined Clark Kent.

And then there was Wolf.

"Of course we know Wolf," Ryan said. "Our ID and firework plug. Wolf*gang*!"

Wolf's lips curled into a smile. "Not my name but I'll take it from you."

He slapped hands with Ryan before throwing a lazy nod in my direction.

I didn't know Wolf that well—I only interacted with him when doing business—but I'd always found him vaguely interesting, which is a rare thing to be in this town. He was attractive, but not conventionally, with his slightly too long grayish-brown hair and his startling blue eyes. He was always on the outskirts of things, doing who knows what, but whenever I did see him, he was almost always laughing and having fun.

My kinda guy, I decided.

He was the first one to sit down, carelessly lowering himself onto the bench before sliding all the way down to me. I glanced at the silver rings on his fingers and caught myself thinking that if I hadn't decided to completely swear off boys after my disappointing experience with Tristan Mattaliano, I would go for someone like Wolf next. I liked that he didn't seem to care about what was trendy, topical, or even what was considered normal. Too bad he had a terrible smoking habit. Contrary to the rumor that I'd started smoking when I was nine, I despised smoking with all my guts.

Wolf made himself comfortable and after a second of hesitation, the other three followed.

"So . . ." Ryan started, amiably turning to look at Tyler, "I hear you're turning our Cairo into a star?"

"Oh, yeah." Tyler let out a nervous laugh. "Well, my uncle is. He wants to meet her on Friday."

"At a party," Cairo added, looking pointedly at me and then around the table. "A party. Am I the only one who thinks that's sketchy? Meeting a teenage girl for a job at a party?"

"Hey," Tyler cut in. "It's a launch party for a client's clothing line! I promise it's not as creepy as it sounds."

Cairo raised her eyebrows, and Tyler turned his hands out. He was slightly more comfortable now, talking to her. He'd stopped his fidgeting and there was a smile on his face. So they'd reached *that* level of friendship, I observed. Guys were often intimidated by Cai until they spoke to her and realized she was—and I'm quoting here—"one of the bros" (again, *not* my words). It was always sweet to see the shyest of them open up and relax around her.

"This is just what these people do," Tyler continued. "He just wants to see you in person to decide whether it's a yes or a no. Plus, he said she could bring a friend."

"*A* friend?" I repeated.

"How about friends, plural?" Ryan asked.

Cairo grinned and raised a finger. "I'll only go if everyone at this table is invited."

"Everyone?" I repeated, looking around at Clay and Sid. The whole table seemed a bit excessive.

"Yes, everyone," Cairo said. "I need you two to be there, that's a given. And then obviously Tyler has to be there, and he'll likely want Clay and Sid, right?"

Tyler nodded.

"Which means Wolf has to be there because technically this is his pack."

"Pack?" I asked, turning to Wolf. "You have a pack? I thought you were more of a lone Wolf."

"No way," Ryan said, grinning. "You think this guy operates so successfully on his own? He has his people help him, his Wolf-gang!"

The nerds snickered while Ryan echoed "Gangganggang," in a purposefully obnoxious way.

Wolf, who'd probably heard it all, gave us a tired look and shook his head. "I will give this party a swift miss if this is what I'm gonna have to deal with."

"Wait," Tyler interrupted. "So I really have to call my uncle and tell him eight teenagers are coming to his industry-level party?"

"Yep," Cairo said with a pleasant smile.

Tyler was at a loss for words. He hung his mouth open and unintentionally made a croaking noise, which elicited laughter from around the table.

Everyone seemed to relax after that. After some time, the conversation turned, inevitably, to Mattaliano's party and as it went on, I sensed Ryan closing off more and more until he stood up a full ten minutes before lunch was over.

"Hey, well it was nice meeting you all," he said, adjusting the strap of his bag. "But I've got to make a quick locker stop."

I looked up at Ryan, his thinly veiled gloom almost visible behind his weak smile. Lunch was almost over and I hadn't had the chance to crack him.

"I'll come with you," I said.

"No, no," he said, "there's no need. I'm gonna make a trip to the bathroom on the west wing and I know you've got classes on the east. Bye, guys."

"But—"

He was off before I could say another word. I caught Cairo's eye and she lifted a shoulder before Tyler pulled her into another conversation. As soon as Ryan disappeared through the cafeteria doors, I pulled my phone out.

> Hey, whats up? You ok?

The message was marked "read" and then the screen showed that he was typing. He was typing for a long time. A few minutes went by before I finally received a reply.

Yeah, I'm fine

I scoffed. Was he really trying that with me?

> Yeah, right.

> Intervention at ur place after school

This time, he responded immediately.

> Can't today, got
> rehearsal w/ the band.
> But, I'm fine, I promise!

No response. I sighed. Of course he couldn't pinky promise: he was lying.

Since Ryan had band practice right after school, I had to call my mother to pick me up. Like a freshman.

Or like someone who didn't have a fully functioning car sitting at home in their garage.

As she pulled up, I heard the hum of a woman's voice coming from within and immediately groaned. She was listening to one of her podcasts, which meant I would have to silently scowl to a discussion on interior decorating the entire ten-minute drive home. Which is exactly what happened. But my spirits were instantly lifted as we arrived at our gate and I saw the most beautiful view in all the world: my online shopping, all pink, white, and stacked by the front door, ready for me to open.

I sprang from my seat as soon as my mother put the car in park and headed directly toward the largest box of the pack.

"What are these?" my mother asked, stepping out of the car. She frowned at the sight of the seven boxes. "Hermès? Aisle by Ailee? Loli. Did you really need seven of them?"

Mom hated it when I shopped excessively. She'd grown up without a lot of money so she'd learned to be extremely cautious with it, even after her acting career took off. My father had also grown up without a lot of money, but he had the exact opposite philosophy. He'd grown up surrounded by rich kids with flashy things, so it made him happy to know he was able to give his daughter everything he never had.

Sure I liked to shop and dress, but it's not like I was some kind of spoiled label brat; I mostly wore my outfits for the dissonance. Running away in third grade wouldn't have been as iconic without my Paciotti flip-flops; car surfing wouldn't have been worth it without my Versace pumps. Just like Ryan had his music thing, I had my clothing thing. It would be a tragedy to do something dangerous in a bad ensemble.

Mom's phone rang and she dug a hand inside her purse, stumbling over the boxes as she went inside. I grabbed both stacks of boxes and crept upstairs to unpack my goods. I had just tossed the last box in the trash when the doorbell rang.

My breath caught. For some inexplicable reason, my first thought was that he'd found me. The Mystery Voice. I knew we'd promised not to try to find each other; but I also knew that he was a stranger, of yet undetermined morality, and that it wouldn't be too hard for him to find me if he really wanted to. All he had to do was ask around, figure out who really threw that party . . .

I wiped my hands on my pants and flicked my hair aside, trying to push away the irrational thoughts spiraling around my head.

But when I opened the door, there was no formidable stranger, only Cairo, cradling a bike helmet as she leaned against the wall. Her hair was wild, and her brother Kyle's motorbike was perfectly perched against the gate behind her. I raised my eyebrows. Kyle only let his little sister borrow his bike on the rarest of occasions.

"Yet another perk from your party," she explained. "Long story. Can I come in?"

I stepped aside and Cairo walked in the way she always walked into my house: making a direct beeline for the kitchen. This time, however, after grabbing two packets of chips and a glass of lemonade, she stopped in the foyer and picked up a few magazines too.

"Model research?" I asked.

She nodded. "Model research."

She squinted at *Vogue* as though it were written in a foreign language.

"It's actually why I'm here," she said. "I have no idea how the hell to do any of this stuff, and I have to figure out how to look pretty for Keene & Co."

I grinned widely and clapped my hands together. She didn't need to do anything to look pretty, but I wasn't going to push it right now. I'd been dying to dress Cai up for *years*.

Unlike myself, Cairo didn't care for makeup, brands, or clothing—she was on the self-described "butch side of femme."

"Okay, let's do a switch," I suggested. "I'll give you makeup and a couple of fashion tips in exchange for your poetry notes."

"Deal," Cai agreed. "But warning: you're actually going to have to start doing the work soon. Novak's making us memorize a poem for our final."

I groaned. None of the poems we'd read in class were remotely interesting. They were all just pretentious words organized in complicated rhythms. Now I had to commit a bunch of them to memory.

"You feel that?" Cairo said, teasing. "That's exactly how I feel about dressing up."

In my room, she collapsed on my bed, flipping through the first magazine until she came to a full-page ad. She pulled a face.

"Don't," I warned, settling in my chair.

"I didn't say anything!" she retaliated.

"But you made a face."

"Okay, before you give me a lecture on internalized misogyny, it's not that. It's just . . . bizarre to me. I mean—this is a soda ad!" She turned the page around so I could see the model, who was in full makeup and twisted in an odd position. Either they had photoshopped her or she was able to fold herself in a way that would make a pretzel cry.

"I don't know, man," I said. "Maybe the soda was so good she started dancing for joy and got stuck?"

Cairo snorted and turned the page. "You sound like Ryan when you say stuff like that."

At the mention of his name, all memory of Ryan's weird behavior sprang back to the forefront of my mind. I half-heartedly picked up the second magazine. "Speaking of . . ." I started. "Are you sure you don't know what's going on with him?"

Cairo swept the page with her eyes. "I wouldn't stress, Lo."

"Well, I am stressing," I said, annoyed. Why was I the only one who seemed to care about this? "The guy's gonna rub his eyes off if we don't get to the bottom of this. Earlier today you said of course something happened at the party—what did you mean?"

"Nothing. I just meant he only started acting weird after the party."

"So it can't be Babble then."

"I don't know," Cai said. "But I'm sure he'll tell us what's up when he's ready." She tossed the magazine aside and picked up a new one. "Speaking of the party, what's the update on our Letter Boy?"

I put a mental pin in our conversation, allowing the topic change only because I had been dying to discuss the mission I'd set for MV. I closed the magazine and rearranged myself on the bed, trying not to look as giddy as I felt at the mention of his name.

"I dropped his letter off this morning," I said. "I thought I'd start off by giving him a code to crack so I could figure him out, you know? I have no idea where his threshold is, what his boundaries are . . . I have no idea what kind of person I'm dealing with."

Cairo nodded. "A code's a good starting place. Test out his smarts."

"Exactly," I said. "Let's hope he's got them. The letter's sitting between the pages of a book in the library."

"No way," Cairo said with a smile. "I have never heard anything more rom-com in my life."

I frowned. "No romance, remember. It was barely even a book—it was a textbook. And it was not a love letter, so you can completely scratch the 'rom' out of that sentence."

"So . . . what did it say?" she asked.

I shrugged, not wanting to give her another chance to turn me into a movie trope. "Nothing much."

Dear Non-Entity,

What are you hiding? Your reasons for being in the closet couldn't possibly have been more complicated than mine. Did you kill someone? Judging from the way you ended your last letter, all emo and "maybe I am a monster," I wouldn't be surprised. In fact, I hope you did kill someone. That way your story would actually be worth all this dramatic secrecy.

You know, we met for less than ten minutes but there are two things I already know I admire about you: 1) you don't do or say things just because they're nice or necessary, and 2) you're not the type of person who would think it's crazy to elaborately steal a necklace that's already yours. Don't be too flattered though, I'm still trying to figure you out.

I get what you mean about old things dying but if I'm honest with you, I don't really care about it that much. Once, this girl who sat behind me in homeroom was talking about how she wishes she lived in the fifties so she could curl her hair, hit the derby in a puffy dress, and share a large diner milkshake with her friends and I turned around and told her that she could literally go out and do all of the above and more any time she wanted. I think I said, "Don't blame the time period, blame yourself for being boring," and I'm willing to bet she hasn't been to a roller derby in a puffy dress once since then.

Also, I have to say, I completely get why "the art of letter writing" died. This is, like, my third attempt at writing this stupid thing and my hand is cramping up.

Anyway, I read your sob fest about old things dying and I noticed you like Led Zeppelin, so I included a little temporary gift for you: an ace of spades signed by Robert Plant himself.

Given our extensive history, I trust you'll give it back.

Sincerely hoping you'll give it back,
A. Stranger

CHAPTER
9

TRACK:
SUNNY
Bobby Hebb

It was stupid of me to give The Mysterious Voice the rest of the week to complete his mission—three days was way too much time for me to sit still and wait.

Waiting made me jittery.

Maybe I'd given him too much time? He'd probably figured it out in one day, and now we were both sitting around wasting time, waiting for Friday. Or maybe I hadn't given him enough time at all, and the clue was too hard. There were three cemeteries in the area, maybe he'd been searching for Sarah Walsh's tombstone for days with no luck. Or maybe he was going through some dusty archive at the Woolridge Town Hall, looking through the records of every single person who had died in this town since it was founded in 1860. A fact that I now knew due to my extensive planning.

My worrying got to its worst on Friday, D-day, when it occurred to me that I could've typed the ISBN wrong, or that someone could've used the textbook and discovered the letter before he'd gotten there, or worse, someone could've taken the textbook out of the library. It wasn't like me to worry. I hated it. I was so wrapped up in my unnecessary stresses and the anticipation of whether I would ever talk to him again that I completely forgot about Cairo's plan to lower the median age at Michael Keene's party.

She sauntered over to my locker as soon as the bell rang, walking in that overly relaxed Cairo way through the crowd. When she reached me, she crossed her arms and leaned against my neighboring locker.

"So," she breathed, "turns out Wolf has this huge minibus with like eight seats. He's offering to drive us all there and back."

"What?" I frowned while racking my brain for any sane reason why Wolf would ever need to drive us anywhere and then I remembered. "Oh crap. The Keene party is today?"

Cairo studied me with passive, green eyes. "You forgot."

"Of course she forgot. She's too busy thinking about Letter Boy." Ryan, whose locker was three down from mine, smirked and pulled his door open.

"Great, Ryan. Do you want to maybe say that a little louder?"

I glanced at the guy opening his locker on my other side, and then at the girl at the water fountain. Who's to say he wasn't MV? Or that she wasn't one of his friends? I sighed. At this rate, I'd have to ban all MV-related conversation from the school premises.

"Trust me, I know," Cairo replied, stepping away from my locker and moving closer to his. "She's been pestering me with her worrying all week long."

"Worrying?" Ryan slung his backpack over his shoulder, walked over to me, and lifted the back of his hand against my forehead. He frowned. "Something is definitely not right here."

"I'm just fine, thank you," I said, batting his arm away. As much as I hated to admit it, he was right. How could I possibly explain— without sounding incredibly stupid or like some horrible teenage cliché—that I'd felt better understood by The Mysterious Voice in five days than I'd felt by most people in my life?

I couldn't. So I didn't. Instead, I turned to Cairo and switched lanes. "So. Wolf has a minibus, huh?"

"Of course he does," Ryan mused. "He's got everything. The guy's like a dodgy handyman the way he churns out spare metal parts and useful services between his distribution of burner phones and barely legal uppers."

The thought of Wolf, of all people, driving all seven of us in a minibus to a fancy party made the prospect of going ten times more enticing. It was just the perfect amount of chaos to subvert my worry spiral.

I slammed my locker door. "Fine by me. I don't have a car anyway."

"Uh—you have my car," Ryan said, looking hurt. "My car is yours until you get yours back, remember?"

"Only because you owe me for covering for you," I reminded him, as if either of us had forgotten. "Besides," I continued, "no amount of pickups, drop-offs, or car borrowing could ever replace the freedom of having your own vehicle."

"Okay," Cairo interrupted, "so it's a yes to the minibus?"

"Yeah, I guess I'm in too," Ryan conceded.

Cairo smiled and flashed a casual thumbs-up before disappearing into the after-school crowd.

Without thinking about it, I pulled my phone out to check the clock for the umpteenth time that day, stopping myself just as the screen brightened. I don't know why I kept looking; it wasn't like the date would miraculously change.

Ugh. Thank goodness for Keene's party. I really needed the distraction.

Baby Blue was the first car any of us ever had and the first real thing that any of us ever really earned. Ryan worked three summers, saving every penny he was given from eighth grade to sophomore year just to afford her, so naturally he loved her more than anything. She was old and very obviously used but he was incredibly proud of it. He wasn't even the tiniest bit jealous when my parents bought me a brand-new Porsche a few months later.

I opened the door on the passenger side and lowered myself in, taking in the familiar homey smell of old leather and ocean-scented car freshener.

"Well that was easy," Ryan said, getting in the car and closing the door behind him. "No argument? No fight? You're just . . . in the passenger seat voluntarily?"

I shrugged. "I'm feeling generous today."

Ryan smirked. "More like you've finally accepted your fate."

It was more like I wanted to get home as fast as possible, and I knew that an argument over driving would only take more time, but I decided to let Ryan think whatever he wanted to think. I didn't need him catching on to just how antsy I really was.

He leaned back and propped his left leg up beside the wheel the way he usually did when he drove, and then he picked his phone up and scrolled before settling on a song with the image of a tan woman against a mustard yellow background as its album cover.

"Song of the day?"

"Yep," he said, looking over his shoulder to reverse out of the parking lot.

I reclined my seat as the song started and closed my eyes under the sun's warm rays. Through half-open lids I watched the sun shine different shapes and patterns against Ryan's hands as he drove, the passing trees flickering shadows against our car. Ryan tapped the wheel, humming along to the singer's brass voice, and I decided I liked this one.

When we arrived at my house, Ryan headed for the bathroom, and I went straight to my laptop. It was stupid, but I just had to check AnonChat, at least once. Just in case he was online too. When the page loaded, my heart sank:

> ### AnonChat
> — We're sorry. There are no online users
> with the interest: Frozen Mudpies —

"You know it requires him to be online at the exact same time as you."

I glanced up at Ryan as he entered the room and promptly collapsed on my bed. "Yeah. I know."

I don't know what I'd been expecting—an awe-inspiring moment of magical telepathy? I sighed and wheeled over to Ryan who'd started an absent-minded scroll down some timeline on his phone. His eyes stayed glued to his phone as he chewed on the inside of his cheek and laughed at a looping video on his screen.

Friday-Afternoon-Ryan seemed to be doing much better than Wednesday-Morning-Ryan. He was better rested, less agitated, and there was a small, easy smile on his lips as he looked down at his phone. Something must've changed.

"Ryan, what happened at the party?" I blurted.

It was stupid. A rookie-level mistake. The key to unlocking Ryan was to sound lighthearted and nonchalant; interrogation and serious conversation were pure Ryan repellant. But I'd been waiting so long that I just couldn't help myself.

Ryan faltered for a fraction of a second and then looked up at me with flawlessly affected cluelessness. "What do you mean?" he asked.

"Don't try that on me," I said, scowling. "You've been acting off all week. I gave you time to allow you some space but that time is up."

I kept my eyes trained on him. He looked aside and laughed nervously. "Lo . . ."

I waited. "Yeah?"

He ran a hand through his hair and was just about to say something else when the door flew open.

"I thought I heard voices up here!"

I twisted in my chair, exasperated at having been interrupted.

My mother was standing in the doorway with a cup of coffee and the wide, loving smile I knew she'd be wearing on her face. Like everyone in town, my mother absolutely adored Ryan. Somehow, even after all the wrong things we'd done together over the years she still believed *he* could do no wrong.

"Aunt Nance!" Ryan returned the smile. It was his classic angel special, reserved mostly for adults and getting out of trouble.

My mother tucked a strand of her perfectly maintained hair behind her ear and put her hands together. "Are you two eating here tonight or at the party?"

"Probably both," we said in unison.

She laughed. "Okay, Lollipop. I'll get dinner started then." I cringed at her use of the childish name mash-up Ryan and I had coined as kids. We used to think it was the coolest thing ever that "Loli" and "Pope" joined to make lollipop. Embarrassingly, after all these years, our mothers had never let it go.

She went to close the door but suddenly stopped, putting on her best authoritative face, which was really her worst authoritative face around Ryan.

"Ryan, I hope you're not letting Loli drive your car."

"Mom," I said, groaning. "Stop. We get it."

"Of course not, Mrs. Crawford," Ryan lied. "I'm keeping Baby far out of her reach."

He was good. I would never have believed that that same face had handed me the wheel on the way to school that morning.

"Good," Mom said. "And don't let her boss you around either."

"I don't boss him around," I argued. "Mom, don't you have somewhere to be?"

My mother shared a knowing look with Ryan before she closed the door. I let out an exasperated sigh and rolled my chair all the way back to my desk.

"I hate lying to Nancy," Ryan said, when her footsteps reached the end of the hall.

I shot him a stern look. "I hope you don't think we've moved on from talking about the party."

He shifted on my bed and craned his neck, squinting across the room at my still-open laptop screen. "Woah, Lo . . . your laptop screen is flashing."

"What?" I rolled toward my desk and stared at the screen in disbelief. "No. Way."

I sat in awestruck silence until Ryan appeared above my shoulder. He peered down at my screen. "No kidding."

Somehow, stupidly, miraculously, even though the chances were one in a million and slimmer than slim, it had worked. At that exact moment in time, MV just happened to be trying to contact me too.

AnonChat
— You are now connected with someone who
likes Frozen Mudpies, just like you! —

You: Hello?

Stranger: wtf?

You: What!!

Stranger: tf?

You: How did this happen?

Stranger: I've been refreshing this page for like a day to try get a hold of you

You: A bit desperate. And slightly embarrassing. Did you find the letter?

Stranger: Yep. Found it yesterday.

You: I'm gonna need some kind of proof.

Stranger: Proof like what? The fact that Sarah was born in 1868? Or am I supposed to find it funny that you hid the letter in a textbook on psychopathy and criminal behavior.

You: Well, now that you know where it is feel free to read it.

You: I was worried that you wouldn't find it. I thought maybe the clue was too hard.

Stranger: Oh, I would've found it. Even if it meant skipping class and roaming through that graveyard all night long.

You: You know you're really not doing well to support your whole 'I'm not a creep' campaign

Stranger: Oh man. Then I guess this is a bad time to bring this up.

You: Bring what up?

Stranger: The fact that we need an entirely different mode of communication if we want this thing to work better.

"Like what?" Ryan asked aloud. I'd forgotten he was reading over my shoulder.

Stranger: Texting would be so much easier.

I paused. My hand hovered over the keyboard.

You: Texting?

Stranger: You've got a phone, don't you?

Stranger: We should exchange numbers. That way we can just let each other know when a letter has been dropped off or picked up.

"Bad idea," Ryan said over my shoulder.
"Why?" I asked.
"Too personal. You can ID phone numbers. Easily."
I thought about it for a while. "I don't think he'd do that. I mean—he's the one who is so hell-bent on our identities being kept a secret."

"And if he changes his mind? Calls you? Looks you up in the phone book? Perfect invitation for a stalker."

Even after his use of the word *stalker*, the benefit far outweighed the risk in my mind. I turned back to the screen and started typing.

You: Okay.

You: Same rules of anonymity apply.

"'Okay'?" Ryan repeated. "No. Not 'Okay.'"

"Hey," I said, turning around to face him. "MV may be good, but we're better. He has no idea what he's up against. And if it ever gets bad, we've got Wolf."

"Wolf?" Ryan repeated, his face scrunched up. "What good is Wolf? He's skinnier than I am."

"Have you seen that kid's face? He has like . . . scratches and weird scars. I'm sure he's had to threaten some people in his line of work."

The computer dinged and I turned back to see what he said.

Stranger: Obviously

You: And we're only allowed to communicate in emojis.

Stranger: Uh . . . no to the emoji part

You: What? It works. We send a mail emoji for 'you've got mail,' a wind emoji for when you've picked it up, and obviously you can type out your riddles or whatever if you need to.

Stranger: No, no emojis.

Stranger: Damn, I should've known you were an emoji person.

You: What's that supposed to mean???

Stranger: . . .

Stranger: That you use emojis

You: And??? They're there to be used

Stranger: Hey don't get offended, I was just saying.

The stranger then sent me a sequence of ten numbers that I assumed were his cell phone number. I deleted the angry message that I'd begun to type and sent my number in return.

Stranger: Just checking, in case I have to call this whole thing off—do you also use reaction gifs?

You: This conversation has gone on for much longer than it was ever supposed to.

You: Save the talk for the letters.

AnonChat
— You have disconnected —

Ryan took in a sharp breath. "I can't believe that when I'm standing over your dead body and your parents ask what happened, all I'm going to have to offer them is that I tried to warn you and you didn't listen."

"Calm down," I said, swiveling around in my chair. "A guy who hides at a party is no match for me. Now. On that topic. What were you saying before my mom came in?"

He looked stumped for a second, then seemed to remember. "Oh, yeah. I was just going to tell you to stop worrying about it—I just haven't been sleeping well lately, that's all." He ran a hand through his hair. "Probably won't sleep well ever again now that you've given your number to a stranger."

I sighed, turning back to my desk. "All right, here." I pulled a piece of scrap paper from my desk and started writing on it, then I handed it to Ryan. "Does this help?"

Ryan held the paper up so he could read it. "*Here is written proof that the accused, Ryan Pope, did his best to warn the deceased, Loli Crawford, about giving her number to strangers, but she refused to listen.*"

Ryan nodded, folded the paper, and put it in his pocket. "Yeah, I'm keeping this. It's perfectly vague enough to come in handy for whatever you do next without my permission."

CHAPTER

10

TRACK:

TEETH

Cage the Elephant

We left my house for Ryan's with only twenty minutes to get ready before Wolf was meant to pick us up. Somehow, between homework, dinner, pointless talking, and jamming to good music, we had lost complete track of time, and I ended up having to bring my makeup supplies to the Pope's to get ready while Ryan showered.

After a good ten minutes, Ryan came down the stairs wearing a casual blazer jacket and jean combo, hair slightly wet. I lowered my mascara wand and turned from the mirror in the sitting room just as a battered teal minibus pulled up in the driveway and honked.

"Yikes," I commented. "That's Wolf's whip?"

There was a clash in the kitchen and Ryan's eyes widened. "We've got to get in that minibus before Helen sees it or the whole night's canceled," he hissed.

I took one look at the rickety minibus, and I knew he was right. Mrs. Pope, with her many anxieties and narrow-minded predilections, was not going to like the look of that.

We both reached for the door handle at the same time and sprinted out the door toward the vehicle, Ryan with his shoes still in hand, me with my hair loose and wild in my face.

The side door to the minibus slid open, and Wolf hung his arm out the window. He removed the toothpick hanging from his mouth and tossed it, watching me with squinted eyes as I ran around the front of his vehicle and climbed into the empty passenger seat.

"Go, go, go!" I shouted as soon as I was in. With no hesitation, Wolf reversed, and the car was moving before Ryan even had a chance to slide the door shut.

Cairo looked from Ryan, who was lying across the seats in the middle, to me. "Helen?"

Ryan pulled himself up in his seat. "Didn't want to risk it," he said, breathily.

Wolf glanced in his rearview mirror. "Blond? Stiff haircut, pastel clothes?"

"That's her," Ryan answered.

"I think you've been caught, man. She ran out the house and stared after us."

Ryan groaned. "Well, I've got a nice long lecture waiting for me when I get back home."

"Hey," I said, clicking my seat belt in. "At least we made it out the door this time."

We neared a cross street and Wolf turned the corner so violently, all the little trinkets on his dashboard scattered noisily to the side.

"Easy, man," Ryan said. I glanced in the big circular mirror stuck to the dash and watched as he winced and rubbed his head.

Wolf barely registered the turbulence or his disgruntled passengers. He simply shuffled his hand through the mess between the front seats and pulled a new toothpick out of a small brown box.

"We've got one more stop before we head to the party," he said, placing the toothpick between his lips. "The boys are all hanging out at Killinger's."

The boys. I twisted in my seat to check if there was enough room for all three of them to sit in the crowded garbage and chaos of Wolf's car, and when I did, I was surprised to find Cairo wearing the makeup I'd given her a couple of days before. It was perfect. She'd done it just the way I'd shown her in my room: a subtle lip gloss, a light touch of mascara, and a thin stroke of liner that made her green eyes stand out. It was all just enough to highlight her features without covering the significant splatter of dark freckles that made her Cairo.

"Nice makeup, Cai," I commented. "You're gonna crush it tonight."

"Thanks," she said with a wink. "Would've been better if you'd done it though. Believe it or not, this under-eye smudge was an accident."

The car slowed down outside a small, narrow house, and Tyler, Sid, and Clay all walked out to the beat of Wolf's incessant honking.

They looked different from how they had looked awkwardly standing in the cafeteria at school. Probably because I'd never really bothered to see them as anything but three unimportant scraggly looking guys.

Tyler actually looked really cute dressed up. His hair was lightly gelled, and he wore a good pair of leather shoes as opposed to the worn-out sneakers he had been wearing before. He smiled and bumped fists with Cairo before climbing in next to her.

Sid was equally as fresh and bright-eyed in a white golf shirt and pants. He wasn't nervously hovering anymore; he even smiled before climbing in the back. And Clay, who was bent over his cell phone, looked surprisingly okay in his dark shirt and black jeans ensemble. He actually dared to make brief eye contact with us in his visual sweep of the vehicle before climbing in after Sid.

"You ready?" Tyler asked, looking at Cai.

Cai shrugged, calm as ever. "Ready as I'll ever be."

Wolf jerked the minibus back in motion, and we all held on as he swerved into the right lane. When everything was right side up again, he reached a hand out to fiddle with the stereo, and the system cracked and buzzed as he skipped through the stations. When we entered the freeway, he tore his eyes from the road and held them on the radio a little too long for my liking. Cairo was right to not bother being nervous about the party—it was clear we were going to die before we got there.

I glanced in the mirror and saw, quite predictably, Ryan starting to get antsy.

Not because of the driving, of course, but because of the music.

I counted three seconds of incredible self-restraint before he leaned over the divider. "Hey," he said, propping himself up and leaning an arm on either seat. "Don't worry about the music, I got it."

He fell forward onto the sound system, then reached for the end of the black cord running along Wolf's right leg and plugged his phone in, inciting a loud crash of rock music. I cringed at the sudden noise and watched in the mirror as Tyler eyed the situation nervously.

"The cops aren't gonna like the look of that," he shouted over the guitars and drums.

Wolf switched lanes and Ryan lost his balance, leaning all his weight on top of me. "Sorry," he shouted over the music. I couldn't tell whether his apology was directed toward me or Tyler. "Just give me a second. I have to queue the rest of the songs."

He straightened himself up again and in the brief window he created, I caught a glimpse of Wolf, slyly texting by his thigh.

"Hey!" I shouted, gripping onto the roof handle. "Eyes on the road, outlaw."

Wolf expertly darted his thumb across his phone, pressed send on whatever he had been typing, and slid his phone back into his pocket as the vocals started on Ryan's song. Ryan sat back down in his seat, red in the face but satisfied.

I took a deep breath in and straightened out as soon as he was out of my face. At least one of us was at ease. But even through the chaos of Wolf's driving and Ryan's obsessive compulsion, I was thinking about MV and our last AnonChat.

I'd saved his number in my notes, but there was no way in hell I was messaging him first. Why should I? It was his turn to drop a riddle or a clue. I had no reason to text him at all, so I decided I would wait until he did.

I heard snickering behind me, and I glanced in the oval mirror to see Tyler and Cairo huddled over something I couldn't see, their bodies barely illuminated by the passing streetlights on the highway. Farther back, a cold white light shone from Clay's phone onto his face. I hadn't even noticed how much the car had darkened until I realized it was the only thing that kept those back rows from being covered in total darkness.

After ten minutes that felt like ten years, we arrived at the event building. Wolf drove to the underground parking lot and stopped by the valet, where the man at the desk—"Eddie," according to his name tag—eyed the minibus with barely hidden distaste. As we climbed out, he snatched the keys from Wolf, not even bothering to fake a smile before getting in and starting the engine.

"Hey!" I shouted, knocking on the driver window. Eddie looked up. "Watch the attitude, man. You might not like the car, but this is Michael Keene's nephew."

Tyler winced and Wolf snickered as we headed toward the elevator. "You didn't need to do that," Wolf said, once the minibus disappeared around the corner.

"I did," I replied, pulling my coat over my shoulders. "You might be okay with being looked at like that but I'm not."

"Guys, elevator!" Cairo held the door open and waved us over, stepping aside only once Tyler pressed the button for the ninth floor and we were all inside. I snuck a quick look down at my phone to check for any updates and took a sharp breath in.

"What?" Ryan whispered.

I shook my head to signal that it was nothing, but I felt like doing jumping jacks, because fifteen minutes ago, I'd received three texts from an unknown number.

> Testing testing

> Stranger? You there?

> You know, I wouldn't be surprised if you gave me a fake number.

Ryan continued to look at me questioningly, but I ignored him and turned to Cairo instead. He'd made it clear he hadn't approved of my newly textual relationship with MV, and I wasn't in the mood for another telling off just then.

"You ready?" I asked Cai, flashing her a smile.

She nodded. I was amazed at her composure.

"I just hope he's not a perv," she said, arranging her top.

"I promise, my uncle is not a perv," Tyler asserted.

"Well, that's what anyone would say about their uncle," Cairo responded.

"Not anyone," Wolf said, matter-of-factly.

We all looked at him with varying looks of consternation before the elevator dinged and the door opened on the party.

I'd expected the doors to open at the end of a hallway or near an elaborate entrance, but the doors opened right onto the top floor of a wide, two-storied ballroom with humungous floor-to-ceiling windows that looked over the darkened city.

Tyler stopped to give the guard standing at the side our names, and the rest of us stepped out into the buzzing atmosphere, looking around in awe.

The room below was filled with small circular white tables and littered with adults in semiformal wear, all of whom were chatting, snacking, and drinking to the soft piano music coming from the center of the bottom floor. Ryan's eyes followed a waiter holding a tray of crispy crab rangoon.

"Slap me with a branch," Cairo said.

Wolf reached out toward an open tray and grabbed a handful of rangoon, stuffing one in his mouth before offering us the rest. Clay took one, inspected it, and took a bite before mechanically surveying the room.

"Hey!" Tyler exclaimed, pushing out from behind Wolf and enthusiastically pointing over the rail in front of us. "I see my uncle! Come on!" He grabbed Cairo's arm, and she looked down at his hand, blinking, before she decided not to care and let him take her through the crowd.

Wolf craned his neck and zeroed in on another waiter with a full tray spread before slapping his stomach. "Okay," he said. "You kids have fun, I'm getting food."

Wolf left and Sid immediately turned to Clay, looking slightly sick. "I need the bathroom," he said. "Come with me?"

Clay nodded, still surveying the room through his square glasses, and they both walked off, leaving Ryan and me standing over the railing.

He smiled, a slow, dangerous smile. "Care for a drink?" he asked, holding an arm out. I grinned and hooked my arm in his.

"Why not?"

As we descended the fancy staircase leading to the bottom half of the party, I swept the room with an impatient eye. The party was beautiful and the guests just as dazzling, but I was itching to pull my phone out and respond to MV's messages. I needed my next mission.

At the bottom of the staircase, I spotted a restroom on the far right of the room. A bathroom break was the perfect opportunity to check my texts away from Ryan. "Hang on a second," I said, loosening my arm in Ryan's. "I've gotta make a quick trip to the bathroom."

Ryan nodded. "I'll be at the champagne table when you're ready."

I was three quarters of the way there before I slowed down and pulled my phone out, unable to keep myself from replying any longer.

> Yep, it's me.

> Now let's get down to business.

I pushed the bathroom door open just as three heavily perfumed women were walking out, and I kept my eyes on the screen. He was typing.

> Ouch. Cutting straight to the chase.

> What do you want me to do? Ask what you're wearing?

The restroom was empty. After checking my fake lashes in the mirror and adding a tad more lip gloss, I turned around and pushed myself up onto the sink's marbled surface. He'd sent another message.

> What if I do?

> Or what if I just wanted to see how you are?

> Save it for the letters.

> Oof. Cold.

> Hey—you're the one who was all, 'Woe is the 21st century, if only one could goeth back in time and puteth pen to paper'

The door opened. A woman who looked as though she were in her midforties shuffled into the first cubicle.

> I'll ignore your impertinence but only bc you have a point.

> It's no fun sneaking around and leaving letters if we have access to each other through our phones anyway.

> Exactly. So, you can either give me that clue or delete my number.

I hopped off the counter, took one last look at my reflection, and walked back out into the party. My phone buzzed again.

> Touché
> Next Mission—

> ●●●

He continued to type, and I stood outside the bathroom, craning my neck in the direction of the champagne table. Ryan was in an obvious spat with the guy manning the table, who was shaking his head with his arms crossed. Ryan's arms were up in defense, as if to say he was innocent. It looked like one of those rare occasions where Ryan had found someone impervious to his charm.

"Listen, kid. I'm not going to say it again," the man warned as I sidled up to Ryan.

"I really don't know what you're talking about," Ryan said, eyes wide. "I was just going to ask where the bathroom is."

The man stared Ryan down for a few seconds and then he uncrossed his arms and turned to point out the marked signs at the end of the room.

"Straight down there," he grumbled.

"Thanks," Ryan said with a polite smile. The man didn't change his expression. He simply raised his eyes to look far across the room and recrossed his arms. Ryan rounded the table and headed toward the bathroom. I followed him.

"Well, that was a predictable fail," I said.

A wide, rakish grin spread across Ryan's face, and he clicked his tongue. "Oh, Loli. My dear, sweet, precious Loli. Are you growing soft or getting old?"

He pressed something hard against my side and I reached down to discover an entire champagne bottle pushed firmly into the fold of my dress. I smiled and wound my arm around the bottom of it. "Table," I decided. "Quick."

We shuffled away until we were a safe distance from the champagne guardian, and then Ryan nodded toward an empty table in the corner. We did a casual sweep and when we were sure the coast was clear, we ducked, lifted the tablecloth over our heads, and scuttled underneath.

"Presto!" Ryan said, holding his pinky out. I grabbed it with mine and laughed as I straightened out my dress.

"We haven't had to do that since Aunt Ruth's Thanksgiving in ninth grade," he said. "Remember?"

"Oh yeah, with the last quarter of the pumpkin pie?" I asked.

"Yep. That was a crazy dinner. My cousins still argue over who took those last slices to this day." Ryan held the bottle up and squirted. It was half empty; it must have been used to pour into the champagne glasses on the table. "It's only half full. Here. Go for it."

He held the bottle out to me, and I grabbed it and took a swig. The bubbles sparkled in my mouth and down my throat. I handed the bottle back to him. "Closet Boy texted me," I said when I'd swallowed it all down. So much for keeping it secret. I could never hide exciting things from Ryan.

Ryan raised his eyebrows. "Already?"

"Yeah, already."

He wiped his mouth. "Jeez. Anything newsworthy? Did he accidentally drop a clue as to who he might be?"

"No. No clues," I said. "It's strange. I don't want to know who he is, but at the same time it's the only thing I really want to know."

Ryan threw his head back in mock frustration and placed the bottle firmly on the ground. "Why is everything so complicated with you?" he said, sighing. "It's simple. We want to know who he is."

I frowned. "No, it's not simple. You weren't in the closet that night, so you won't get it."

"Oh really?" Ryan raised his eyebrows. "Enlighten me then."

"It wasn't just like meeting someone regularly. It was . . . weird and unique and wrapped in secrecy and I can't just . . . yank the door open on us and ruin it forever."

"Yeah, you can," he said. "It'd get us to the most interesting part faster."

I let my hands fall to my sides in frustration. "Come on, Ry! Think about it! There is no one interesting in this town. I'd get bored of him in a second if he were real. But right now, he's . . . enticing and interesting and mysterious because he's just a concept. He's just a voice and a bunch of words on a page that I can twist and make into anything I want."

Ryan took another swig and didn't say anything for a while. "If I didn't know any better, I'd think—" He stopped short.

"What?" I asked.

He looked at me and seemed to be weighing something in his mind before he shook his head. "Nothing."

"No," I insisted. "What were you going to say? You'd think what?"

Ryan's eyes searched mine and then he looked back down at the bottle. "No really, it was nothing. I was just thinking about who it could be and . . . you've got a point. It'd suck if it turned out to be some guy we already know."

I watched him take another sip. "Yeah."

"I mean, imagine if it turned out to be someone like Scott or Connor," he prattled on. "Someone like Mattaliano."

"Ugh," I groaned, leaning backward on my arms. "Don't even joke."

Ryan's eyes grew wide. "What if it was Mr. Robinson!"

I snorted. "That's the only outcome I can think of that I'd be fully satisfied with."

Ryan laughed. "I would want, no, I would *need*, front row seats to that."

I grabbed the bottle from him and readjusted my legs so they didn't fall asleep.

"Hey, speaking of front row seats," Ryan continued. "I haven't told you about the deal we just got for Babble."

"Yeah?" I said, taking a swig. "What deal?"

"I managed to get the VIP balcony row for our friends and family."

"Ooo," I cooed. "Fancy."

"Very fancy. And very hard to reserve. The owner of The Ivory says if you're VIP you've got to come on time or he has the right to give the seats up to the elderly and disabled, so no last-minute trouble causing on that day, okay? Put it in your calendar."

He was pointing a finger at me and trying to look stern which always made me smile.

"Hey." I took Ryan's hand and looked into his eyes. "I'll be there. I'm always there, aren't I?"

Ryan smiled. "Good." He took another drink, long and steady, and then he put the bottle down.

"Now let's go find Cairo and make sure Tyler's uncle isn't a perv."

We crawled out from under the table and into the fresh air, narrowly missing a couple fully decked out in Bulgari. Ryan nudged me and pointed toward a nearby table, where Cairo was chatting with an older Asian man with a well-trimmed beard. Michael Keene.

"There they are," Cairo said as we approached. "My bodyguards."

Michael Keene laughed. "Well they're not doing a very good job, are they?"

He held out his hand. "Michael," he said, giving us each a quick pump of the arm. "I was just telling your friend how fantastic her face is. Isn't it just fantastic?"

I smiled politely, waiting for Ryan to take over. Small talk with adults was his area of expertise. I almost always ended up saying something that upset them.

"It really is, Mr. Keene," he said, turning to face Cai. "We tell her that every day."

"And not only that," Keene continued, "but she has such a keen eye for detail. Do you know, she pointed out my latest . . ."

I tuned out of the conversation and reached into my purse for my phone. I'd been holding out on reading the text, but it was probably best to read now. For all I knew, he'd already hidden the package and it was due at midnight.

> No riddle this time.
> The mission is simple:
> Today I got my "phone"
> confiscated in Mr. Brink's
> class (you know how he is)

I did know how he was—absolutely vicious. Mr. Brink loved confiscating people's phones. He must have gotten some kind of sick pleasure out of it because his confiscations were ludicrous; I mean, he took phones away from people who were just texting in the hallway, even if they weren't in any of his classes. I also knew that Brink was notorious for locking these confiscated phones in a large metal drawer underneath his desk for however long he deemed fit. Usually it was just until the end of the day, but in what he considered "severe cases," he had been known to hold onto phones for a week.

> I need you to get my "phone"
> out of his desk by the time the
> bell rings for the end of the
> school day on Monday.

I guessed from the quotation marks on the word *phone* (and the fact that he was texting me) that it wasn't his real phone. The letter must've been attached to the "phone" in Brink's desk, which he'd purposefully gotten confiscated. I smiled to myself. I had to give it to him; this was a good one.

"Have you guys tried the quiche?"

I clicked my phone off as Wolf—followed closely by Sid and Clay—suddenly appeared right next to me, resting one arm on my shoulder and the other on Ryan's. "I don't know how they get that fluffy texture both in the crust and the filling."

"Please! Eat as much as you'd like, kids," Michael Keene said. "And while you do, Cairo and I are going to call her parents to get their permission for our shoot."

Cairo paused. "Wait. So . . . it's a yes?"

"Of course it is," Keene said. "We don't just want you, we need you."

Cairo looked between Ryan and me, and we stared at her, equally as stunned.

"Come on," Keene said, heading toward the staircase. "Let's go get you started."

A short while later, the group sat outside Keene's office as he talked next steps over the phone with the Dahmanis. Tyler had been allowed inside, but the rest of us were banished to the hallway. Wolf, Ryan, and I formed a triangle around a tiny buffet of stolen food that Wolf had laid out on a couple of napkins. We'd left spaces for Sid and Clay to join the feast, but in true antisocial form, Sid had chosen to sit against the opposite wall, and Clay had opted to pace the carpet with his hands stuffed in his pockets.

I grabbed a tiny quiche from Wolf's napkin buffet, opening MV's text messages again as I took a bite. There was nothing new of course, but I sent him a thumbs-up to let him know I had read his texts.

Suddenly, a loud and hollow wail reverberated all around us. I looked up from my phone in alarm to find Wolf stretching his arms up above his head, leaning back as if to punctuate his monstrous yawn.

"I'm sorry," he said, registering my expression. "I haven't properly recovered from that stupid party. That night was the type of wild I might never recover from."

"Ha," I said. "You can say that again."

"Hey, can we try to avoid the topic of the party tonight?" Ryan asked.

I looked at him and was surprised to find that he was visibly annoyed, not even bothering to coat his request with his usual amiable charm.

"What?" I asked. "Why?"

"Because it's all anybody's been talking about all week."

"Okay," Wolf said. "I'll change the topic." He folded his fingers together in a way that perfectly framed the big silver rings on his middle fingers and placed his knitted hands across his stomach. "Tell me, Pope, what's your deal with music?"

Ryan looked taken aback. "Deal? What do you mean?"

"In the car, you got so itchy to change the tune. And when I made a sharp turn, you held onto that dial like it was the steering wheel."

"I just love good music," Ryan said. "And I'm a firm believer in the fact that you can't play bad music during a good moment."

Wolf nodded. "I hear you. If movies can have great scores, why shouldn't life, eh?"

"Exactly!" Ryan agreed. "That's what I always say. If something great is happening, why not throw some Hans Zimmer in the background?"

"Or some Enya," Wolf added. "I always imagined the movie of my life starting with a good Enya masterpiece."

A look of displeasure set on Ryan's face, like he'd just tasted something bad. "No, no, no, man. Not Enya. If your life were a movie it would start with something . . . more sinister and provocative." His eyes brightened and he snapped his fingers. "If your life were a movie and you had to have a theme song, it'd be 'Clint Eastwood' by Gorillaz."

Wolf let out a wheezy laugh and straightened against the wall. "Okay, I'll take it," he said. "And you? What would your movie start with?"

'Oh, I think about this a lot," Ryan started. "There's this song, 'Pipeline,' by The Ventures that I would like to think works for me but I think it'd probably be a self-titled era Cage the Elephant song."

"What about them?" Wolf asked, pointing to Sid and Clay.

Ryan hesitated. "I'd have to get to know them better. It's a process. Give me a few weeks."

"You know me," I said, suddenly interested. "What's mine?"

"Easy. We've always said it was—" he stopped.

"What?"

"Well, it used to be that Keri Hilson song, remember? But . . . that's not right anymore. You've grown out of it." He narrowed his eyes and his expression dimmed.

'No," I said in disbelief. "Are you seriously drawing a blank? You? The human jukebox?"

"No!" he protested, although it was very obvious that he was. "No, no, you don't get it: the song has to *sound* like you at this moment in time, and it has to capture your entire personality. I can't just shoot out any old tune, it has to be . . ." He trailed off and pulled up his phone, frowning as he swiped, tapped, and scrolled through his music library.

By grabbing his phone Ryan had broken the social seal. Wolf flipped open his knocked-up burner first, followed by Sid who quietly slid his phone out of his pocket. Clay stopped his mindless pacing and took his phone out before sliding down the wall next to Sid, and then I buckled and looked down at my phone too. I was pleased to find I'd received another text.

> Ugh. I'd said no
> emojis—remember?

> For you maybe,
> but not for me.

I typed out a sequence of emojis—just because—and the office door opened just as I pressed send.

"Come on, guys," Cairo said, waving two papers in the air. "Let's bounce."

We said goodbye to Mr. Keene on the ninth floor, held the elevator as Wolf ran in for more food, and less than ten minutes later we were all back in the minibus.

"Thanks for coming with me, guys," Cairo said, pulling her seat belt strap down.

"Of course, Cai!" I smiled. "You know we're always here for you."

Wolf held up his fresh bounty. "And I got free food out of it, so really I should be thanking you."

I snorted. The party really was the gift that kept giving. Who would have thought I'd be in a minibus with Wolf and his friends, driving back from copping a modeling gig for Cairo?

Ryan put on some mellow tunes for the drive home. Through Wolf's circular mirror, I watched him lean back and stare out his window, totally content.

"Hey, Wolfie," I said, still eyeing the circle on the dashboard. "What's with the mirror?"

Wolf glanced at me and then looked back at the road. "What's with it?"

"Like, why is it here? To show you when someone's hiding behind a seat, waiting to jump out at you?" I asked, sarcastically.

Wolf blinked. "Well. Yeah," he said plainly.

I looked at him, waiting for him to say he was joking, and when he didn't, I turned back to see Ryan and Cairo looking equally nonplussed. Cairo was the first to break. She put her hand to her mouth in an attempt to stifle her laugh but instead amplified the burst of air that escaped her lips. Her trumpeting immediately set Ryan, Tyler, and me off, and we were all laughing, ignoring Wolf's orders to shut up until he purposefully swerved into the wrong lane and the laughter turned into horrified screams as we yelled for him to stop.

CHAPTER
11

TRACK:
PIPELINE
The Ventures

The next morning, I stood in my room debating over whether it was a good idea for me to make my weekly Saturday morning trip to Westerns or not.

I decided not. My Saturday morning trip to Westerns was the one surefire thing MV knew about me, and I didn't want to risk the possibility of him secretly scoping me out. Sure, we'd made a promise not to go looking for each other, but what good was the word of a stranger?

So I looked up other places I could go, scrolling through boring coffee shops and diners, before it occurred to me that I was moving my entire schedule around because of a boy. The concept was so disgustingly horrific that I closed my phone and immediately decided I would go to Westerns after all.

When I went downstairs to announce that I was leaving, Mom pursed her lips. "Okay," she said. "I'll drive you."

I stared at her. She continued typing on her laptop.

"Uh . . . I'm just going to Westerns."

"I know."

"I'll be back in two hours."

"Sure."

"So can't I just drive myself?"

"No."

I frowned and tucked my hair behind my ear. "What? Why not?"

"You know perfectly well why not."

I stared at her. "Mom, that makes no sense at all. You let me drive to Westerns last week."

"Well your father and I spoke and we decided that that was a mistake."

"What? Why?" I asked. "I mean sure I took a little longer than I'd said, but I came right back home after the Popes'."

My mother stopped typing and looked at me over her glasses. She was tired, I could tell, and I knew she hated it when we disagreed. Despite our differences and the fact that I was a "difficult daughter" (her ex-therapist's words, not hers) we didn't fight often. The three of us actually got on really well.

It's why the rules were always a little loose, and the punishments, no matter how fiery upon issue, were usually brushed aside. Although it seemed she'd forgotten that part this time.

"I'm simply enforcing the rule, Naloli. It's no good having a car taken away if it's still available to you."

I sighed, frustrated, and sat down, immediately pulling my phone out. "Fine," I huffed. "I'll get Ryan to take me."

"That's fine by me. As long as you stick to the rules," she said. "Okay?"

"Fine," I acquiesced.

Ryan pulled up fifteen minutes later, and I was surprised to see Cairo waving from the back. She lived a little farther away from us, so she rarely joined us on these trivial trips.

"Don't mean to scare you, Ry, but there's a model in the back of your car."

Cairo pulled a face as I climbed into the front seat, but I knew she was just as pleased with the outcome as I was. "We knew you'd land it." I beamed.

"There was no chance you wouldn't," Ry agreed.

Cai covered her face with her hair. "Pleeeaase cut the mush before I die."

Ryan pulled the car forward and I leaned back, pulling my shades over my eyes. "I hope you guys aren't expecting an adventure or fun road trip."

"We know, we know," Ryan said, turning the volume down. "Westerns is your 'you time.' We'll leave you to draw, or plot, or whatever it is you do on your own, and we're going to the mall."

"You know what I was thinking?" Cairo cut in, leaning between our seats. "Hanging out with Tyler's friends yesterday wasn't bad."

"It was surprisingly fun," Ryan agreed. "They pass the hangout test."

"Anyone can pass the hangout test," I said. "I mean, the jocks passed the hangout test, and they're as basic as it gets. It's the Loli test that counts. We've got to figure out whether they're ride or die or whine and cry."

"Good point," Cairo said, sighing and lying down across the back seat. "The last person who passed the hangout test failed the friendship test."

There was a moment of silence as we thought back to Noel Sang screaming and begging not to have to get on top of the car.

"You know what?" Ryan said. "Cut him some slack. At least he tried."

Cairo sighed. "He's so sick on stage with that guitar. It's a shame the attitude doesn't carry in real life. I liked him."

Ryan looked torn between defending his friend and agreeing with us. In the end he just reached over and turned the music up.

We arrived outside Westerns twenty-five minutes later, and as Ryan slowly drove up the grimy street, I pulled my bag strap over my shoulder just as the scratchy twang of an electric guitar sounded from the radio.

"Hey, wait," Cairo said suddenly. She was sitting up now, squinting out the back window. "Isn't that Will Hudson?"

I shut the door immediately. "What? Where? Here?"

"Right there." She pressed a finger against the window in the back seat, which didn't help at all, but I looked anyway and spotted

him. All tall, dark skinned and polo shirt wearing as usual, standing by a table in the middle of the café.

I frowned. How was it possible that I had never seen a single
Woolridge soul at Westerns until now?

I froze.

Maybe it was because up until recently I had never told anyone about it. "Ryan," I said, low and urgent over the sound of the
beachy guitar. "GO!"

Ryan turned from the radio to look at me. "What? Why? I
thought you guys were cool."

"We are cool," I said, reclining both myself and the seat farther
than usual. "But you need to GO!"

Ryan switched into drive with a confused look on his face, and
I mumbled under my breath. My sanctuary had been infiltrated.
The era of Westerns was over.

As Ryan drove around the corner, I hoisted myself up again.
"Wait," I said, mind racing. It couldn't really have been *him*—
could it?

"What?" Ryan looked from the road to my hand on the door.

"Go around again."

"What?" Ryan asked, again. "Round back to the front of Westerns?"

"Yes! Quick!" I said, frantically. "But do it slow."

He took a right, and then the next right, and then we were
right in front of Westerns again. I took my sunglasses off and
crouched down on the floor so I could peak over the top of the
door through the window. Will was sitting by himself, reading
a book. That's all I got before we passed him, and I was staring
down a dirty alley.

"Go again," I demanded.

"Uh—can I ask what is happening?" Ry asked.

"She's looking to see if he's there with someone," Cairo said.

"No, I don't care about all that. Hurry, Ry! And slow it down
this time."

"I'll do it if you tell me what's going on!" he said, exasperated.

"What's going on," I snapped, "is that I'm realizing that it could be him."

"Who?"

"*Him*."

"Ahhh," he said, nodding slowly.

"What?" Cai asked.

"Closet Boy," he replied.

We rounded the corner again and I eased back up onto my seat.

"Think about it," I said. "No Woolridge kid ever comes here. No one. Up until now I have never, not even once, seen anyone from the Grove in this vicinity. Why would anyone drive out so far just to sit in a dump like Westerns? And don't you think it's a little odd that someone is showing up now, a week after the party? I told MV I come here every Saturday morning. It's the only surefire way he could track me down."

Ryan and Cai looked at each other and then back at me.

"Well. Damn," Ry said.

Cai tapped our seats. "What are you waiting for? Hit the pedal, Pope."

The third time we circled, the three of us gravitated to the right of the car to get a better look. We watched as Will turned a page.

"You really think Will is Closet Boy?" Ry whispered.

I thought back to the closet, the witty, flirtatious phrases and lines. It made sense. Will and I always had good back-and-forth.

"Has to be," I adamantly concluded. "Who else actually likes this place? Plus, he was here around the same time last week too, just waiting to disarm and perplex me. Think he's aiming for round two."

"Look," Cai said. "Look at the table: three cups and two plates, yet only one of him."

"A.k.a., he's been here for a while," Ryan concluded.

"Waiting for me," I spat.

"Obviously," Ryan said, craning his neck. "Just look at how he's sitting in the middle of the room, facing the door."

"What the hell?" I exclaimed. "This is such a blatant breaking of rule number one!"

We all silently stared out the window, cruising by at a snail's pace. Suddenly, as if he could sense us, Will looked up from his book and out the window. I ducked with gravity-defying quickness, and Ryan hit the accelerator, causing the car to lurch so suddenly that Cairo and I both slammed into the leather in front of us.

When we were a good distance away from Westerns, I sat back up in my seat, rubbing my head. No car, no Westerns, and no more mystery to The Voice.

I couldn't think of a worse start to the weekend.

"He looked good," Cai offered.

"So?" I asked, shooting daggers at her over my shoulder. "He always looks good."

I pulled the mirror down and fixed my hair. "And, unfortunately for him and every other one of my exes, so do I."

Ryan snorted. "Wow. Beauty, brains, and humility. What do you lack?"

"A thrilling mystery," I mumbled. "The promise of adventure."

"There still is the off chance that we are wrong," Ryan offered.

"Doubt it. This is real life, Ry. The answer is usually the one you work out. Things are more often staring you in the face than hiding."

"Blue Monday" was playing before we even stepped under the flashing neon lights at Dizzy Arcade. It was too much of a coincidence to be an accident, so Cairo and I simultaneously turned to look at Ryan, whose face was washed completely blue under the fluorescent light.

"Jukebox app," he explained, shaking his phone. "Timed it perfectly."

After the trip to Westerns had proven to be both a bust and a huge blow to my spirits, we'd collectively decided the only fitting course of action was to drown our angst in decadent fried food, colorfully adventurous milkshakes, and excessively syrupy mixed drinks.

The music pulsed around us, and I felt the whir of the machines beneath my feet. I'm sure once upon a time Dizzy's was a normal family diner, but after its retro revamp, it had become a place for teenagers of all ages to come and socialize, creating an environment with all the drama and fun of school without the assignments and bells. The food was amazing, sure, but people mostly went to Dizzy's to see and be seen. I didn't need to bother squinting through the flashing neon lights to know that the place was packed with almost everyone we knew. It was the opposite of Westerns in every way.

"Ah," Ryan said, taking a deep breath. "Smells like home!"

A couple of kids at a table nearby waved to us, and Ryan smiled and waved back. I, however, was not in the mood to be civil, so I slipped my sunglasses on and followed Cairo to our usual booth. As we slipped in, some guys at the table next to us nudged each other and pointed our way.

"Why do underclassmen always stare at us," I complained, pushing the menu out of my way. I already knew what I wanted; it was always the same thing.

"If you don't want to be stared at, you have to stop doing things that make people point and stare at you in public," Ryan replied.

"Rude," I mumbled.

"True," Ryan shot back.

Our usual drinks arrived almost immediately: a floating brownie atop a giant milkshake for Cairo, a green soda float for Ryan, and an overly saturated Shirley Temple with extra maraschino cherries for me.

"Same food order too?" the waitress asked. We all nodded in response, and Ryan clapped his hands together. Dizzy Arcade was the one place he broke his perpetual diet for.

Cairo swallowed a monstrous gulp of her milkshake, and I picked a cherry from the top of my Shirley Temple, finally content.

'So," Cai started. "Will Fricken Hudson, huh?" She ran a hand through her hair. "You know what? Let's have a toast. Or—the opposite of a toast. A sad clashing of drinks for the end of our short-lived, riveting mystery."

She raised her giant milkshake bowl, and we followed suit.

"To what could've been, and to what isn't. In memory of our short-lived adventure." We all clinked our drinks together and took a drink.

"I know this wasn't my story or anything," Cairo continued, putting her drink down, "but I'm actually really disappointed. I was hoping for . . . more magic. An adventure. Maybe a little romance, some twists and turns . . ."

I swirled a spot of dark red syrup and took a long melancholic sip. "I know."

"Buut," Ryan cut in, "as I said in the car, how do we know it's him for sure? You don't have some doubt at least? Like, for starters, the fact that you dated him but somehow didn't recognize his voice the night of the party. Sure it was dark and your vision was impaired, but you're not deaf."

"Maybe not," I said. "But I dated him in freshman year, before his last crazy wave of puberty, and I think I've spoken to him like once after his voice broke."

"Dammit," Cairo said. "I really wanted to do a mission with you."

"Same," Ryan said.

I picked up a cherry and put it between my teeth. "Actually, Ry, I think I might need you for this next one. The last-ever one."

"Yeah?" Ryan leaned forward. "What's the task?"

"I need to get a fake phone out of Brink's confiscation drawer."

He laughed. "Oh, man. That's good."

"Since you have Brink Monday morning, I was thinking you could keep an eye out. Stay alert, watch where he leaves his keys lying around, whether he leaves the drawer open, etcetera."

"Sure," Ryan said. "And if he happens to leave the classroom— I'm pouncing on it."

"Uh, no," I said. "Don't do that, that's cheating. You can try to get the keys if you can though. The plan is to slip in before he locks up for lunch, but it'd be good to have them just in case the drawer is locked or I get to the classroom too late."

"Okay fine," Ryan said. "I'll try to get the keys."

"Good." I bit into my final cherry. "Because I am not failing this mission. I have to finish this on top."

"Of course," Cairo said. "What other way is there to finish?"

I may have sounded confident, but my chest ached at the prospect of a lost opportunity: no more mystery, no more adventure, no more promises of excitement. Only deceit and disappointment.

As I sipped my drink, it occurred to me that deceit could have been his plan all along.

This was his game after all; maybe he'd always intended on giving himself the upper hand while I blindly played by his rules. He knew my Saturday morning routine, he knew where he could find me if he wanted to—I knew nothing about him.

Was there a chance he'd been in the café when I'd gotten the letter? Could he already know who I was? If he'd been hiding his true intentions, what else could he have been hiding?

My straw made a hollow sound as I got to the bottom of my drink.

I resolved that I was not going to let him have the upper hand.

I was going to win by finishing my mission and calling the game off.

CHAPTER 12

VENUS FLY
Grimes (feat. Janelle Monáe)

It was second period on the day of my final mission, and Ryan hadn't texted me any updates on the Brink situation.

I'd excused him from texting me during first period (for obvious Brink/phone related reasons), but I'd expected him to send me the details as soon as the bell rang.

Second period came and went, and by the time third period came around I was getting antsy. I had just over an hour until lunch, a.k.a. just over an hour until I planned to get into Brink's classroom before he locked up. But now I had no idea whether I could, because Ryan hadn't texted me yet.

When the bell rang for my fourth period gym class I rushed out into the hallway and sent the third string of punctuation marks since second period.

????!!!!???

Hey! Sorry, only just switching on my phone

What the heck Ry? I'm dying out here.

I just had a chem test!

Oh. Okay how did it go?

Fine. But I think I messed up one ph/ poh calculation.

I mean with Brink—did you get a key? Did he leave the room?

Nope, sorry. None of the above. The guy is relentless—never left his desk once.

I glanced up from my phone, exasperated. What now?

Good news though— found out he keeps the drawer unlocked. Meet you outside the gym after class?

I was typing a response when my phone pinged with another text message. I froze. It was MV.

You get the letter yet? You only have three periods until time's up.

My annoyance flared. I shouldn't have responded. I should have left it and waited to reply after lunch when I did have the letter, but the feelings I'd been holding in all day forced my thumb to act before I could think otherwise.

> Well I haven't sent a message saying I have, have I?

I clicked my phone closed. Another buzz.

> Woah, Rob. Cutting it close over there.

> Whatever. I'll get it in the end.

> And if you don't?

I paused. Now that I knew he had broken the rules, it didn't matter whether I got the package on time. I would win the game as soon as I ousted him for cheating; completing the final mission was simply another thing to throw in his face.

> Oh don't you worry— I'm definitely winning this thing.

> This is the last package. As soon as I get this one we're done.

> What, have we already lost our spark?

I had the good sense to ignore that message and respond in the affirmative to Ryan.

Forty-five more minutes. Forty-five minutes until I got the letter and officially broke it off with MV forever.

My second-tier friends, Jalissa and Brianna, waved me down as
soon as I entered the gym. It was a shame—I would've liked for
them to have passed the test, but they'd stayed second-tier after
Jay complained about Ryan's "constant loud music" and Brianna
proved that she couldn't run for peanuts.

I dodged a flying basketball that just narrowly missed my head
and glared at the kid who had thrown it. Whoever thought it
would be a great idea to have two gym classes going on in one
gym needed to be fired; just because the gym was big enough for
it, didn't mean it needed to happen.

And that's when I saw him.

Will Hudson, shooting a ball into the basketball net on the
other side of the court. His teammates cheered when it shot
through in one clean swish.

"Hey, Lo," Bri said, standing up from a downward stretch.

"Uh . . ." I paused, confused, looking between her and the team
of boys across the gym. "How long has Will Hudson shared this
gym period with us?"

"I'm pretty sure he's been with us in this gym all semester,"
Brianna answered. "Why?"

I shrugged, trying to act casual and not like I'd been in a
secret correspondence with him for the last week, and lowered
myself to the floor to join them in stretching. "I never noticed
him before."

"Girl, that's because you never notice anything," Jalissa chided.

Brianna laughed and I narrowed my eyes.

"That's not true," I said. "I was the first person to notice your
eyebrows last week, remember?"

"That's because you wanted to know where I got them done.
You only notice things when they have something to do with you."

I rolled my eyes. "You say that like it's a bad thing. At least I
mind my own business."

"Okay, I hear you on that one," Jalissa agreed. "We need more people like that. Did you hear that Sammy . . ."

I looked across the court and watched Will glide across the shiny wooden floor, weaving in and out of bodies and flying into the air.

Will Hudson.

It had been a while since I'd really spoken to him. Two years. Not including our time in the closet, of course.

I watched him, contemplating if it would be a good idea to go right up to him now, in person, and let him know that it was me and that I already knew it was him and that it was all his fault for breaking the rules and trying to find me in Westerns right at the time he knew I'd be there. Watching his face as he realized he lost the game because of his own dishonesty would be the sweetest victory ever.

Suddenly the temptation became too hard to resist.

I stood up, ignoring questions from the girls as I strode across the court, dodging birdies, rackets, and volleyballs to get to him. He had walked away from his game to grab his phone and a towel from the bleachers, which he was using to wipe his face down when he turned to find me standing behind him with my hands on my hips.

"Woah," he said, stepping back in surprise. He squinted at me for a second before he realized who I was and smiled. "Loli Crawford," he said slowly, tossing his towel over his shoulder. "What's up?"

I studied his expression for anything that would suggest that he knew I was the girl from the closet, but there was nothing. Just smooth, perfect skin, dark, teasing eyes, and a haircut fresh enough for the Whole Foods produce section.

"I didn't know you had gym this period," I said, keeping my face neutral.

He raised his eyebrows. "Well . . . I do."

"Hmm," I said. "Fancy that."

Just as I'd suspected, his voice was unplaceable. I'd either have to catch him in a lie or back him into a corner. I shifted my weight, contemplating where to start. The party? The closet? Westerns?

"I heard you went to the party."

He grinned. "You mean the one at The Golden Eagle's house?"

I tried not to roll my eyes at Mattaliano's nickname. "Yes. That one."

"Of course I did! My boys texted me saying his place was bumping. Obviously I had to come through." Will's phone buzzed and he glanced at the screen. "My mom. Gimme a second."

As he began to type a response to his mother, I was struck by an immensely brilliant idea.

His phone. It was right there, in front of me.

All I needed to do to catch The Mysterious Voice in action was give it a call.

I whipped out my phone and tapped on MV's number, staring Will down as the line rang—

And rang.

Will continued typing, and the sound just continued to ring in my ear.

Then, suddenly it stopped. My heart stopped cold; someone had picked up. And it wasn't Will.

"Hello?"

The Voice was muffled. Quiet. As though trying not to be heard by anyone nearby. "Rob?"

I cut the phone, fast, feeling light-headed due to the crushing weight of realization.

I'd been wrong. It wasn't him.

Across the court, Coach Burns blew her whistle and shouted for the class to gather round.

"Ah, crap," Will said, glancing up from his phone. "Look, I've got a bet going with Madden for this first round so I gotta go. Nice seeing you though."

He jogged over to the bleachers and my phone buzzed with a text

Hey—did you just call me on purpose? What's wrong?

I closed my eyes, heart and mind racing. If Will wasn't The Mysterious Voice, and MV had in fact remained true to his word, we were once again in equal running, gunning for a place at the top. And I was trailing.

The clock on the scoreboard hit 12:30, and I steeled my resolve. I had to get that phone. Fast.

Ryan pushed off the wall he'd been leaning on in the hallway outside of the gym and immediately fell into step with me.

"It's not him," I said.

"What?"

"Will. He's not MV. I called him during gym class and his phone didn't ring."

"Well hey," he exclaimed. "That's great news!"

He was right, it was a spectacular turn of events. The news had been such a shock to my system I hadn't allowed myself to feel relief.

"But it means we absolutely have to get the phone, *now*," I said. I thought back to the haughty texts I'd sent earlier in the day. I was starting to regret saying anything at all.

We were now speed walking toward Brink's classroom, half jogging down the hall.

"Okay," Ryan said, "I was thinking that when we get there, I should just say I lost something urgent and need to look for it. Knowing Brink and his impatient self, he'll probably leave for lunch and give us the keys to lock up."

"Sounds good," I replied.

Unlike me, Ryan was held in the greatest esteem by the school staff, which didn't make sense considering how much trouble we both got into. It was either blatant misogyny or that stupid, charming smile.

The second bell rang, and we picked up our pace, racing down the staircase to the second floor without breaking into a full-fledged sprint. Running in the hall was a punishable offense that Ryan and I had agreed to never commit again. We didn't care much about the mark on our school records (we'd ruined any chance of leaving high school spotless long ago), it's just that the thought of getting yet another detention for one of the most boring misdemeanors ever was pure agony. If we were going to sit in detention it was only going to be for an offense of the highest quality, something top tier that would make the wasted time we spent sitting in a classroom worth it as we relived every moment of our glorious misdemeanor.

When we finally reached Brink's classroom, my stomach dropped. The door was closed, and he was nowhere in sight. I tried the door. Locked. "Nononono."

Ryan looked up and down the hallway, out of breath, eyes searching through the crowd. "Classic Brink," he mumbled. "He probably dismissed his students early just to get away from them faster."

I leaned against the door and slid down, letting my head bang against the door in defeat. Ryan slid down next to me, hair wild, cheeks red.

"Hey," he said, through fast, short breaths. "Let's Operation Swiss Eye it."

I lifted my head.

Operation Swiss Eye was a classic tactic, something we used to do when one of us was in trouble and needed the other to distract the adult in charge while it was taken care of. Like the time Ryan and I completely trashed the living room while his parents were away, and they pulled up five hours earlier than we expected? I ran outside with some incoherent sob story about how I needed them both to take me to my dad's office thirty minutes away, giving Ryan an hour to put the house in order.

Or the time I sprayed my mother's expensive perfume before a date, and she knocked on my door? Ryan shot out of my room and told her he was about to be sick, giving me enough time to sneak to the bathroom for a toilet spray to cover up the scent.

Ryan moved onto his knees, turning fully toward me. "Listen. We'll come back here as soon as the bell rings for last period. I'll pull him aside with a really complicated question, and while he's explaining it to me you walk in with the other students and get the phone from the drawer."

I looked at him. "You think it'll work?"

"Definitely," he assured me. "I'll make sure to pull him around the corner so he can't see you inside."

I thought about it. Losing the last mission was not an option. This was the only viable way.

"Okay," I said, reaching a finger out. "Let's do it then." Ryan grabbed my finger and we both stood up. "Bathroom and then lunch?"

"Sure," he replied. "I'll text Cairo with an update."

I left him in the hallway by the cafeteria, promising to only be a second as I fixed myself up. I smoothed my hair, checked my teeth, and was just applying a fresh coat of gloss when there was suddenly a loud, terrible noise.

An unbearable, ear-throttling, blaring noise, accompanied by flashes of red and white along the tops of the walls.

I stared at myself in the mirror, gloss half raised, red and white flashing above my head, and then I bolted out the bathroom door, bumping directly into Ryan.

"Hey!" he said, frowning at the ground. I'd accidentally ripped his earphones from his phone and "Venus Fly" pumped from his speakers at top volume.

"My bad," I mumbled, picking up his earphones. He grabbed it from me and hurriedly plugged an earphone back in his ear.

"This is not a drill. Follow procedure and make your way toward the closest exit. This is not a drill. Follow procedure and make your way toward the closest exit—"

I looked up and down the hallway, taking in the words and the flashing fire alarm lights before locking eyes with Ryan. He looked just as bewildered as I felt.

Someone screamed. Shouts arose all around us as the few students still in the hallway spun around haphazardly. A nearby teacher raised her voice to tell everyone to calm down and leave their belongings inside.

I continued staring at Ryan, completely frozen. If this was a real fire, and the building was cornered off for the rest of the day, I was going to lose the game.

"Come," Ryan said, tugging my arm, "let's get out of here."

I shook my head, my breathing shallow. "No. No. Brink's classroom. He could've gone back."

"For *what*?" Ryan demanded.

"His lesson plan? A lunch box?"

"Loli," Ryan said. "There's a fire."

"I'm getting that phone," I said, resolute.

"Nalo—"

I turned and booked it down the hallway, struggling against the erratic stream of students and teachers hurrying toward the nearest exits. I didn't have to turn around to know Ryan was right behind me. Mostly because I could hear him screaming my name over the siren.

Brink's room was just as locked and empty as it had been before, and unfortunately, he was nowhere in sight.

Ryan swore and ran his hands through his hair as he caught his breath.

"I can't lose," I muttered. "We need to get in there. I'm *not* losing."

I spotted a fire extinguisher on the opposite side of the hallway and paused, an idea forming in my mind.

Ryan followed my gaze and immediately caught on to what I was about to do. "Woah nonononono!" He took hold of my arm and pulled me back. "You are not about to break Brink's window! I won't let you."

"Let go of me!" I snapped, jerking my arm out of his grip. His phone fell from his pocket with another violent clack, and the same song leaked out, playing undeterred underneath the sirens and interspersed instructions.

"Lo, stop!" he pleaded. "It's not worth it. There are cameras everywhere. You'll get in serious trouble."

He grabbed my other arm and yanked me back, causing my legs to give way, and we both collapsed on the floor.

"Ryan!" I yelled, trying to push him away. "Get OFF!"

It was just like elementary school all over again, like all those wrestling matches we used to have at recess. Only this time, Ryan was winning, by a landslide.

"Loli, just listen to me! I've got another idea. We'll get the letter for you, you just have to LISTEN!"

I stopped struggling and Ryan waited a second before he was sure he could let go. When he did, I pulled back from him, sliding away from the tangle of our legs as he opened his mouth to speak.

"Hey, you two! Clear the building, now!"

A teacher I'd never seen before was striding toward us, pointing at the exit with a frustrated look on his face. "Come on, come on!" he yelled, clapping his hands.

We got up off the ground, and before I knew it, we were being ushered out of the building.

As we reached the bottom of the staircase, I contemplated how terrible it would really be if I pushed past the teacher and booked it all the way back up the stairs. I gave him the once-over, sizing him up before I was distracted by a tap on my shoulder.

"Look," Ryan whispered as we exited the building. "It's him! Do you see him?"

I scanned my eyes over the scattered heads as our guardian teacher disappeared into the crowd. Brink. About a yard away.

"I see him," I replied. "So what's your big plan, Pope?"

Ryan didn't answer. I turned to look at him and found that he was gasping for air, eyes wide and panicked.

"Ry?" I asked, worried. "You good?"

"I . . . I need my asthma pump."

"What?" I exclaimed, incredulous.

A couple of students turned our way, people gasped, someone

screamed. I narrowed my eyes at him. Ryan hadn't had an asthma attack since the third grade.

He turned a conspiratorial eye toward me, and it clicked. Of course.

He was initiating Operation Swiss Eye.

"Oh no," I shrieked, slipping suddenly into the role of panicked and concerned friend. "Get a teacher! Someone get a teacher! Mr. Brink! Mr. Brink!"

Brink looked up from a few feet away and stalked over, his eyes narrowed.

"Mr. Pope?" he asked, taking in the scene. "What's wrong?"

"He needs his asthma pump," I sputtered.

"Well then . . . doesn't he have it on him?"

Ryan shook his head. "No," I translated.

Brink furrowed his bushy eyebrows. "Where is it, boy?"

This was the most compassion I had ever seen him exhibit.

"I left it—" Ryan wheezed, "class—classroom."

"Whose? Which teacher?"

He pointed at Brink and then lowered himself to the ground, hand on his chest.

"I'll go get it," I offered. "I'll be fast."

"No one is allowed to enter the building," Brink said. "Strict rule. This isn't a drill, kids."

"He's got severe asthma," I shrieked. "If I don't go in, he's going to suffocate! And that will be on you."

This wouldn't have worked on any other teacher. I was sure there was some rule or something somewhere in some teacher handbook that advised teachers to never let a student reenter a burning building. If not, I was pretty sure that was at least the right thing to do as an adult in this situation. But Brink, the meanest, grouchiest, laziest teacher in the world, never did something when someone else had already offered to do it for him. He sighed and scrambled for his keys.

"Hurry up, you gotta be fast. If you're not back in five minutes, I'm sending help after you."

I grabbed the keys and ran back into the building, flying up the stairs as the lights flashed and the sirens screeched all around me. An absolutely putrid smell greeted me as I reached the second floor along with a slow, thick, darkening smoke hanging in the air.

The fire was spreading. It really wasn't a drill.

I coughed and shuffled through the keys until I found the one marked "Classroom 217." I turned to Brink's door and jammed the key in, twisting and twisting it until the door clicked open. I ducked in, safe from the noise and pollution of the hall.

Finally, thank God, I was in Brink's room. I lurched toward Brink's desk, amused by the fact that I was probably the only student to ever think those words.

I was making it.

The school was literally on fire, and I was making it.

I scrambled over to the drawer, heart racing as I yanked the handle. My heart plummeted. It was locked. How could the drawer be locked?

I looked around the classroom in desperation, my chest spiking with every ugly ring of the alarm, until I remembered something that sent a euphoric sear up my chest: the keys. I had Brink's entire chain of keys with me.

I jumped up from behind the desk and ruffled through his papers until I found the keys at the corner of the desk where I'd absentmindedly left them, then I shuffled through each bronze and silver piece, trying to find a label or a mark that would differentiate the one I needed from the rest. Apart from the classroom key, they were all unlabeled and indecipherably color coded. I don't know what I'd expected—a key marked "Free Cell Phones Here"?

I tried the first key, then the second, and I squealed as the third key slid in perfectly. The lock twisted, and I pulled the drawer open to reveal the infamous red crate that was filled to the brim with phones.

iPhones to be specific. Every single phone in the drawer was some recent version of the iPhone, making the chunky old plastic Nokia stick out immediately.

Thank God for basic rich Woolridge kids.

I grabbed the tattered Nokia and popped it open at the gap on the side. Inside was a small, neatly folded piece of paper with the words *For You* written in lovely dark cursive on the front.

Mission accomplished.

I crawled out from behind the desk and scrambled over to the door, peering out the window in distress. The glass was now completely clouded with thick, black smoke. I had to get out fast. As I shoved my nose into the crook of my arm and pushed the door open, the sickeningly sweet taste of smoke crept through my mouth and stung the back of my throat, causing me to sputter and cough as I felt for the exit. My hand found the smooth metal bar through the haze, and I pushed desperately against it before I even considered locking Brink's door behind me.

He wouldn't mind if I left his door unlocked to save my life, right?

After stumbling down the stairs and out of the building, I spotted him standing farther down along the evacuation route with his arms crossed. Something in the arch of his back told me he would mind.

"Hey," Ryan said, coming out from hiding around the corner. He'd been miraculously healed from his asthma attack and was now the picture of perfect health. "You get it?"

I coughed and nodded, barely able to contain my grin.

Ryan didn't return the smile. He breathed out, long and hard, then closed his eyes.

"What?" I asked, lowering the phone.

"Nothing," he said. "We just risked our lives for a piece of paper from some guy. I think I'm allowed time to recover."

I stared at him, surprised at his uncharacteristically surly response. "Some guy? You were all in this morning—"

Two fire engines came careening around the corner, cutting me off. Everyone surrounded the edge of the parking island to get a better view of the action, and I watched in awe as police cars screeched round to the front of our school. My phone buzzed.

So . . .

Did you manage to get
the letter in the end?

I turned slightly away from Ryan and took a discrete picture of the Nokia and the letter inside, feeling a smug satisfaction as the image went through. The satisfaction was dampened somewhat by Ryan's sullen reaction, but how many people could say they'd successfully broken into Brink's drawer? And during a literal school fire? I imagined MV's surprise when he realized I'd managed to retrieve the package at the most impossible time of the day. What, he thought a little hurdle could stop me?

Then it came to me: an ecstatically sickening feeling that leapt from the chamber of my heart and crept along my arteries, leaving me completely cold.

No.

There was no way. Right?

It would be ludicrous, ridiculous, beyond absurd of me to imagine let alone consider the possibility that he'd set the fire. That the reason I was standing there, wheezing, covered in soot, and watching firefighters run into my school building was because of an insatiable desire to end up on top. One, quite like mine, that would do any and everything to ensure it.

The sirens stopped and firefighters in masks ran into the building. I frowned, forcing myself to push the idea out of my mind because, of course, I was wrong.

This was only a game and that would be stupid.

CHAPTER
13

TRACK:
TRAIN SONG
Vashti Bunyan

We were quiet on the drive home. Sweet and sullen folk filled the silence as I watched the darkening sky, wondering if it was going to rain and trying not to think about everything too much.

Thinking too much was becoming an unwelcomed hobby of mine, and it was only proving to be dangerous as I jumped to wild conclusions. Of course the fire had nothing to do with MV. The rumor was that it was started by Mrs. Janvier, who'd been caught smoking in the teacher's lounge again.

What was true, however, was that I'd greatly underestimated The Mysterious Voice. This afternoon had proved that he was much more on my level than I'd anticipated. He was cutthroat.

I knew I was out of bounds for continuing to play a game during an emergency evacuation, but he had overlooked my rash behavior. In fact, judging from his text—he'd expected it.

I had a feeling anyone else in my situation might have been concerned, but I relished in the unique thrill of the moment. It suggested that somewhere out there was another person who was just like me.

At home, I collapsed on my bed and pulled out my phone. MV had sent a message in response to my photographic proof.

> You did it. I'm impressed.

> You doubted me. I'm insulted.

> Forgive me my doubtfulness, it's just there was a bit of a gigantic obstacle in your way today.

> And you still made it. You're something else.

I grinned, feeling proud of myself once more. I really did pull it off, despite the odds. And he was proud of me. The Mysterious Voice was proud of me. My chest glowed.

> Why did you call me today?

The glow dimmed. I had no idea how to explain that one. A butt dial? A dare? After racking my brain, I finally settled on the truth.

> It was a mistake. I thought I'd found you, so I was testing my hypothesis.

My message was marked as read almost immediately after I sent it, but he didn't start typing for a while. I felt his presence as we both stared at each other through our screens, doing nothing. After a few seconds, he started typing.

thought we promised not to go out of our way to find each other.

I wasn't actually trying to find you

I thought you were secretly trying to find me . . . so I tried catching you out first

What? Why would you think that?

I saw this guy from school at Westerns on Saturday and totally freaked out

So . . . some random kid sitting in a café prompted you to break the rules?

I paused, stunned at the turn of events. *Break the rules?* How had we managed to completely flip the script and make *me* into the rule breaker?

I didn't break the rules. I was protecting myself.

> I thought you were tricking me and I got scared, okay? It was an honest mistake.

There was a moment of quiet on both of our ends. Then he started typing again.

> I would never go to Westerns on a Saturday morning because I know that's your time

> I'd never break the one thing holding all the excitement of this agreement

My thumbs hovered over the screen as I considered his words. Before the Will situation, I'd also thought that the most intriguing part of our game was the question of our identities. But now, after witnessing his fervor through the fire, and being forced to consider his actual identity, I was beginning to realize that the person behind the mystery was far more intriguing than I could have expected. He was also unpredictable. *Unknowable.* I reined my thoughts in as I tapped out a response.

> That's the tricky thing—I don't actually know what you would and wouldn't do

> I don't even know what you look like

Hm. Valid point. We're going
to have to change that

What do you think
about meeting at the
junior-senior prom?

I sat up in my bed, feeling a sharp brightness behind my chest.
It was happening. We were actually setting a meeting date. But
. . . *prom?*

Way too cliché.

You got a better idea?

Literally any other day.
How about June 23rd?
The night after exams?

Okay, June 23rd. I'll
save the date.

Our meeting cannot and
will not be boring, MV.

It has to be Dramatic.
Cinematic.

Okay, on what scale?
Romance? Tears?
Betrayal?

All of the above.

Well we've got the betrayal and the romance down.

Betrayal?

Yes. You broke a rule going for my identity today.

Agree to disagree. Romance?

Don't play coy, Stranger.

One broken rule opens the door for many more.

Careful, Voice...

Funny, I was going to say the same thing to you.

I read over our exchange a second time that night, mulling over his words as I burrowed under my covers. It wasn't lost on me that something fundamental had shifted.

One broken rule opens the door for many more.

There was an unwritten promise behind those words: a thinly veiled threat.

I had broken the seal by questioning his identity, and he had propagated it by breaking one of my rules and implying romance.

The promise, the threat, was this: No more rules. If you dare try to find me, I'll find you first.

It was an unofficial free-for-all.

Dearest Stranger,

I thought I'd let you know that I spent an entire day in the Grove Cemetery looking for your Sarah Walsh.

I skipped school the day after you gave me the assignment, grabbed a drink and some snacks from the kitchen, and just wandered around the cemetery for about twelve hours.

It was quite nice, actually. Walking around and reading the various stones. During my lunch break I sat in the grass staring at some guy named Thomas Wilkinson, wondering what all these people did with their lives and thinking that they can't really have done much if they ended up dead in Woolridge.

Anyway, I was halfway through googling some of the more recent residents when I realized that we had a town website with records going back to the days before our independence. All I really had to do was type Sarah's name in and sift through the several dozen that have existed in this town until I got a birth year that created an existing ISBN.

Now, I have a question for you. Did you draw that . . . seemingly cosmeticized skeleton monkey on the envelope of the last letter? It's really good. I should've known you were an artist of some sort: the arrogance, the terrible outlook on life. I've always been a really visual person, but since I could never draw that well I took my eye for visual art and turned to film.

I got into photography back in middle school (shortly after I realized I was no good at drawing) and I fell in love with it. It was all grand to learn the technique and how to take a good photo, but what really grabbed me was the way you can manipulate an image or a sequence of images by dabbling in editing and playing with tools to enhance and evoke the message you want to put out.

So I guess in a way I agree with you just a little on the whole technology front. Not that I'm all for it or that I'm "boring" as you so kindly put it, but I guess we do have a little to be grateful to technology for.

P.S. Calm down, I didn't kill anyone. I'll tell you my closet story soon enough.
P.P.S. Thanks for the Zeppelin card. I promise I'll give it back soon.

Yours,

X

CHAPTER 14

I LOVE MY BOYFRIEND
Princess Chelsea

Unfortunately, the school did not burn down. They simply closed off a small section of the second floor that was damaged for repair. Then, instead of giving us time off to heal from the trauma, all we got was a two-hour delay the next morning. According to Superintendent Anne Lisenby, there was no time to lose for finals.

"Only Woolridge would make us go to school the day after it was almost burned to the ground," Ryan complained.

The three of us were sitting in the cafeteria at a table far away from our tertiary crowd—to allow for some privacy. I'd filled Ryan and Cairo in on Will's innocence and the ominous ending to my last conversation with MV, and Cairo immediately decided that we needed to take action.

"Best public school in the state my ass," she said, laying a bunch of napkins on the table in front of her. "Anyone have a Sharpie?"

Ryan produced one from his backpack and Cairo popped it open.

Her plan was to gather all the information we had on MV and see if we could suss him out. Ryan seemed just as determined as Cairo in getting to the bottom of it, but I was ambivalent. Sure, I wanted to know who he was, but we had a meeting date now—a full and proper way of ending things. To know who he was defeated the purpose of the letters.

But . . . *One broken rule . . .*

"Okay," Cairo started, "here is what we know about The Mysterious Voice so far." She scratched out a star for the first bullet point. "Number one: he mentioned the prom, so we know he's either a senior or a junior."

"Right," Ryan agreed. "We also know he likes film and photography."

Cairo nodded and wrote "film/photo" as her second point.

"He's pretentious, presumptuous, romanticizes the past, and is slightly arrogant," I offered.

Cairo snorted. "You only think so because he called you arrogant," she said. "And what's wrong with romanticizing? Everyone idealizes something or someone."

"We know he was at the party," Ryan offered. "And that he's more of a loner than a socializer."

"How do we know that?" Cairo asked, tipping her head sideways as she held the marker up in the air.

"Well, first off, Lo met him in a closet," Ryan said. "Then there's the fact that he's always immediately there when she texts him. And then there's the way he talks: so offhand like he doesn't care if you're offended."

"You're right," Cai said, resuming her list. "He doesn't seem to care about crossing lines or boundaries."

"Exactly," Ryan agreed.

I thought about how he sent me into a stranger's house, how he asked me straight up for my number. I thought about his lack of concern about the school fire.

"Oh!" Cairo exclaimed, raising her finger. "And we know that he has a crush on Lo."

She wrote "likes girls" and I snorted.

"Wow," I said. "I thought we were only outlining cold, hard facts."

"It's a cold and hard enough fact to me," she said. "He keeps bringing up the fact that you're supposedly flirting with him, he slipped in the word 'romance' and—who hasn't at one point had a crush on Loli Crawford?" She winked at me and underlined the words.

I cut eyes to Ryan, who cleared his throat and jumped in, avoiding eye contact. "She has a point," he said. "It's like that beauty privilege thing."

He was referring to a debate we'd had in health class on intersectionality. Some brainiac had suggested that in addition to race, class, and gender privileges, attractive people carried some privilege too. The teacher wasn't very happy to equate levels of hotness to the gender problem, but the kid raised some pretty good points and ended up with half the class on his side.

I stared at Ryan, incredulous.

"What? It's a real thing," he said with a shrug.

"Yeah . . ." I said slowly. "Except you're forgetting that this guy has literally never seen my face."

"He doesn't need to see your face, he's gotten a clue from the way you act," Ryan started. "It's like we broke down in health class; people with privilege act entitled to the means for which they're of privilege. They never have to ask for things they know are theirs. Like a super-rich kid never has to ask to go to school and get educated, pretty people often have terrible manners and say things like, 'Don't fall in love with me,' to people they've never met before."

Cairo chuckled. I rolled my eyes. "Okay that's not exactly how I put it in the letter. I said *no flirting and no sappy love confessions.*"

The two of them shared a look.

"I was establishing a boundary!"

Cairo's chuckle turned into full-on laughter, and Ryan began to crack up too. I looked between them, offended. "Are you guys laughing at me?"

That threw them into fresh hysterics. "We are one hundred percent laughing at you," Cairo said, wiping her eyes. "I mean—who *says* things like that?"

I folded my arms. "I had just finished with Mattaliano, okay? I was not in the mood for another love interest. I don't think I ever will be."

"Really?" Ryan asked, raising his eyebrows.

"Yes," I said, matter-of-factly. "I'm done with boys."

Ryan, who had almost slipped out of his seat during his fit of laughter, readjusted himself, suddenly subdued.

"Oh please," Cairo interjected. "You? Done with boys? Your eyes linger on Hamilton's face when you see a ten-dollar bill, Lo. You're never going to be done with boys."

Ryan cracked a small smile. "Good one, Cai."

Cairo raised the napkin in the air. "Okay," she said. "This isn't much, but it narrows things down a lot. I think we could actually find this guy."

I bit my lip. "Can we hold off on an actual search?" I suggested. "I mean, I like having the list as insurance, but I don't know if I want to actively go looking for him."

Cairo frowned and placed the napkin back on the table. "But what if he actively goes looking for you?"

"I don't think he will, as long as he's sure that I am not. Finding me doesn't seem to be a rule he's intent on breaking."

"Okay," Cai said, acquiescing. "We won't go out of our way looking for him, but we'll keep an eye out just in case."

She folded the napkin neatly and tucked it in her pocket just as I sensed a presence approaching our table.

"Hey uh . . . can I join you guys?"

I looked up. A tallish guy with floppy black hair, a black beanie, and a really sick Guns N' Roses T-shirt stood behind Ryan, holding his lunch under his arm with clearly feigned composure. Usually Noel had a sure, strong presence—what with the reputation of his band and his good looks—but ever since the car surfing incident, he hadn't been able to look me in the eye.

"*Sang!*" Ryan grinned and turned around to slap hands. "Yeah, come on, there's lots of space."

He moved down to give Noel room and Noel sat down right opposite me.

"Noel," I said in acknowledgment. He nodded at me uneasily. "I hope you've had enough time to recover?" I asked.

"Recover" was the word my parents had used when they told me about the condition he'd been in the day after the incident, but what he'd had to "recover" from I couldn't tell you.

That night was one of the best nights of my life.

Just picturing Ryan and me poised on top of our cars, music blaring out the windows as Noel and Cairo raced down the street, gave me a rush of adrenaline. Cairo's scream as she threw her hand up out the window, the stars in the black sky above us, the rushing wind in my hair—perfect. The only blemish on the night was Noel hyperventilating on top of Ryan's stationary car. Stationary. The car hadn't even been moving yet.

And he'd been the one who had insisted on doing it.

Noel cleared his throat. "Yeah, I have, thanks."

"Well, that's good to hear," I said, pleasantly. "Because I haven't."

"Lo . . ." Ryan warned.

"I'm guessing," I continued, "it's because being robbed of a car lasts longer than a momentary panic attack." I folded my arms. "Do you know that I had to take the full blame just so Helen didn't ban you from playing at Babble? I saved you both."

"That's actually why I'm here." Noel dug into his jean pockets and produced two small green pieces of paper. "Your VIP tickets," he explained. "I wanted to personally give you two yours. You get to sit in the balcony and avoid all those sweaty people you always complain about."

Cairo grabbed hers. "Thanks, Sang."

I glared at Noel before snatching my ticket from his hand. He sighed.

"Look, Lo. I'm sorry. I really am. If you want, I'll go speak to your parents an—"

"Don't sweat it, Sang," I said. "What's done is done. Thanks for the tickets."

He smiled, looking a little relieved. "No problem. See you guys at the concert!"

The bell rang. I clicked my lunch box closed and looked between my friends, an idea brewing in my mind. After having to rummage through Brink's desk for my last mission, I wanted to treat MV to something equally as risky.

"You guys free at seven tonight?" I asked.

"Nope," Cai replied. "Team dinner."

"I'm free," Ryan said.

"Good," I said, standing up. "I think I'm gonna need your help putting my next letter in place."

Wolf's garage, a stand-alone parking shelter, wasn't much to look at, but it was filled with all sorts of random junk and equipment for his business. It was our first stop whenever we needed to pick up anything questionable—fireworks, plasma torches, drinks, a couple of new fakes. Wolf had everything. He was like Woolridge High's dark fairy godmother.

Ryan switched off his headlights as we approached it, winding up a dirt road surrounded by trees. When we reached the clearing, he turned off the engine and parked in front of the garage door. I surveyed the dark shadows outside the windows, shapes and figures cast by the trees and crawling things of the night. It was always slightly spooky here.

"You sure he has one?" I asked Ryan. "It's so specific and arbitrary."

"Yeah," he replied. "I saw a whole line of them decorating the inside of his garage when he fixed my exhaust pipe."

I turned to look at him. "Wait—Wolf fixed Baby?"

"Yeah."

"I thought you took her in to get it done professionally."

"Well, I was going to and then Wolf said he could fix it for cheaper."

"Does Helen know about this?"

"Of course Helen doesn't know about it."

"I can just imagine what she'd think about her son—"

"Ugh, Lo, please. What gives you the right to—"

"—endangering his life by paying some random teenager to fix his—"

A loud knock on the window made us both jump up in our seats and scream.

"Easy, kids. It's just me." Wolf leaned an arm on top of the car, and Ryan laughed as he lowered the window.

"Well," he said, "if it isn't the Big Bad Wolf himself."

This time, instead of cussing or rolling his eyes, Wolf grinned. "In the flesh."

"I thought you were just going to send one of your guys out," Ry said. "Thought you'd have bigger fish to fry."

"Send someone out?" Wolf looked offended. "To my two favorite customers? Never. Only the best for you two."

"Aw, thanks, Wolfie!" I sang, leaning forward in my seat. Wolf rested both arms on Ryan's window and winked at me.

"I doubt we're your favorite customers," Ryan said. "You probably get one hundred times more money from Mattaliano and his stoner buddies."

"It's not about money," Wolf replied. "It's about character. And you two have more character than anyone in this town. Who else calls for a simple college contact and throws the best party Woolridge has ever seen?" Wolf pulled an arm away and produced a shiny green bottle from seemingly nowhere. "And who else would call me asking for a single green glass bottle at the first crack of dusk? Only you two."

The bottle glinted in the moonlight as Wolf spun it in his hand, and then he reached through the window, stretching over Ryan, to hand it to me. It was perfect. Exactly what I'd envisioned for the mission

"So," he resumed, "what is it the two of you are up to tonight, with one shiny green bottle?"

Ryan glanced at me. "It's a little bit of a secret mission, I'm afraid."

Wolf laughed and hit the top of Ryan's car. "Only you two!" He placed a toothpick in his mouth and tapped the roof of the car again. "Well, have fun. Don't trash the car too badly this time."

He backed away from the car, still facing us, before waving

and disappearing into the black mouth of his garage. Ryan started Baby and began a slow and careful cruise up the dirt road, squinting into the dark.

"Ryan. Why aren't you driving with your lights on?"

"Don't know," he answered. "Wolf's rules. The text said to only switch our headlights on when we hit the road."

"Hm." Wolf had never made us do that before. But then again, we'd never come to his garage so late at night.

It took us about fifteen minutes to get from Wolf's garage to our last stop of the evening—the Woolridge Country Club. During those fifteen minutes, I swallowed my pride and my hatred of rhyming couplets, and with the help of Google, a couple of historical websites, and Ryan's lyricism, I drafted a quick riddle clue for The Mysterious Voice:

> Sent by sailors and lovers through the ages
> Now just a bridge between two teenagers
> I float in a pool, public as the ocean
> From dusk to dawn I'll remain in motion

I hated it. A lot. But I muscled through the hate by reminding myself that a riddle was perfect for my old-timey idea. When the riddle was done, I sent it through with another text to inform MV that he had until 6 A.M. the next morning to find the package. Let's see how he fared with a time crunch.

Ryan and I drove past the country club's entrance, following the curve of the hedge past the humungous golf course and the tennis courts until we saw the top of the big white gazebo by the swimming pool. The WCC pool was the only part of the country club open to the "public," i.e., all certified Woolridge residents, making it the only open pool in town. Even in its generosity, our town perpetuated exclusivity. We stopped a few yards in front of the hedge, and I rolled my letter up in a tight scroll, squeezing it through the mouth of the bottle. Then we left Baby with music humming, engine still running behind us. The Pope Way.

As we neared the hedge, I twisted the cork into the mouth of the bottle, pushing hard until I was sure it wouldn't come off in the water. I held the bottle up to inspect my work, admiring its deep emerald depths one last time, and as I did, I caught Ryan looking at me, hands buried deep in the pockets of his brown leather jacket. I knew what he was thinking. "Wanna throw it—"

"Of course I want to throw it in," he cut in.

I laughed at his predictability and he smirked. He always wanted in on the action.

"What happens if I miss?" he asked. "What if I throw it and it lands on the ground and just shatters all over the place?"

I grinned. "Then I guess it'd be easier for MV to get the letter."

Ryan scoffed. "You're ridiculous, you know that."

I shrugged. "Sometimes in life you have no option but to risk it."

He paused, looking down at my shoes, and in the brief quiet between songs, he lifted his gaze to mine and opened his mouth as though he were about to say something. A slow and boozy bass spilled from the car, interrupting the quiet, and he seemed to shake himself out of it.

"We could try getting off the ground a little," he suggested, looking back at the car. "It'd heighten our chances of making it in the water. Follow me."

He jogged back toward the car and climbed onto the roof. "Loli, come on!" he shouted. "You can just about see the end of the pool from here! All we'd have to do is try to aim it toward the middle."

I walked in his direction and he pulled me up to join him on top of the car. The soft bass line drifted up from the car speakers. I moved the bottle to the hand closest to Ryan. "Ready?" I asked, watching his hair rustle in the wind.

He slid his fingers over mine as the echo of a woman's voice wrapped around us, and then he closed his hand over the neck of the bottle, just under mine. His hand was warm and soft, a complete contrast to the cold hard glass pressing against the inside of my palm. I looked down at our hands, grateful for his presence, which was always there when I needed it. Then Ryan abruptly moved his away.

"Actually, I think you have to throw it," he said.

"What?" I asked. "Why?"

I turned to look him in the eye, but he looked straight ahead, focusing on the hedge.

"Because it's your game. It's only right that you do it alone."

I glanced back down at my hand and gripped the bottle tight. It would've been more fun to do it together, but I didn't want to push it.

"You ready?" he asked.

"Always."

"On three," he said.

"One . . ."

"Two . . ."

I raised my arm above my head, propelled it quickly forward, and let the bottle fly up into the vast black sky. Ryan winced as it soared in the air, and I watched, still and expectant, hoping I'd swung hard and straight enough. The bottle disappeared behind the hedge, and we waited for a sound, any sound—a crash, a cry, a yelp, and then, after what felt like hours, we heard a soft splash and a discreet "bloop."

"Oh my gosh," I sputtered, eyes wide. "I did it."

Ryan laughed and held his hand up in the air. "You did it!"

"I did it!" I squealed, smacking his palm. "Wooo!"

My voice carried through the wind and rang out into the night, long after I closed my mouth. I whooped again, just to hear it echo, and Ryan stilled. "Lo, stop."

I ignored him and yelled again, letting my voice carry through the rustling trees.

Ryan put his hand over my mouth, which immediately made me laugh. "Stop, Lo. The guards!"

I stopped laughing. The guards.

Ryan, Cairo, and I had history with the WCC security guards: they were terrifically skilled at catching the three of us. We couldn't afford a run-in with them so late in the school year—not if we wanted to spend our upcoming summer days swinging golf carts and lounging by the club pool.

Ryan took one look down at my widened eyes and began to laugh.

I peeled his hand off my mouth. "Shh!" I hissed, trying and failing to suppress my own laughter. "The guards, dumbass. We've got fifteen seconds to get away before Barney comes."

Ryan straightened up but he was still laughing when he said, "Probably about ten." He nodded his head to the right. "His shed's just over there."

I looked down the road. Crap. He was right. "Well let's go then!"

We jumped off opposite sides of the car in unison before sliding in through Baby's open doors. When we closed the doors, I looked out my window and saw three flashlights winding their way up the hedge behind us.

"Ryan . . ." I warned. I turned to find that he was fiddling with the radio. "Ryan!"

"I got it, I got it," he said, and then he turned the music up, jerked Baby forward, and swung onto the road.

Dear X,

I kinda like the way you ended your last letter with an X. It's so perfectly fitting. Not just because X is a stand-in for the unknown, but because X has always been the scarcest, most mysterious letter in the alphabet.

The X got me thinking about treasure maps and pirates and all those things I used to fantasize about when I was little, and then I had this amazing idea: to mimic my favorite adventure story trope of all time and leave you a message in a bottle.

I thought you might appreciate it, with your flair for old practices and romantic ideas.

When I was younger I remember thinking about how awesome the concept of a bottled message was, but when I really think about it, I can't actually remember where I first heard of the concept or why I first thought it'd be cool. I'm guessing it was all the pirate movies I used to watch.

Anyway, I don't actually have a hidden chest of treasure but I doodled one for you as a substitute, which leads me to my answer to your question.

Yes, I draw. I wouldn't say I'm an artist, since I kind of hate that word, but I do draw. I've been drawing for, like, ever. Not the classic portrait-y, real-life stuff; more abstract weird cartoons and comic strips. I don't really know what to do with the whole drawing thing though. The closest I've come to figuring it out was when I dabbled in tattoo art a while back.

I don't talk about my drawing often because I don't really like people looking at me as though I'm an "artist," that whole thing doesn't match up with who I think of myself as being. I have to be that hard, dangerous girl who instills fear and desire in the hearts of everyone she comes in contact with. I don't like people picturing that girl sitting down with a pen and a book, drawing all by herself. Idk.

Going back to the topic: this whole message in a bottle idea got me googling and I learned a lot about messages in bottles. There's a whole history to it that I think you'd really like. Like, did you know that ancient philosophers used them to test the directional pull of the ocean? Or that at one point opening bottles with a message in them was a crime? There are hundreds of stories about people sending them out looking for pen pals, or just looking to share their life stories and experiences with people on the other side of the world.

I kind of found that part a bit sad. Maybe it's just me but I'm almost 100% positive that the people who put so much effort into writing letters and sending them across the ocean are the ones who most want to receive a message in a bottle themselves.

In the end those people settle for sending one out. And then they have to wonder whether their package was ever appreciated, whether it was ever even received.

Anyway, I hope to God that you're appreciating mine at least because it's really hard to write on this stiff paper.

Sincerely,
A Girl Across the Ocean

DAZED AND CONFUSED
Led Zeppelin

There are few things worse than waking up with a dying phone.

My phone had just enough juice to wake me up at seven in the morning before it flashed 1 percent, flickered, and died. After the excitement of yesterday's mission and almost getting busted by the security guards, I must've fallen asleep before I got a chance to plug it in for the night. I reached for my charger, but it wasn't plugged in by my bedside where it usually was. Had I moved it downstairs? Taken it to Ryan's house? I sighed. Great. The 6 A.M. deadline had passed. How was I supposed to get updates from X with a dead phone?

The answer? I wouldn't.

The whole day, while the school was abuzz with prom chatter, caused by a couple of spectacular promposals, I was on a mission to find just one single available charger to check my texts. It was only at the end of the day that I managed to find a girl who let me use hers, just before she had to leave for track practice.

Ryan caught me at the school entrance. "Hey, did you hear about Zoë's prom ask? With the carriage and the roses spelling P-R-O-M?"

"Uh-huh," I said, holding down on the power button on my phone.

"It was actually really sweet. Seeing them get so excited made me think that maybe—"

"Ahh!" I exclaimed as my phone sprang to life. "Sorry, Ry—my phone's been dead all day. I just need to check my texts."

I ignored the low battery warning and the slew of unimportant notifications, scrolling down until I saw two texts from an unknown number, all sent at three in the morning.

> I'm soaking wet and I'll probably dream of getting chased by guards for the rest of my life but—I got it.

> I'm guessing this is payback for the trial you had to go through in getting the last letter.

I smiled. He'd made it.

Below the texts was a photo of the green bottle lying in the grass. I zoomed in, chest fluttering. I'd been holding that bottle just hours before, and now it was in whatever dimension X existed in, in the hands of a complete and total stranger.

"Hold on," Ryan said. "Is that Cai? What is she doing outside the band room?"

I glanced up from my phone. Sure enough, Cairo was standing at the side of the west wing. The answer became apparent as we circled the band room's large window only to discover Tyler, Wolf, Clay, and Sid leaning along the windowed ledge.

"Hey!" Wolf exclaimed, spreading his arms. "Now it's a party."

My ears picked up the sound of music playing from someone's phone: a static rumbling of bass, drums, and electric guitar dropping together in a steady beat.

"That's a good song," Ryan said, pointing at Wolf's phone.

"One of my favorites," Wolf agreed. He smiled and drew from

the cigarette wedged between his ringed fingers. I turned away, trying to disguise my disgust for Cairo's sake.

"What are you guys doing out here?" Ryan asked.

"This is our spot," Tyler said. "We come out here whenever we need fresh air—"

"Or a smoke."

"Or endless screen time," Tyler added.

I jolted at the mention of screen time. I had about 3 percent battery power, and I hadn't responded to X's text.

The conversation turned to complaints about our school's stupid phone policy, and I tapped out a reply.

> I'm impressed. You did it with such short notice too.

He responded in a matter of seconds.

> If I've managed to impress you then maybe the physical and psychological trauma of last night was worth it.

I suppressed the smile that threatened its way to my face.

> Careful. My friends are starting to think you have a little crush on me

Wolf's sharp laughter pulled my attention from my phone. He tossed the lighter over to Clay, and I refrained from commenting on the smell or the major health risk that smoking was—again, for Cairo's sake. Instead, I dug into my pocket and pulled out my fruit punch gloss, which I held in front of my nose to mask the grimy smell of smoke.

"So . . ." Tyler said. He was either expertly ignoring the smoke or completely unbothered by it. "Are you guys going to prom?"

Wolf straightened up and scoffed. "Have you ever seen me at any of the high school dances?"

"I'm not asking you, genius," Tyler mumbled.

There was a moment of silence before I realized he was asking the three of us. "Oh, I don't know," I said. "I haven't really thought about it."

"I mean . . . we might as well," Cairo said with a shrug.

My phone buzzed and I glanced down at my screen.

> You've told your friends about this?

>> Not everyone.
>> Just two. Haven't you?

> Kinda. You came up once after the party but that's about it. All they know is I've been talking to some girl.

>> 'Talking to some girl'?
>> Sounds scandalous

A gentle nudge on my side caused me to look up from my phone.

"What do you think, Lo?" Ryan said. "Should we go?"

I scanned the circle. Everyone else was chatting amongst themselves. "What? Do you want to?" I asked, a little surprised. We hadn't gone to a school dance in a long time. Not for any particular reason—we just always somehow ended up finding something better to do the night of.

Ryan smiled and puffed out a surprised laugh. "I guess I do."

"You know," I began, "we could probably throw a party a million times better than the prom."

"I know," Ryan replied. "But it'd also be nice to do something a bit . . . you know . . . normal sometime. Just kick back, relax, and be kids at a high school dance."

I couldn't think of anything worse to do with my time, but I knew, judging from his busy fingers and his casual shrugging shoulder, that it was something he really wanted to do—even more than he was allowing himself to let on. My mind flashed back to the sight of his red eyes and his tired frame from days before—the last thing I wanted was to see him upset again. So, instead of voicing my thoughts, I smiled and said, "Sure. Let's do it."

But everyone knows prom night complicates things more than it ever fixes them.

CHAPTER

16

TRACK:
ALWAYS FOREVER
Cults

What had always bugged me about having a best friend who just happened to be a guy was all the unnecessary overreacting from other people.

The winking, the nodding, the suggestive phrases, and the knowing looks (oh God, the *knowing looks*) were so constant and relentless that by the time I was twelve I was sick of it. I still remember the rage I felt toward Andy Guthrie and his snickering photocopies, in sixth grade, when they kept calling me Ryan's wife. One day, to put an end to it, I turned to Isaiah Patten in the middle of gym class and told him to be my boyfriend. And so began my long string of attempts to put an end to the scrutiny created by everyone's adherence to an extremely boring and predictable heteronormative standard.

Lately, I'd been pretty good at ignoring the comments. Last year I didn't get all riled up when everyone started hypothesizing that Basilica's latest ballad, "Imagine Us," was about me. I just rolled my eyes and moved on. And in January, I'd managed to bite my tongue when Dr. Trader, the school's principal, called Ryan my "little boyfriend" before sentencing both of us to a week's worth of detentions (another story for another time).

I was getting good at ignoring the blatantly stupid stuff, but when it came from the ones we loved and trusted I couldn't help getting a little heated.

"Oh, don't start," Ryan groaned, reading my expression perfectly. He closed his bedroom door as much as possible without actually shutting it, which only made me madder. Helen probably thought the open-door rule was completely justified now that we were going to prom together.

"I knew this would happen," I fumed, shaking my head. "I knew it the moment I saw those flyers go up."

"Calm down." Ryan shrugged his backpack off his shoulder and tapped his laptop to life. "All Helen said was that she was glad we were going to the prom together."

"Yeah. With a knowing smile. Did you have to tell her as soon as we got home from school?"

"You know how my mother is. Besides, our parents were going to find out sooner or later. I mean . . . it's the prom."

"Exactly! The dance our parents have been hinting toward our whole lives! And now we have to endure their smug faces and exchanged glances."

I collapsed on Ryan's bed and sighed, staring up at the ceiling. "I don't think I can stomach seeing my parents' reaction when we tell them."

"I don't think you're gonna have to worry about that." Ryan moved toward his speakers. "Helen's probably texting Nancy as we speak."

I groaned and sprawled my arms above my head just as music began to flow softly from the speakers. Ryan ran his hands through his hair before collapsing right next to me on the bed. We lay there for a while, listening, and then Ryan turned his head to look at me.

"What?" I asked, flatly.

"I know it's nothing," he started, "but it's really bugging me that I can't think of the perfect song for you."

It took me a full ten seconds to remember our conversation outside Michael Keene's office, at Cairo's model audition. "You're still looking for that?"

"Of course I am. I need answers."

"Wow." I knitted my hands over my stomach. Typical Ryan with his careful precision and his desire to make everything right. "I've never seen you so stumped for a song before. I thought you had all the music in the world flowing through your veins and absolutely everything in perfect order up there in your head."

Ryan puffed out a short breath of air. "So did I."

He said it with such a surprising amount of gloom that I immediately turned to look at him. He pulled at one of the bands on his wrist, biting the inside of his cheek, looking infinitely sadder than I'd expected him to. Jeez. I knew he liked music but it wasn't that serious.

He glanced up from his wrist and I met his eyes. All hazel and warm and vibrant and . . . home. A funny look crossed his face, and he reached out to touch my necklace, picking it up by the oval-shaped pendant at the nape of my neck. He smiled softly.

"Of all the impressive things we've done together, I think the thing that shocks me most is that you've managed to keep this thing after all these years."

I looked down as he held the pendant between his thumb and his finger, twisting it so that the engraved *L* was facing me. If only he knew just how much effort keeping it had taken.

"I'm surprised it was never, like, caught in some fence while running away."

"Or taken by the wind all those times we've sped in the Porsche," I added.

Ryan laughed. "Or . . . I don't know. Forgotten in some hurry to get to the next place."

I frowned, inching away from him. "Forgotten?" I repeated. I may have nearly lost it, but forgetting it was never on the cards. "Never. I pinky promised, remember? This necklace is our friendship."

Ryan let go of the pendant and turned on his back to look up at the ceiling. I followed suit. We lay there for a while listening to the music, and I thought mostly about how much I hated the song that was playing. I hoped, for the artist's sake, that the bubble gum tone of voice and the saccharine lyrics were ironic.

"Remember that time I climbed your roof when my parents came over to pick me up, just so I could avoid having to go home?" Ryan asked after a while.

I grinned as I recalled listening in on Mrs. Pope's panicked calls to the police station while we lay on blankets on the roof. She'd said he had to be home by five, but I wanted him to stay for dinner, so we brought snacks and planned to wait the two hours out.

"Our first mission," I laughed.

"How about that time we baked all those cookies for Ms. Vella after her divorce? Remember? We left them outside her door with an anonymous note and then ran away after pressing the doorbell so we could watch her pick them up from behind a tree?"

"Yeah," I said quietly. "I remember that."

"That was my favorite one, I think."

I raised an eyebrow. He said that a lot, and about a different story each time.

"Now, Ryan and Loli take on the prom," he joked.

I laughed. "That hardly counts as something adventurous."

"I would beg to disagree," he said. "We're both venturing into completely uncharted territory."

His words mixed and mingled with those of the song, twisting and wrapping themselves together as it crescendoed. I stared at the ceiling, contemplating them all.

Unfortunately the next mission wasn't as action packed or adventurous as we'd hoped.

"We're watching . . . a movie?" Cairo's voice was flat and unimpressed.

"No," I replied. "Well. Yes. But we're not just watching a movie. The movie is the letter. We have to decode what it says."

It was Wednesday evening, and the three of us were sitting in my living room with our homework and three boxes of pizza spread out all over the coffee table. Ryan and I were sitting on the floor with our work directly in front of us while Cairo sat on the couch, a great distance away from the orange binder she had pulled out and placed on the coffee table. She leaned forward on the edge of her seat, legs spread and elbows facing outward in classic Cairo fashion, and she narrowed her murky green eyes at me. Somehow, even in a simple billowy white tank top and camo pants, she still managed to look stunning.

"Let me get this straight," she said, bringing her hands together. "You two got to visit Wolf's lair, jump over a hedge, throw a bottle in a private pool, and run away from guards, and the day I come all we get to do is watch a movie?"

Ryan smirked and scribbled something in pencil on his math worksheet.

"I actually think it's kind of cool," I said, pulling the sheets of paper I'd printed out and laying them on the table. MV had texted me rows of movie time stamps arranged in the order of a soon-to-be sentence and I'd printed them out to make it easier to decode. Cairo squinted at her sheet, finger trailing the second line of text:

Row 2: 01:07:05; 00:48:17; 00:26:56; 00:07:05; 01:39:27; 01:28:09; 00:56:23.

"Don't confuse yourself with the numbers," I advised. "All we have to do is watch the movie, write down the sentence or phrase that is said at all these times, and voilà! A secret message."

"Like a spy decoder," Ryan suggested. "Except we also get to watch a movie."

"Okay," Cairo said. "I'll bite. What movie is it?"

"Some movie from the nineties," I answered, turning on the TV. "*Wicked Jam.*"

"*Wicked Jam?*" Ryan lifted his head from the throne of pillows he'd created in front of the screen and pointed at the TV with his pen. "I've heard of this before! It's supposed to be really good."

"A cult classic," Cai added with a nod.

"Well let's hope it is," I mumbled, easing into my space on the couch. I grabbed my fluffy pen, my notepad, and the clicker, pulling my copy of the time stamps close. "You both got the times written down in chronological order?" I asked, double-checking.

Ryan shot a thumbs-up from the ground. Cairo grunted a yes through her mouth full of pizza.

I smiled, satisfied. "Good. Let's decode this thing." I took a deep breath and pressed play.

Wicked Jam was weird. It was too artsy, too loud, too violent, and with all the pausing and rewinding we had to do to write down the appropriate words and phrases, it took much longer to finish than we'd anticipated.

The story followed four young twenty-something white guys who weren't happy with the rules of society or whatever, so they decide to quit their jobs and live in a secluded forest all alone and isolated for a while, until they kidnap a girl passing through the forest. After months in captivity, she somehow convinces them to go back out into civilization, and the next thing I knew they were all robbing a bunch of people and murdering each other.

The movie ended on a black screen with a horribly loud rock song playing over it, and I grimaced as the credits started to roll. I guess it was supposed to be some thought-provoking commentary on life but all it did was leave me feeling queasy. I thought the girl deserved revenge.

"Well that was," Ryan paused, struggling for a word before he settled on, "something."

Cairo put her notebook aside and stretched her arms. "I liked it," she said, beginning a yawn. "I think it's one of those movies you have to watch twice."

"I think once was good enough for me." I grabbed the clicker and lowered the volume on the closing credits.

"Hey!" Ryan complained. "That's actually a really good song!"

I didn't want to keep the movie on for longer than it had to be, but I turned the volume up a little just to keep him quiet. "So," I began, flipping my notebook open on the coffee table, "what do we have?"

It took us forty minutes to compare notes and construct the letter, but in the end, this is what we came up with:

(The Assumed "Dear Robyn")

I really enjoyed (. . .) your last (. . .) message. It came as quite a surprise (. . .) and I think it was worth (. . .) the harm (. . .) I had to endure.

   I also feel sad (. . .) for those who send (. . .) messages (. . .) in (. . .) bottles. (. . .) I doubt a single one of them ever (. . .) got what they wanted.

   I was surprised you even thought about those people (. . .) until (. . .) I realized why you did.

   Because (. . .) you identify with them.

   You know what I think? (. . .) I think we are (. . .) really different. But I think (. . .) we're both (. . .) nomads (. . .) in one way or another.

   I roam (. . .) away from places and people. You stray (. . .) away from (. . .) moments.

   You're scared to wait (. . .) because (. . .) you're afraid they'll never come.

                                        (The assumed "From MV")

"Damn," Cai said. "He's got you down to a tee."

I hastily folded the final draft and put it away in my bag.

"No, he doesn't," I objected. "He doesn't even know me."

"Well he knows a lot about you for someone who doesn't know you," Ryan mumbled.

"That movie was surprisingly good," Cairo said, stretching across the coffee table for a slice of pizza. "I should've known it though. Wolf said it was his favorite movie of all time, and everything that guy likes is a riot."

Ryan and I both turned to look at her, startled.

"This is Wolf's favorite movie?" we asked simultaneously.

"Yep." She nodded.

"How do you even know that?" I asked.

Cairo shrugged and took a bite of her pizza. "They were all talking about it after school and Wolf said it was his favorite movie and that I should watch it. I said I'd think about it, but I forgot until now."

Ryan raised his eyebrows. "Well, that's a weird coincidence."

"Not that weird," Cairo returned. "It's a cult classic."

There was a moment of silence as we turned this information over in our minds.

Ryan and Cairo packed up shortly after the credits ended. When they weren't looking, I scrunched the letter into a ball. It was no use.

The contents stayed fixed in my mind until we said goodbye.

Much later, after Ry and Cai were long gone, I stared down at the glowing contact I'd semi-jokingly saved as "Unknown."

For a moment I was tempted to tap his name. I wanted to know what he meant when he said that I strayed away from moments. I wanted to tell him he didn't know me. I wanted to rip him to shreds. I wanted to hear him out. I wanted to agree, to disagree, to say something, maybe all these things, and I could if I wanted to; he was right there on the other side, accessible and available to me at any time.

I tapped "Unknown" and started a message, thumbs darting around the keyboard before I came to my senses and pulled them away from the screen.

What the hell was I doing? Late night chats and unwarranted personal text messages were never the plan. It was the letters for him and the missions for me, nothing more.

I was not supposed to want more.

I cleared the text, sent him the required photographic proof of our decoded letter, and went to bed before I could check for his answer.

CHAPTER

17

TRACK:

THE DENIAL TWIST

The White Stripes

Something was up with Ryan. Again.

He'd been fine all of Wednesday; fist-bumping in the hallway, stealing food from people's trays at lunch, and practically skipping on his way to Noel's place after school for band rehearsal.

But then Thursday morning came. I knew as soon as I approached Baby that something was up. The car didn't throttle or reverberate with the heavy bass of a promising day, it merely hummed at an appropriate volume. I adjusted my sunglasses and practiced a bright smile in the reflection of the car door before getting in.

"Hey!" I stopped cold at the sight of him.

His eyes were red and raw, and his usual "carelessly tousled" hair was just a disheveled blond mess, as if he'd been tossing and turning all night and hadn't bothered to run a comb through it that morning. I tore my eyes away from him and set my focus on the dashboard where I noticed the most jarring thing of all.

The radio was playing.

The radio.

Ryan was listening to the radio.

"The devil's commercialized, recycled backwash" was playing freely inside Ryan Pope's car. The hairs on my arms pricked up.

"What's up?" I asked, trying to sound casually cheerful and not at all concerned or suspicious.

He cracked a weak smile. "Nothing much."

I blinked, trying to calm the sense of panic this was giving me—like the world was twisting upside down. Was he even aware that the radio was playing? I didn't want to risk bringing any attention to it.

"How'd band practice go yesterday?" I asked, carefully.

There was a beat. "Uh, yeah. It went well."

He turned his head to the left to watch for oncoming traffic, and I watched him for a while, debating whether it would be a good idea to ask him if he was okay, before I decided to leave it for now. I knew Ryan Pope. Letting him know I could tell he was upset would only make things worse.

I managed to hold it in all the way until after school, when he drove me home to the sullen sound of a yogurt commercial. Screw it, I thought, watching him pull away. I'd given him more than enough time and space. Ignoring things may have been his way of dealing with things, but confrontation had always been mine.

When I arrived at his house, the kitchen door was wide open, and Mrs. Pope was just lifting a tray out of the oven.

"Lolly!" Helen slammed the oven door shut with her free arm and waved away a faint cloud of smoke. "I need to get that thing cleaned. How are you, sweetie?"

"Good," I answered, edging my way toward the oven. I peered into the tray and furrowed my brow. "Are those cookies?"

"Yes," she said, gently lowering the tray to the top of the stove. "And they're white chocolate chip because"—she paused and glanced up at the ceiling before lowering her voice—"he's in a bit of a funk."

I raised my eyebrows. If there was anyone Ryan could successfully deceive, it was Helen Pope. Her anxiety-prone nature had forced Ryan to learn exactly how to evade and elude her in order to cause the least possible amount of stress or worry, even when it came to the little things. And since he was usually only doing things that would either stress or worry her, Ryan had become a very good liar. One especially tailored for Helen Pope. I couldn't imagine what was going on if even *she* could pick up that some-thing was wrong.

Mrs. Pope opened a drawer and grabbed a spatula to scoop the cookies up. "Here," she said, lining them on a plate. "Take some with you when you go upstairs."

I glanced down at the dried fruit packets in my hands, choos-ing not to state the obvious. We both knew about Ryan's strict, self-imposed dietary habits, but I guess she figured it was worth a try.

"Do you know why he's upset?" I murmured, already trying to read her expression for faults and cracks.

She shook her head. "It started a little over a week ago, and I thought I'd give him his space for a few days because—well you know how he is. He clams up as soon as anyone even attempts to bring up anything tough. But just as I was planning to confront him, he got better and I put it out of my mind. Only now it's started up again . . ."

She cast a worried glance up the stairs and I nodded. Her story mirrored mine exactly.

As I turned to go up the stairs, I went to grab a cookie and immediately dropped it back onto the plate. Helen gasped as if it were her hand and not mine.

"Ouch!" she said, rushing forward. "They're still hot, sweetie, wait until they cool down! And please pass that message on to Ryan. Knowing him, he's going to do the exact same thing."

Radiohead wailed from the crack underneath Ryan's door. It was loud at the bottom of the staircase and only got louder as I got higher up the stairs and closer to his bedroom. He couldn't hear me knock, he couldn't hear me yell, and he didn't hear the door creak when I pushed it wide open.

I gaped at the state of his usually immaculate room—it was as "trashed" as trashed could get for Ryan Pope: clothes strewn all over the floor, empty water bottles lining the windowsill, bowls gathered on his bedside table. As I stood there, I realized I had never seen his bed unmade before. The sheets were ruffled and tossed as though he'd been sleeping in them all day. Ryan lay on top of them, scrolling down his phone.

"Wow." The song came to an end just in time for my surprise to be audible.

Ryan jerked his head up with a start, surprised, probably, to hear a noise other than loud depressing music.

"What a clichéd picture of a sad teenage boy," I teased.

Despite the fact that we were indoors and it was warm, he was wearing a blue hoodie with the strings pulled tightly at the ends. He looked like a babushka doll. I smirked. It was cute.

"Except you're supposed to be hopelessly staring at the ceiling and not your phone," I continued. "Maybe absentmindedly throwing up a basketball."

"I actually did that for a while," he said. "You just missed it."

I walked farther into his room, kicking a clear path from the door to his bed. "Cookie delivery from Helen." I shoved the plate and the dried fruit toward him. "And healthy snack delivery from, well, me."

"Ooo, nice," he said. "I thought I smelled something sweet." He placed the cookie in his mouth and tore open the fruit packet as he got up to lower the volume on the speakers without any mention of his diet.

"Hey, I have to show you this song," he said, pulling the cookie from his mouth.

I nodded, relaxing a bit. A song recommendation was a good sign. The quietly somber song that had started was stopped abruptly and interrupted by the burst of an electric guitar.

"The Black Keys?" I asked.

"Nope. Cage the Elephant," he said, flashing his phone at me. *It's Just Forever*, the screen read. I frowned. I didn't like it. It was too loud and definitely not the right mood for this conversation.

"Ryan . . ." I started. "Are we going to talk about whatever's bothering you?"

He let out a dismissive laugh and collapsed back onto the bed. "Nothing's bothering me," he said.

"Really, Ryan?" I glowered. "You're seriously trying to tell me that you're okay? You're up alone in your room on a weekday, blasting Radiohead. Your eyes are red from rubbing them so much. And you didn't even hesitate when I offered you that cookie."

He looked away from me and swallowed. "Lo, I . . ."

"Are you worried about Babble?"

"What?" He looked surprised. "No! I'm literally counting down the days until we perform."

"Then why are you so upset?"

"I—I'm not upset," he hesitated. "I'm just . . . confused." His voice cracked on the last word and he cleared his throat to cover it up.

Okay. That was manageable. There were worse things to be than confused; the three of us could work through any difficulty together. "About what?" I asked.

"Everything," he said. "I don't know."

He took a deep breath and ran a hand through his hair. I lowered myself onto the other end of his bed and waited for him to go on.

Finally, he looked up at me and sighed. "Okay. I'm just going to get this out of the way so that you're not annoying about it: this story is about something that happened with Julia Flynn."

I gasped. Julia Flynn: a.k.a. Ryan's first ever crush and all-around dream girl. Also the girl he was rumored to have been with at the party.

"But you told me that nothing happened with Julia during our party debrief!"

"I didn't want to get into it."

"So the rumors are true?"

"No! Just—listen." He threw up his blue hood and pulled the strings so that only little tufts of blond hair could poke out.

"After about . . . an hour of DJ-ing, I realized I hadn't seen you for a while, so I left the booth and looked around for you for a bit. I looked everywhere downstairs and outside before I figured you'd probably gone upstairs, so I went up and searched every single room only to find that you weren't there either."

I shifted on the bed so that my legs were crossed and I was facing him.

"Anyway," Ryan continued, "I was about to head back downstairs when I turned around and there she was."

"The girl you've been madly in love with for six years," I teased.

"She asked me what I was doing, and I told her I was looking for you, and then she pulled a face and asked if we were 'a thing,' to which I said no. Then she stepped toward me, getting real close, whispered 'thank goodness,' and before I knew it she was kissing me."

Ryan stopped. "Ugh. Lo. Don't make that face."

My cheeks actually hurt from how much I was grinning. "You kissed Julia Flynn! One of the most sought-after girls in our grade! And you didn't tell me? I can't believe this."

Ryan let go of the strings on his hoodie, eyes downcast. "I didn't know what to do. It was weird and uncomfortable and wet, and I didn't like it, so I just pulled away and told her I wasn't interested."

"Wait . . ." I paused. "I'm confused. What's the issue? You've had a crush on her since, like, middle school."

Ryan threw his hood off. "I've never had a crush on Julia Flynn, Lo."

I stared at him, completely confused. "What do you mean?"

Ryan shrugged. "I picked her name randomly in sixth grade because everyone was pestering me for one."

"But—" I opened and then closed my mouth, completely stunned by this information.

Ryan continued. "And I know Julia's a beautiful girl—one of the prettiest, I think. So why did I hate it so much? Why was my only instinct to push her away? I mean even she was baffled. I doubt she's ever been rejected by, well, anyone. She looked at me with this confused expression and was like, 'What's your deal? Are you gay or something?' And I was still thrown off by the kiss, so I just went 'uhh,' and she went 'that'd explain a lot,' and stormed down the stairs. When I finally got back downstairs to the party, Rod Stevens and a bunch of other kids gave me pats on the back, congratulating me for coming out."

I paused, digesting the contents of this story. "So . . ." I paused, trying to find the right words. "You're embarrassed about your awkward kiss with Julia? And . . . you think you might be gay?"

It was Ryan's turn to pause. "Yes. No. I don't know. I just—"

"I can't believe," I interrupted, "that I threw a party so iconic that Cairo became a model, Mr. Robinson lost his job, I became a secret agent, of sorts. Perfect Kathy started dating a skater and you realized you might be gay. I think I saved us all like . . . ten years of maturity and figuring things out the hard way."

Ryan shifted on his bed. "Lo . . . I'm not gay."

Although he didn't sound too convinced when he said it.

Then, something I had never even thought to consider occurred to me. "Ryan."

"What?"

"Had you never kissed anyone before Julia?"

The possibility of Ryan having never kissed anyone before was a complete shock to my system. He was so popular and so well liked that I'd always assumed he simply chose not to share his adventures with me because he didn't want to make things awkward and uncomfortable.

"I have," he scoffed. "Obviously. I just don't particularly . . . want to. I don't really care for any of that stuff."

I raised an eyebrow. "Names," I demanded.

Ryan heaved his shoulders up and sighed in frustration. "I'm not giving you names, Lo."

"Well, I need to know who and how if you want help figuring out what's going on."

"You need to know who and how?"

"Yeah, I need to know the context and the circumstance. For example, if it was, like, Ashley Holmes on a dare at some awkward eighth grade party, then your situation is self-explanatory, and there's no need to stress."

That didn't seem to help; he only looked more confused. I unfolded my legs and scooted closer to him. Ryan had always been particular—that's the way I'd always perceived him. He needed just the right song for the moment, just the right amount of balance to his diet, and he needed just the right girl to ask out. At least, that's what I'd believed.

"Look," I started. "It might seem as though kissing is all about the lips but before you even get to that stage there needs to be some sort of contextual tension, some pent-up feeling or emotion that builds up just before—or you might as well just call the whole thing off."

Ryan threw his head back and looked up at the ceiling. "God help me."

"You need that tension," I went on. "The classic will-they-or-won't-they situation."

As I said it, my mind unwittingly went to MV and his threat of romance, before I shook the thought from my head. No. There were greater matters at hand.

I placed both arms in front of me on the bed and leaned forward so that our heads were inches apart. Ryan's breath caught. He looked panicked.

"Are they going to do it?" I said in a low tone. "Or better yet, Am *I* going to do it?"

He held my eyes. I held his. I probably would've kept holding them forever if he hadn't looked away.

"Geez, Lo—"

"Shh." I reached my arm out and directed his head back to face me. "Step one. Prolonged eye contact."

I looked into his confused, muddy green eyes for a few seconds, and I couldn't help but smile. The mopey expression he'd been sporting all day had disappeared, and in its place was his frozen look. The same look he got every time I suggested doing something he thought was crossing the line and he didn't know how to stop me.

I focused on the freckle under his left eye and leaned in so there was only a centimeter of space between my chest and his arm. His eyes dropped down to my lips and back to my eyes.

"Wha—"

He stopped and I felt the warm air from his breath hit my face. I knew what he was thinking, what he'd wanted to say: *What in the world are you doing, Lo? Are you really going to kiss me?*

I looked down at his lips and moved the arm I was leaning on so that it was behind his back. Neither of us said a word.

"Lollipop!" Mrs. Pope shouted up the staircase. "I'm heading out! If you see Cody playing Xbox report to me immediately!"

"Sure thing!" I shouted back. I kept my eyes on Ryan's lips.

The front door slammed shut. I heard Cody run down the stairs to the sitting room, and that's when I decided to stop being stupid. I laughed a little and pulled away from Ryan, springing off of my arms to sit back on my legs, but the gap that slowly widened between us was immediately closed again by Ryan rushing forward to kiss me.

The force of it pushed me back so hard, I had to lean on my arms for support.

The song changed.

For a second I was completely stunned, and then I got it. I knew exactly what he was doing. It was what he always did when I went too far. Like the time in first grade when I told him I'd drop his last birthday cupcake in the lake if he didn't give me his night-light, and he reacted by throwing the cupcake into the sand to show he didn't care. Or the time I threatened to call his mom and tell her about his secret candy stash when he wouldn't let me pick a movie, and he told her about it himself and proceeded to click on his choice of film.

Ryan smiled slowly, watching me as he backed up to his side of the bed. I cleared my throat and brushed my clothes down, trying to appear calm, collected, and nonchalant. My heart may have been violently hammering in my chest, but I was not about to give him the satisfaction of an outward reaction.

"And?" I asked, matter-of-factly.

He shrugged. "Meh."

I frowned and kicked him in the leg.

"Ouch!" He winced and rubbed the spot where I'd hit him.

"Well then I can one hundred percent tell you that there's definitely something wrong with you and not the people you've been kissing." I sniffed. "This is the thanks I get for doing charity work."

Ryan laughed. I smiled. Mission accomplished.

We decided to go downstairs to get snacks (and to check that Cody wasn't playing Xbox in the basement) and then we sat in Ryan's room, pretending to get homework done but really just scrolling through social media and listening to the rest of Ryan's Mope Playlist.

"You know," he said during the silence between two songs, "there doesn't have to be something wrong with me if I don't like that stuff."

"Yeah, I know," I said. And I thought of saying something funny to ease the seriousness, something like: "There'd be something wrong if you did like that kiss, Ryan," but I couldn't bring myself to utter the words.

CHAPTER 18

INSTRUMENTAL

At home that evening, my parents were both working in the living room: Dad on his phone talking through a contract, Mom typing on her laptop with a look of extreme concentration on her face. Not wanting to disturb them, I quietly headed straight up to my bedroom.

My room was quiet. I didn't like quiet. Silence brought forward an unwelcome slew of thoughts—about middle school crushes, the ugliness of peer pressure, and the taste of Helen Pope's cookies in my mouth. I cut though them all by pulling my phone out and tapping the last message I'd received from The Mysterious Voice.

> Perfectly executed, 007

He had sent it in response to our decoded *Wicked Jam* letter. I had let the text sit in my pocket unanswered all day.

There were two reasons for this, three if you wanted to be technical:

1. The deadline was for midnight, which meant I didn't really have to respond or do anything else until then.
2. His brief response was proof that our texts were naturally reverting back to their original purpose, and I wanted to keep it that way. No more banter-filled chats. Just a simple text to alert the other: a notification really, rather than a text message.
3. I understood. The rest we'd save for the letters.

Before I went to bed, I emptied one of my old Scrabble boxes out on the ground and picked out the fourteen letters I needed for my next package. When I was sure I had them all, I tied them in a little drawstring bag with a card that read:

To You,

--- --n- --o- --

Respectfully,

a Stranger

It was a succinct one-sentence letter with a difficult puzzle and an easy enough clue, which I texted to him as soon as I was ready:

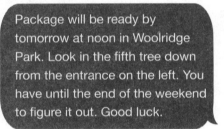

Package will be ready by tomorrow at noon in Woolridge Park. Look in the fifth tree down from the entrance on the left. You have until the end of the weekend to figure it out. Good luck.

Short and simple. No messy emotions.

I sent the text and crawled into bed, trying not to think about him and failing miserably. *You're scared to wait for moments because you're afraid they'll never come.* I scoffed, pushing his words out of my mind.

The audacity it took for a complete stranger who didn't even know my first name to try to read me was astounding. Who did he think he was, trying to tell me what I felt? Why I did the things I did? I turned over in my bed, my arms crossed against my chest, and when I'd settled in a comfortable position, my phone buzzed. I froze and I closed my eyes, fighting the urge to pick it up. Because there was a third reason I hadn't texted him that day.

I liked it too much.

Not just the game, the missions, and the fun, I liked it, *him*, the whisper in the dark, the ink scratches on the paper, the loftily detached text messages with comments and jokes: everything that made him The Mysterious Voice. I liked him just as much as I liked the fun and the adrenaline, and I hated it.

CHAPTER 19

TOP DOWN
Kari Faux (feat. Leikeli47)

Almost as soon as I realized that Ryan was doing bad enough for his mother to get involved, it occurred to me that I could use his pain to our advantage. Well, everyone's advantage really. My Porsche was a blessing to anyone who set eyes upon it.

"I thought I was still dreaming when you texted me this morning!" he shouted from the top of the driveway when I pulled up to his house the next day. "How in the world did you get this to happen?"

I pulled my shades down to the end of my nose so I could look at him over the top.

"Never question your blessings, Ry. Only count them."

But of course there was no way I was going to confess that I'd manipulated my parents with a sad story about how he was suffering through some personal stuff, and maybe I should give him a ride to school instead of making him pick me up in this difficult time? I swear my mother almost cried when she heard Ryan was down. She really would do anything for the boy.

Ryan grinned and shook his head before running down the slope. As he got in the car, all hyped and charged up, flashes of the scene in his bedroom flickered in my mind. I forced the images out and abruptly turned the music up—my choice this time—before speeding away.

First to the park to drop off the package for The Mysterious Voice, and then down Bel Avenue, taking the long way to school so we could enjoy our ride the proper way: with music blasting, wind blowing through our hair, and dozens of curious eyes trailing us as we drove by. I snuck a look at him as we rounded a corner. He was leaning back with his eyes closed and a small, easy smile on his lips. I smiled. If it wasn't the car, or the music, something seemed to be working. Ryan was happy again.

After a painfully average Friday at school, the three of us decided to start the weekend right by going to Dizzy Arcade.

"Ugh, I missed that." Cairo sighed, leaning into my seat. I knew exactly what she meant. The freedom of driving fast down the highway without a roof was incomparable to anything else.

I played my song choice again on the way to Dizzy's, and Cairo stood up in her seat with her arms in the air, screaming as we took off down the highway. I laughed and looked in my rearview mirror to see that Ryan was grinning too.

When we walked in, the lights were blinking and music was playing, but it wasn't as busy as it usually was on a Friday afternoon. I looked around beneath the veil of green light. The place was basically ours. Our usuals were brought to the table less than five minutes later, and after we had all had our first few sips, Cairo sat back and assessed Ryan.

"Well, you seem to be doing a little better," she said.

I looked up from my plate and caught Ryan stealing a glance at me. I had told Cairo that Ryan needed someone to talk to, but I hadn't told her the specifics of our conversation, or about the kiss—that wasn't my story to tell. She was better at these things than I was and definitely more knowledgeable about the topic at hand. I wondered whether Ryan would bring the kiss up in front of her, as casually as it had occurred. I wondered whether he'd thought much about it at all.

He was looking slightly better today. Still a little rough around the edges (judging from his eyes, I doubted he'd had much sleep) but otherwise his laughter had been genuine, and his cloud of gloom had lifted.

"Yeah, I uh . . . I was kind of dealing with some things that I think I've mostly sorted out."

"Yeah?" With her straw, Cairo drizzled milkshake over her brownie. "Is this to do with that Julia Flynn rumor?"

Ryan choked and I looked at Cairo, surprised at her abruptness.

"Look, Ry. I know difficult conversations aren't your favorite thing and that you don't like to worry anyone, but I hope you know that you can come to us at any time and we won't feel burdened. In fact, we'll feel the opposite, because . . . we love you. Right, Lo?"

I nodded. "Yes. Yes, we do."

The table was silent for a moment. Ryan kept his eyes trained on Cairo's shriveled straw wrapper. "I, uh . . . I don't know what you've heard," he started, "but the rumors are kind of stemmed in truth." He paused, struggling for words.

"You're gay," Cairo said with a shrug.

"I don't think so. I just don't really want any . . . thing."

"So you're asexual," Cairo said.

"Asexual?" I asked.

"Yeah," Cairo said. "It's a thing. Some people don't experience sexual attraction or show any desire for it. That sound like you?"

"A little," Ryan said. "I've actually been considering the fact that I might be demisexual."

Cai grabbed her phone and tapped it a few times. "Here," she said. "There's like a whole diagram of branching subgroups. You could be demi, greysexual, aromantic . . ." She tilted her screen in his direction, flashing a colorful chart with the words "Ace Spectrum" at the top.

"Welcome to the alphabet club, my dude," Cairo said.

Ryan grabbed her phone and eyed the chart. It made so much sense in retrospect: his vague responses about girls, his indifference about Woolridge hookups. Why hadn't I considered it before?

"Thanks, Cai," he said, smiling gratefully. "And thank you too, Lo."

"For what?" I asked, taking a sip of my drink. "I didn't do anything."

He smiled wider. "Of course you didn't."

Our conversation was abruptly interrupted by a loud clash followed by a yelp from the center of the restaurant. We all turned toward the noise.

"What the heck was that?" Cairo asked, craning her head to peer around the corner. "Who dare interrupt this special moment?"

Over her shoulder, a few kids got up from their tables to get a closer look, their expressions troubled and curious.

"I'll go find out," I said, sliding out of my seat. "Be right back."

I walked away from the table and headed toward the growing crowd. Practically everyone in our corner had gotten up to see what had happened. I pushed through the wall of kids to get to the middle of the crowd, and when I finally reached the center, I saw the cause of the commotion.

Some kid was sitting on the ground, holding his head in his hands. Blood ran from his mouth down the front of his shirt, and his glasses, which I guessed used to be on his face before the accident, were now lying on the floor shattered and broken.

I backed away slowly as a waitress rushed toward him with a frozen ice pack and a roll of paper towels. The kid lifted his face. Despite the blood and the lack of glasses, I realized I knew him. It was the blond nerd, Sid Oakes. One of Cairo's new friends.

He took the paper towel from the waitress's hands and then someone swooped up behind him, lifting him from beneath the arms. It was Sid's other half, the dark-haired nerd, Clay. He raised Sid from the floor, cigarette in his mouth, and lifted him onto a bar chair.

People whispered amongst themselves and slowly walked back to their tables, casting looks behind them. I thought of turning around and walking away too—but then I thought of what Ryan would say when I got back, what he'd say if he was standing right next to me.

I sighed and walked toward them.

Sid's eyes were shut tight as he held the ice packet to his head, mouth pressed closed to suppress the blood. Clay stood in front of him with a hand on either shoulder, bending low to talk to him.

I stepped closer, concerned. "Hey, are you okay?"

One of Sid's eyes popped open. Judging from the thickness of his waylaid glasses and the amount of pain he was probably in, I guessed he couldn't see me.

At the sound of my voice, Clay stepped to the side, looking back with an expression of confusion, which turned to indifference when he saw it was me. "Yeah, he's fine. Don't worry about him."

"You sure?" I asked, looking at Sid. "If you two need a booth to sit at while you wait for an ambulance or something, we're right up front over there."

"Thanks," Clay said. "But we really are fine. I'm going to call Wolf and head to the hospital just to check it out."

Knowing Wolf, he could've been anywhere in Woolridge doing who knows what.

"You know . . . I have a car—"

"Listen." Clay stopped and turned to look down me. I could see his gray eyes through his glasses. They were tired and impatient. "Wolf's just over at Woolridge Park getting some business done, so if I call, he'll be here in less than two minutes. Don't worry about us."

I raised my eyebrows. "Okay . . ."

He turned back to face Sid. I headed straight toward the booth. So much for helping. As I neared the table, Cairo cleared her throat and Ryan shut up. I slid in next to Cairo and they both looked at me, with weird expressions on their faces.

"It's Sid," I said, picking one of the cherries from my drink. "I guess he slipped and bumped his head."

"Is he okay?" Ryan asked.

I waved my cherry dismissively. "Yeah, yeah, I offered my help and made sure everything was fine before I left. They say Wolf's coming."

As if on cue, Wolf pulled up outside. After barreling down the freeway in it, I would recognize the rattle of his minibus anywhere.

All three of us turned to look as he hurried into the restaurant. He rushed toward his friends, and he and Clay lifted Sid up from his seat, moving him through the restaurant and into the minibus.

"Guys," I said, frowning. "What time is it?"

"Like, four or something. Check your phone, I don't know."

I pulled my phone out and saw that Cairo was correct. I also saw that MV had recently sent me a text:

> Package collected. Will alert when message is decoded.

I stared at the screen.

"Did you hear me, Lo?"

"What?" I asked, slowly looking up from my phone.

"I was talking about Basilica's new song," Ryan said, looking slightly hurt. "I think it's the best song we've ever written. It's very different from our normal stuff and a bit out of genre but I think you'll like it."

Wolf and Clay slammed the minibus's doors, and I looked back out the window. "Yeah, I'm sure I'll like it too," I answered, staring after Wolf's minibus even as they pulled away. "Don't I always?"

I barely listened to Ryan and Cairo as they went on about Babble and new songs and what other bands were playing. All I could think about was how remarkable of a coincidence it was that Wolf returned from Woolridge Park around the same time MV texted me that the package had been collected.

chapter 20

TRACK:
KILL OF THE NIGHT
Gin Wigmore

Later that afternoon, we headed to Ryan's to lounge around and play one of Cody Pope's "forbidden until you're older" video games. Cody had received them as a Christmas gift some months before, and he very cleverly allowed us to play them before he was "older" because it meant he could watch and sometimes join in when Helen wasn't around. And lucky for him, Helen was not around.

I sat next to him on the couch, scrolling on my phone as Ryan and Cairo screamed and yelled at the screen.

"Can I have a turn?" Cody asked.

"Not risking it," Ryan replied, eyes glued to the screen.

"But I watered Mom's petunias like you asked," he complained. "I even put the gloves back in your car."

"You used her gloves?" Ryan asked, turning from the screen. "You don't need gloves to water flowers, Cody." He sighed, compassion getting the best of him. "Okay, fine. We'll let you play later tonight."

"Wait, we're still going to Raycher's tonight, right?" I asked, lowering my phone onto my lap.

"Yep," Cairo confirmed. "To share the humble peace offering of our presence."

Our third-tier acquaintance, Matt Raycher, had been passively salty in the cafeteria after he found out we were involved in planning Mattaliano's party. It made sense—until last week, Matt

Raycher's "mad ragers" had been unbeatable. We figured it would help calm things to show face. I even promised I'd give his friend a stick 'n' poke when we arrived.

Ryan tossed his controller to the side as Cairo stabbed him and took the prized Dalusite Dagger from his arms, and the screen erupted into bright words and cheer. Cairo shot up in her seat, whooping and cheering, and I watched the scene in great amusement.

Then, my phone buzzed.

My heart leapt in my chest. It was him. The only contact set to vibrate on my phone.

I cursed my body for the incredibly Pavlovian response and picked up the phone.

> Except of course, that I do.

> Know you, I mean.

So he'd decoded the letter. My fingers didn't hesitate a second to respond.

> What ever happened to responding via letter? Is that not a thing anymore?

> Ah. So it wasn't all in my head. You stopped texting me on purpose.

> No, we both stopped texting each other.

> Did we?

> Yes. Because we realized there was no point in doing all of this if we can just text each other on the side

Well I want to end this texting hiatus.

Talking to you is usually the best part of my day.

Cairo and Ryan screamed a bunch of unintelligible words at the TV screen as I read the last message. I felt a quick, dangerous heat inside my chest as I sent a winking emoji and a black heart. It was the same heat I felt when I jumped off bridges, ran away from guards, climbed over gates.

Except, of course, when you use emojis.

"Lo! Are you watching this? Cairo is getting absolutely obliterated."
"Hold on a sec."
I watched as MV typed and was just about to put my phone in my pocket again when he sent a very different, completely unexpected text.

I hope you're not busy tonight because there's been a slight change of plans.

Your next delivery will be at the park in same tree trunk at 10PM SHARP. Await further instruction.

I frowned, confused. What?

> Wait what does that mean? Is 10PM the deadline or is it being dropped off at 10?

> Man. I miss the days of AnonChat where I could just log off and leave you to your own devices.

> Just make sure you're there at 10.

> "Stranger has disconnected"

"Wait, Lo, did you just miss that?" Ryan asked, turning around to face me. "Cairo was just completely knocked out!"

I lowered my phone. "Ha, really?"

"Yeah! And she was so close to finishing. Oh man, that was really bad."

Ryan packed up, laughing, and Cai moved the pillow she was screaming into off her face so she could kick him.

"Ow!" he yelped. "What's with the two of you and hurting me?"

10 P.M. Tonight. It was inconvenient, and I'd have to make it up to Raycher, but I didn't have a choice. "Hey, guys," I cut in, "I can't make Raycher's anymore. Something's just come up."

Ryan raised his head over the coffee table. "Why? What's come up?"

I paused, mind racing. I knew if I told them the truth they'd want to come. That's how it worked. And something about this unconventional mission told me I shouldn't bring them with. This time, I wanted to go alone. All the mission consisted of was

simply picking up the letter, and the letters themselves were private. Between us only.

'Just something," I said. "You guys can go on ahead to the party
though."

Ryan gave me a strange look. I was acting suspicious. I looked
away from him, afraid he'd be able to see through me if I met his eye.

"Cool," Cairo said. "Just keep us updated if you change your mind."

I glanced at the digital clock underneath the television. It was
8:46. I reached for the car keys in my bag and paused. I had struck
a deal with my mother: I could drive Ryan to school and back,
sure, but that the car better be back home around dinnertime.

Yikes. I didn't want to push her beyond her limit. Not after
she'd just warmed up to the idea of me driving my car again.

"Hey, uh . . . can I borrow your car, Ry?" I asked. Somehow, I
found it in me to look at him again.

"What?" he asked, lowering his controller. "Can't you use your
own?"

"Not really. I have a curfew."

Ryan's eyes cut to Cairo. She raised her eyebrows.

"If I let you drive Baby, how are Cairo and I supposed to get to
Raycher's?"

"Raycher's is like a seven-minute walk from here," I pointed out.

"Yeah, but it's still my—"

"Please!" I begged, bringing my hands together. "I'll be grateful
forever! You know the reason I don't have a car in the first place is
because I took the full blame so you could do Babble."

Ryan brushed a hand through his hair. He looked annoyed, but
I'd gotten him with that one.

"Fine," he acquiesced.

I smiled sweetly, got up off the couch, and headed for the key
rack at the front door.

"You're the best!"

I gathered my things as they prepared for another round, and as
I turned at the door, I caught Cairo shooting Ryan a pointed look,
which he chose to ignore as he hit play.

Oh, and cover up. It's a little cold out.

Ha. Where was your concern for my comfort when you wanted me to break & enter into a stranger's home?

CHAPTER
21

TRACK:
COME TOGETHER
The Beatles

By the time I arrived at Woolridge Park it was ten o'clock, right on the mark.

I turned Baby's engine off and got out, taking a swift look around as I shut the door. It was deadly quiet. No kids running around, no suburban-mom hiking groups, no dogs barking: just me and the wide avenue of firm oak trees tunneling straight ahead. Even though I would never admit it to him, I was glad I took MV's advice. The leggings and the long-sleeved shirt I'd pulled on were exactly what I needed to protect myself from the chill in the air.

I'd also made sure to grab a sweater and the can of pepper spray that I kept in my purse. Just in case.

I switched my cell flashlight on and walked up the gravel road toward the fifth tree to the left—the same tree I had left my last letter in—just as he had directed.

As I neared the tree trunk, I shined my light in the hole to ensure there weren't any animals hiding inside, and then I stuck my hand deep inside and grabbed the top of what felt like a brown paper bag.

It was a bigger package than usual. I squeezed it gently to see if I could discern what it was through the paper. The parcel had the weight and feel of a disappointing Christmas present: like clothes, but not heavy enough to be anything good.

I tore the paper open, reached a hand in, and touched something small and woolen.

I thought it was a beanie before my fingers slipped through one of the holes in the front. I blinked. It was a balaclava. And tucked inside it was the smallest rectangle of a note.

Meet me. Tonight. 10:15pm. 5th tree from entrance at W. Park. Wear this.

X

I dropped the paper bag. A quick hot pang flashed from my chest to my stomach.

The Mysterious Voice was here. And he wanted to meet me. Right now. Without warning.

He wanted to meet me again.

An animal cried in the distance, and I shivered, looking out into the expansive darkness of Woolridge Park. What was he doing? We had already made plans to meet on the last day of exams. Why was he switching it up?

I considered my options. There were only two:

1. I could turn and walk away, thus admitting cowardice and losing the game immediately, or . . .
2. I could stay, put the balaclava on, and see what MV had in store for me.

The choice was obvious.

I bit my lip to suppress the widening smile on my lips and my pulse rose to a sickening pace: there was nothing I wanted more than to stay and face the unknown.

I switched my flashlight off and glanced behind me, my senses on high alert for anything strange and out of place in the dark blue field—and that's when it decided to hit me. The only thing that could possibly make me think twice about meeting MV like this.

I shifted my feet and rubbed my arm as I scanned the parking lot, frustration welling up inside me. My skin would give me away. I was one of seven dark-skinned Black girls in my grade—a balaclava was not going to do well for concealing my identity. A small slip of skin could narrow his pool down significantly, he'd be able to place my identity within minutes.

I groaned and looked up at the sky, cursing the lights in Woolridge for being so damn reliable. A breeze fluffed through my hair, sending another shiver down my spine.

And then I remembered Cody and Helen's petunias.

I tightened my grip on the balaclava and sprinted back to Ryan's car, frantically wielding his keys to unlock his trunk.

Thanks to our miscellaneous adventures (and in part to Helen and her obsessive tendencies) Ryan's trunk was like a mother's handbag; he always had hand sanitizer, granola bars, binoculars, a change of clothes, random containers, two pairs of sunglasses, garden gloves, and a pair of sneakers.

Thank Helen. I grabbed the gloves and shuffled through all the miscellaneous items, pulling out a pair of sunglasses and one of Cody's bandanas that we had as a remnant of his cowboy phase. I decided he was completely forgiven for all the times he used a lassoed rope to tie me up in my sleep.

I glanced at my phone for the time. 10:07 P.M. Eight minutes until I met MV.

Heart racing, I quickly forced the sweater over my head, pulled on the balaclava, stuffed my hands into Ryan's grubby gloves, slipped the sunglasses on, and tied the bandana around my mouth. When I was properly suited up, I hesitated and grabbed the pepper spray before shutting the door. The game was on.

He was three minutes late.

I stood by the oak tree, trying every nonchalant pose I had as I waited for him, but after two minutes I gave up and leaned my back against the bark, popping the cap of my fruit punch gloss to bide the time.

Then, finally, a car turned in at the opposite entrance. There was the familiar sound of loud music boxing against car doors as it drew near—it was a familiar song, too, but I couldn't put a name to it. I capped my lip gloss and straightened as the yellow headlights lazily swept across the park and down the avenue of trees. As he slowed into a parking space, the lights beamed through the fence, holding a dirty yellow haze for a few seconds before flickering off, engine still running.

My cue. I took in a deep breath and kicked off of the tree.

It was a weird feeling, walking toward something I didn't know, couldn't see, and could only faintly hear. I let that feeling draw me closer toward him. The muffled beat of the song grew louder as I walked down the wide avenue of oak trees, and the sound swelled around the tinny vocals giving the song a dreamlike effect.

I watched a tall, dark figure rise from the vehicle. The music spilled out in brief clarity before he abruptly ended it by closing the door. The headlights flashed twice, illuminating me fully in the process. For a moment, everything was still.

Then, I made slow, deliberate strides toward the dark outline next to the car, stopping about ten feet away from it, at the mouth of the gate.

We stared at each other for a moment, though there wasn't much of each other to actually look at through our disguises and the static blue night.

"Robyn?" The Voice asked.

His voice was unsettlingly steady and calm, just like I remembered it. "You know," I folded my arms and stepped closer to him. "You promised me that when we met it was going to be something big. Something . . . heart-stopping."

The Voice laughed—only he wasn't just a voice anymore. He was a tall, black shadow with a sharp, fantastic laugh, moving slowly toward me. He stopped when he was close enough for me to reach out and touch him.

"When we meet," he said calmly, "I promise it'll be heart-stopping."

I scoffed. "When we meet?"

"Yes," he said, unmoved. "When we meet. Because this . . . is not us meeting."

"Really? What else would you call this?" I signaled to the space between the two of us.

"Just another anonymous conversation."

I laughed, incredulous.

"And maybe the greatest mission to date," he added.

He didn't sound like Wolf, or Will, or anyone I knew, for that matter. His voice was strange, and it was muffled enough that he could have been anyone.

I stared at the dark outline wavering in and out of sight against the blue background. "I'll bite," I said, placing my hands on my hips. "What's the mission?"

He smiled. I couldn't see him, obviously, but I heard it in his voice when he said, "You'll see. Follow me."

The shadow turned on its heel and walked down the slope of the parking lot, heading straight toward the main road that ran along the park. I hesitated and then followed him, out of the parking lot and down the road, staying a good distance behind him as he tore down the path ahead. His strides were so long and fast I had to jog to catch up.

"Tired?" he asked, when I finally caught up to him. "Having second thoughts?"

"No," I said defensively. "I just have to get used to this whole . . . following thing."

"Hmm." He reached for something in his pocket, but he must have thought better of it because he let his hand fall again. "You like being in control, don't you?" he asked.

"Yes," I replied. "It's the only way to make sure I'm never let down."

We approached a crossroad and MV took a left. "On that note, what's the plan?" I asked, running to keep up with him.

"You're going to fail the mission if you keep asking," he warned.

"You can't just make up new rules on the spot," I said.

We turned left down the next street. He slowed in front of

a darkened house that appeared to be floating on the soft warm glow coming through the large rectangular basement windows.

I stopped next to him. The light from the basement window revealed that he, too, had taken the precaution of wearing sunglasses, and their golden rectangles reflected in each lens as he stared down at the window. I followed his gaze and was surprised to see about six guys, not much older than us, sitting at a big round wooden table and playing poker. I recognized one of them, Joey Ocasek, a Woolridge High graduate from the year before. He tossed his cards on the table and stood up, proudly sweeping an arm around the table to collect his money while the table erupted with various exclamations.

"MV, I do—"

"Oh, man. Don't call me that. It sounds terrible out loud."

I smirked. He was right, it did sound horrible. "Okay, then. What am I supposed to call you? Boy I Don't Know? Mr. Stranger? X?"

"X doesn't sound half bad," he said.

I snorted. "Yeah it does. It sounds full bad. Like some cheesy superhero or villain."

He shrugged. "Well, if I'm dressed the part . . ."

An obnoxious laugh sounded from inside the basement. The dealer dealt the next round before MV—*X*—turned to me. "Okay," he said, voice suddenly low. "Follow me and do exactly as I do. When I say the word 'karma' you run, okay?"

I nodded, forcibly rejecting the discomfort of driving blind. I hated not knowing where we were running, why, and what from, but this was a mission, and X was right next to me, studying my every move through darkened lenses. I had to coolly pull through if I wanted to eventually win. "Got it."

X scuffled over to the right, where he signaled for me to follow him down a concrete flight of stairs I hadn't noticed before. I followed him down, heart humming in my chest as he reached a wooden door and pressed an ear to it. I heard the sound of a zipper being opened as I reached the last step, and then X placed something small and heavy into my gloved hands.

"Careful with this," he whispered. "Stay close to the door."

And before I even had time to look down at the object he'd placed in my hands, he bust the door open and ran into the room, shouting for everyone to freeze.

The players looked up from their game, only slightly startled by the interruption. They appeared unperturbed at first, as though loud interruptions like this were common occurrences in these games, and then one by one they stilled. Well, all but one guy who continued to play until someone nudged him, and he looked up from his cards to register the two completely covered faces and the cocked handgun pointed right at them.

I stood frozen in the doorway, and as X neared the playing table, I forced myself to look down at my own gloved fingers to confirm my suspicion that I was gripping a gun too.

A gun.

I brushed a finger over the tip and black ink smudged across Mrs. Pope's glove. A fake gun? If it was, I didn't know whether to be relieved or more panicked than before.

X steered his gun around the table in a slow, steady motion and the guys slowly started to raise their hands. One of them even stood up and backed up against the wall. I swallowed and tried to hide my shaking arms by extending them fully.

"You," X said, "with the ponytail. Take the money and start putting it in the bag."

He tossed a folded paper bag onto the table, and the guy with the ponytail slowly stood up and started sweeping the stacks of money inside.

The other players eyed X warily as the stacks audibly hit the bottom of the bag. Some of them looked at me, standing at the door. I stood as still as I could, with my fingers tight around the grip, managing just enough will to keep the barrel aimed at the table.

When the table was about halfway cleared, X ordered "You With the Ponytail" to stop and to leave the bag at the edge of the table.

Ponytail obeyed X's order, and when he was seated, X looked back at me and then at the table. "Robyn?"

I blinked a few times before realizing what he wanted me to do, and then I inched slowly forward, keeping the gun pointed at the table. My breath was shaky, and every step I took felt as though it would lead me over the edge of a cliff, but when I reached the table, I confidently grabbed the bag and backed up as fast as I could.

"Tell Leo not to take things that aren't his," X said. "Karma might not be so kind next time."

I didn't need to hear the word "karma" to bolt out of that room. I stumbled out of the doorframe and shakily reached for the concrete stairs, climbing and tripping up them as fast as I could. When I reached the top, I ran a couple of yards before I heard a door slam and watched as X appeared, racing up the stairs two at a time.

"Run!" he barked.

"I am!" I yelled back, and then I ran the fastest I had ever run in my entire life.

I fell forward into each heavy stride, attempting to put as much distance between myself and the house, the street, and the neighborhood as fast as I could. My legs felt like hot rubber, and my heart beat hard against my ribs as I flew down the street and out across the main road toward the park.

I ran past the parking lot, through the oak trees, across the field, and up the slope of the hill, stopping only when I was certain it was just us and no one was after us. Then I dropped the gun on the ground, ripped my bandana off, and leaned forward, placing my hands on my knees as I fought to catch my breath.

I heard X run up the hill after me and, though I barely had enough breath to whisper, spun toward him, ready to fight. "What," I said, wheezing, "THE HELL IS WRONG WITH YOU?"

X collapsed onto the ground, ripping his sunglasses off and splaying his legs out across the grass.

"What did you just make me do?" I shrieked, still breathing fast even though I was thinking more clearly. My legs were buzzing, and my arms were still shaking, so I put a hand on my chest and tried to get all the energy out by pacing and breathing in slowly.

"Calm down," X said. "It was nothing you haven't done already."

"What's that supposed to mean?" I snapped.

Instead of answering, X placed the money on his stomach and stared up at the sky. At the sight of the maddeningly peaceful look on his face, suddenly—finally—logic kicked in.

I strode over to where he lay on the ground and stood over him with one leg on either side of his body, and snatched the bag from his stomach. I was a lot of things, but a felon was never going to be one of them.

"I'm going back," I hissed. "I'm taking all of this off, and I'm dropping the money outside the door."

As I moved to walk away, he grabbed my left leg. "Hey! You've got to calm down—this isn't stolen. We didn't steal." I made another move to leave but his arm was tight around my leg. "It's like the situation with the necklace!" X explained. "The money was mine to begin with."

I stopped trying to free myself. He relaxed his grip. I stared down at him, anger pulsing through me. "So what?" I spat. "That makes it okay to trespass, threaten people, and steal? That was not a friendly party, and this," I said, jiggling his bag of money, "is not just a necklace."

I gave a frustrated sigh and rested my arms on the top of my covered head. "This is way out of my league. I don't risk my life committing mindless crimes. What if one of *them* had a gun? What if someone had shot at us?"

"I staked the situation before we got there. No one had a gun."

"Well, someone could have!" I shrieked. "Do you think I've ever handled a gun in my life?"

"No," X returned. "But then again, neither have I."

I lowered my arms from my head and looked down at him, remembering the paint on Helen's glove. "They're not real," I said, confirming my initial suspicion.

He nodded.

There was a long silence. I stared at him, breathing heavily, mind racing. Then I dropped the money bag to the floor, reached for the nearest gun, and angled the muzzle at his neck as I knelt over his chest.

I kept it nestled just under his neck as I straightened myself up. "Not real?" I repeated.

He didn't move. I looked into his eyes, dark, devoid of color.

"Yes," he said. "Not real."

And then, maybe because of the adrenaline or the ridiculousness of the situation—the ski masks, Ryan's trash gloves, the fact that we'd interrupted a random game of poker—something deep inside me bubbled up and came out in spurts of laughter. I couldn't contain it: I laughed and laughed and laughed, and then he was laughing too, and I was rolling off him and lying on the ground, laughing.

"You are terrible," I said when I finally came around. "Absolutely despicable."

"It was fun though, wasn't it?" he asked.

"I refuse to answer your question," I replied. "It might reward your stupidity."

"I think it's too late for that," he said. "You've already done that by laughing."

I looked up at the starry sky and felt like I was wedged right between the ground and the universe, on top of the world but just below the rest of the galaxy. I laughed again, and in another wave of ecstasy I curled my fingers around his. He squeezed my hand tight, and it was just as well that I couldn't feel his skin through the rough interior of Mrs. Pope's glove because that was our thing, wasn't it? To be there but not really, to be close but worlds apart. The cloth was just another buffer, like the screens of our phones, like our complete ignorance of each other, like the darkness of a closet.

"What's with us and meeting in the dark," I said after a while.

"I don't know," he said. "But I like it."

I snorted. "Why? Because you can continue to hide your grotesque form from me?"

"No," he said. "Because anything is possible in the dark."

I was going to ask him what he meant by that, but as I stared up at the pitch-black sky through dark glasses, I realized I already knew. It was all possible: the supernatural, our wild imaginings of the future, who we were. All of it was possible because of the dark's concealing nature.

"I used to be afraid of the dark," I said suddenly, unexpectedly. "But then . . . one day something changed, and I started to crave the very feeling I used to fear."

I let go of X's hand and pulled myself closer so I could rest my head on his chest. He was still for a second and then he placed a hand on top of mine. Then, suddenly, before I could even think about doing it, I whispered: "You were right."

He didn't say anything in response.

I squeezed my eyes shut and took a deep breath in. "About me straying from moments. I get this feeling sometimes," I began. "When everything is still and quiet I get this urge to do something . . . something drastic. So I avoid quietness and stillness at all costs, and I tear through everything with as much noise and action as possible. My mom says it's because I'm young, but if that's true . . . well then, I should be terrified, because it's the only thing that makes me feel alive."

I bit my lip as soon as the words left my mouth. I don't know why I said it. I didn't even know if it was true. I'd never let myself go there before.

The Mysterious Voice, X, The Stranger, Whoever He Was, drew a thumb across my wrist, just underneath my glove. In his pensive silence I felt understanding.

"Well," he said, "then I promise to deliver missions that leave very few moments for stillness. At least for the next few weeks."

I sniffed and a laugh burst from my lips. "Promise?" I asked.

"Cross my heart."

Just got home. Did you make it back alright?

Yeah, I'm home.

Good.

Good. Sleep tight, X.

I think I love you

You don't even know who I am, you idiot.

And? Has that ever stopped anyone before?

Good night, X.

TRACK:
FEELING MYSELF
Nicki Minaj (feat. Beyoncé)

When I woke up on Saturday morning, everything from the night before felt like a strange and distant dream. Like it was all something I'd thought up long ago and only just been able to recall. My mind's murky eye whirred through the poker game, running into the night, lying on the grass, laughing, *I think I love you . . .*

It was a dizzying feeling, sorting through my emotions after the events of the previous night. I needed to do something exciting to counteract them, something out there, something Loli. So I got a new hairstyle.

Early Saturday morning, instead of grabbing my drawing utensils and making my weekly trip to Westerns, I sat in a salon chair for six hours, doing homework, writing my next letter, and watching the mirror as the hairdresser twisted through synthetic purple strands with incredibly strong and well-practiced fingers. Around hour three, after she had finished a good portion of the back, my phone beeped. Ryan's ringtone. My heart sped up. I hadn't yet told him what I'd ended up doing the night before.

Hey—are you alive?

Yeah I'm alive. Why?

> Just checking. You
> never got back to us
> last night. You good?

I felt a flash of guilt. He was right, I hadn't gotten back to them after my adventure. But this was *not* the kind of story you wasted with a text.

> Sorry! Yeah I'm all good.

> Need a ride to
> Westerns?

> Ha. Thanks but it's a
> NO for Westerns. I've
> learned my lesson after
> last week.

After last night, I'd forced myself to shake the vision of Wolf and Clay carrying Sid at Dizzy Arcade out of my head, along with the rest of my suspicions about X's true identity. I liked not knowing. I had the rest of my life to know. And I liked the vision of us we'd left in the park—X and Robyn, wearing masks, lying in the dark, unknown to each other and the rest of the world.

When my hair was finally done, I stepped outside the salon and made a beeline for my mother's car. She'd pulled up in her Range Rover as the hairdresser started to dip my braids in a bowl of boiling water. For the last fifteen minutes, she had been sipping a caramel Frappuccino while speaking with someone on the phone. I ran up to the door just as she ended her call, and when I pulled it open, she gasped.

"Loli!" she exclaimed. "It looks amazing!"

I flicked some of the long purple braids from my shoulder and flashed her a smile, trying not to wince as the long curtain of hair pulled at my freshly planted roots.

"Ooh, I've got to show the girls," she said, raising her cell phone to take photos as I got in. "Shauna and I were afraid it would look a mess but—look at you!"

I rolled my eyes, fastening my seat belt. "When have I ever allowed myself to look a mess."

"Oh, you like to act all haughty and little-miss-perfect, but I've seen you in some pretty bad places, Naloli. Don't you ever forget it." She laughed that playful put-you-in-your-place mother's laugh. "I still have pictures from your seventh-grade fashion walk."

I gasped, eyes wide. "You would never."

She lifted her shoulders, as if to say, "Maybe."

I jutted my chin out. "As far as I'm concerned, if you want to retain your rights as my mother, you have to burn those photos."

She was too busy flicking through the photos she'd just taken to respond.

"And don't send those to the girls," I added.

My mother paused and slid her sunglasses up into her hair. "And why not?"

"Because," I said, grabbing her phone, "then Helen will show Ryan before I get a chance to, and I want to see his first reaction."

Mom sighed and lowered her phone into the coffee holder. "Fine," she said. "I'll just send them to Shauna then."

"You know . . ." I started, "if you gave me back my car for good, I'd let you send the photos to whoever you want."

My mother turned the steering wheel and looked up and down the road, watching for oncoming traffic. "My goodness," she muttered. And then she put on a whiny voice. "'Don't send the photos, burn the photos, only send these photos, don't show Helen, give me my car back' all in one conversation?" She shook her head. "You are a piece of work."

Unfortunately for me, the next time I saw Ryan was Monday morning before school. Between my six-hour hairstyle, his erratic

Babble rehearsals, and a small last-minute movie premiere I was forced to attend with my parents, it was impossible to coordinate a time that we were both free—and then, suddenly, it was Monday.

When he pulled up in front of the house, I bounced out the front door with the sort of pep only a new hairstyle could give you, spinning around twice before climbing in.

"Loli Crawford lives," he announced. His hair was deliberately tousled, his eyes were bright, the aux was plugged in, and a contrary grin played at his lips. We were back in business. Our conversation at Dizzy's must have done the trick.

I settled into my seat, nonchalantly flicking my hair over my shoulder, only narrowly missing his face with the long purple strands.

"Hey!" he exclaimed, wincing as he jerked backward. "Watch it."

I stopped shifting in my seat and stared at him expectantly. He blinked. I tilted my head forward.

"Uh . . ." he began, slowly narrowing his eyes. "Why are you moving your head like that?"

I dropped my arms to my sides and continued to glare.

"You hurt your neck?"

My expression must've darkened significantly because Ryan immediately dropped the act and grinned that teasing grin he did when he was trying to annoy me and knew it was working.

"You're the worst," I hissed, hitting him on the shoulder with my arm.

He snickered and ducked out of the way. So I got up on my knees and hit him again.

"Ouch!" he shouted, leaning forward on the horn. "Loli, stop!"

His shoulder hit against the horn a couple of times, letting out a noisy staccato blare as I crawled out of my seat to attack him.

"OW, stop! Lo, get OFF. I'm sorry—"

I ignored his pleas for peace, jabbing him underneath his rib cage until he peeked out from beneath his raised arms and seemed to catch sight of something behind me.

"Nancy! Thank God, help me!"

Sure enough, Mom had flown out of the house, all robed and bonneted up with a frown on her face.

I paused on top of him, watching his stupid smile turn into a pained grimace as he tried to signal to my mother that it wasn't his fault. My mother focused her eyes on me and shook her head. I fell back into my seat.

After she'd walked back indoors, I dragged my icy eyes over to Ryan, who was grinning and leaning his back against the car door. I'd messed up his signature purposefully disheveled hair—now it was just disheveled.

He sighed. "Okay, okay. I guess I now have to perform my reaction to your hair."

He ran a haphazard hand through his hair, cleared his throat as he looked aside, and then turned to me with a gasp. "Loli?" he asked, eyes blinking. "Oh my g—I literally didn't even recognize you. Wow. Your hair looks amazing!"

I shook my head and looked straight ahead, trying not to smile. "The Academy are disgusted," I responded. "They refuse to acknowledge that performance, let alone nominate it."

Ryan righted himself in his seat and raised his left leg up beneath the wheel in optimum Pope driving position.

"Okay, fine, in all seriousness your hair looks sick," he admitted. "It actually looks so good that I'm already tired of all the attention you're going to get today. You're going to look perfect at prom."

The last sentence sent an unexpected warmth to my face, and I felt strangely embarrassed. Ryan didn't seem to notice. "I've got the perfect song for right now," he said, scrolling through the music on his phone.

When the song started, I laughed and pulled my shades down. "Okay, I get it," I said. "Please, feel free to drive."

After one last glance at my new hair, he did.

"Nice hair," Cairo commented, nodding toward me in approval. It was lunchtime and since we'd spent so much time apart over the weekend, the three of us had decided to get a table just for us.

"Thanks, Cai," I said, and I smiled.

Ryan had been right: everyone loved it. Since first period, I'd had to swat at least a dozen wondering fingers and dodge twice as many hair pats.

Cai ran a hand through her brown hair and let it fall back over her face. "My long hair days are over. The hairstylists wanted to put extensions in for my shoot, and I had to tell them about my never-beyond-the-chin rule. I can deal with eyelashes and makeup, but I cannot deal with hair touching my back."

I lowered my sandwich. "Wait—you had the shoot this weekend?"

Ryan didn't seem surprised at all. I must've missed something through all the X drama.

"Yep." She nonchalantly tossed a grape into her mouth. "It was enlightening. First, I learned that I am not built for the modeling industry, and then I learned that I might have to learn to be built for it because I got a fat wad of cash and free photography lessons from Michael Keene himself."

Ryan, who'd been struggling to keep his kale from falling off his fork, shoved a piece in his mouth. "When can we see the photos?"

"No idea," Cai answered. "But I managed to secretly take a few photos of that screen-thingy when no one was looking. Look."

She passed her phone over the table, and I gasped as I swiped through the pictures. "Damn, Cai. You should've posted these on your story."

"You know very well I have no idea how to do that," she said, taking her phone back. "And that I would never care to."

"Wait," Ryan started. "Who drove you there?"

Cai counted on her fingers. "Tyler, Wolf, and Clay, in the minibus."

"No Sid?" Ry asked. "Is he okay after the incident at Dizzy's?"

"Yeah . . . they said he was recovering at home. I think Clay was missing Sid a little because he was extra standoffish, but Tyler and I had a fun time. I figured it could be a learning opportunity since they both do a bit of photography, and I really want to get involved."

Cai bit into her sandwich and fixed her green eyes on me. "But, hey, you texted saying you had something to tell us—what happened?"

I glanced between the two of them. They watched me intently, waiting for an answer. "I met The Mysterious Voice," I said, a smile on my lips.

Cairo stopped chewing and Ryan leaned forward on both elbows.

"Are you serious?" he asked.

I cast a glance over my shoulder, to make sure the coast really was clear. "Well," I started, "I met him but I didn't meet him. Not really . . ." Then I told them everything. Well almost everything.

I'd dismissed X's near love confession, chalking it up to being lost in the moment. It was entirely understandable; I had been too after the night we'd had. Despite my myriad emotions, including my disapproval of him tricking me into his mess, X's text had made my chest glow. I didn't need to tell Ryan and Cairo either of those things. It was exclusively mine and X's moment to be lost in.

So I focused on the letter, the balaclava, the faux robbery, and the fact that I went back on Sunday to hide X's next letter at the very house we'd robbed.

Cairo smirked, her eyes alight. "You didn't."

"I did," I said, leaning back. "I had to remind him who he was dealing with and put him in his place after the stunt he pulled."

Ryan gathered himself in his seat. "Lo . . . This guy obviously has bad blood with those people. What happens if he gets recognized and caught?"

"What would have happened if I'd been caught 'robbing' people with a balaclava and a faux gun in my hand?" I rebutted.

Cairo shrugged and leaned back. "Touché."

"I needed to show him that I'm not his loyal little sidekick. That I'm not automatically his because I went along with some . . . twisted plan."

Cairo smiled at me over her box of apple juice with her

all-knowing eyes. "You 'needed' to be in control again," she said. "That's what it is."

"Maybe it's for the best," Ryan decided. "You don't want to end up unknowingly at some psychopath's service. He could very easily assume—"

"That I'm willing to do any and everything and to go down with him?"

"Exactly," Ryan agreed, picking up a forkful of kale.

Cairo snorted. "You guys are either meant for each other or meant to be kept very, very far away from each other." She paused. "You and The Mysterious Voice that is."

I ignored the weird look on her face and went on. "It's probably the latter. I can very easily see myself going too far and becoming a criminal just to keep the game going."

"Oooh, imagine that," Cairo said with a lowered voice. "X and Robyn, the modern-day Bonnie and Clyde."

I winced. "Ugh, don't."

She looked between the two of us, catching Ryan's raised brow, and nodded. "Oh. Right."

Bonnie and Clyde. Ryan and I were likened to those two whenever we did anything remotely interesting together, and we were completely sick of it. Were there no two other people who did anything noteworthy together? No others who ever misbehaved or were as strongly devoted to each other? The phrase was tired. I mean, Helen and Nancy called us Bonnie and Clyde if we did so much as take an extra cookie from the cookie jar.

Cairo shrugged. "You know what I mean."

Ryan stabbed a fork through cucumber and feta, looking disproportionately upset. "You know I'm all for fun missions, but I think you should be more careful. A robbery? A fake gun? We don't know this guy."

I scoffed. "Yeah, that's kinda the point."

He looked at me. "I'm being serious. If Friday night taught us anything, it's that we should be on guard."

I frowned. "Since when did we ever let other people scare us off?"

"I'm not saying we should be scared, I'm saying we should be cautious."

I folded my arms. "So you don't think I'm—"

'Hey, I'm not trying to argue," Ryan cut in. "I'm just saying you should loop one of us in next time. Both of us want to see you win this, but more importantly, we want to see you safe."

I bit the inside of my cheek. "Well you don't have to worry about me," I huffed.

Ryan stuffed his fork in his mouth, I took a bite of my sandwich, and for the few remaining minutes of the lunch period the three of us sat in a silence punctuated only by the noisy slurping of Cairo's juice box.

Dear X,

Funny hiding spot, right? I thought you might appreciate a little throwback to our first and last crime together.

I hope that as you stood at that door, searching around the window ledges for the letter, you felt the same amount of fear and panic that I did when you handed me that fake gun.

It was nice meeting you on Friday but I think I need to remind you, or tell you if you didn't already know, that I am on my own team, first, foremost, and always.

If we're going to continue this . . . whatever this is, I need you to communicate and be open with me. All the best teamwork in history has only been accomplished with clear communication, and the best partnerships have thrived on honesty and transparency. So next time you have the grand idea to pull off a heist, I'd appreciate a heads up.

That night, when I got home and took off my balaclava, I reflected on the way you handled things that night by weaponizing omission, and I realized there's so much you haven't told me.

If you've made mistakes or are afraid to tell me things, just be honest. I hate dishonesty. Dishonesty is for those who aren't brave enough to choose a poison and stick with it. Dishonesty is for people who are ashamed of themselves.

So, what else are you hiding that I should know?

Sincerely,
O
(Get it? Because X?)

CHAPTER

23

TRACK:

CHERRY COLA
Kuwada

"This song is making me want a Coke," Cai murmured, raising her head slowly.

I hummed an agreement and closed my eyes, lying still so I could effectively absorb the sun's golden rays.

Summer was just around the corner, and Woolridge had reached a surprising eighty-five degrees, so naturally, we'd decided to go to the country club pool to cool down after school—only none of us had actually gotten in the water. I was sunbathing under a large white sunhat with sunglasses on, Ryan was sitting up in his chair, fixing a poolside playlist to blast from his portable speaker, and Cairo was tossing and turning in her pool chair, growing restless.

Finally, she sat up and looked over the top of her glasses. "That's it," she announced. "I'm going in." She stood up, fiddling with the orange Moroccan scarf she'd tied over her swimsuit before pulling it off.

"Hey," she said, blocking the sun with her eyes. "I see Raycher's car. And I think I see Kathy too."

I sighed. Their arrival guaranteed an assortment of third-, second-, and non-tier individuals from school as well. "Well," I mumbled, "those ten minutes of peace were fun while they lasted."

"Welcome to summer!" Cairo said, and she spread her arms and fell backward into the pool.

The peace lasted five more minutes and ended when an encroaching presence on my right side blocked my sun. I sighed. "You're in my sun," I uttered without opening my eyes.

I heard Ryan put his equipment down and stand up. "Jalissa! Connor!"

I heard a soft slap followed by a louder one. When I opened my eyes, I saw the aforementioned Jalissa and Connor hovering above us in their bathing suits, gripping towels and portable chairs.

"Can we join you guys?" Connor asked. His eyes nervously flickered to me and then back to Ryan.

"Yeah, man, of course," Ryan said.

"Nate, Todd, and Jay are coming through too," Connor added.

Ryan was saying something about how we had more than enough space when I got distracted by my phone buzzing. I picked it up immediately.

> Hypothetically, if I were in jail right now, would you have enough money to bail me out?

I lifted the sunglasses from my face, panic briefly pricking in my chest as I reread his text, and then I immediately relaxed.

> Well clearly you're not in jail bc you're texting me.

> I very well could be after the stunt you pulled.

"Lo?"

The sound of my name threw me off guard, and I looked up from my screen. Jalissa and Connor had pulled a bunch of chairs around our three, creating a very big, very unnecessary circle. They looked at me expectantly.

"What?" I asked, not unkindly.

"Uh, nothing," Connor said, flushing. "I was just saying your hair looks sick."

I smiled. "Thanks, Sullivan."

Ryan interjected, explaining that my hair had taken seven hours to do, and I sensed the conversation leaning dangerously close to turning into a braiding explanation, so I tuned it out and scrutinized the words on my screen before responding.

> If you were in jail maybe you'd deserve it. How would I know?

> •••

X started typing. He was typing for a while. I watched Kathy Summers and her new guy splashing each other in the shallow end of the pool until his next text came through.

> I know I'm supposed to 'save it for the letter' but I'm sorry for throwing that curveball on Friday

I stared at the screen in surprise. I hadn't expected an apology so easily.

> Okay. Apology appreciated.

> I'll be more open from now on

I'll start by baring it all in this next letter. I think you're going to like it. It's a confessional.

MV tells all? I'm captivated.

But hey, if I promise to be more honest, you have to promise to be more reliable.
No more mind games and trap missions.

Hm... I'll think about it.

Because I think we had a good thing going: A Pulp Fiction, Bonnie and Clyde type thing.

You literally. Couldn't. Have picked a worse thing to say

Why? Not a Tarantino fan?

'Bonnie and Clyde' are a tired example of partnered miscreants.

We need alternative options

Harley Quinn and the Joker?

No

Honestly, I don't care what you say—Bonnie and Clyde are iconic. They went against the grain, fought the hardship that was brought their way, and made their lives their own. Can you imagine being so unaffected by the world? So dangerously devoted to someone?

Imagine being so in tune with someone that 'a criminal life on the run' was just what you were about to say.

I drifted my eyes over the crowd of friends that had gathered. Nate was rubbing sunscreen on Rachel's back and dodging splashes from Matt who was already in the water. Jalissa was perched on her chair, laughing with Brianna. Bri wiggled her fingers in my direction and I smiled back. And then I found Ryan.

He was resisting being dragged into the pool by Ricky Schwartz—second-tier friend and Basilica's drummer—who was losing the tug-of-war.

Can you imagine being so unaffected by the world?

I didn't get it. Was following your own uncontrollable desires something to be praised? I myself had never had a problem being true to myself—it was the easiest thing to be.

So dangerously devoted?

I snorted. You could hardly give credit to Bonnie and Clyde for being in love. Everything is easier when you have someone by your side.

Ryan finally pulled away from Ricky and caught my eye through the oiled-up limbs and half-naked bodies. He raised an eyebrow.

I shrugged.

He put his arms out.

I nodded, deciding to yield, and he started making his way through the crowd. "You ready?" he asked when he reached me.

I grabbed his outstretched hand and let him pull me up. "Hold on," I said. "Glasses." I set my shades aside and got in position. I knew what was coming. "Okay, ready?"

Ryan nodded and got in a similar stance.

"Set."

And before either of us could even think the word "Go!" we pushed off the ground, sprinting toward the pool, and dove in. Last one to the other side had to go out and get the towels when swimming was over, and I was not about shivering at the side of a pool.

I won the race—as I always did—and we spent the rest of our time on the big white pool floaties (with cup holders), sipping on lemonade that Cairo bought from the snack bar.

The three of us probably looked like the picture of utter relaxation: floating on our backs and holding on to each other's floaties so none of us drifted away. As we bobbed in the water, I realized I never felt more at peace than I did when I was between these two.

On my left, Cairo shifted. Her leg squeaked against the plastic as she sat up. "Have you guys ever tried sneaking to the pool area after hours?"

"Once," I replied. "The guards caught us, unfortunately."

'Man," she mused. "This place would be so sick at midnight. With that blue light on?"

"And the fountain?" Ryan added.

"Without all the extra bodies," I put in. "And the noise?"

Ryan's floaty twisted sideways and he wiped his hair from his face. "Too bad it closes at seven," he said.

There was a lull until Cairo dipped her hand in the water and squinted our way. "You guys wanna try it again sometime?"

"Yes," Ryan and I said in unison.

She snorted at our synchronized agreement, letting go of my floaty in the process. The sudden shift in weight tilted me and I yelped, leaning dangerously to the side as I reached out for stability and accidentally let go of Ryan's floaty. Cai laughed and paddled over, scrambling to link back with me, almost knocking Ryan out in the process, and as the two of them splashed and scrambled to get back together I thought for the hundredth time that X was wrong. Bonnie and Clyde weren't worthy of any sort of praise. They were lucky; they had it easy. They had each other.

I'm planning your mission right now, and I think I should warn you that I wasn't kidding when I said I was going to up the ante.

I hope for your sake and mine that you're not just a big talker

Be careful what you wish for

You know I'm rarely ever careful.

Edgy.

But there's a very high chance you could fail tomorrow's mission, so you might have to learn to be.

I don't think I need to remind you that if you fail once, this is all over. No meeting.

Up the ante. Bring it on.

CHAPTER 24

TRACK:
ANTITAXI
La Femme

Noel Sang was staring at me.

Sure, I was used to catching short surreptitious looks from anxious underclassmen and random guys but . . . not like this, and certainly not from Noel. From the moment I'd walked into fourth period study hall and sat down at a computer, he hadn't quit his ogling. I squinted at the words on my computer screen, feigning ignorance because of my promise to Ryan that I would go easy on him.

Finding a good poem to memorize for finals week was impossible enough without Sang's penetrative gaze boring a hole in my head. I'd designated my hour of free time to scouring the internet for a half-decent, non-pretentious piece of poetry that wasn't completely soul-sucking but so far, not so great. After about twenty-five minutes of skimming the names of dead people and ignoring Noel, I quit my tabs and stormed over to his side of the lab.

"Okay, Sang," I said, sighing and collapsing into the chair next to him. "What gives?"

Noel, who was now staring intently at his computer screen, affected surprise at seeing me. "Oh, Loli! Hey!"

"Cut it out," I ordered, scooting my chair closer to him. "What's going on?"

He blinked. "What do you mean?"

"You've been staring at me for the past half hour."

His eyebrows went up. "Have I?"

"Yes, you have!" I hissed, a little too fervently. Upon seeing his alarmed expression, I took a deep breath.

"Noel. Please. You and I just came out of a rough patch, one that I, frankly, am still recovering from. So can you just cut the bull and let it out? For Ryan's sake."

His lips formed a line and then he looked around helplessly. I sorely missed the days I used to see him as a badass, guitar-shredding genius.

"I was just . . . p-planning for Babble," he stammered. "And I was wondering whether I should ask you to design our outdoor banners or not, you know, since you didn't design the posters this year."

I raised my eyebrows. "Really? That's all?"

"Really," he replied.

I watched him for a while. "Okay," I said. "What are you guys thinking?"

Noel's shoulders relaxed. "Well the thing is . . . I'm not sure yet. That's why I didn't ask you," he said quickly, "because I'm still thinking about it."

His knee bounced as he absentmindedly drummed his painted fingernails on the chair.

"Okay . . ." I said.

He was still acting weird, no doubt, but my interest was quickly fading, and I had work to do. "Let me know if and when you decide," I said, gathering my things to go, but I'd barely taken a step away when he let out a loud, computer-lab-friendly whisper.

"Wait!"

I stopped in my tracks, annoyed. "What?"

"Uh—just . . . the owner of The Ivory said he has the right to give away our VIP tickets if you don't come on time—"

"I already know about that. What are you trying to say?"

"Well. When you come to Babble, you have to sit in those seats, okay? It's our last show with Ricky and Space before they gradu-ate, and we have new songs and . . . Ryan really wants you to get there on time and have a good seat."

I glared at him. "You don't need to tell me that, Sang. I know, okay?"

I walked back to my seat to resume my fruitless research. For the rest of class, Noel kept his eyes trained on his screen, where they belonged.

The rest of the day passed in relative monotony. It was a gray, sludge-like blur of finals revisions, practice packets, and continued prom chatter, which only slightly piqued when it came out that Thade Logan had finally uploaded his vlog from our party. Everyone huddled to watch the video on their phones, trying to spot as many people as they could from Woolridge, but I couldn't bring myself to be fully swept up in the excitement.

X had promised a mission for today, and he'd yet to send a single text.

I'd checked my phone at least twice every hour since I'd woken up, but it remained unsettlingly text-free. Where was he? He couldn't have forgotten, and I definitely wasn't mistaken. His clear promise of a mission had glowed bright on my screen all day.

When the last bell of the day rang, I headed straight for the parking lot, passing the corner where Ryan and I usually met, as I tried to beat the end of the day crowd. I was going home the old-fashioned way, via Nancy, to free up some time for Basilica to rehearse for Babble. With the show only two weeks away, the band was using every second they had to prepare.

I stepped out into the parking lot, squinting in search of my mother's black Rover. When I didn't see it, I pulled my phone out, glancing down at the glossy black screen seconds before it buzzed to life.

> Package delivered. X marks the spot. You have until 3pm to show proof of receipt—tick-tock.

My heart jumped. Just below the text was a photo of a cartoon map with road marks and footprints leading through a forest to an island with a lone palm tree. Just underneath the tree was a big red *X* written on the sand.

My heart skipped. I recognized the lake: Lake Waban. 'Ridgers had been sailing, waterboarding, canoeing, and bonfiring there since the beginning of time. I knew, from firsthand school-skipping experience, that it was a twenty-minute drive from here and a forty-five-minute walk if I took the shortcut through the forest.

I glanced at the time: 2:40 P.M.

I had twenty minutes.

"Crapcrapcrapcrap!"

I dropped my bag on the floor and opened my conversation with my mother, trying to decide whether it would be a good idea to get her to drive me to pick it up. I pictured her expression as I tried to explain this nonsensical detour. No. Too risky. Even if she did agree to take me, I had no way of preparing her for if X had set something wild up, and I wasn't in the mood for grounding part two. As much as she wanted me and Ry to go to prom together, I wouldn't put it past her to ban me from it.

I sent her a quick text instructing her NOT to pick me up, then I ran back into the building, dialing Ryan as I pushed through the crowded hall.

"Pickuppickuppickup," I urged, running a frantic eye over the people cluttering the hallway. And then, by luck, by chance, by some God-given miracle, I spotted Ryan making his way down the main stairs with a big box of musical equipment. Relief poured through me.

"Ryan!" I shouted. I fought my way toward him, ignoring the complaints from the people around me, and shouted his name again.

Ryan looked up, surprised. "Lo!" he exclaimed. "What's up?"

"I need your car," I said, cutting straight to the chase. "It's an emergency."

Ryan stared at me. "Loli, I have band—"

"I know, I know!" I interrupted. "It's just I have a package to pick up, and I have to get it by three. Three, Ryan! Or it's over."

"Uh," Ryan lowered the box and looked around, flustered.

"I'll be quick," I assured him. "We'll make it in time, and hey— you said to loop you and Cairo in if I need you, right? Well, this is a mission that I need you for, and it's a treasure hunt this time. Isn't that amazing? It's like the perfect adventure."

Ryan shifted the weight of the box in his arms and fixed his eyes on me, his expression desperate and complicated. "Lo, seriously," he protested, "Mr. Donizetti said we can only have this equipment for two hours and practice starts at three—"

"Well you can be a little late, can't you?" I pushed, panicking.

Ryan considered it for a moment. He propped the box on his knee and ruffled his hair out of his eyes. "Treasure, huh?"

"Yes. A treasure hunt." I caught the smallest spark of interest in his eye, so I kept going.

"With a map and everything. See? The package is buried on the island at Lake Waban."

I flashed my phone in his direction and just like that I had him. His eyes drifted toward the time and then widened. "Jeez—we have like fifteen minutes!"

"I know!"

"Okay, let's go. Quickly!"

I grabbed a dangerously teetering music stand and a piece of unidentifiable music equipment that looked like it was about to fall out of the box, and resumed pushing through the crowd of slow-moving bodies. We weaved and shoved until we were outside in the parking lot. My chest tightened with excitement. Baby was in my direct line of vision.

"Keys!" I yelled. Ryan tossed them over without hesitation.

After we packed the equipment in the trunk, I peeled out of the parking lot at high speed—until we hit after-school traffic.

I groaned. We did not have time for traffic. I glanced over my shoulder and thought fast. The only other way to Lake Waban was the hiking route through the forest. Forty minutes by foot. We had about thirteen.

The car in front of me inched forward.

I bit my lip and thought my way through the hiking route. It was less of a hike and more of a walk, something I remembered thinking back in middle school when someone held a sleepover camping trip in the middle of the woods. I was pretty sure I'd seen a parked car next to the tents. Which meant that the path had to be wide enough for a car. Right?

I cast another glance over my shoulder to make sure that the road was clear, and then I put the car in reverse. "Ry," I said. "I think we're going to need music." Ryan looked up from his phone as I made a rough three-point turn and hit the gas, headed in the opposite direction.

He twisted in his seat, head swiveling between the traffic behind us and the road ahead. "Uh, Lo . . . Where are you going?"

"The forest path."

He looked at me. I didn't return the gesture.

"I'm sorry—did you just say the fo—"

"It'll be fine," I said, trying to sound confident. I needed it to be true. "Remember that sleepover? With Ms. Dickinson's Jeep? That car was bigger than this pile of metal, and it survived without scratches or anything."

"Yeah, that's because 'that car' was a Wrangler!"

I swerved into the trail parking lot, and Ryan slid left as I floored it past the trail sign onto the dusty forest path. Baby shook violently as I forced her over the rocks and roots by the entryway, spurting up clouds of dust as I pressed harder on the accelerator.

"This is a really bad idea." Ryan's voice shook with the vibrating car. He gripped the side door as it jiggled us around. The space was a little tight, and I felt the branches, sticks, and stones flick against the metal, but Baby had survived countless other adventures. Baby would be fine. I hoped.

After a few minutes of headache-worthy jostling, we came out on the other end with four minutes to go.

"Three minutes," Ryan announced as the digital clock on his dashboard ticked to 2:57 P.M. Chest pounding, I pulled the car to a stop and looked out over the water. Darn. The island was farther out from this side of the lake; it would take much more time to swim over from this end.

I gripped the wheel and chewed my lip. Ryan's music coaxed me. "I'm driving round," I decided. "It's the only way I can swim from the shore to the island in time."

"Well then . . ." Ryan sanctioned. "GO!"

The sound exploded from Ryan's speakers as I hit the accelerator and started around the lake, speeding over the uneven grass and curving round the bend, leaning dangerously close to the trees and shrubbery on the left but doing well to avoid the rock obstacles and ridges—at least until Baby suddenly slowed with a lurch and began to lag on the left side. I pressed down on the accelerator as hard as I could, but all the car did was make a loud noise and jerk forward.

"Mud," Ryan announced glancing out his window. "Go left, it's drier there."

I turned the steering wheel all the way left and pushed hard on the accelerator. The engine complained as the car fought against the slippery terrain, but we slowly dragged ourselves along the edge until both sides of the car were on dry land and then, suddenly, finally, we were on the other side of the lake.

My heart beat uncontrollably. We were facing the dock and the little island just beyond it.

"Two-fifty nine," Ryan said. "You can do it, Lo."

There was no way I would make it there and back through the water.

I eased my grip on the steering wheel and, looking out at the ramped dock, I figured out a way to make it. "Okay," I said, trying to keep my breathing steady. I gripped the wheel tight.

Ryan must have read the intent expression on my face because he followed my eyes toward the lake and then back to me. "Loli . . ." he began slowly, evenly.

"Ryan," I replied in a similar even tone.

"You can't do that."

I shifted gears and reversed for greater distance, then I put the car in drive and faced forward again. "Get out."

"Lo—"

"Ryan!" I shouted, losing patience. "Get Out!"

"No!"

"Fine by me," I replied, "'cause I'm going with or without you."

"THIS IS MY CAR."

"Five!" I shouted. "Four. Three—"

Ryan swore, winced, and closed his eyes.

"Two! One!"

I stepped on the pedal, and the car made a horrific sound before lurching forward, hurtling toward the dock at full speed. We jerked up the ramp, and I kept my foot on the pedal as the dock rolled out in a white blur beneath us. I tried not to think about the fact that we were going to leave solid ground and turned the wheel in the direction of the island as we sped toward the end of the dock. The white blurred beneath us as the wheels ground against the concrete, and then the white was gone, and there was just blue and near silence as the thrashing of loud music temporarily muffled in my ears.

I fought the urge to close my eyes, watching as we soared. I think Ryan was screaming, I think I was too. If there was ever a moment I thought I was going to die, if there was ever a moment I felt the most alive, it was this one.

And then we sunk through the air and landed in the water with a horrifying splash.

The water jostled the car and rocked us back and forth. My heart sank at the prospect of us having landed in the middle of the lake, but as I peered over Baby's nose, I saw that we had landed on the bank of the island and were teetering on its shore.

It was still 2:59.

Without thinking about what I'd done, or what was happening, I pushed the door open and stumbled out into the shallow water, frantically splashing and running up the sandy slope toward a giant red spray-painted *X*.

"Grab my phone!" I shouted over my shoulder, and I fell to my knees over the X. I scooped up handfuls of hot red-and-yellow sand, pausing only to catch my cell phone when Ryan tossed it over. I dug and dug until my fingers scraped a flat, white envelope, and then I snapped a haphazard photo and pressed send just as the five and nine on my phone's clock turned to double zeros.

There was an ugly crank of something metallic shifting in the background, and I collapsed onto the sand.

I made it. I did it.

"Loli . . ."

Still sitting in the dirt, I reached for the white envelope and inspected it. "So much for treasure," I said. "I don't think there's anything in here but the letter."

I barely registered the rapid glug-glug-glugging sound behind me until Ryan's anguished groan caused me to turn around. I slowly stood up as I watched the last of Baby Blue slide backward and disappear into the water.

Then there was a silence.

"I guess we're going to have to swim after all," I said, in attempt to ease the tension.

Ryan looked dumbfounded.

"Hey," I said, stepping forward. "Don't worry about it. We'll get you a new one, I promise."

Ryan didn't say anything, just stared at the ripples of water. "Right," he said. "Yeah. No. It's fine. I'm fine."

I eyed him, uncertainly. Baby was drowning before us and Ryan was fine?

"Are you . . . are you sure?"

"Yeah." He nodded. "I'm sure."

His bright, tinny tone worried me. There was no way he wasn't more upset. I knew how much work he'd put into getting her, how much time and money he had spent maintaining her, and there was all the effort his parents had made to help him get her too.

"I'll tell your parents you had nothing to do with it," I added. "You were rehearsing for Babble, and I took your car without your permission and I totaled it. I'll tell my parents the same story, and they'll get you a new one, no problem."

He didn't respond. We stared out at the water as Baby let out one final gurgle. When all signs of life were gone, I waited a solemn three minutes before I waded into the water with the letter held above my head.

When we were both safely on shore, I dialed Cairo and arranged for her to take Ryan to Noel's on Kyle's motorbike. She arrived within a matter of minutes, and as soon as they were gone, I dialed the police.

"Woolridge Police Station."

". . . Patrick?"

"Speaking."

"It's Loli."

There was a pause, some rustling, and then a sigh. "Heavens to Betsy. What is it you've done this time?"

Dear O,

Yeah I get it, X and O. Nice one. Since we've both got a bit of humor about ourselves—how did you like my pun?

"X marks the spot." I laughed at that one when I sprayed that giant X in the sand—it was super meta.

Anyway, I know I already said this over text but I'm sorry I lied to you. I promise I'm not as insidious as you make me out to be and that I'll be honest from here on out. Well. As honest as we are allowed to be with each other. And I thought I'd start out by confessing my sins:

Sin number 1: Yes, the fire at school was me. I'm guessing that's what you were alluding to at the end of your letter? It wasn't dangerous, I'm not an idiot.

I lit the fire in a tin trash can so that it wouldn't catch or spread, and I placed the can directly under a smoke detector in hopes that it would cause just enough hysteria to evacuate the school before it was inevitably put out by the sprinklers.

Some dumb person must've freaked out and knocked it over in all the panic.

Hopefully now you can see that I didn't set out to burn the school or to hurt anyone —I did it just to create a little obstacle for you. You were being so unbelievably arrogant that day, sending those texts saying how easy it would be for you to get the letter, and how you were going to stop sending letters to me as soon as you got the package.

I thought you could do with some light humbling.

Sin number 2: Well, this one isn't really a sin, but it's a confession just the same.

The day we met, you asked me what I was doing sitting in a closet at a party, and I didn't tell you because I didn't know how to put it into words exactly. I still don't really know how to put it in a way that doesn't sound pretentious or creepy but I thought I might as well try.

You know that feeling you get when you're either hanging out with friends or socializing at a party but you still feel lonely? I get that sometimes, but instead of feeling lonely, I just feel . . . unreal. Like I'm some impostor who is only allowed to observe the human experience and doesn't ever get to live it.

Then this one time I overheard my mother and brothers talking in the kitchen and it helped me realize that sometimes it helps a little to remove myself from situations and observe them from the actual outside first—hence the sitting in a closet.

So that's what I was doing. Listening to the muffled music and tidbits of conversation, the yelling, the smashing, the screaming, the laughing, and taking it all in as an outside party who is there but not participating, not felt, not seen. And then, just as I start to feel deprived, I can simply open the door and go back out into the noise and become a part of it again.

And I haven't forgotten what I texted you the night we lay on the grass together. I'm going to try and prove it to you.

Sincerely,

A Seemingly Real Person

CHAPTER

25

TRACK:

GHOST

The Acid

To say that my parents were upset would be an understatement.

I won't get too into the gory details because they're pretty depressing, but I will say that my mother literally cut my driver's license up in front of me.

The display was a bit much, if you ask me. I already felt awful for totaling Ryan's prized possession, and it was made worse by the fact that he kept swearing he was fine when I knew he couldn't be. On top of the unnecessary theatrics, my parents wanted me to go over to the Popes' and apologize to the entire family.

I thought this was a bit much since Ryan—who had paid for the car out of his own savings—had already been taken care of. We'd gifted him a brand-new, bright red apology 'Stang that he'd already christened "Ryder." Though my parents had covered the cost, they'd also drained my spending account so I could personally "help" to pay it off.

The only grievance Ryan seemed to have was whether he could recover all the important things he'd had in his car—namely the school's music equipment, his phone, and some old tapes he always kept in the glove compartment. The school equipment was recovered with minimal damage (which was compensated and paid for), his phone was fine after a few hours of soaking in a bag of rice, and his music . . .

Well. That's what streaming services are for, right?

After all the damage and the money that was spent, the only person who was actually impressed at the incredible grandiosity of the feat I had managed to pull was X. I told him all about the whole car fiasco (omitting the fact that it was Ryan's car that got totaled and not mine since I didn't want him to trace Ryan's popular new ride back to me).

> Wait so the car actually landed on the island?

Yep, I typed out, collapsing onto my bed. It was late, and I was preparing for bed by slipping on my pajamas and wrapping my long purple braids in a scarf. I put on my Go-To-Sleep playlist and leaned against my pillows.

> And you and your friend weren't hurt??

Not really, I responded. Both Mom and Officer McNamara made me go to the doctor for a checkup after I told them my neck was spasming a little. I knew Ryan had gone for a checkup too. I wondered whether he was okay.

> Damn.

> You know I'm starting to think you're not afraid of anything.

> Funny. I was thinking the same about you.

You're sorely mistaken.

It doesn't happen often but I've found I do get afraid sometimes.

For example, lately, I've been afraid of you.

I snorted. I couldn't tell if he was joking or serious. When he didn't add anything to that last message, I let out a puff of air, slightly surprised, and continued typing.

Really? Me?

Do I need to remind you that you set the school on FIRE.

That little fact from X's letter had stopped me dead in my tracks when I'd read it. I had told myself it was delusional to think he had anything to do with the fire—but he had after all. The explanation that he hadn't done it on purpose was sound enough to assuage my initial shock, but there was still that lingering doubt I'd come to expect with X.

I resumed typing, adding more points.

Or that you made me a criminal, caused me to break my car . . . I could go on

Yeah, and you never flinched once.

Most people have a breaking point when it comes to me.

My eyes flickered away from the screen. After years of failed Loli Friendship Tests and disapproving parents, I could more than relate. The phone buzzed and captured my attention again.

So . . . what's your Achilles' heel? Where would Delilah need to angle her scissors?

Idk . . . I'm not really scared of physical things . . .

But in middle school there was this scary story someone told me about this little girl hiding from a rogue bear in the closet of an abandoned house.

It was terrible, the way this kid told it. With all the waiting and the creaking and the peering through the crack of the door. Anyway the bear caught her in the end and ever since that story I've been afraid of abandoned houses.

Really? Not bears?

> Abandoned houses are way scarier than bears. They're so . . . eerily quiet and still.

> And they get you stuck in floorboards so predators can catch you.

There's an abandoned house on Glen Rd that looks like it hasn't seen life for decades. Do you know the one I'm talking about?

I knew exactly the one he was talking about: small and gray with broken windows and a dilapidated fence. We went there after Nick Van Der Waal told that stupid bear story. Someone dared us to go in right after Nick finished his story, and those of us brave enough had crept up to the gate and scattered around the backyard. I remember standing alone in the quiet dark, realizing everyone else had run away. There wasn't a single sound, no sign of life. I called my mom to pick me up soon after. It was the one time I ever backed out of a dare.

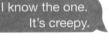

> I know the one. It's creepy.

Perfect. Let's meet there.

> What?

I think we should meet at the creepy house.

> That way we'd both be facing one of our fears.

> Ha. Ha. Funny but I'm going to have to say no.

> Come on! It'd include all our favorite things! Trespassing, secrets, the dark . . .

> And it'd be the perfect melodramatic background for our story.

> How is that not good enough?

I sat up in my bed, mulling it over.

> You want it to be exciting, right? What's more exciting than fear?

I glanced at the time and my eyes widened. Two in the morning? When did it get that late?

Okay. I'm in. I typed hurriedly, then pressed send before adding:

> Abandoned house. Midnight. The day after final exams.

> Perfect. See you there.

I turned off the light, placed my phone facedown on my side table, and pulled my bed sheets up to my chin, but I couldn't fall asleep. It wasn't the music—music was the only way I ever fell asleep—I just kept thinking about that house and about X, replaying the entire conversation over and over in my head.

After a while I sat up, feeling the eerie pulse of a new song. Hues of darkness ebbed around me; patches of purples, blues, and blacks surrounded me, seeming to beat in time with the song. The colors were so stubborn I could still see them even when I closed my eyes. I sat there for a while, waiting the song out.

I used to be afraid of this, I thought with a sad laugh. The helpless, intangible dark. Fear's a funny thing. I used to run from the feeling—now I relished it when it spiked up my chest in cold flashes every time my phone buzzed or whenever the screen said that X was typing.

He was scared of me, he said. I was scared of him too. He was sharp, unpredictable and he had an unprecedented hold on me.

I shuddered and buried myself back underneath the sheets, wondering if fear could be mistaken for something else.

Dear Mysterious X,

I've never been more disappointed in the revelation of anything in my entire life. That's what you've been hiding? A deep life reflection? You could've just sent that same explanation in the first letter and gotten it over and done with instead of having me wonder all kinds of things.

That being said, I do kinda get where you're coming from. That going-to-the-bathroom-alone-at-a-party feeling where you seem to exist in between realities is weird. Except I don't enjoy listening to the muffled music and the voices, I prefer it all loud and in surround sound. I always bring a friend with me to go to bathrooms just so I can avoid that very feeling.

Your last letter got me really messed up—not on the deep existential closet stuff, but with the casual mention that you have an actual family??? A living breathing mother and brothers??? You??? X? The ever-elusive being??

I have parents too, surprise surprise. You'd think with all the trouble I get into that we'd either butt heads a lot or that they'd just give up on me and let me do whatever I want but it's neither. We usually get along pretty well. Sometimes they bring the hammer down but it's never so fast I can't see it coming or stop it just in time.

I don't have siblings, although my friends are basically like siblings to me; we've grown together, we annoy each other a lot, and we love each other. As far as I'm concerned that's exactly what siblings are.

I hope you like the whole secret letter with invisible ink idea, I'm surprised it wasn't the first thing we ever did. I could've planned this whole thing in a hell of a sicker way if I actually knew you or had any idea where you lived, but oh well.

There's always the future.

Always,

[Redacted]

CHAPTER 26

PURSUIT
Sylvia Plath

I didn't mean to find out X's identity. It just happened, and there was nothing I could do to stop it.

I wish I could have though. I wish there'd been some big warning sign in the sky telling me not to go to Connor's party but I couldn't, and there wasn't, so I ignorantly went about my day like it was any other: laughing with the third-tier at lunch, scratching sketches in my notebook during class, and most notably, plotting how exactly to carry out the plan for my next letter, because I'd had a genius idea: invisible ink. I was shocked we hadn't thought of it before—it was, like, the number one secret letter thing to do.

Ryan and I drove to Gags Galore to buy invisible ink after school, and I wrote my letter on the front of a prom poster I'd ripped off the school bulletin during lunch. When I was done, I flashed the UV light from the back of the pen over the letter and smiled. It was perfect. The words I'd written around the bigger bolder print were almost indistinguishable but very clear when washed underneath the bluish-purple light. No one would notice a thing.

Ryan insisted on driving me to drop off the packages—first at the blue mailbox opposite Westerns to discard the UV pen, and then at school, where I hung the poster back up on the school bulletin.

It looked inconspicuous enough hidden amongst the dozens of brightly colored and over-the-top school activity posters. A plain old white prom poster with slight tinted markings wasn't going to catch anyone's eye.

I sent the text to X on my way out of the building.

> Postman came and you've got mail! After pick up you might want to check out the school bulletin. Deadline = Friday 7pm.

When I got back home, I forced myself to sit down at my desk and start a serious search for my poem study. Finals were around the corner—it wasn't something I could put off anymore. I'd only narrowly escaped Mr. Novak's title-sharing exercise at the end of English class when the bell rang, and as I walked out of his classroom, I'd made a vow to at least have a title by the end of the day.

Now, I typed: "poems that aren't about flowers," "poems that don't suck" and "edgy poems" into the search bar. Nothing good came up.

I sat in my chair, alternating my attention between Instagram and stale literary sites, scrolling through the similar-looking stanzas with the similar imagery until finally, I stumbled upon one that was different. I read the first two lines and bookmarked the page.

There is a panther; stalks me down
One day I'll have my death of him

It was dark, it was twisted, and it was so vivid I felt as though the words were my own. The poem made me feel the way I did when I got that familiar buzz in my pocket or in my chest. I couldn't for the life of me figure out why.

A loud jingle broke through my thoughts. I reflexively reached for my phone. Connor.

> Ayyy Lo wassup?

> A bunch of us are gonna chill at mine in a bit. We got fondue, beer, and this kid I know is gonna bring fireworks. Come thru, bring the squad.

I'd barely finished reading when I got a message from Ryan in the Cake Tier group chat, followed by a reply from Cairo.

R You guys down to go to Connor's?

C yeah sure

> I probably shouldn't w/ all this work I have to catch up on

R Ahhh. Ok. Be responsible, hit those books.

C haha we'll catch you up on anything good that happens.

> Nah no need. I'm coming.

> **C** lol we know. of course you're coming. when have u ever said no to something bc of hw?

> **R** Want to arrive late and leave early as usual?

>> Ugh you two know me so well

> **R** Unfortunately for us. Pick you both up around 8!

It was one of those rare occasions where it really was just a small gathering.

There were about twenty kids total, and the atmosphere was a chilled hang out kind of vibe. Most of the party was squished on the living room couches, sitting on each other's laps, and spilling over onto the white fluffy carpet into a crowded circle where someone was passing around a packet of nacho chips and a bowl of home-made guac. The non-couch people were standing on the outskirts of the group, chatting animatedly with drinks and mini plates of chocolate-covered strawberries and marshmallows in their hands.

When Cai, Ryan, and I walked in, both couch-crowder and drink-stander alike turned to either wave or shout a greeting.

"Hey!" Nate bellowed, standing up from his seat. "Loli, Pope, and Diamond are here!"

"It's Dahmani," Cai said, correcting him with an amused expression on her face. "But hey, I'll take the jewel."

She slapped Nate's outstretched hand and we proceeded to greet everyone as we made our way through.

I smiled and waved at the faces I recognized, and as my eyes swept around the room, I found a few faces I wished I hadn't. Namely Kathy Summers, Julia Flynn, and Tristan Mattaliano.

I glanced at Ryan to see whether he had noticed Julia, but he was too busy holding some kid down in a headlock, laughing as they were both brought to the ground by Chase Castle.

Typical. Ryan was everyone's man.

I turned my attention away from the playful brawl and let my eyes drift past Mattaliano just as he looked up to see me. It didn't surprise me that he was there. These were his people as much as they were mine, probably even more so.

I grabbed a soda from the drink table, continuing to look past him, until my eyes happened upon someone who did surprise me. "Wolf?" I called out in disbelief. Wolf looked up from the couch he was leaning on and a grin took over his face.

"Hey!" he exclaimed, straightening up, arms wide. "It's my favorite customers."

"Biig Baad!" Ryan rushed forward from behind me, and the two embraced each other with that weird handshake body slam guys do.

"What are you doing here?" I asked. "I've never seen you at one of these before."

Wolf shrugged. "Trying something different. Tryna live a little on the wild side this year."

Cairo grinned. "Well, if you're looking for wild, the Sullivan household is just the place to be."

Wolf chuckled and I snorted. Connor Sullivan was the least exciting person one could ever encounter. He was the cookie-cutter perfect Woolridge resident.

"Hey!" Connor yelled from across the room. "Fondue's in the kitchen!"

"Thanks, man!" Ryan replied. And then to us: "You two stay here. I'll scoop a bowl for us."

"I'll join you," Wolf offered, throwing an arm over Ryan's shoulder.

They turned around and disappeared into the kitchen, leaving Cairo and me to attempt to find a seat in the mess of people.

Caroline Sanchez must've been in the middle of a story when we walked into the living room because she opened her mouth and blinked impatiently as we sat down. A few people around the room shushed and threw in a couple "go on's."

". . . Anyway," she said eventually, "that's why he hasn't been in school lately."

She sat back on the couch and quirked a shoulder before biting into her nacho chip.

"Wait, really?" Julia said with a furrowed brow. "I didn't even notice."

"Wow," a girl said, nodding slowly. "That makes so much sense."

I looked around, confused. "Who hasn't been in school?"

"Bryant Leabo," Caroline answered, beaming with the pride of having captured my attention. "And I don't think he's coming back anytime soon. He says he's finally found his passion."

"Well cheers to Leabo!" Jake Ucci raised a beer, and a couple other guys raised their drinks in solidarity.

"It was that party," some guy said, lowering his beer.

Nate laughed. "It all comes back down to that damn party!"

A bunch of his guys laughed and slammed drinks together, and the rest of the room hummed in agreement.

"Man." Nico Apa shook his head. "I wish I'd gone. That party's all anyone's talked about for weeks."

"Dude," Nate tried and failed to hold on to the big couch before leaning over its back, "you missed out. Everyone has a story from that night. Literally everyone. Did you know that Ross Ma lost a toe? I watched it happen, man."

Connor winced from his futon. "I was there for that. I think I'm scarred for life."

"And Allison Schuenemann started going to church after that party," Nate continued. "Allison freaking Schuenemann. She's a completely different person. I saw her praying for someone in the hall just the other day."

Cairo and I exchanged a smirk as a murmur went around the room.

"Hey," Nate said with a sloppy smile on his face. "I've got an idea. How about we go around the room and everyone shares the craziest, most ridiculous story they have from that party. Winner gets a case of beer."

The giggling and murmuring started up again.

"I have a story," Cairo piped up. Everyone turned to look at her.

She leaned back, resting her arm on the back of the couch and recounted the story of how she ended up modeling for Michael Keene. I couldn't help but smile as jaws dropped and people scrambled for their phones—either to text their friends or to google to make sure that it was *that* Michael Keene.

After Cairo, some kid said he heard someone stayed in the Mattaliano house for week after the party without anyone noticing. Mattaliano confirmed the rumor, adding that it was an exchange student who didn't know how to get back to their place and was too embarrassed to ask for help.

Each story shared was more ridiculous and unbelievable than the last, and most of them I'd already heard a few times, but I couldn't help but feel a sense of pride as they were told again. I was responsible for this. All of the merriment and post-party enjoyment. Of course, I couldn't publicly take credit for it—Mattaliano was continuing to bask in unmerited glory—but it felt good to know it was all happening because of me.

Maybe after X and I finally met, I could simultaneously take my credit and have the greatest story of them all.

Jake was in the middle of enlightening the room on how exactly he'd lost his clothes that night, when Wolf and Ryan finally came back in. They were snickering amongst themselves, each holding two bowls of warm, liquid chocolate as they neared the couches.

"Where the heck have you two been?" I asked, laughing through my frown.

"Well," Wolf said, glancing at Ryan and then back at me, "we thought it would be a good idea to try and move one of the machines into this room but . . ."

"Let's just say, trying to move a flowing fondue machine is a fon-don't," Ryan joked, lowering himself to a space on the floor just by my leg.

Connor's smile faded, and he shot them a questioning look that Ryan waved away with a reassuring hand signal that everything was fine.

"What are you all cackling about?" Wolf asked, licking chocolate off his finger.

"Oh." Jake burped. "We were just sharing the weirdest stories we know from The Golden Eagle's party."

Ryan squirmed uncomfortably before glancing at Julia Flynn. I glowered at her, immediately protective of him, but Ryan's never-had-a-problem-my-whole-life smile never left his lips for a second. If I didn't know better, if I hadn't caught that squirm, I would've thought he was at his most relaxed, having the time of his life even.

A sinister smile spread across Wolf's lips. "Ooo!" he breathed. "Have I got a good one for you."

"Well, please," Nate encouraged. "Go ahead, share it."

The room sat in silence, watching Wolf with intrigue and curiosity. Having Wolf, of all people, with his carelessly abrasive attitude and his tattered, gray clothes, sitting on the couch between suburban Barbie and Ken was an anomaly that warranted everybody's full attention.

Wolf twisted the big silver ring on his forefinger with his thumb and looked around the room with a relaxed gaze, as if he were surrounded by nothing but the closest of family. "You guys know Clay Killinger?" he asked. There were a few hesitations, a lot of *no*s and some undecipherable noises. "Really tall?" he added. "Always carrying a camera?"

"Looks like a zombie-fied Clark Kent?" Ryan offered. It was a joke, but the description was accurate enough that a few people nodded and made sounds of recognition.

"Yes," Wolf said chuckling. "Zombie Clark Kent. We were running a few, um, errands before the party, so we arrived together, and we ended up spending most of our time partying together—which is to say we stood outside with a few drinks, smoking and talking with only a few short dance breaks in between. Anyway, after one of these breaks he comes back outside with this crazy story about how he met some girl in the coat closet who was trying to steal a necklace, only she didn't know he was in there watching the whole thing—"

I stilled.

It happened so carelessly and the moment was so fast and meaningless that I almost didn't believe it had happened. Everything in my chest tightened and plummeted into my stomach. Wolf continued to talk, and the room continued to laugh, but I didn't hear a word.

This wasn't supposed to happen. I didn't want to know. I wanted to wait for the big moment, like we'd planned. I wanted the fun and the magic of not knowing to continue and grow and congeal. I wanted a big dramatic reveal.

I wanted to be in that coat closet a little longer.

I kept a passive smile on my face as the room carried on. I felt like screaming, but I didn't. I didn't even think, really. I just laughed when everyone else laughed even though everything was strange and out of focus and I had no idea what Wolf was saying.

I felt Ryan and Cairo looking at me, but I didn't acknowledge them. I only smiled and tried to keep my breathing steady.

"And the bizarre thing is, through all of this, they still don't know who the other one is!" Wolf ended emphatically. "How bizarre is that?"

"Dude—are you serious?"

"How have I not heard this story before? I thought I'd heard everything."

"Who do you think she is?"

I sat still as dozens of detailed questions and awe-filled comments erupted throughout the room, and I smiled widely until finally the next story was being told, and I could finally move my legs and it was safe to get up, grab my things, and just go.

TRACK:
DAZED AND CONFUSED
Led Zeppelin

Clay Killinger.

I turned the name over in my head all night, and even though I knew exactly who he was and what he looked like, I tracked down his social media and scrolled through the pages of photography and random edits to find a photo of his face. There were only two photos of him on his entire Instagram account: a face-obscured self-portrait of his reflection in the mirror, taken on film, and a candid taken at a bowling alley. I alternated between the two, trying to match everything I knew about him to his face and name.

Clay Killinger.

Was it actually him? I kept an eye out for him the next day, detouring from my normal route to go past Mr. Brink's classroom and through the senior wing, hovering by the activity bulletin, hoping I'd catch him when he came to collect the letter, but he was nowhere to be seen. I needed to see him. I wanted to make sure he was real and to smooth the worry that things would never be the same as they had been that night on the grass.

Cairo and Ryan tried their best to cheer me up at lunch by distracting me with pictures from the new Aisle campaign and telling me all about Connor's alleged crush on me. They'd known better than to say anything last night when they'd chased after me and taken me home. Now, they were talking a mile a minute about anything and everything but X.

"He got the fondue machine for Loli *specifically*," Cai said, continuing on the topic of Connor.

"Did Nate say that?" Ryan asked. "Because Nate's not exactly a trustworthy source."

I let them continue, still mulling over my recent discovery. Would I even like him? This "Clay" that X presented to the world? Would I actually want to spend time with him? I couldn't remember being particularly impressed by him before. I'd never really paid him much attention.

Then, moments later, I was presented with the opportunity to do just that. Wolf, Clay, Tyler, and Ross entered the cafeteria and made their way toward a table by the exit. My chest squeezed at the sight of Clay. I had to do something. I had to at least confirm it was him.

Before Cairo or Ryan could say anything, before I could give it a second thought, I grabbed my things and strode across the cafeteria with absolutely no idea of what I was going to say.

"Loli!" Wolf exclaimed when I arrived at his side. "What's up?"

"Nothing much," I said, sweeping an eye around the table.

Everyone had turned to look at me—everyone, that is, except for Clay Killinger.

"I just thought—" I tried and failed to tear my eyes away from his rigid form. "I just thought I'd mix things up and join you guys for lunch today."

Wolf slid down the bench to make room for me, but I walked around the table and set myself directly in front of Clay. Finally, he looked up.

Lightning sparked all the way to my fingertips for the few seconds our eyes met. I forced myself to look away, lowering into my seat with what I hoped came across as indifference.

A conversation started—something about bad SFX aliens in film—and I dared myself to look at Clay again. Right as I did, his phone sprang to life with a Zeppelin ringtone. I'd never really taken care to look at him before; he was always just that random guy I lumped in with Sid. But now, looking at him and knowing who he was, he seemed completely different from the person I'd remembered him as. The tall and skinny nerd that had previously existed in my peripheral vision was completely gone.

His shoulders were broader than I'd remembered, his arms more defined than I would've given him credit for, and—surely the tight angle of his jawline could only have been crafted by a surgeon's scalpel? I watched as he reached for his apple, curling his fingers across the red surface before taking a bite.

I'd always thought his placid expression seemed diffident and detached, but now as he quieted his phone and glanced up at me through the dark strands of hair that fell just over his glasses, his gaze was cold, sure, and indifferent. It was daunting, but I pressed forward.

"Clay," I said in acknowledgement.

He nodded slightly before giving a short, concise, "Loli."

I nonchalantly ripped open a salad dressing packet. "I don't think we've really ever spoken before."

He looked at me, eyes unmoving. "No." He grabbed his sand-wich with his free hand. "We haven't."

He shoved his phone in his pocket and lifted the strap of his backpack onto his shoulder. As he did, something in me jolted. If he was X, my letter was floating around somewhere in that big black bag.

I had to get in there. I needed official, definitive proof of X.

I grabbed my phone, meaning to text Ryan plans for an Opera-tion Swiss Eye, when suddenly, Clay got up from the table.

"Hey, man. Where you going?" Tyler asked.

Clay, who had seemed just about ready to sprint out of the cafeteria, suddenly froze. He no longer looked as bored and dis-interested as he had before. He stared out in the space behind me for a couple of seconds and then seemed to shake himself back to attention.

"I, uh . . . I have a few things I need to do before class," he replied.

"Ah okay,"Tyler said. "See you soon."

And then Clay was off without another word.

I faced the empty space in front of me, bewildered. He'd been so close—just within my reach—and just like that, he was gone. I hadn't been able to get the confirmation I needed. Panic rose in my chest, and I stood up from my seat. "That reminds me. I also have some business to take care of."

I grabbed my things and stepped away from the table, but as I did, I felt something fall down my back. A long, purple synthetic braid flitted to the ground and curled by my feet.

Ugh. Perfect. My brand-new hair was already starting to fall out.

I grabbed the braid in one swift movement, shoving my annoyance aside. Clay was getting farther and farther away. I needed to follow him closely if I wanted to get into his backpack.

I tightened my fist and sprinted through the cafeteria doors, looking desperately up and down the hallway until I spotted a tall dark figure turn around the corner to my left.

I lunged after him, forgetting our "No More Running Detentions" rule, dodging students and backpacks until I reached the corner. I rounded the bend just in time to see him duck into the third classroom down to the left, and then slowly, carefully, I crept toward it, stopping just in front of the door to peer in. The classroom was empty except for Clay and a teacher with short white hair and frameless glasses.

Clay had placed his bag on top of a desk at the edge of the room. He was standing by the teacher's desk in the corner, talking privately with him. I turned away from the scene, pressing my back up against the wall. Jaume Taplin and her friends greeted me as they walked by. I was smiling tightly, thinking only about that backpack and how to get to it, when the two voices inside the classroom grew louder and closer.

". . . but that would only be for the scholarship," the teacher was saying.

"Yeah, I got that . . ."

"We can go and check in with your guidance counselor before class starts if you'd like?"

Clay stepped out of the classroom—without his backpack—followed closely by the teacher. Holding my breath, I slid closer toward Jaume's cluster of friends as they passed. I stared after them in disbelief. Problem solved.

After they rounded the corner, I slipped into the classroom, rushing straight toward Clay's charcoal backpack. I hurriedly unzipped it and reached a hand inside, pushing aside books, pens, erasers, unidentified cases, charger cords and then . . .

A sharp paper corner. My breath caught. I pinched the corner and pulled it out, anticipating my letter but getting something else.

I blinked. No, it wasn't the letter. It was something better: my dad's signed ace of spades. The very one I'd given him at the start of our game.

I lowered my hand back into the depths of Clay's backpack and unzipped the front pouch. My letter was carefully folded within, the UV pen resting right beside it.

The bell rang and I stifled a yelp.

Seniors started to trickle into the classroom. Panicked, I quickly zipped Clay's bag closed and ran out, heading straight into the nearest bathroom where I stood in front of the mirror, trying to regulate my breath and racing heart.

Clay Killinger was X. It was confirmed.

I took a deep breath, running an errant hand through my braids and then I paused, eyes wide. I was still holding the ace of spades between my fingers. Which meant that my braid, my bright purpl braid, the one that could only belong to me, the only girl at school with bright purple braids, was not curled up in my palm anymore.

"No . . ."

I spun around, searching for it on the floor but my searching was in vain. The last time I'd seen it, or felt it rather, was in my hand as I unzipped the main compartment of Clay's bag.

"No . . ." I repeated, sweeping an eye under the sink. "No, no, no, no, no . . ." I shook my head and took a deep breath, counting to ten before I stood up straight in front of the mirror and looked at myself.

This was not the way he was supposed to find out. Our story was meant to end perfectly, just as it had begun. Not with me slipping up by making a stupid mistake, and certainly not with him losing trust in me forever as a result. There was no way he'd believe this was a mistake or a coincidence, not after the Will situation.

I took in a deep breath. I was not going to lose my head over this

If I'd learned anything in all my years of dodging trouble and weaving through tough spots, it was that there was always, always a solution to the problem—even if that solution was unsavory and unorthodox.

I was as resourceful and as unorthodox as they came. I could fix this.

I took another deep breath and looked at the facts.

Yes, Clay Killinger was X.

Yes, I had inadvertently left a trail in his bag pointing toward me.

And yes, there were only two hours left of the school day—but two hours was a long time for a person who didn't mind skipping classes in the name of something important, and if worst came to worst, I knew exactly where he lived.

CHAPTER

28

TRACK:

LOTUS EATER

Foster the People

Two hours later, I sprinted up Winter Road toward Clay's house.

I'd had to stay longer than I'd hoped to get exam notes for Pre-Calc and History, but I'd managed to slip out fifteen minutes before the bell rang with an excused bathroom emergency.

He didn't live far from the high school; I remembered thinking so as Wolf tilted his minibus down Blyton Road toward Winter all those days ago.

I glanced at the time—2:30 P.M. School was out. I had to act fast.

As I reached the outside of his house, I ducked behind a tree to get my bearings. There were no cars in the driveway, just as there had been none the night we'd stopped just before Keene's party, and there was no discernable movement through the windows on either of the two levels. Perfect. I could hide out in or around the house until Clay came home, and then I could make a move for his bag as soon as he left it unguarded.

It was risky but worth it if it meant I had the chance to preserve my identity. Besides, sneaking around was my specialty. "Okay," I said, letting out a breath as I watched the time change from 2:32 to 2:33. "It's now or never."

I stepped out from behind the tree, flicking my hair over my shoulder as I casually and confidently walked over to the front door and rang the doorbell. If someone did happen to be home,

I could always revert to my perfected salesgirl routine and come again later. I peered through the window and rang the doorbell a second time for good measure. No signs of life. I waited five extra seconds and when I was sure no one was coming I tried the handle.

Locked.

No surprise there. I sighed, stepped off the porch, and went down the side of the house in search of an open window, but they were all solidly and firmly shut. As I rounded the house into the backyard, I scrutinized the faded, overgrown lawn and dragged my eyes toward the sliding glass door in the center of a mini patio. My second chance.

After glancing around for nosy neighbors, I stuffed my hands in my pockets and jogged toward the door, trying not to feel too hopeful as I reached for the handle and pulled.

The door stuck right in its place.

I pulled again, harder this time. To my surprise, the door groaned and slid in its groove. I grinned and slipped inside, closing it firmly behind me. "Hello?" I asked the empty house. Better safe than sorry.

I relaxed a little as I took in the tiny space and the quaint furniture. I could see the entirety of the first floor just by standing in that one space. There was a kitchen to the left, a laundry room just beyond, and I could see the bathroom on the right with the door wide open. I glanced to my right and up the narrow staircase covered in blue carpeting. The bedrooms had to be upstairs; there was no room for them to be anywhere else.

I touched the soft brown armchair in front of me and glanced at the old box of a television against the wall. This was X's house. He lived here, with his family, like a normal person.

Clay.

X.

I couldn't bring myself to strictly call him by his real name. To me, he was both Clay from school and the forever unknowable X, melded into one.

My hand brushed along the top of the armchair as I walked

forward, soaking it all in. A large, framed photo hung on the wall beneath the staircase. It featured a small woman with dark brown hair surrounded by three little boys. One, clearly the oldest, towered over her. He had her brown hair and her soft smile, and held the littlest brother in his arms. The little boy looked as though he was squealing with joy, arms and legs spilling out from his older brother's embrace. The third boy, who seemed somewhere between the two in age, was on his mother's right, holding her waist. I recognized the complicated eyes and frigid composure almost immediately.

I moved on through the room, surveying the plush, homey carpeting and the immaculately ordered shelf beside the TV lined with video games. Curiosity got the better of me, and I was bending down to check out the space inside, sifting through old Wii, Call of Duty, and Assassins' Creed games, when the distinct sound of a lock and key made me jump.

A black head of hair bobbed in the window at the top of the front door, a mere ten feet away from where I stood.

Clay.

I bolted up the steps on all fours quickly and quietly, reaching the top just as he opened the door. From the top of the stairs, I heard him shuffle in. I pressed my back against the wall, keeping my breaths as quiet as possible.

When he closed the door, everything was still and quiet again.

I imagined him standing there, smiling smugly to himself the way I always imagined him to be, one step ahead as usual, knowing I was there, knowing exactly who I was.

"Loli?" he'd call out. "Stop trying, I know it's you. I've known for quite a while actually."

I squeezed my eyes shut.

No. It was me.

I was the one who was two steps ahead. I was the force to be reckoned with, the reason he should fear. I was, after all, the one in his house.

I held my breath, waiting for something, anything, to happen

and then finally he moved. I heard his footsteps, heavy and rever-
berating as he walked across the room downstairs. I felt each step
under my feet. He was getting closer.

I needed to find a way to get to his backpack without him sens-
ing me. How was I supposed to do that?

I looked up and down the hall upstairs. There were four doors:
two were wide open, revealing a bathroom and a bedroom with a
childish superhero bedspread. The other two were closed. One of
the closed doors had to be his room.

His footsteps trailed to the other side of the house. I figured
I had just enough time to try the doors. I stretched a leg out and
lowered it slowly, the way Ryan and I had perfected for wooden
floors: as delicately and as close to the wall as possible. I took
another big step toward the door and then paused as I heard his
footsteps return, quicker and louder than before. At that rate he
would reach the stairs in seconds.

I abandoned all attempts to move silently and took advantage
of his loud footsteps by stepping normally toward the door, and
then he was right there.

I heard the creak of the first step, the squeak of the next; just a
few more strides and he'd see me standing there in plain sight. I
twisted the handle of the first door and managed to make out the
corner of some flowery patterned bedsheets through the tiny crack
in the door. Not his.

As Clay neared the top of the staircase, I caught sight of his
shadow against the wall. I jerked backward and practically threw
myself through the last remaining door, immediately falling on
top of a pile of clothes as I did. He was upstairs now, in the hallway. Without a second thought, I wriggled through the clothes,
twisting and pulling my body along the floor with my forearms.
And then I forced myself under his bed. I pulled my toes in just as
I saw his feet stop by his door.

Hot blue waves of fear shot through my chest as his feet inched
closer to the bed. His black-and-white shoes looked like eyes, and
they were staring right at me. I stared back.

"Uh . . . Hello?" he said.

I was caught. Of course I was caught. He'd heard a noise. He'd seen me. He'd found the braid—

"I'm not stupid, you know," he said. "I don't know how many times I have to tell you."

He crouched, dropped his backpack. A quick, white flash of a hand. "I know. They come every Friday. I left it out this morning and they took it. Stop worrying."

He walked toward his desk and a cool relief like I've never known before flushed through my body. He hadn't seen me; he was on the phone.

"Yeah, I'm gonna be home." Pause. "I don't know. Homework? A movie? I'm only here until six and then I'm going out with some friends."

I cursed internally. He was going to be here until six? Three hours was a long time to wait under someone's bed. I had to figure out a way to get him out of his room.

"Okay," he said, ending the conversation. "Bye."

Clay—X—cut the phone and then there was silence. I had barely recovered from the terror of such a close call when something buzzed against my leg. I started.

A buzz meant a message from X.

Thankfully the loud vibration was drowned out by the cascading sound of typing on a laptop and then a song playing. The Killers. I raised an eyebrow. He and Ryan would get along.

With the music on, I was sure I could move without being too noisy, so I reached down into my pocket and glanced at my phone.

> I'm about to write my last letter. Crazy, huh?

I frowned. The last exam was on Thursday, six days from now. We had plenty of time before then for a few more missions.

Confused, I typed a What? Why?

Clay's phone dinged. He responded within seconds.

> Because. You've got exams. I don't want to interfere by messing with your head and risking your life.

> Ha. Since when did you care about risking my life?

"Since I realized I liked you." He said it quietly, to himself. I watched his ankles, the movement of his black jeans. All he typed was:

> There's a time and place, O.

I smiled. And even though it was sweet and it made my stomach all warm, and even though I love spice and knowing things I shouldn't, I suddenly wanted to be out. This was an entirely new level of nosy that I was not prepared for. What would happen if he decided to get dressed? Or—

I switched to a chat with Ryan and sent at least ten butterflies in a row.

> Wow. Nothing could possibly warrant that many emergency butterflies.

> Don't freak out but I'm trapped under X's bed and I need you to come by.

> ...

Wtf Loli

It's a long story, just please come! Bring ur car!

What do you want me to do??

Idk, distract him?? Help!

K I'm omw

I breathed out. Ryan was on his way. Clay stood up, leaving his phone on his desk, and walked over to his bed. The bed bulged slightly, and I winced, quickly getting my phone out to distract him by keeping the conversation going.

Wait—don't you have exams?

I asked, even though I knew he didn't, and I knew why because I knew who he was. His phone dinged and he climbed back off his bed to go check it. A few seconds later my phone buzzed.

Nope, I'm a senior. Seniors don't have exams since we're practically already in college.

You're a senior? That's some risky information sharing, X

Ha, right. You've basically got my identity all figured out.

I basically do, I said. Your name, your address . . .

He swiveled in his chair. It was getting too real. I changed the topic.

Btw, I found a poem in the end. And I actually really like it.

Really? By who?

Doesn't matter who, the point is that I finally found something I like.

. . .

I stared at those three dots and bit my lip. I couldn't share the poem with him. It felt strangely . . . personal. Expository. Confessional, in a way. I hovered my finger over the screen, trying to figure out what to say next when the doorbell rang. I skimmed Ryan's most recent texts.

Cue awkward conversation.

You better hurry. Car's parked round back on the side of the road by the yard.

Clay got up from his chair and left to answer the door. As soon as I heard his steps fade down the staircase, I reached a hand out from underneath his bed, grabbed his bag, and wriggled out into the open air.

"Oh, hey! Clay . . ." I heard Ryan's voice downstairs and mentally counted down the time I had left. Probably thirty seconds. Clay didn't seem like the chatty type.

I reached into my back pocket for the card and placed it exactly where I'd found it. Then, I wriggled my hand around the bottom of his bag until I felt the thick braided strand of fiber running along the side of his backpack.

"There you are," I whispered, pulling it out and stuffing it into my pocket. Once I was satisfied with my card placement, I zipped up Clay's bag and climbed onto his bed. I could see Ryan's brand-new bright-red car through the window, idling on the road along the side of the house.

As a new song started on Clay's speakers, I opened the window and slid down the slope of the roof the way Ryan and I used to before Helen forbade us from climbing her house. I reached the edge and peered over the rain gutter. There was no way. I couldn't safely reach the ground by myself. I was two people short.

I swung my legs over the edge and tried dangling them a little to get myself amped, but I knew, judging from the distance and my previous experience, that it was a bad drop. I pulled my phone out.

> Ryan! Help!! Stuck on roof.

I inched farther over the edge of the roof until my backside was teetering over it like a seesaw. Maybe I could do it . . .

There was a crash, some loud voices, and then Ryan was running down the street.

"Ry!" I hissed.

"Shh!" he said. He looked back from where he had come and

then ran over into the backyard, stopping right below me with his arms raised.

"Okay, come on. I've got you."

I wiggled further off the edge. We'd done this before, I kept reminding myself, trying to forget that before, we were smaller and had placed garden chair pillows on the ground just in case.

"Come on, Lo! I've got you!"

I eyed his outspread arms, remembering that they were stronger and more practiced than they had been before—and then I pushed off the edge of the roof.

The two seconds I spent in the air felt like an eternity, but Ryan caught me in his arms. We stumbled backward before he put me down on the grass, out of breath.

"Are you okay?" he asked, holding me out at arm's length. His hazel eyes looked concerned. My breath burned in my lungs; his fingers burned on my shoulder.

"I'm good," I assured him, heading for the car. "Let's go!"

When I slid over the brand-new leather seats, I laughed in complete disbelief. "Lotus Eater" was playing in Ryan's car too.

Now that he was sure I was safe, Ryan's concern was eclipsed by exhilaration. He hopped in the car and hit the accelerator, screaming, "What the hell was that!"

I matched his grin and laughed again as we swerved around the corner. And then I told him the whole story: from the moment I left the cafeteria to the moment I texted him, begging for help.

Ryan shook his head at me, smirking the entire time. "You need to be stopped."

"But what about you?" I asked. "What happened at the door?"

"Oh, I made something up about Wolf not answering any of my calls, and I asked him if he knew where he was."

"And that crashing sound?"

"I asked for a cup of water, and it accidentally spilled as I got an urgent call from my mother," Ryan said matter-of-factly. I raised an impressed eyebrow. He caught it in a side-glance and chose to ignore it. "I said I was sorry, he said it was fine and that he'd clean it up, and then I ran out to save you from breaking your bones."

I pulled a face and nestled myself into the curve of the strange new seat's tightly bound leather. Nothing like Baby's comforting plush. "Needing your friend's help to get off a roof? Not hot. Rookie move."

Ryan shrugged. "Everyone needs a partner or a teammate. Even you."

"Yeah," I said, "but imagine if I'd jumped off of the roof straight into your car and just hightailed it right out of this neighborhood."

"Hmm," Ryan agreed. "Now that would've been hot."

I snorted and he smiled before averting his eyes back to the road.

Not for the first time since it happened, Helen's cookies, Ryan's bedroom, and memories of The White Stripes playing in the background infiltrated my thoughts.

I shook them away.

What lull, what cool can lap me in / When burns and brands that yellow gaze.

"Meh," I said, eyes skimming over the expansive sky and the road ahead. "Hightailing it would've meant leaving you behind. And I'd never do that, no matter how amazing it looked."

Ryan snorted. "Touching."

I smirked, turning to face him, and then I held out my finger. Ryan glanced down at it.

"Ride or die, right?" I asked, watching his face.

He wrapped his finger around mine. "Ride or die."

CHAPTER

29

TRACK:

GETCHOO

Weezer

I didn't get much sleep that night. I hadn't had much sleep since Connor's party.

There was way too much going on in my head. Too much to consider in light of everything that had happened in the past forty-eight hours.

First, Clay was confirmed to be X. Second, I'd snuck into X's home and made it out by the skin of my teeth. And third . . .

X really did like me. I'd heard him admit to it, out loud in the quiet of his own room. I didn't know what to do with that information. I didn't yet know whether I liked him.

Instead of sleeping, I shot up from my sheets and blared Ryan's rock playlist in my earphones as I paced my room, lay on the ground, stared at my reflection in the mirror . . .

I was feeling chaotic.

I wanted to sprint down the street in my pajamas and head wrap until all the activity and excitement in my head smoothed out again. I wanted to wake Ryan up and tell him to take me on a ride wherever he wanted to go, with the windows down and the music on as loud as it could go. On a normal night I would've gone for the second option—I knew Ryan would be down to take me no matter the ungodly hour—but no amount of driving was going to quiet the feeling.

The only thing that might, I thought, was him.

X.

I grabbed my phone from my nightstand and stared at his contact, letting my finger hover over the call button.

Unknown.

For him, everything was still the same. I could still be any and everyone in the world. I liked that. I had all the power. I had control.

I could easily block his number and disappear from his life, and he would never know who I was, ever. Or, I thought, I could just say screw it all and go to him right now in the middle of the night. After all, that is what we wanted, right? The big dramatic reveal.

I got up from the ground to switch on the overhead light, and with the luminescence came a dose of reality. Of course going to him was a stupid idea. And so was thinking I could ever detach myself from X and this twisted little game we were playing; at this point, he had me so hopped up on adrenaline that I needed him more than he needed me.

I glanced at my reflection in the mirror once more, noting the thick purple braid poking out of my head scarf, and then, without even realizing what I was doing, I pulled the scarf off and grabbed the scissors in my middle drawer.

I needed a distraction. I opened the scissors and closed them on a bunch of braids on the side of my face, relieved at having something to occupy my mind, if only for a few fleeting minutes.

When I woke up the next day, I immediately knew it was late; there was no music, no whirring, clinking, or slamming in the kitchen, and no enticing smell wafting up the stairs to wake me. Bad sign.

I sat up with a start and looked at the time, running my hand through my freshly undone hair. 1:30 P.M. I relaxed. There was more than enough time to stop at the salon.

But still, something didn't feel right. There was something about the day I was missing. Some big thing just in the corner of my mind . . .

Babble.

"Ohhh Crap." I grabbed my phone. "Crap, crap, crap!"

Noel Sang and his absurd anxieties about my Babble attendance were not going to be confirmed today.

I ignored all the notifications I'd accumulated throughout the morning and tapped on Basilica's official Instagram account to view their story. Ryan, Noel, Ricky, and Basilica's keyboardist, Space, were at The Ivory already goofing around the stage with their instruments, spinning with their guitars, absolutely buzzing with energy. I tapped through their story, a little confused.

Usually the band had practice at Noel's during the day and only went to the venue when it was time to set up and start the long line of mic check rehearsals with the other bands, but they were already at the venue. I frowned. Why were they already at the venue?

That was a question for another time. Now, I had to get ready for the show.

I stumbled out of bed, dialed the salon, and gathered all my best drawing utensils as I haphazardly got dressed.

I'd been planning on doing a nice big poster for this year's show, complete fangirl-style with bubble letters and hearts and everything, to hold up in the crowd. I'd have to do it at the salon.

Mom gave me a ride there on her way out to run errands, and three hours later, when my hair was finally done, she pulled up in front of the salon with a checked off list.

"No braids?" She tucked a straight dark curtain of hair behind my ear. "I liked them on you."

"No time," I replied, carefully placing the finished Basilica poster on the back seat.

Mom glanced back at it and smiled. "You know, despite all the mess you get that boy into, I've always been proud to see what a wonderful friend you are to him."

I sighed. "For the hundredth time, Mom. I don't 'get him into' any messes. Ryan gets himself into more messes than you'd expect."

I felt her eyes on me as I stared straight ahead. I figured she must be giving me her "are you serious?" look before launching into a tirade on Baby and how I'd destroyed it, but when I finally looked at her, she had an expression on her face that I couldn't read.

Pity? Pride? She brushed my hair out of my face again and pursed her lips. "You know, you're a beautiful girl, Naloli . . ."

I groaned. "Mom, please, I know, I'm 'gonna be a real heart-breaker,'" I said, jokingly. "You can tell me all of this later, right now we have to get to The Ivory so I can watch Basilica rehearse before the other bands show up."

Mom started the car, still watching me. "Okay, okay," she conceded. "Just don't . . . break more hearts than is necessary, okay?"

I pulled the seat belt across my chest, thinking of the situation with X. I wasn't sure exactly what she meant, but I'd never planned on toying with anyone's emotions. I didn't dignify her prodding with a response.

We pulled into the parking lot at The Ivory, and I climbed out of the car as soon as the engine stilled. Mom did the same.

"Uh . . ."

"Calm down, Loli," she said. "I'm just going to catch up with Margaret before I drive back home."

"Fine."

I turned to fix my hair and lip gloss in the window's reflection. When I was satisfied, I followed her through the club's front doors, smiling as the familiar staticky sound of Basilica reached my ears.

Then it hit me: I hadn't been to a single Basilica practice all year.

Usually, I would've seen and heard the set so many times, I could've yelled every lyric back up onto the stage from the audience. This year, all I knew about the set was that it was six new songs and that one of them, as Ryan had mentioned that time at Dizzy's, was supposedly the best song they'd ever written.

I would've blamed it all on not having a car or X being too much of a distraction, but then I realized something else: Ryan hadn't asked me to a single rehearsal. The realization stung. I was supposed to be his best friend. Why did it feel like he was pushing me away?

As I stepped farther in, I realized that it wasn't an original they were playing—it was Weezer. They must've been doing one or two covers as part of their set.

I waved at Mrs. Sang as my mother greeted her in the foyer, and then I pushed open the doors to the performance space, letting the overwhelming sound of bass and guitar wash around me and through the open doors into the hall.

I walked down the aisle, miming a round of applause. As I approached, the beat tripped over itself and the bass slowed to a halt as Ryan looked up from his guitar. He squinted down from the stage in disbelief.

"Loli?"

The entire song came to a lethargic, staggered halt as Ricky and Space stopped playing their instruments. Noel turned to silence the band.

"Hey," Ryan said, laughing sheepishly. "Uh . . . What are you doing here?"

"What do you mean?" I shouted up at the stage. I lifted my sunglasses into my hair and smiled up at them. "I came to listen to the last rehearsal."

Ryan shifted the strap of his guitar and glanced at Noel, who eventually stepped forward. "Sorry, Lo. I know you usually watch us rehearse, but today you're going to have to wait for tonight."

I snorted, pulling my sunglasses off as I sat down in the front row. "Funny, Sang."

I crossed my legs and stared up at them, waiting for practice to continue. When it didn't, and Noel's expression failed to soften, I frowned. "You can't be serious." Silence. "You're kidding, right? I thought we were cool, Noel?" Noel was fast becoming my least favorite person. Ever.

"We are cool," Noel said. "You just can't sit in on this rehearsal."

I sprung up from my seat. "Since when did I ever need permission to sit in on rehearsal?"

"Heyheyhey . . ." Ryan took the guitar off his shoulders, hopped off the stage, and grabbed ahold of my shoulders in attempt to remove my fiery gaze from Noel.

"Lo," he said slowly, looking back and forth between my eyes, "you know you'll always be our favorite groupie."

"Groupie?" I scoffed, eyebrows raised. "I am not your groupie. I was there when—"

"I know, I know you've been here since the beginning, you developed our logo, you're not a groupie, jeez it was a joke, okay? Just—please, please let us have this? We have a lot to get through and I promise it'll all be worth it in the end."

I forced myself to tear my eyes away from Noel and zeroed in on Ryan's honest expression instead.

He grinned, a playful, disarming smile. There was a reason Mom called him the fire extinguisher. I took a deep breath in and wondered for the first time if her comment was an underhanded insult directed at me.

"You guys aren't even famous yet and you're already acting like total jerks," I mumbled.

Ryan smiled even wider and patted my back, knowing full well he had cracked me.

"It'll be worth it!" he shouted as he jumped back on stage. "I promise!"

I rolled my eyes and turned back toward the door.

"Oh, and nice hair," he added as I walked up the aisle. "Everybody, tell her how nice her hair looks."

"Lookin' good, Lo!" Space shouted.

"Love it," Ricky said.

I was so focused on expressing myself with a finger in the air that I barely registered the sudden appearance of a form in front of me as I pulled open the doors and stumbled directly into someone's chest.

The person grabbed both sides of my arms, smoothly pushing me away from their body. Even though it was gentle, my annoyance reignited immediately. I hated being manhandled.

"What the—" I struggled out of their grip, ready to fight, when I looked up and saw a familiar Cheshire Cat grin.

"My favorite customer!" Wolf beamed.

I stepped back and smoothed down my hair. "And it's my favorite . . . whatever it is that you are."

I was relieved that it was him and not anyone else; Wolf was touchy with everybody—I once saw him kiss Principal Trader on the cheek after a meeting in his office. I liked to think it was some weird European thing that must've been passed down to him from his family.

It probably wasn't.

Wolf flickered his gray eyes from me to the theater doors. "Where are you running off to now? You set the theater on fire?"

"Very funny," I said with a wry smile. "But no, no fires today. Only Babble. Really, I should be asking you what you are doing here."

Wolf nodded, tilting his head down as he placed a toothpick in his mouth. "Same as you," he answered. "Babble. I had to drop some stuff off for one of the bands, but now I'm off to the library."

"The library?" I snorted. "You? Yeah, right."

Wolf chuckled. "It's not for me actually. It's for Killinger."

I stopped. An unexpected cold air rushed through my chest.

"Clay?" he tried, gray eyes peering through the mousy strands of hair that hung over his face. "You remember him, right? He came with us to Keene's party? Sits with me at lunch sometimes?"

I attempted to cover my shock by clearing my throat. "Yeah," I said, coughing. "Yeah, sure. Clay."

Wolf glanced behind him toward the door and then back at me. "I've got to go. I'll catch you back here in about an hour, right?"

"Yeah," I said. "Right."

Wolf nodded and backed up toward the door, and as he turned to open it, I ran forward. "Wolf, wait!"

I caught up with him, and he turned to face me again. This was exactly what I needed. A chance to size Clay up and get a sense of what he was really like. A chance to see if it'd be possible to like him too.

"I uh—I just remembered I have to go to the library too."

He raised his eyebrows. "The library?" he said. "You? Yeah, right."

I snorted at his use of my own words against me. "Yeah, wise guy. The library." I pushed the doors open and he followed me. "I'm not a complete miscreant, you know. I'm on the honor roll."

"Really?" he asked, impressed. "Huh. You learn new things every day."

I climbed into the front of his minibus and immediately looked down at the circular mirror reflecting the back of the car, remembering how I'd glanced into it that day two weeks ago, watching the ominous white glow on Clay's face.

Wolf climbed in and started the car with his seat too far away, and his arm resting out the open window. He looked behind him and backed the car up, and I watched him in shock.

"Uh . . . aren't you going to put your seat belt on?" I asked.

He half-heartedly reached for his seat belt and absentmindedly fumbled the buckle as the car swerved out of the parking space and around the lot.

"Jeeeeeez," I complained, grabbing onto the sides of the car. The car straightened and Wolf's hand was still struggling at his hip, so I sighed and leaned forward to help him click his buckle into place.

Wolf laughed, the kind of laugh I knew was at me and not with me.

"You know," he said, "with your reputation, I wouldn't have expected you to be such a stickler for rules." He didn't say it in a rude way, just an honest, open way. Which was exactly why I liked him.

"I'm a fan of rules that keep me alive," I replied, looking out the window.

When we arrived at the library, I followed Wolf past the children's section, all the way down to a winding staircase at the other end of the building that led underground. I raised my eyebrows. I didn't know the library had a basement.

"Ladies first," Wolf said, nodding down the stairs.

I smiled at him sarcastically and started slowly down the twisting stairs with a hand on the rail and my neck craned in anticipation.

The yellowing white wall spun before me as I descended the steps, going faster and faster until it raised like a curtain to present Clay in the open space; five shelves down, standing at the end of the row with his head bent over a book. He looked up from the leafy text in his hands as we drew nearer to him, and his expression soured upon realizing Wolf had brought company.

"Hey, man," Wolf said, either completely unaware or not caring. "Look who I bumped into."

He pulled a chair out from the table closest to where Clay stood and collapsed onto it, kicking out the nearby chair and sprawling his legs across it.

Clay's eyes flicked to me. My heart nearly stopped. It was ridiculous, but even with the full knowledge that I was the one in control, I couldn't help but feel like he was still somehow playing me.

"What's up, Killinger," I said, following Wolf's lead by plopping into a chair.

Clay looked back to his book and then closed it with a finger to hold his page. He walked slowly over to the table and smiled slightly before nodding in my direction. "Loli." His eyes held mine. They were vibrant, blue, and alert.

"What you reading over there?" Wolf asked, craning his neck.

"Not so much reading . . ." Clay trailed off. I saw a large piece of white paper sticking out from the side. "Rather rereading some good passages."

"*Gone with the Wind*," I announced, reading the spine. "Controversial choice."

Clay turned the book in his hands, suddenly grave. "The amount of great literature blighted by racism never fails to disappoint."

I smiled internally. It was such an X response. "I haven't read it," I admitted. "But nothing I hear about it is ever good."

He looked at me, and I thought he might make a snide remark about my ignorance of the book, but he didn't. Instead, he said: "Considering the ideological rhetoric, I think that's fair."

I held his gaze for a second, thinking there was hope yet.

Wolf slammed a foot on the table between us, then crossed one leg over the other. "I bumped into Loli at The Ivory. Turns out she has work to do in the library too."

"I did," I confirmed. "I mean, I do."

"Really?" Clay glanced at my off-white clutch. "What work do you have to do?"

I faltered, adjusting the strap on my shoulder. They were the first words he'd said to me in person that were completely unprompted. "Just some stuff I have to take care of. Upstairs."

"Hmm. Book fines?" He placed the book down on the table and watched me.

"Yeah," I softly echoed. "Book fines."

To my surprise, he smiled. "Those things have a way of sneaking up on you."

It was surreal, standing there as myself, looking openly at him. I could see him so perfectly: smooth dark hair, bright blue eyes, coal-gray shirt. He was looking at me too, only he couldn't see me the way I saw him: in the fullness of all our past interactions and confessions.

I stood up and clutched my bag. "Yeah," I agreed. "I should probably go deal with it right now. I'll be back."

I made sure to look calm, composed, and collected as I made my way toward the staircase, and then I ran up the stairs to the main library floor where, having no actual book to return, I wandered aimlessly before deciding to get a little something to eat at the store across the street. As I bought myself a drink and found a bench to sit on just outside the main entrance, I tried to figure out what to say once I got back downstairs. It was the perfect opportunity to speak to him as a civilian. There would be no games, no trickery, no outsmarting or double thinking, I could finally get the inside scoop. But as I sat there sipping my cherry cola, I realized that all the things I wanted to ask him were things I couldn't. Like what had initially drawn him to Western's and whether he meant what he had texted the night we crashed the poker game.

I think I love you.

I tossed my empty soda can in the trash and was about to head back into the library when I almost bumped into Wolf again.

"Loli!" he exclaimed. "Perfect timing. We've got to get back now. Traffic's picking up and Babble starts soon."

"Where's Clay?" I asked.

Wolf shrugged. "He told me this morning that he needed a ride from the library but now he says he's a little busy."

I looked at the doors and then out at the street. Basilica and Echo Air, the two best bands at Babble, always played either first to amp up the crowd, or last to make sure people stayed. Basilica was the crowd-winder this year and on top of that, I had a time-sensitive VIP ticket. I had to be there on time.

But there was never going to be another moment like this one, a time before Clay and X had completely melted into the same person, a time where I was at liberty to do as I wanted with him while he had no idea who I was.

I bit the inside of my cheek. If I made it quick, I could make it back in time. "Don't worry about me," I told Wolf. "I'll get a ride to Babble."

"You sure?" Wolf asked.

"Yeah, I'm sure."

He nodded a salute and went off in the direction of his car. After going back into the library, I paused at the top of the stairs.

> You've been quiet. Where the hell have you disappeared to? Getting cold feet about meeting in person?

I descended the stairs, lagging as he typed his response.

> Cold feet? Never. I'm just giving you space before exams.

> I never asked for space. And the letter?

At the bottom of the staircase, I found Clay sitting at the table, bent over his phone, typing. He locked his screen as soon as he noticed me walking toward him. Mine lit up with another message from X.

"You didn't go with Wolf?" Clay asked, stuffing his phone into his bag.

"Nope," I replied, pulling out a chair. Much to my dismay, he continued gathering his things. "Wait. Are you leaving?"

"Yeah," he said. "I'm gonna head out."

He grabbed *Gone with the Wind* and placed it back on the shelf. I sat in the opposite chair, trying not to let any emotion show. "Well," I said, pretending to write a text message. "See you around."

And just like that he was bounding up the stairs.

I waited for the sound of his footsteps to soften, and then I pushed off the chair and sprinted toward the shelf where he'd placed the book. It didn't take long to find—the book was thick, bright red, and the letter stuck out at the very top. Before I could open it, my phone buzzed.

> You'll be happy to know that the last package has been delivered in the town library.

I typed, smirking to myself.

> I think I need a little more than that.
> Give me an author, a quote, a genre at least.

> Since when has this ever been that easy?

Hey, I gave you an
ISBN!

Frankly, my dear, I don't
give a damn.

I opened the cover. I'd never read the book, but I recognized the line. Dad and Ryan had once taken over an entire lunch discussing the positive and negative cultural impact of the movie, and I remembered one of them saying it was the first movie to ever have a curse word in it.

The book fell open on the page where the letter was stuck on with sticky stuff, and a red arrow pointed up from the letter to the words just above it:

I love you, Scarlett, because we are so much alike, renegades, both of us, dear, and selfish rascals. Neither of us cares a rap if the whole world goes to pot, so long as we are safe and comfortable.

I read through the entire paragraph and then it came again: the overwhelming urge to run toward him.

Only this time I did.

I unstuck the letter from the book, shoved the book back on the shelf, and flew up the stairs, not knowing what it was exactly that I wanted or where in the world I would end up.

As I reached the top of the stairs, I caught Clay exiting from the back entrance. I went after him, not thinking, just moving.

I pushed the door open a crack and spotted him about twenty feet away, walking with one hand in his pocket, and one occupied with a cigarette. Heart racing, I followed him.

Just ahead of me, Clay stopped. He dropped his cigarette, put it out with his foot, and then looked to his right. I froze, contemplating my next move. I could reveal myself right here and now; the moment was dramatic enough.

Clay moved his head slowly, squinting up at the sun right as my phone buzzed with a call from Mom. That's when I noticed the time.

It was 6:03 P.M.

Babble started at 6:00 P.M.

An insurmountable amount of panic rose within me. I should have long been there by now. I squeezed my eyes shut and answered the call, ducking behind a nearby tree.

"Loli?" my mother asked. "Where are you? You're supposed to be up top in the VIP seats, remember?"

"I know," I said, wincing. "I know."

"Ryan saved them specially for you, you better hurry!"

"I'm at the library."

"What?"

"I got a bit distracted, and I'm at the library now and I need a ride."

"Naloli," she said, slowly. She was angry. "Are you serious right now? You found your own way there, you're going to have to find your own way back."

"What?" I sputtered. "No!"

I heard a soft drum solo in the background. She must've slipped out of the venue. When she spoke again her voice was loud and clear. "Naloli, it is the beginning of Ryan's set, and I am currently the only one representing our family."

"Mom," I said, trying to match her tone, "the only reason I even need a car right now is because you took mine away!"

"And whose fault was that?" she asked.

I looked out from behind the tree. Clay was gone.

"Now," Mom slowly continued, "I'm going back inside to the concert. I will see you later."

And then she cut the line.

I looked down at my phone, horrified, and then I let out a frustrated scream. Perfect. Just perfect. It was Babble and I wasn't there for the opening.

CHAPTER 30

CLOSE TO ME

Ellie Goulding (feat. Diplo & Swae Lee)

Wolf wasn't kidding about the traffic. I arrived at The Ivory twenty-five minutes later, and after a rushed attempt at retrieving my poster from Mom's car (which was, unfortunately, locked) I entered the building both breathless and poster-less.

It wasn't the end of the world, I assured myself. Ryan would understand. He always did.

I flashed the guard my ticket and prayed that my seat hadn't been taken as I ran all the way up the stairs to the VIP area where Cairo, Helen, Cody, and my mother were sitting. I sprinted to the front row and managed to slide into my space without either mother noticing.

I took a deep breath in, relieved. The moms couldn't get mad at me if they didn't know when I'd come in. Cairo, on the other hand, I couldn't deceive. She frowned as I brushed up against her arm, and I felt her staring at me as I cupped my hands around my mouth and shouted the lyrics to "Midnight Arrangement" in support. It was an oldie, one of my favorites.

"Where the hell have you been?" Cairo shouted over the noise.

I turned to look at her briefly before averting my attention back to the stage. "I got caught up."

"On Babble Day?" she asked. "Jeez, Lo. Of all days to get caught up."

"Look," I said, looking back at her again, "I tried. It wasn't my fault—I got distracted trying to catch Clay and I los—"

"Clay?" She shook her head and turned back to the stage. "Man. You better not mention that to Ryan when he asks where you were."

I blinked, confused. Cairo rarely let anything bother her, and she never got into anyone's business if it wasn't hers. What did it matter to her if I was late to the concert? And why would Ryan take the time to ask me where I was? It really wasn't that big of a deal. Some friends—hell, some parents—never even made it.

I turned back to the stage and watched as Ryan signaled to the band to do their final song, the last of the duo encore act. They must've done all their new songs in the beginning because yet another song I recognized started playing, a crowd favorite.

When they finished, I screamed louder than anyone, jumping up and down with my hands in the air. Ryan looked up at the seats, sweating, a smile on his face. He made eye contact with me, and I did a golf swing to let him know that he'd hit it out of the park.

A short guy with glasses got on stage and started making really bad jokes as the next band prepared, and I reached over Cody to tap my mother on the shoulder.

She started and turned around to face me. "Oh good, you're here."

"Yeah, I'm here," I said. *No thanks to you.*

"Oh, Loli!" Helen gasped. "When did you arrive?"

"I don't know, twenty minutes ago?" I lied.

I ignored Mom's raised eyebrows and put my hand out. "Keys. I need to get Ryan's poster."

Mom paused and stared me down.

"What?" I asked as she kept looking at me. "Oh, come on. I promise I won't take the car."

She dropped the keys in the palm of my hand, and I ran back down the stairs and out of the venue, all the way down to the car. As I grabbed the poster from the back, I heard a couple of familiar voices behind me and spun around.

Noel and Ryan were walking out the front door with some guys I recognized from one of the other bands. They slapped palms and the other band members headed toward the side of the building, waving back at Ryan and Noel as they departed.

"Maybe next time!" Ryan shouted after them. Noel snickered and said something to Ryan, who gave a weak smile in return, and then Ryan looked up and saw me. His smile faltered and he stopped in his tracks.

Noel looked up and stopped walking when he saw me too.

I wiggled the sign and walked down the hill toward them, trying to ignore the hollow feeling in the pit of my stomach. "Can you believe I forgot this in the car!" I said. "Dumb, I know. But hey! Basilica kills it again!" I pumped the sign up and down. Ryan didn't move. He didn't bother to crack even a fake smile.

Noel awkwardly waved a hand. "Hey uh . . . I'm gonna go . . . inside."

He ran back toward the doors at a speed faster than Ryan's car the night he chickened out of surfing. Typical.

I lowered the sign. Ryan was now looking down at the ground, absentmindedly kicking his shoe against the gravel.

"Hey," I said. "You guys played really well today."

He scoffed.

"No, really," I said, putting the sign under my arm. "You were good! 'Midnight Arrangement' was the best it's ever been, the highlight of my week for sure. You guys were amazing."

"Come on, Loli," Ryan said, sighing. "I saw you sneak in at the end of the set."

"What?" I said, feigning confusion. "No, I'm sure I was there for more than that . . ."

"Loli."

Ryan stopped looking at the ground and looked me dead in the eye. This was a new expression, one I'd never seen before. I didn't like it one bit. I shut my mouth.

"I asked you for one thing," he said. His voice was low and dangerous. "One thing, Lo. I've been running around with you all month—hell, our whole lives, and I ask you for one thing and you don't show up."

"Hey!" I narrowed my eyes. "I've been there for you loads, and this is the first time ever in three years that I've ever missed a concert. What, I accidentally miss a few songs and suddenly I'm the worst person to ever exist?"

Ryan looked back down at the ground, he sucked his cheek in, and then he looked back at me with a new sadness in his eyes. "You killed Baby, Loli."

I blinked, surprised at the change in direction. There was a momentary silence and then he continued. "I literally screamed and begged you to stop, and you just ignored me and did it anyway. Without thinking about the consequences or how it might affect me, you just went ahead and destroyed her."

His voice cracked and the cardboard poster wobbled as I lowered it down to my side. Here it was. The true expression of his feelings that I'd been waiting for. I'd waited for him to react the way he should have for days, and now that he was, I didn't know what to say.

"You know what?" Ryan started, shaking his head. "You're the best kind of friend. You bring the life to the party, you're cool, you're kind when it matters, and you fight with everything you've got for the ones you love. But you put yourself and your . . . your *need* before everything and everyone every single time."

"That's not true," I countered.

"It is," Ryan asserted. "And I can deal with you being bossy, stubborn, and self-righteous . . . I know how to handle all of that. You ran my car into a lake and failed to tell me when you lost my grandmother's necklace . . ."

I stilled, trying to figure out how he could possibly have found out about the necklace, and then I remembered Wolf at Connor's party.

I'd been so wrapped up in him revealing X's identity that I'd forgotten he had also given away the reason I was in the closet that night in the first place. I felt a twinge in my chest. "I got it back," I said softly.

"I can forgive all of that," Ryan continued. "But this? This is the final straw." The sides of his mouth twitched. "You weren't there when I needed you the most."

"Goodness, Ryan," I said, laughing weakly. "Come on. I'll be there next time." I lifted a pinky, but he didn't make a move.

Slowly, I lowered my arm and crossed it over my torso, smarting from his rejection. "You know, you don't make it easy to be your friend either," I said, getting annoyed. "You hide things, and you don't express your feelings, and it's not easy to know what to do about it all the time. It's frustrating."

Inside, a band started up the muffled cover of a pop ballad. Not the right track for this moment at all. I scoffed and shook my head, letting my frustration grow. *You weren't there when I needed you the most?* That is like . . . a top-tier movie cliché of a sentence."

Ryan didn't laugh. He only looked at me with eyes as clear and as resolute as I'd ever seen them, and he swallowed. "I can't be friends with you anymore."

My heart sunk deep into my chest. I was not expecting that. "What?" I whispered. There was a five second silence. "What do you mean?"

Ryan fidgeted. "I've been . . . having a really tough time, and after this . . . I can't do it anymore, okay?"

The worst thing in the entire world was seeing Ryan Pope upset. Knowing I was the reason why this time twisted up my insides. I wanted to cry.

"Guess I've officially failed the test," he said.

"No," I objected. "No, you passed the test, remember? You pass the test, over and over again. Every day."

He shrugged. "Then maybe you failed mine."

"Ryan."

I stared at him, waiting for him to realize the weight of what he was saying and to take it back. He didn't. "I righted all those wrongs," I pointed out. "I got you a new car, I got the necklace back—and the concert was a mistake, okay? Look, I made a poster!"

"It's not that," he said. "It's not any of that."

"Then what is it?" I demanded.

"It's you, Loli!" he said.

"Me?" I asked, heat creeping into my face. "Me?"

"Yes, you! You destroy everything you touch, and you never show any remorse!"

I stepped back. Anger twisted his face, and I felt it growing inside me too. "Me?" I repeated. "Why does everyone always put the blame on me as if you're not right there with me every time!"

"You're right," Ryan said, stepping forward. "I am always right there with you. I'm there being the only one who stops for a while to think about what we're doing, who it would affect, and whether it's okay or not!"

I laughed, bitterly. "Well maybe that's your issue. Maybe if you relaxed more, you wouldn't be so confused about whether you like boys or girls or whatever the hell is going on with you."

I knew I had gone too far, but so had he.

Ryan's temple pulsed and he set his jaw. He swallowed and I knew he was trying not to cry. "Wow," he said. "You know, I should've listened to my parents and every person who ever told me not to be friends with you over the years."

His words pierced through me, and I felt tears prick behind my eyes. People had said that to him? Mr. and Mrs. Pope had said that to him? "If I'm so horrible, why didn't you just listen to them and leave when they told you to?"

"Because Loli, I—!" he shouted and then stopped. He struggled with what he was about to say and eventually let it go back down, but I felt it all around me. It was as good as screaming it out loud.

I looked at him and suddenly felt a terrible, dangerous anger. He was ruining it. He was ruining it all. "You were right to say that it's over," I spat.

"I know," Ryan replied.

There wasn't a scrap of sadness left on his face. It was clear this was something he had considered before, which felt like another punch to the chest.

"But before I go, I just want to say this one last thing: Stop running, Lo. From clichés, from life . . . It's so much work trying to be above everything all the time. Go, I don't know, cry at a rom-com. Listen to the top forty. Appreciate a bouquet of flowers." There was a brief silence as he looked at me, searching my face. "Go and just . . . grow the hell up."

And there it was. The last time Ryan Pope and I ever spoke. It was painful and horrific: because for the first time in my life, he was not on my side; because I was the reason his eyelids were reddening and his lashes were wet; because when he walked away, for the first time ever, I felt really, truly, and utterly alone, and everything was still.

Dear Thief,

I'm going to assume, judging from what I know of your relationship with literature, that you've never read *Gone with the Wind*.

The book famously has an abhorrent outlook on the Civil War era, which is a terrible source of pain for me because it has one of my favorite literary quotes of all time: the passage, highlighted above this letter, right where the arrow is pointing.

I thought you'd like an example of a renegade pairing that is slightly less clichéd than Bonnie and Clyde.

You remind me of the main character, Scarlett. You can read the book to decide whether this is a good or a bad thing. There's nothing more effective than brevity, I believe, so thus concludes your final letter. Kind of. I decided to leave a secret note for you somewhere out there; the real last letter.
Let me know if you ever find it.

Yours forever,
X

CHAPTER

31

TRACK:

NOTHING

Once, in seventh grade, I shaved all my hair off after some kid said Black girls weren't pretty with short hair. My hair went from being twelve inches long to completely gone, and though I proved the kid wrong by continuing to look flawless, the feeling was odd. I could feel every cold whisper of air on my bald scalp and kept having "ghost hair'"moments where I'd try to flick my hair back or reach to tuck a strand behind my ear only to find that it was all gone.

Being in school without Ryan felt exactly like having ghost hair.

When I woke up on Monday, I had no notifications from him—not even the automated song of the day. He must have cleared the queue for the rest of the year. Before my math exam, I went straight to his locker the way I always did in the morning. I only remembered the situation as I approached and saw that he wasn't already there.

I kept drafting funny texts and only catching myself in the middle of a sentence, I'd capture snaps just to realize I couldn't send them as I found his name on my friends list. And on top of that, every single social interaction without him felt out of sync: Ryan was the conversation stabilizer, the one who smoothed things over when I said something borderline problematic, the one who politely steered the conversation to a close without being rude when I was tired and done talking to other people.

I could get along fine by myself, but it was suboptimal. It just wasn't the same.

The next day was pretty much the same as the first; constant locker avoidance, two exams, no texts all day, and the silent treatment from Ryan. He sat with Basilica at lunch. The closest thing we had to an interaction was when we passed once and made the briefest eye contact in the hallway. My hand instinctively made a fist for our usual hall passing fist bump, but he steered clear of me, continuing his conversation with Ricky.

When I got home that afternoon, I pulled out a jar of maraschino cherries and sat by the kitchen window, staring out at the street as I wallowed in my situation with Ryan. Ghost Ryan Syndrome was the worst thing I'd ever experienced. I missed him.

"What's up with you?" Mom asked, grabbing her keys off the hook. My father followed shortly after her, trailing a suitcase down the stairs.

"Nothing," I lied.

"Okay . . ." Mom said, taking in the cherries. "We came to say bye, baby. Dad's flying to New York for the week, and I'm driving out to the Hills for on-site meetings."

She gave me a hug. Dad kissed me on the forehead. "Call Ryan and Cairo round if it gets too quiet, okay?" Mom said.

I nodded. She hovered at the door, then finally left. The house fell silent.

Then my phone buzzed.

> So . . . you didn't get the letter.

> I had a hunch my clue would be too hard.

I grabbed my phone to reply. Through all the drama with Ryan, I'd totally forgotten to send proof of receipt.

> Of course I got the letter, what do you take me for?
> I just didn't have time to send proof to you.

No proof = failed mission

No, I typed, indignant. I was more vigilant than that.

> You didn't give a time frame. So I can't lose.

Touché

Hey, have you been back to Westerns?

> No. You?

Yeah. I went recently and it was like coming back home. You should definitely do it.

Home. The situation with Ryan had me feeling particularly displaced.

> I need that. I've been having a crappy day.

Why? What's wrong?

Just. Someone I know is acting up.

Acting up how? Do I need to come over and

I'm sorry did you just use *emojis*??
I don't know what's real anymore.

I thought I'd sacrifice my dignity to make you laugh.

You laughed the night we stole my money back. Remember?
I do. It was a nice laugh.

Ha. Well maybe you'll hear it again tomorrow.

Tomorrow.

Tomorrow. It was slowly becoming reality. The day I'd dreamt about every night for the past month was right around the corner; tomorrow was the night we revealed ourselves to each other. Ryan had promised to be on high alert for any butterfly texts in case the meeting went south or any sort of danger occurred.

I sat, staring at my phone, trying to decide whether or not to text him when a rapid series of loud knocks rang throughout the house. I jumped out of my seat and ran toward the door.

There was only one person I knew who knocked as forcefully as that. Of course she would be the one to drag Ryan to my door, as usual, and force us to fix this mess. I paused in front of the mirror on the way to the door just to make sure I looked okay, and then I flung it open—

Cairo stood leaning on the wall with her arms crossed. Alone. No Ryan.

My heart sank.

"You are an idiot," she said, uncrossing her arms and stepping in.

My eyes gave the driveway one last sweep, catching only Kyle's motorbike before I shut the door. "Well, hello to you too," I said.

"There's no time for unnecessary 'hellos' in the middle of a crisis." Cairo walked into the lounge and fell backward onto the couch, letting out a huge sigh before leaning forward and running her hands through her hair.

"Loli," she started, looking me straight in my eyes. "You. Need. To go over and apologize to Ryan."

I narrowed my eyes. "I did!"

"No." Her gaze was fixed and her voice was authoritative. "You didn't. And do you want to know how I know that you didn't? Because you never apologize."

I tried to think back to our fight. I was sure I'd apologized somewhere in there? I showed him the poster, and I explained that my tardiness wasn't purposeful—surely he understood that I was sorry?

I fiddled with my necklace. Cairo's eyes followed my hand to my neck.

"You're still wearing it," she said.

"Yeah," I said. "Why wouldn't I?"

"Because this is bad, Lo. It's probably worse than you've realized if you're still wearing the necklace. If you don't go over and apologize in some big way, it might be over for real. I mean, at this point, after everything you've put him through recently, you'd be lucky if he even considered your apology."

"Well I'm not going to apologize," I said, turning away from her.

"Uh . . ." Cairo waited, confused. "Why not?"

"Well first off, he said I was destructive."

"Which is true."

"He called me selfish!"

"True again."

"And he told me that he should've stopped being my friend a long time ago!"

"Again," Cairo said, listlessly waving a hand, "all of the above is true."

I cut my eyes at Cairo.

"I'm just telling it like it is," she said, shrugging. "And, hey, would you look at that! I've just said all the same things about you and we're still friends!"

"Hmm. Don't be so confident about that," I mumbled.

Cairo stood up. "Look, just . . . go and apologize, okay? For once, admit you're wrong. Or you might as well take that necklace off and burn it."

When I arrived at Ryan's, Mrs. Pope opened the kitchen door with a polite smile on her face. A powdery white apron covered her daily clothes. Though she looked slightly less glamorous than usual, she was still beautifully bright and alert.

"Loli," she said, stepping down a step. It was impersonal. Restrained.

"Hi, Mrs. Pope," I said. It was the first time I'd seen her since I'd driven her son's car into a lake. I cursed myself for failing to send an apologetic edible arrangement. "Is . . . is Ry home?"

I shifted from foot to foot. I'd never had to stand outside, waiting to be invited in. But the way Mrs. Pope was guarding the door gave me no other choice.

"I need to speak to him," I added.

Mrs. Pope stepped out and closed the door behind her. "Loli," she said softly, and suddenly she was my "Aunt" Helen again, the one who had fed me and comforted me and laughed with me all these years. "You know I love you. Right?" she asked.

"Uh . . . yeah," I responded.

"Good. Because I do. You are like the daughter we never had."

There was a silence as she smiled at me softly. "So I feel comfortable telling you that you've got a lot of thinking to do before you come back into this house."

That sentence, so filled with love and charged with meaning, smacked me right between the eyes. I felt my face heat up, tears prickling behind my eyes. "Uhm, I . . . I'm sorry about the car," I said. And I really was. "I'm sorry about everything," I said. "Can I . . . can I just talk to him?"

Mrs. Pope walked down the steps and put an arm on my shoulder. "Yes, you can talk to him. Just maybe not today, okay? Give him some time. Some space to breathe. I think you need some time to think through some things too."

I blinked, quickly running a hand under my eye before a teardrop fell.

"Okay," I said. "Okay." I nodded and walked away from the house, rounding the corner to order a car just as I felt the first drop of rain. Ugh. Typical.

On the drive to Westerns, the driver took a wrong turn down a one-way street. I watched the raindrops streak the window as he fiddled with his GPS, thinking about the last time I sat inside the café the day after the party—after I met Clay. So much had changed since then. I'd put so much effort into getting my necklace back; how strange it was to think it was all for a friendship that no longer existed.

The driver didn't seem to be getting any closer to fixing the directions, so I thanked him and got out of the car, figuring it'd be easier for me to run the two blocks instead. I braced myself against the pouring rain, folding my arms as I sprinted toward the oasis that was my favorite crappy, deserted coffee shop. Westerns was meant exactly for moments like this.

Inside, I ordered my usual and sat by the window with no notepad to distract me from my thoughts, just the gray wet outside filtered by the grainy rain.

And then I saw them.

The bright red words spray-painted in a familiar loopy calligraphy on the brick wall in the back alley.

X's final letter.

I think I love you

— X.

I'd lost the best thing I had, so suddenly. It felt nice to know I'd gained something in its stead.

On my way out, I picked up the badly hidden spray can and added a "too" and an O at the end.

CHAPTER

32

TRACK:

SPECIAL

Angel Olsen

"Oh, Loli, please. Can't you recite that in your head?"

I unfolded the paper in my hands and glared at my mother for interrupting my recital. "Mom," I said, straightening the paper out, "this is my entire English exam. I have to know every single word if I want to pass."

"I know," she said, glancing over at me from the driver's seat. "But . . . death? Burned women? Did you have to choose such a grim poem?"

I sighed, trying to remind myself that this was the last day of school before the summer. One more exam and then it was sunshine and beaches, and most importantly, X.

I was trying not to think about that part too much though. My brain was already fried enough with finals, falling out with Ryan, X's secret message, and my spray-painted response. I didn't have time to think too deeply about the fact that I was meeting him that night, and I sure as hell didn't have the time to question why the thought of meeting him terrified me so much. So I buried my mind in the poem I had to learn, reciting the lines by memory.

"*I hurl my heart to halt his pace, to quench his thirst I squander blood—*"

"There are other poems out there, you know," Mom interrupted. "Beautiful poems, lovely ones."

"Well this one's the only one I could stomach," I said, sighing. "And it *is* lovely, Mom. It's about love."

Mom looked wary. "Love? Doesn't sound like it to me."

"Love isn't all flowers and birds, Mom." I folded the paper and put it away. "Sometimes it ruins you. Or it leaves you no choice and comes for you when you don't want it to."

Mom didn't say anything more. She just looked over at me, amused, before focusing back on the road.

I closed my eyes and started again from the third stanza. Mom had always been safe, stable. I wouldn't expect her to understand what it was like to want and deeply fear something at the same time.

When I arrived outside Mr. Novak's classroom, Cairo was loitering outside, reading from a marked-up sheet of paper.

She glanced up as I approached her. "Hey," she said with a smile. "Think you're ready?"

"Barely," I said. "I am ready for the summer though."

"Hear, hear." Cairo followed me as I sunk to the floor, eyeing me worriedly. "You good?"

I thought about giving some wise-ass answer, but I didn't have the brainpower. "I went over to Ryan's after you left yesterday," I said. "To apologize."

"You did?" Cairo asked, looking mildly surprised. "What did you say?"

"Nothing. Helen wouldn't let me in. She stood in front of the door practically yielding a shotgun and baring fangs."

"You're kidding," Cairo said, her eyebrows high. "Damn. That's heavy."

"Yeah," I said.

I still wasn't over it. The Popes had never turned me away. They'd stuck by through peanut-allergy poisonings, gum in hair incidents, homework stealing, car stealing, skipping school, the works, because they were family.

Mrs. Pope's actions had confirmed what I'd feared. It was too late to fix things with us. I'd ruined everything.

An unexpected tingling sensation tickled my nose, so I pulled out my paper and started reciting the poem again from the second stanza. Cairo took the cue and pulled her paper up too.

Two hours later, school was out and we were free, but I couldn't bear the thought of sitting in Dizzy's for a celebratory end of school feast without Ryan, so Cairo suggested we order it to go and bring it all over to her house.

Staying at the Dahmani's was always an experience. The house was small and always very loud because everyone was always shouting. It was Kyle and Zakaria mostly; Cairo managed to steer clear of scraps with her siblings most of the time, though I had no idea how. Those boys loved to fight. Hell, they even fought with Sami, and he was literally two years old. But today when we walked in, the house was quiet.

"Wow. Where is everyone?" I asked.

Mrs. Dahmani took a deep breath. "School. Work. Play group. And who knows where Kyle is."

"Don't ask questions, just be grateful," Cairo said, shrugging her jacket off.

She grabbed our bags of food, and I followed her up the stairs to her room where we spread the food out on her floor.

"You know, I almost choked in there." Cairo tore apart a chicken tender. "I legit forgot how the poem started."

"How is that possible?" I laughed. "'*Shall I compare thee to a summer's day*' is literally the most memorable line in the history of poetry."

Cai shrugged and wiped some excess ketchup from her finger onto a napkin. "It's possible," she said "'*Can I compare you to a summer's day?*'"

I rolled my eyes. "Please. The poem is short and easy. It's why you picked it."

"Well. That. And I wanted to put on a funny accent, look out contemplatively, and hold an arm out." Her expression turned serious, and she lifted a hand into the air. "'*Though art more lovely and more temperate,*'" she pronounced.

I winced. "If I were Mr. Novak, I would fail you so fast."

Cairo ignored me and reached for more fries. "You know, I kinda want to meet whoever Shakespeare was talking about. Just to see if he was exaggerating or not. I mean—I've been around a long time, and I can't think of anyone I could compare to a summer's day."

I shrugged. "Must be a love thing," I said, but my mind immediately went to Ryan and the bright, radiant warmth that followed him everywhere he went. I bit into a fry, forcing myself not to prolong the pain by thinking about him.

"Hey—" Cairo said, nudging me with a toe. "Speaking of lovey-dovey stuff . . . how are you feeling about tonight?"

"Good," I said, taking a sip of my drink.

But really, the mention of "tonight" made me sick to my stomach. It made no sense—I'd laughed with him, joked with him, stayed up all night texting him. I'd watched him from afar, held his hand, and told him things I was scared to admit to myself, but for some reason the thought of him looking at me, knowing who I am, the thought of being alone with him, terrified me.

"Good," Cairo said, breathing out. "Because I'm terrified."

I looked up at her, surprised. "You? Why?"

"Well, besides the fact that you're meeting some guy, alone, in the middle of the night—" I rolled my eyes. "This guy . . . Loli . . . he's next level."

"And I'm not?" I asked.

"No, that's the thing. You are. This whole time it's like you guys have been in this race to out crazy each other."

"And?"

"And, I'm scared it's not going to end well. You do whatever he says just because you don't want to seem incapable—"

"I don't do whatever he says," I interrupted.

"Yeah," she countered. "You do. And you don't check to see if what you're doing is okay because you're so wrapped up in the game and the story."

I looked down at Cairo's box of food. She had stopped eating to watch me.

"Chill, Cai." I swished the syrup in my drink. "I'll be fine. I can think for myself."

"You know, Ryan—" The room stilled at the mention of his name. Cairo continued. "He texted me today. Asking me to be your lookout."

I paused, straw between my lips. "He did?"

"Yeah, and he told me to tell you that there is strength in giving up and letting go sometimes. Only he told me not to tell you those words were from him."

I felt a flicker of hope. Offering me advice was a good sign, right? Even if it was unwarranted. "You guys act like I'm five years old. I'll be fine, okay? Clay is not going to kill me, and we aren't going to embark on some wild heist. We're just meeting."

"Okay," Cairo said. "Just make sure your phone tracking is on."

"Phone tracking?" I gave her a skeptical look. "I can't decide whether you sound more like Ryan or my mother."

At five o'clock in the afternoon, seven hours before my meeting with X, Mom picked me up from the Dahmani household. She drove the scenic route home and I felt every single second tick by as I looked out the window.

By 5:13 P.M., I had lost my mind.

I tried watching a movie to pass the time, but I couldn't stay focused, so I switched it off and ran upstairs to my bedroom. I paced for a while before deciding to get some drawing done, which I did until I got frustrated at my shaking hands and tossed down the pen.

At around 6 P.M., I got up and looked through my wardrobe, reasoning that I probably needed all six hours I had left to pick the perfect outfit. I needed something that was girly but not too girly, logical but not boring, and badass without being too much. I settled on ripped black skinny jeans with a long-sleeved crop top and my new Margiela sneakers.

I stared at myself in the mirror with both hands on my hips. This really was it. After weeks of anticipation there were no more games, tricks, or secrets. Tonight we saw each other for real, for the first time, and the mystery was over.

At 11:45 P.M., my calendar reminder woke me up with an alert. *Reminder: Meet X.*

It was time.

I lurched out of bed, falling to the floor in my haste, and ordered a car. My plan had originally been to walk to the abandoned house, amped up by Ryan's Kick Ass Playlist, but there was no time for a power stride to The Temptations anymore.

"Okay," I said, giving myself a once-over in the mirror and reapplying my fruit punch lip gloss. "This is it."

I grabbed my phone and tiptoed down the stairs, careful not to let a floorboard creak as I left the house and snuck into the car I'd called. As I pulled the seat belt over me, a surreal feeling washed over me, as though I were living in a daydream.

I stared out at the trees as we drove, focusing on the blurred and mangled branches cut out against the soft purple sky, and I recited the poem to keep my brain from thinking about all the things I didn't want to. When we arrived at the house, I untangled my earphones and plugged them into my phone. I needed the extra courage.

The driver leaned forward in her seat and looked up at the rickety wooden building. "You sure this is the right address?"

"Unfortunately," I mumbled, opening the car door.

"Sweetie," the driver started, turning in her seat to face me, "it's late. You sure you'll be okay out here?"

I cast one look out into the black. My eyes fixed on the building I'd been avoiding practically my whole childhood. "I'll be fine." I shot her a self-assured smile. Even I was surprised at the confidence in my voice.

When the car drove away, I was left standing alone in the shivering cold, with nothing but the ugliest house in the world to keep me company. It was hard to find anything becoming about the site of my one-and-only failed dare. I crossed my arms and looked up and down the badly lit street, focusing on the busted-up yellow streetlight that flickered on and off intermittently. It was eerily quiet. No movement, no sound—and no X. I looked down at my phone.

I'm here, I typed. Where are you?

He responded immediately.

> Still on my way

Still on his way? I folded my arms and looked up and down the street again before my phone buzzed.

> Why?
> You scared?

> Yeah, genius. That's the whole reason we're here.

> Are you standing out on the street?

I tensed and glanced behind me. A vibrant yellow light shone directly over two trash cans and a bush. There was no one there. Though sneaking up unannounced sounded like just the type of thing X would do.

No, I lied.

> I'll bet you are.
> Don't wait for me go on inside.

I stuffed my phone in my pocket, annoyed that he would assume I wasn't in the house already. As I put my earphones in, it struck me that going into the house alone after all these years could be my redeeming moment. The years-old dare would officially be fulfilled.

I stepped forward, grabbing the rotting gate's wood pane and lifting it slightly as I pushed it open and wedged my way through. The gravel on the path leading up to the door was cracked and uneven. I had to step carefully between the muddy cracks so I didn't trip or ruin my new shoes.

When I reached the door, I looked up at the house and reached between my earphone wires to grab the oval pendant on my necklace. Then, out of the corner of my eye, I spotted something creeping slowly up the street; a car without headlights, cruising silently at about five miles per hour.

I ducked and shuffled to the shattered window on my left. I didn't know who or what it was, but I figured I was safer inside than out, so I crawled through the window with expert ease, making sure not to touch the shattered glass at the edges.

When I'd made it safely over the shards of glass, I turned to look back over my shoulder. There was no car anymore—not that I could see anyway—and the street was silent again. I breathed a sigh of relief and turned around to finally face the interior of the house.

Everything was steeped in black, torn only by the dashes of yellow light that shone through the dirty broken windows over doorframes, ceilings, and corners. Distorted shadows of trees, telephone poles, and lines webbed their way across the darkened room. I moved through them, trying to get my bearings before X arrived. Sure, the discolored shadows were freaky, but they were better than total dark.

Within a minute or two, my eyes adjusted, and my pulse went from pounding frantically to thrumming the way that I liked. I breathed again. This wasn't so bad. I could see where I was going, and I could tolerate the stillness with music in my ears.

I followed my shadow across a long wall until I emerged into a wide room. My eyes locked on a tall silhouette a hundred feet ahead of me.

It was him.

Of course he'd lie about not being in the house. What else did I expect?

Heart racing, I dug into my pocket and turned the flashlight on my cell phone on, raising it slowly from the ground to his face, only to illuminate a sideways cabinet in the room just ahead. Huh. Typical. He wasn't even here yet and he was messing with my head.

I moved my phone around the new room. The place was surprisingly well furnished: run-down chairs, a dilapidated table, a torn-up couch, all covered with a thick film of dust and connected by cobwebs.

I inched my way around the downstairs area. Somewhere between being frightened by the false alarm and walking around the house in comfortable silence, I had gotten my confidence back. There was nothing to fear. Not in the house anyway.

I was itching for something more. And so, because it was invitingly dangerous and probably not a good idea, I crept over to the rickety staircase just ahead of me and started a slow and steady climb up to the second floor.

I tilted my flashlight over the banister pickets, moving it around the floor in a sweeping motion as I reached the top of the stairs. There were no bears there, just three doors: two closed and one wide open.

Goosebumps ran along my skin. The open door seemed like an invitation. Like a welcomed dare.

I walked directly toward the room with the open door and cautiously stepped in, sweeping the light around the space. It was nothing special, just a small, empty room with yet another broken window and a wardrobe in the corner. I shined my light over the floor, highlighting the piles of dust and dried leaves mixed in with scattered shards of glass. A cold breeze blew through the window. A bitter scent flowed in, mixing with the scent of rotting wood and stale material. I closed my eyes, taking it in with a frown before flinging my eyes open again in the dark.

In between the undertones of wood and dust, something familiar was hidden, something I was just on the brink of distinguishing when a door slammed downstairs. I froze. And then there were slow, deliberate footsteps.

My phone buzzed.

> I'm here.

My heart spiked at the sight of those two words. No near accident, no shade of black, nor imaginary bear had ever sent shivers down my spine the way those words did.

A creak, then a crash, sounded downstairs. I backed farther into the room, hands shaking as I switched the flashlight off.

> I know.

There was the sound of a chair scraping the ground and another crash.

> Come and find me.

I slipped my phone into my back pocket and stared straight ahead, curling my hands into fists as I waited for him to come up the stairs. A faint electric guitar played beneath the drumming in my ear, and I let it play instead of cutting it off.

X's steps got fainter and fainter as he searched the house, and then they got louder again. Then, after a sickening silence, came the steady beat of his soles climbing up and up the stairs. Although I couldn't see him, I could feel his presence on the other side of the wall. My throat pulsed. I couldn't breathe. I didn't.

He must have gone around the banister because I heard him walk slowly as he looked for me in each of the rooms; the first one, then the second, and then his footsteps made their way to my room, unmistakably pointed in my direction. And then he was there, right in front of me.

His silhouette stood tall and black in the doorframe, save for the burning ember at his lips. I knew he could see me. I had deliberately stood half darkened by the square of the window, the light illuminating a portion of my face, watching him as he stepped closer, into the striped shadow of the streetlight.

Even though he was standing in front of me, I could only see one quarter of his face—dark hair, glasses, a gray eye, and the red dot where his mouth should've been. He reached for his cigarette and pulled it out.

At the sight of him, blood rushed to my ears. All I could hear was this thin but piercing screech, like the squeal of an electric guitar. Drums. Cymbals. Every instrument, all at once building and building as he stepped into the light. I yanked my earphone out and stuffed it in my pocket.

"Well, shit," X said, blowing out heavily. "If it isn't Loli Crawford."

He stepped forward, tossing the cigarette butt out the crack in the window. Then he stood up straight, fully illuminated by the yellow light. I followed suit, stepping one foot closer without breaking eye contact.

"Are you surprised?" I asked, looking up at him. He was tall. Really tall. I always hated people who were taller than me. They made it harder for me to be convincingly intimidating.

He looked me up and down. "Mostly. But if half the things I've heard about you are true, then I guess I shouldn't be."

"Oh?" I asked, feigning surprise. "What things have you heard?"

"What things haven't I heard?" he asked. "Broken hearts, broken bones, sworn enemy lists . . . I don't know, none of it ever had enough substance or value for me to remember specifics."

I scoffed, taken aback. "Excuse me?"

"I mean, you have to understand." He fumbled in his jacket pocket. "As soon as I hear about anyone from your usual table, I zone out. I couldn't care less about those people."

"Well," I said, "since we're being honest, at one point in time I couldn't have cared less about your people either, Clay Killinger."

He laughed. "Well, at least we have that in common."

He put a white stick in his mouth and brought a lighter up to his face before flicking it alive. I grimaced, displeased at the sight. The flame illuminated his entire face for a few seconds, and I watched as he focused on lighting his cigarette, brows furrowed in concentration, before he drew in, looked back at me, and exhaled in the direction of the window.

"We're going outside," he said.

"Outside?" I repeated in disbelief.

He nodded, taking another drag.

"And the house?" I asked.

"What about it?"

"What was all of that for if we were just going to leave anyway?"

"Therein lies the eternal philosophical question." I scoffed. He smiled. "You conquered your fear, didn't you?" he asked.

"I guess," I replied. Then I raised my chin and looked him over, remembering his comment about me being his biggest fear. "Did you?"

His fingers pulled away from his face and he exhaled. "I'll let you know."

I narrowed my eyes at him. I knew what fear looked like. I saw it on the face of every underclassman, every nervous jock, every informed and underprepared teacher, and every wary parent in Woolridge. There was not a single sign of fear or worry on his face; he was as comfortable as anyone could be. It occurred to me that he hadn't used a light in his search through the house. I wondered for a second whether he had any fears at all.

X looked down at me. "You ready?"

I sighed, uncrossed my arms, and walked past him, out the door, down the stairs, and into the night.

Clay's steps were so long, I had to speed walk just to keep up with him. After two blocks of feeling like a hamster on a wheel, I decided the only way I was ever going to keep up with him was if I grabbed onto him, so I did. I slipped a hand under his arm, and he glanced down at me, before looking forward again.

"Wow," he said.

I looked up at him, cheek on his arm. "What?"

"It's just . . . surreal," he replied, blowing out a puff of air. "No offense, but when I think Loli Crawford I think pouty rich girl who plays with guys' hearts. Not badass mastermind of adventure and thievery."

"Really?" I grimaced. "Wow. You must be new or something."

"I am," he said. "Only started at Woolridge this year."

"Right," I said nodding. "That makes sense." I looked up at him again and he glanced down at me. "On the other hand, when I think Clay Killinger, I think hopelessly boring snively nerd who doesn't know how to talk to people."

Clay grinned. "Ouch."

I shrugged. "It's the truth. You and Sid are like, Wolf's shadows." We walked a few steps in silence and I glanced down at our stretching shadows.

"You know, I told Wolf about this."

"You did?" I asked, acting surprised. "I thought you hadn't told other people."

"Well, I did. I told Wolf, Sid, and my older brother. They all thought it was hilarious. Except for Sid. He thinks it's the greatest love story ever told, the big romantic."

"The *greatest* love story?" I asked, raising my eyebrows.

He angled his head at me. With the passing light it was too dark to see his face. "What? You disagree? All we're missing is the climactic kiss."

The climactic kiss.

It was exactly the kind of kiss I'd established with Ryan those days ago: *contextual tension, pent up feeling or emotion . . .*

Somewhere nearby there was a loud popping sound and I started, letting go of his arm.

"Let's hope those were fireworks," Clay said, stepping forward and grabbing my hand. "Come on, we're almost there."

He pulled me along to a cul-de-sac leading on to a hiking trail I'd never been down before. There were no lights anymore, so I slowly followed in his footsteps with one hand on his shoulder and the other still resting in his. It was unnerving, suddenly having to trust him like this. That feeling was something I was going to have to get used to.

After a little while, we deviated from the path and he led me down a small hill, being careful not to trip over the rocks and the sticks poking out in the dark. There was no light except for the moon and the distant glow of a window on the horizon. Clay stopped and angled me toward a huge boulder.

He heaved himself onto it before offering me his hand. "This," he said, pulling me up, "is my second-favorite place in Woolridge Grove. It's the place I go when I need to be alone and get away from it all."

I uncurled my legs so that they were flush against the rock and leaned back on my arms. Clay moved closer to me, mirroring my pose. "Wow." I stared out into the impenetrable navy blue. "This view is amazing."

"You're hilarious," Clay said. "But I think we've learned that you don't always have to see something to appreciate it."

We sat quietly for a while, listening to the sound of nearby river water and the breeze rustling the leaves. Clay moved his knee so that it knocked against mine and I looked at him. The stark blue light from the sky washed over his face. Something in my chest stirred. What I'd wanted so badly all these weeks was finally right in front of me—not just the missions and thrills, but a chance to look X directly in the eye. He looked right back at me, with eyes wide and unreadable. His gaze drifted to my lips before meeting mine again.

"I got your message," I said.

"I know," he said, and suddenly he pulled away to reach into his pocket for a cigarette. "And I got yours."

When he flicked the box open, it was empty (thank goodness), so he closed it and put it back.

"Well," I began. "Is it true?"

"You're asking if I really love you?"

"Yes."

"I do."

"How?" I demanded. "How do you know? Until a moment ago, you didn't even know what I looked like."

"It didn't matter."

I laughed. "How does that not matter? And don't say it's not about looks. Life is solely about looks."

"Well, *my* life is solely about trying not to let myself be bored to death."

"Ha," I said, shifting my arms. "Now *that* I can relate to. Trying not to die of boredom is a hard job to take on when you're living in the Grove."

He paused. "Have you ever thought about running away?"

"Thought about?" I snorted. "More than thought about it: I did when I was in third grade. Not successfully though. My friend started crying when he realized we would never get another one of his mother's homemade brownies, so we had to make our way back home."

Clay breathed out, looked at me passively. "Is your friend Ryan?"

Hearing his name felt like a stab to the heart. "Yes."

"Is he the one who gave you the necklace?"

"Yeah," I said.

"So you're Ethel then."

"What?" I asked. "Ethel?"

Clay looked at me. For the first time, he looked visibly interested in something I'd said. But for some reason, instead of prodding at it, he retreated. "Nothing. My mistake."

We listened to the water for a while before he started up again. "Have you . . . never opened the locket on that necklace of yours?"

"No. I made a promise not to open it until he gave me the key . . ." I hesitated. "But . . . I guess none of that matters anymore. We aren't friends anymore."

Saying it out loud felt like another stab, a puncture to my soul. I didn't want to think about it anymore, so I shifted closer to X and moved his arm so that I could lay my head on his chest.

"What about you?" I asked. "Have you ever tried to run away?"

"No," he said. "I should have though."

"Should have?" I repeated.

"Yes. Should have. A long time ago something bad happened, and the thought crossed my mind. But before I even had a chance to do it, my decision was made for me."

"That's . . . cryptic."

"Mysticism. What we do best, right?"

I smiled. "Right."

"You asked me why I love you," he said. "It's because we're different, you and I. You're the only person I could ever ask what I'm about to ask."

"Another mission?" I teased. "The game is over, X. Now it's all hand-holding and emojis."

Clay stirred. "It doesn't have to be."

I lifted my head from his chest to look at him. "What are you about to ask me?"

His expression was serious as I looked into his eyes. "Run away with me."

It wasn't a question. The corner of his mouth dared me to say no. "Run . . . away," I repeated slowly.

"Yes. Leave it all behind and come with me on the greatest adventure of our lives. I've been planning on going for months, and I've saved enough money to last us a year at least. I've got it all planned out."

I stared at him, stunned. "Where to?"

"Where to?" he repeated, amused. "Look at you, asking about a plan! We don't need a destination. Just ourselves and the thrill of throwing it all away."

I thought about it. It sounded exactly like something I was always meant to do—like the real version of the thing Ryan and I had been playing at all these years.

Mom and Dad would survive. They had their careers to keep them busy for the next century. Cairo was strong; I didn't think my leaving would really have that big of an impact on her. And the only person I would've ever considered staying for was already gone.

"I'd understand if you don't want to go," Clay said. "I mean you're from the Grove. It's all fun and games playing around your safe neighborhood with your parents having your back at every corner . . ."

I frowned. "What are you trying to say?"

"I'm trying to say that you've never really been in any real danger."

"Oh, and you have?" I asked, moving away from him.

"I'm just saying. I'd understand if you had reservations. If you wanted to keep your options open in case you get scared and want to come back home after the summer."

I folded my arms. "If you're trying to convince me with some sort of reverse psychology, you've failed. You have no influence over my decisions. I choose what I want to do and when I want to do it."

"Okay, Robyn," X said with a smile. "It's up to you. As long as you let me know before the end of the day tomorrow because when Friday night comes, I'm gone."

"Friday night?" I asked. "That's the night of the prom." I don't know why I mentioned it. It hadn't mattered to me until Ryan had suggested going.

"Were you planning on going?" he asked.

"No," I said. "Well. Not anymore."

Clay smirked.

"Oh, don't act like you're above the prom," I sneered. "There was a time you wanted us to meet there, remember?"

"That was only because I thought you might want to go."

"Right," I said with a laugh. "Lousiest idea you've ever had."

"Hey, even Thomas Edison had some bad inventions."

We sat in silence on the rock for a few minutes. "I'll think about it," I said. "And I'll let you know tomorrow."

"Fine by me," he said. "There's no strict deadline for this one."

We spent the rest of the night walking through the woods, talking about all the times we had been in each other's presence

in the past couple of weeks, and all the ways we could've accidentally given ourselves away. Then I told him about all the things I
couldn't in my letters: about Ryan, about Cairo, about my parents
and how it was growing up without any siblings. He then told
me about his life: his estranged father, his overworked mother, his
distant older brother.

I shared all my best "friendship test" stories, and he shared some
of the mischief he'd caused at his old schools. Although, truth be
told, a lot of what he had to share was startling; he shared stories
of school suspensions, damaged property, and a near brush with
juvie as a result of arson. While my stories were rooted in fun, his
all seemed to be rooted in destruction.

At around three o'clock in the morning, Clay walked me back
to the abandoned house. "Here we are. Back at the tower of your
fears." He looked down at me and touched my cheek lightly. "See
you Friday, right?"

"Maybe," I said. "I'll let you know."

At home, I went through the short version of my nighttime routine and paused to touch the oval pendant at my neck. After a
moment of consideration, I reached back to unclasp it. It had to
come off sooner or later.

I held the chain in the palm of my hand and turned the pendant
over two or three times before my fingers found the protruding
ridge. I needed to see the thing that had piqued Clay's curiosity.
I didn't feel guilty as I jammed my nail between the space in the
middle. Our biggest promise had already been broken.

Friends for life.

After a few failed attempts at prying it open, I grabbed a pair
of tweezers and jammed them in the space at the top. The oval
popped open.

I peered inside, holding it open under the light. There, at the
back of the locket, was a sheet of white paper, glued against one of
the walls. I squinted to read the words written in unfamiliar blue
scrawl, and when I did, I frowned in confusion.

Marry me, Ethel?

Ethel. Ryan's grandmother.

I stared at the words. Why would Ryan make me wait all these years just to read that? I turned to my reflection in the mirror, and as I did, sudden understanding flooded through me. After all these years—

But the revelation was immediately eclipsed by dread as my eyes landed on something white and out of place, just to the left of my reflection.

It's impossible, I think to myself, because he only could've done it after I'd left the house, before we even met. It's impossible, but it's right there: a one-of-a-kind signed ace of spades poking out of the frame of my mirror.

I rang the Dahmani's doorbell twice before Zak came to the door. He didn't even bother greeting me, just screamed up the staircase for Cairo and went back to whatever he was doing before. A second later, Cairo walked down the stairs in a gray USC sweater and green sweatpants.

She scratched her head and raised her hand in a lazy wave. "Sup, Lo."

"Hey." I stuffed my hands deeper into my hoodie pockets and cleared my throat. "I'm ready."

"Ready?" she asked, landing in front of me. "For what?"

"For you to tell me what to do to get Ryan back."

Her mouth turned up at the corner. I didn't like the way she was looking at me all proud and happy like my mother or something, so I averted my eyes.

"Follow me."

I followed her into the living room, passing Zak who, I was surprised to learn, was doing homework while listening to a blues and jazz channel on the television.

"We're going to need a drink for this." Cairo went into the kitchen and turned on the kettle. "Coffee?"

"Ugh, yes," I said, groaning and then collapsing onto one of the chairs. "I didn't get any sleep last night."

Cairo's head poked around the wall, and she raised her eyebrows. "Don't think I've forgotten about last night. You're telling me everything as soon as we're done with this."

About three minutes later, she returned with two deliciously creamy mugs of coffee in beautifully patterned Moroccan mugs she placed on the table between us. "Okay." She sat on her chair in that Cairo way, with her legs crossed as though she were sitting on the floor. I never understood how that was comfortable for her. She clasped her hands together and looked somewhere above my head. "Where to start . . . the party?"

"I already know about Julia Flynn," I said, dismissively. "Just tell me what to do to fix things."

"Well first you need to understand the full story," she said. "The incident at the party . . . really messed him up. Yes, because he was slowly coming to terms with something new about himself, but also because it confirmed something he'd known for a long time."

The necklace suddenly felt very heavy against my chest. I shifted uncomfortably. "Remember how there were two times Ryan wasn't himself? The first happened just after the Julia incident which makes sense, but didn't you ever wonder why he got upset about it all over again?"

She moved forward, forcing me to look her in the eye.

"Because of you, Lo. You were this added stress on top of everything else. Those nights he wasn't sleeping he was doing research, talking to other ace people and getting all his emotions out in his writing. He wrote this song about everything he was going through; trying to deal with his feelings, his sexuality, wondering what that meant for him, whether he'd ever be able to be with anyone. And then you, you stupid, brainless gremlin, had the bright idea to kiss him!"

Cairo grabbed a cushion and chucked it at me, hard.

"Ow!" I yelped. "He's the one who did it!!"

"Well you're the one who set it up, and then you kissed him back!"

"Wha—How do you even know about all of this?"

"He told me everything."

"What? When?" I frowned. "Do you guys have a secret group chat without me?"

Cairo rolled her eyes. "It's called a text message, Lo. Not everything's about you. Anyway," she continued, "I won't go into the nitty-gritty because that's for him to say and not me but, dammit, Loli, he loves you."

I hadn't thought it would be possible to feel worse. I looked down at my mug and started thumbing the pattern on the side.

"He loves you and he hates himself for it. I swear you've poisoned or brainwashed him with your ideas or something because he thinks he's failed you."

I could hear Zak's music in the background in the silence that followed. I hadn't considered the possibility that Ryan's reticence could've been partly caused by me. I turned my mug in my hands and stirred my coffee with the teaspoon.

"Anyway," Cairo continued, "he told me about the song he wrote so I asked him to play it for me, and honestly I think it's the best song he's ever written, so I encouraged him to add it to the set list. Noel and Ricky perfected it during one of their rehearsals, and Ryan literally cried when it was done. That's when he decided he was going to tell you. Through the song. They had this whole special moment planned for weeks: confetti, balloons with printed lollipops and butterfly emojis, everything. And then you didn't show up."

I bit my lip and stared down at my blurring mug, wrestling with my emotions. This was all much messier than I'd expected. And most of it was my fault.

Stop running from clichés, he'd said. *Cry at a rom-com. Listen to the top forty . . .*

Fall in love with your best friend.

"Dammit."

Ryan knew me; he knew me better than anyone. He must've

known how I felt. He must've known I would run, that he was better off pulling away first.

And it was sad to admit and to be so mortifyingly predictable, but he was right; because it was at that exact moment that I decided to run away with Clay.

I lied. I said Ryan and I never spoke again. But as with most of the things I do, I did it for the story, and as far as bad things go, it's not the worst thing I've done.

What I did next was.

Clay replied instantly.

I knew you would be.

Back in my bedroom, I dropped my phone so that it was face-down on my desk, and took in a few deep breaths. It was official. Tomorrow evening, after prom, I was leaving Woolridge Grove with X for the great unknown.

Which meant I only had one day to apologize to Ryan.

Bad intentions aside, I really did want to apologize. I wanted everything to be okay between us, just one last time.

I walked over to my speakers and turned Rico Nasty up on full blast, queuing the loudest music possible before I gathered all my good pens, markers, and poster paper for my plan. I found an old radio in the storage room—one of those really old ones with a CD space and a pop-open space for tapes. Perfect.

I called Mom to ask her to get two of the items on my list, but she told me she was busy with work and to take Dad's car since he was out of town (?!?!) (honestly don't ask me about the logic behind that) so I quickly made a stop at the grocery store, enjoying the limited freedom of mobility before I buckled down and worked on my posters. About an hour later, when I was done, I called Cairo to join me in executing my plan.

"You're a goofball," she said, once I'd explained myself. She smirked, lifting up the fluffy teddy bear holding a heart. I felt a twinge of guilt—she had no idea that I'd be gone in less than forty-eight hours.

"You think he'll like it?" I asked, pushing the thought away. "I mean I know he would absolutely burst usually but with everything that's happened . . . I don't know."

"Well," Cairo said, "I guess we're just going to have to find out."

I made her carry the radio (apparently called a boom box?) and the teddy bear on the walk over to the Pope house. When we arrived, I went straight for the backyard instead of wasting time at the front door. We pulled out the garden chairs and quickly set up the chocolates, flowers, and teddy bear so that they each had their own chair underneath his window, and as I stepped back to admire our work, Cairo tapped my shoulder and placed three small rocks into my palm.

"Here," she said, moving the boom box onto her hip. "But don't go breaking the window. That would be extremely counterproductive."

I held the rocks in my hands, positioned the posters, and motioned for Cairo to stand closer to me.

"Ready?" she asked.

I nodded and experienced extreme déjà vu as I raised my hand. It had been a while since I'd thrown a rock at Ryan's window, five years if I remembered correctly. Middle school was a tough time for communication when not everyone had a cell phone. I drew my hand back, trying not to think about how this was likely the last time, and when I let go of the first rock, it hit Ryan's window perfectly.

"Nice," Cai said, and I geared up for another throw. Everyone knows the second throw is the one that raises suspicion. Only after the third throw is there ever any movement. As soon as the third rock hit the window, the curtain rustled a bit—and then there he was.

He looked down at us from through the window, and I saw him throw his head back with a heavy eye roll. I signaled for him to open the window and he didn't. He just walked away and closed the curtains again.

"Okay," I said under my breath. "We can fix that. Press play, Cai."

Cai hit the play button on the radio and at the sound of music, Ryan reappeared.

I raised the first poster over my head. I'M SORRY! it said. Ryan blinked, his expression neutral. I signaled for him to open the window and after a look around and a heaving sigh, he did. I raised the stack of posters up against my chest and switched to the next one, trying to look as remorseful as possible.

I KNOW YOU PROBABLY DON'T WANT TO SEE ME, the second one said.

I KNOW I'M THE WORST FRIEND EVER.

I KNOW YOU SAID YOU NEVER WANT TO TALK TO ME AGAIN. BUT I HAD A TASTE OF WHAT EVERY DAY FEELS LIKE WITHOUT YOU AND I CAN'T BEAR IT.

PLEASE FORGIVE ME.

I'M SORRY FOR THE CAR, THE CONCERT, FOR EVERYTHING SPANNING FROM THE TIME I GOT GUM STUCK IN YOUR HAIR TO THE TIME I MISSED YOUR BAND'S CONCERT.

I'M SORRY. I'M GOING TO TRY TO BE A BETTER FRIEND, AND PERSON, FROM NOW ON.

I HOPE YOU'LL FORGIVE ME BECAUSE I HAVE ONE LAST QUESTION FOR YOU.

WILL YOU [STILL] GO TO PROM WITH ME?

It was gross and it was cheesy, and it would've made me gag in any other context, but it was worth it if it meant I had a chance at getting Ryan back. I looked down at the last card, all swirly and covered in blue glitter, and then I looked up at Ryan, who wasn't even trying to hide the fact that he was grinning like a fool.

I smiled too, unable to stifle my laughter, and I tried not to think about what I was doing, or what I was about to do. I felt tears prick behind my eyes.

Ryan ruffled his hair and leaned out the window. "This is the most clichéd BS I've ever seen in my entire life," he shouted down over the music.

I laughed. "I'm just trying to grow up."

"Well," he said. "I appreciate the sentiment and the absolutely perfect early two-thousands music choice but, Loli . . . I'm going to have to say no."

"What?" I asked, blinking rapidly.

"The answer is no," Ryan repeated.

My smile fell. His didn't. Cairo turned the music down a bit.

"I won't go to prom with you until you say it out loud."

"What?" I asked.

"Say you're sorry out loud, genius," Cairo piped up.

I looked up at Ryan who was standing at his window, waiting for a response. I fought back every urge to push back or retaliate.

"Ryan Alexander Pope," I said, lowering the boards to the ground, "I would like to sincerely, loudly, and publicly declare that I, Naloli Tamryn Crawford, am really, truly sorry. *I'm sorry!*" I yelled it out and threw my hands in the air. The worst part was that I meant it, I meant every word.

Ryan laughed and pushed off the window, disappearing only to appear seconds later at the back door. Seeing him standing there in his favorite black-and-white The Smiths T-shirt, wearing that stupid half smile, made me realize just how much I missed him, and I couldn't help myself. I ran forward and embraced him in the tightest hug known to man, burying my head under his chin.

"I'm sorry," I repeated at least a dozen more times, hoping that some of them would still be good for later.

I looked up from Ryan's shoulder to see Mrs. Pope standing in the doorway, smiling widely and clasping her hands in front of her chest.

I pulled apart from Ryan and put my hands behind my back. "And I'm sorry to you too, Aunt Helen."

Mrs. Pope's smile turned weird and her face crumpled. I looked at Ryan and he gave me the look. Here came the tears.

"Oh, my little Lollipop!" Mrs. Pope said, stretching out her arms. "Come here, dear."

I walked forward into her flower-scented embrace, squeezing my eyes shut until she let go. When she finally did, she sniffed and waved us all inside.

"Come in, girls. Let me get you something to drink."

Cairo and I gathered Ryan's gifts and put them on the coffee table in the sitting room where Cody was playing Minecraft. He only briefly looked up and then went back to his game. Typical.

"Cody!" Mrs. Pope exclaimed, her arms on her hips. "Aren't you going to greet Loli and Cairo?"

"Hi, Cairo," he droned. "Hi . . ." He paused and looked from his mother to me. "Wait. Are we allowed to say her name again?"

Ryan coughed, turning only slightly pink as Mrs. Pope told Cody off for being a smart aleck.

As soon as Helen disappeared into the kitchen, the three of us collapsed into our usual places: Cairo sprawled over the big couch in the middle, Ryan on the chair to the left and me on the one to the right.

"Ahh," Cairo sighed. "Just like the old days."

I snorted. "It's been like, five days." Ryan chuckled and Cairo turned to look at me. "But you're right," I said quickly. "It felt like forever."

"Hey, guys," Cody interrupted, "look at this mansion I built."

We all looked at the screen.

"Hmm. Average mansion, Cody," I said. "You've done better."

"Hey!" Cairo exclaimed, suddenly sitting up. "I've been so busy stressing about exams and dealing with the two of you that I haven't had a chance to show you!"

"Show us what?" I asked.

She pulled her phone out and tapped it a few times before flipping it around and showing us a blown-up photo of her standing against a silver background in tight black pants with a jean jacket hanging off her shoulders. She was wearing a heavy amount of dark makeup with her hair all slicked back, and she looked absolutely gorgeous.

"My photos," Cairo announced. "Keene sent me the proofs via email. He wants me to sign full time so that he can do more shoots with me, and I said sure as long as he agrees to be my mentor."

"Cai," I said, flipping through the photos, "these are amazing."

Ryan leaned over my shoulder. "Yeah," he agreed. "You look like a real model."

"Thanks," she said, grabbing her phone back.

"You better wait two weeks between uploading those and your prom photos," I said. "It's too much. Your followers won't be able to handle it. They'll just drop dead."

Cairo smirked. "So. We're all going to prom now, huh?" She looked from Ryan to me. "Want to rent a party bus?"

"I was thinking more of a limo vibe," Ryan cut in.

"Same," I agreed. I'd only just won Ryan back, I wasn't about to vote against him.

"Okay," Cai said, lowering her phone. "As long as it's big enough for Wolf and Tyler to join."

I raised an eyebrow. "Wolf and Tyler?"

"Yeah. I said I'd go to prom with them."

"Them plural?" I asked.

Cairo rolled her eyes. "Yes. Isn't that what this is? A group of friends going to prom?" She stopped. "Unless . . . unless of course there's something else happening that I'm intruding on . . ."

I snuck a quick look at Ryan. "No, yeah, of course," I said.

"Friends," he agreed, vehemently.

"Does Clay want to join?" Cairo asked.

A spark went off in my chest as I remembered the reality of the situation. "Uh . . . no," I said. "He's against the prom."

Ryan rolled his eyes. "Boring. Also, can I add that it's extremely weird being able to just call The Mysterious Voice 'Clay'?"

"Oh man," Cairo said through a shaky laugh. "Loli is going to have to catch you up. That guy is anything but boring. He almost went to juvie." Even though she seemed chill, there was an uncharacteristic hint of concern in her expression. She'd definitely brought it up in front of Ryan on purpose.

"Juvie?" Ryan repeated. "What for?"

"Something to do with property damage," I said, trying to assuage them. "He has a history of setting fires, as we've seen."

"What do you mean 'as we've seen'?" Ryan asked.

Crap. I hadn't told them. I looked between them both. There was no point in hiding the truth. "The school fire a few weeks ago—"

"That was him?" Ryan asked.

"Yeah," I said. "Can you believe it? He started it to make it harder for me to do the mission."

"That's messed up," Ryan said. "I don't know about him, Lo. Everything you're saying . . ."

"Guys, calm down. I've met him. Hey, you've met him. He's fine. Harmless even." I forced a smile. "I, on the other hand, am not."

Thankfully, Mrs. Pope came out of the kitchen with a tray of lemonade and potato chips, which she placed on the coffee table before us. "Ice for everyone but Cairo," she said with a nod.

"Thanks, Mom."

"No problem. And hey . . ." Mrs. Pope stopped and smiled in the way that mothers do when they know they're crossing the line but are about to risk it anyway. "You know . . . the prom is tomorrow. No pressure but I'm sure a last-minute arrangement could be made for a limo . . ."

Ryan sighed. "Calm down, Mom. We already decided we're going."

"You are?" she asked, practically bouncing in place. "That's wonderful!"

"Yeah, it is. Look, Mom . . ." Ryan struggled for words.

"Oh, yes, of course. I'll go." She scuttled out of the sitting room and Ryan looked at me.

"You know what's coming, right?" he asked.

I nodded, glumly.

"What?" Cairo asked.

But we didn't even need to explain because a second later we heard a cheer and a very distinct "Nancy! They did it! Prom is back on!"

Ryan winced, Cairo snorted, and I started laughing despite myself. I guess the small things don't matter when there are bigger things looming.

CHAPTER

35

TRACK:

ASK ME ANYTHING
The Strokes

"Are you sure you don't want to get a smaller size, Loli? It's bunching up at the waist."

My mother frowned and gave the hem of the dress I was trying on a quick tug. It was an Ailee design: dark blue iridescent silk with a slit at the leg. I had promised to grab Ryan a tie made of the same material, at his request.

"Mom, it's meant to look like that," I said, running my hands along my waist. "It's part of the design."

"Okay . . ." she said doubtfully. "If you're sure . . ." And then she beamed. "My baby's going to the prom! I can't believe it!"

"Mom!" I hissed, shooting her a dirty look as she pulled her camera out. "I said you could come as long as you don't act . . . like this."

"Okay, okay. I'll save the pictures for the pre-party tonight."

I had officially been going to the prom again for less than twenty-four hours, but already my mother and Mrs. Pope had fully arranged a pre-party and a limo long enough to cart a large chunk of the second-tier to the prom. While Mom and I were rushing around getting pretty, Ryan and Mrs. Pope were rushing around trying to get their house ready for a twenty-person pre-party.

I was grateful that my only job was to get my nails and makeup done.

When we arrived at the salon, Cairo and her mom were already sitting in massage chairs, getting their toenails painted. Mrs. Dahmani was lying back with her eyes closed as the chair massaged her, and Cairo was sitting up reading a *Sports Illustrated* magazine.

"Oh, there you are," Cairo said, tossing the magazine to the side table. "I was starting to worry you'd make us late for our three o'clock facial."

She cracked a teasing grin and I sat down next to her. "So I'm not the only one who thinks my mother's prom preparations are over the top."

As if on cue, my mother appeared from nowhere holding a variety of lightly colored polishes. "Keep the colors light," Mom advised. "Blues, whites, and pinks."

"Actually, I was thinking of going for a sparkly black."

Mom stared at me, disapproving. "We'll discuss this later."

When she walked away, Cairo raised an eyebrow.

"She never had a prom so she's acting like today's my wedding day," I grumbled. The nail technician started removing my old polish.

"Well, to her it basically is," Cairo said. "Both she and Helen have been waiting years for you and Ryan to at least humor them by going to a formal together. They're in heaven."

The lady picked up a nail file and started going at my feet.

"Speaking of," Cai said in a lowered voice, "are you and Ryan going to talk at all?"

"We did talk, Cai."

"I mean a real talk," she elaborated. "A talk where you two really sort everything out. And I mean everything. Feelings of love and all." She gave me a knowing look.

I swallowed. Cairo was right: we needed to talk. I had to make everything right before I left and never returned.

I had no idea what to say.

It was strange; on top of all the normal prom worries—dealing with boys, buying a dress, getting the right makeup—I also had to worry about saying goodbye to my friends and family and making sure I packed everything I needed to run away.

I couldn't tell which of the two events was causing me the most stress, but there was no other way. What X was offering was what I'd always wanted—to run, fast and unthinking at lightning speed, to create meaning and tunnel through experiences.

To live.

"Yeah," I agreed, leaning back in my chair. "Don't worry. We'll talk."

After face prep and makeup, my mother and I returned home with only an hour to kill before we had to head over to the Popes'. Mom insisted that the time should be spent on my hair, but I had more pressing matters on my mind than having to decide whether to go bouncy or wavy. Matters like where to find my passport and what exactly I should pack.

I couldn't decide between bringing a fully packed backpack or roughing it with my Dior purse—a bag would allow me to bring a change of clothes, underwear, my hair products, and lotion—but Loli Crawford attending prom with a backpack would do more than raise a little suspicion, so my clutch would have to do. I could buy clothes and all the essentials when we reached our first stop.

I found my passport hiding between the family photo albums and placed it in my clutch next to a bottle of Tylenol and sanitary pads, along with all the cash I had stored up in my room. The bare essentials. I was all set.

At twenty to six, I slipped my dress on and started working on my hair—nothing too fancy. I figured a sultry wave was good enough for both prom and the day I decided to disappear. Iconic.

"Loli!" Mom shouted up the stairs. "Helen's ready for us, let's go!"

I ran down the stairs, stopping briefly as I was blinded by a bright flash that disappeared to reveal Dad smiling at the other end of it.

"Dad?" I started, surprised. "You're coming?"

lo effortttport the

"Of course I am! Can't miss out on my little girl's first prom. And you look so beautiful."

The camera flashed as he took another picture and I winced but I let him have it. Who knew when he'd be able to embarrass and fawn over me next.

"Both of you, come on!" Mom walked into the room and stopped upon seeing me. "Oh, Naloli! You look so gorgeous! Roman, you see this? You see what we made?"

I groaned. "Okay, okay, let's just get in the car."

We headed over to the garage, and as we approached Dad's Land Rover, I stopped and turned to them.

"Wait," I said. They stopped in their tracks and looked at me. "I, um. I just wanted to say. That I am . . . sorry. And I love you."

They paused, dumbfounded.

"What?" Dad asked.

Mom touched the back of her hand to my head.

"Nothing's wrong with me," I said, swatting her away. "I was just thinking and . . . you've always been on my side. Through everything. And I know I can be a lot sometimes."

"Sometimes," Dad muttered, raising his eyebrows.

"Baby, shut up," Mom hissed. "Don't ruin it."

"And," I continued, "I just want to let you know that whatever I do—everything I do, has nothing to do with you as parents."

"Well," Mom said, walking toward the car, "that's good to know, sweetie. Thank you. Now get in the car, Helen is having a field day in my inbox."

We drove the thirty seconds over to the Popes', and I was not surprised to find that we were the first ones to arrive. Mrs. Pope had set up a fancy blue carpet all the way to the front door, which was decorated on either side with arrangements of white and blue hydrangeas. It felt weird walking into the house so formally after years of just bursting in through the kitchen.

"Wow." Mom stepped in and looked up at all the fairy lights. "Helen. You have outdone yourself!"

Mrs. Pope came out from the kitchen, her arms opened wide to embrace us. "Nance, you are a gem," she said. "Thanks for paying for the limo and picking up that tie for Ryan." She turned to me. "And, Lollipop, you are absolutely dazzling tonight."

"Thank you," I said, and I didn't wince at the nickname.

Mr. Pope followed his wife, smiling widely before hugging us all and falling into conversation with my dad the way they usually did to catch up on the weeks since they'd last seen each other.

The mothers whispered, giggling, before Mrs. Pope turned to yell up the stairs. "Ryan! The Crawfords are here!"

There was a scuffle and a thump. "I'm coming!" he yelled. "Sorry!"

And sure enough, ten seconds later he appeared at the top of the stairs. The sight of him made my heart swell. I'd missed him. I'd missed him so, so much.

For once his hair was combed and styled out of his face, which was strange, but it did wonders for him. I caught myself before thinking that maybe Helen had had a point urging him to comb it back all these years. He was wearing the iridescent tie we had brought for him and a very well-fitted dark navy suit, which he smoothed down as he descended the stairs.

"Here she comes," I said, unable to stifle the smile that spread over on my face. He caught my eye and an equally large grin spread across his face.

"The Cinderella-prom moment I've been waiting for all these years," he said.

I stepped forward, putting an arm out the way they did in all those princess movies, and Ryan laughed before hooking his in mine. There was the click of a camera and then a quick inhalation from Mrs. Pope.

"Hold on, hold on, hold on!" she said, stepping forward. "The corsage!"

I blinked and turned to look at Ryan. "You got a corsage?" I asked. "Like a real prom date corsage?"

I didn't think it was going to be a corsage situation. Did friends get corsages for each other when they went to the prom? Were Tyler and Wolf buttoning boutonnieres to each other's lapels as we spoke?

"Yeah," Ryan stated, with mounting confidence. "I did."

I would've bought it, if his skin hadn't betrayed him. His cheeks warmed as he grabbed the box from his mother's hands and popped it open. But I was the one who should've been embarrassed; I hadn't even thought of getting him a boutonniere.

"Hey—" Mom stepped forward and handed me a decorated rose on a pin. "Don't forget the boutonniere, Lo."

I looked at the rose and then at her, stunned. She smiled sweetly and stepped aside just as Helen retrieved the empty box from Ryan's hand.

Wow. The nerve of those two.

I pinned Ryan's flower on his lapel, and he slid the corsage onto my hand as our parents attacked us with a thousand pictures per minute. We took a series of photos—cute, normal ones for the parents and then extra-as-hell poses for the gram—before the guests started showing up and jumping into our photos.

The jocks arrived first, heading straight for the food before walking toward us by the photo area.

"Prom Niiight!" Nate shouted through cupped hands. For some reason they all thought this was the funniest thing ever and suddenly everyone started repeating it. I rolled my eyes as Mattaliano and his boys turned it into a chant.

"Boys, focus please!" Mrs. Pope stood with the camera, trying to get everyone lined up with their dates. The rowdy energy was not great for her artistic vision, but it sure made the photos a lot of fun.

When Cairo and the boys arrived, Mom insisted we get a photo of just the three of us.

"Okay." Cai smoothed her hair behind her ears. It was freshly cut into a dark bob with a middle part, which perfectly framed her face. She slid an arm around my back. "You ready?"

I took a moment to admire her makeup. She'd gone for a slick velvet suit and a red lip with just a little bit of concealer so as not to hide her scatter of freckles. It was dramatic without overdoing it.

As we posed for photos, I pulled them both into me a little tighter than usual.

The limo arrived shortly afterward, fully fixed with LED lighting, a glossy bar table, and champagne flutes hovering over bottles of sparkly cider.

"Woah," Noel marveled, sliding in with his date, Emily. "Okay, this limousine might be glamorous and huge, but none of that matters if we don't have good music."

"Hard agree," Nate shouted from the front of the limo. He extended a hand and pulled the aux cord in Ryan's open palm. "Your time to shine, Pope."

And shine he did. Our limo thumped the perfect party playlist for dancing in a rowdy limo on the way to prom. A couple of the guys got so amped, they stood up and held onto their seats, moving their rear ends in a circle until the limo driver cut the music and threatened to drop them off in the middle of the street. Things were a lot calmer from then on.

Once we arrived at the venue, we joined the line for an attendance check, a security check, and a Breathalyzer test, and the whole time I kept glancing at Ryan, taking in his blissful ignorance and reminding myself that we had to talk about . . . us. I handed my clutch over to the security lady and bit my lip as I tried to figure out what exactly I should say and how to say it.

Ryan looked up from his body search. "What?" he asked, a puzzled look on his face.

"What?" I asked in return.

"You keep staring at me."

I shrugged. "I just missed you, I guess."

His expression softened. "I missed you too."

The security guards nodded for us to go. Inside, the music transitioned from a hip-hop song to a vaguely familiar-sounding pop one.

Ryan grabbed my hand. "Come on," he said. "Let's tear the dance floor apart."

"Actually, Ryan," I said, staying in place. "We need t—"

"Crawford! Pope!"

An arm slid over each of our shoulders, and I looked up to see Matt Raycher smiling smugly down at us. "I thought you two were supposed to be the king and queen of partying," he shouted, running toward the music. "Let's get this thing started!"

He pulled us both into the ballroom and onto the dance floor where his friends were already forming a dance circle. Ryan caught my eye, shrugged, and started dancing. I looked at my watch.

Clay had suggested we meet at a location that was surprisingly close to the venue—it was just a short six-minute walk away—but I wanted to make sure I gave myself enough time. Sneaking out of a well-secured high school prom and not getting pulled into a million conversations was not going to be easy. I assigned myself fifteen minutes to sneak out and arrive at our meeting place, giving me an hour until I had to leave. One more hour before I wouldn't see Ryan again for a very long time.

I took a deep breath and started swaying in time to the music. An hour would be enough. I could eat, dance, and have a good, clarifying, final talk in under an hour.

A couple of songs and a dance-off later, I turned to Ryan to signal to him that we needed to talk but he was yanked away by a couple of his track friends.

Matt caught my eye and shrugged, offering a hand, which I smiled and took as we stepped out of the circle. Now was as good a time as any to make my classic dance-party round. I danced just two steps before I twirled toward him and slipped beneath his arm into the circle to my right, which, I was surprised to find, was made up of a lot of second-tier friends from my cheerleading days. Jade Spring took my arm and pulled me toward her as the chorus hit, and after a few shared dance moves I shimmied over to Pat, who was idling nearby. I made my way around the room, mixing with second-, third-, and even fourth-tier friends, until I found myself right in front of the DJ booth—and then I had an idea like a gift from heaven.

When I finally found Ryan, he was dancing with a group of senior girls. "Hey!" I shouted, tapping his shoulder. "We need to talk!"

"Huh?" He cupped his hands around his ears and then instantly corrected himself by blocking them. It was something we had figured out in eighth grade; when you're trying to hear someone at a loud party, you block your ears instead of cupping them. I didn't know the science behind it, but it worked.

"Talk!" I repeated, and I pointed toward the back of the room. Ryan's eyes followed my hand and then they widened as Cairo unexpectedly popped up from behind me.

"Hey, I've been looking for you two!" she shouted, placing a hand on each of our shoulders. "You get a table?"

"No," Ry shouted, his hands still on his ears. I blocked mine too.

"Well come quick! I hear dinner's almost about to be served."

We left the circle and followed Cairo to a table in the middle of the ballroom. Wolf, Tyler, and Sid were sitting there amongst some of her track friends.

"Hey, guys!" Ry said, sitting down. His eyes ran over the three sitting boys. "Looks like it's everyone but Clay."

"Yeah . . ." Tyler started, "dances aren't really his thing."

"So we've heard," Cai commented.

Wolf hummed contemplatively. He was lying back in his chair with one arm hanging over its side and the other carelessly placed on the table. "Dances aren't my thing either, but here I am."

Cairo looked at me and then at Wolf. "What are you saying?"

"I'm saying I think it's something deeper than that."

I raised my eyebrows. "I think people can decide whether or not to go to prom without it being deep. Ryan and I almost didn't."

"Sure," Wolf said. He turned to his friends. "But have you guys noticed he's acting a little stranger than usual? Yesterday he gave me his treasured record collection. He never used to let me even touch that thing."

Sid nodded slowly, pushing his glasses up his nose. "That is odd," he said. "You know, he gave me some of his photography books yesterday. Said I could keep them forever."

"Weird." Tyler frowned. "I hope he's okay."

Cairo gave me a look as if to say, Do you know anything about this?

My stomach twisted. I responded with a *How could I possibly?* stare. When the food came out, I glanced at my watch.

"Got somewhere to be?" Ryan asked with a raised eyebrow.

I picked up a fork. "I was just checking how long it's been since I last ate because I am starving."

I ate my food almost as fast as Wolf did, all the while keeping an eye on the time, and when I was finished, Cairo stood up and signaled for me to join her in the bathroom. Fifteen minutes before I had to go. I still had enough time to go to the bathroom and then snag Ryan on my way out.

Cairo went into a stall and I went to the mirror to adjust my hair and makeup. I frowned at the slipping clip in my hair, and as I attempted to fix it, my eyes drifted up from my hand to the large window high up in the corner of the bathroom.

It was large. Abnormally so. And it was open just wide enough for a person to slip through . . .

Cairo emerged from her stall, and I resumed fixing my hair until my clutch buzzed. It was a text from X.

> You ready?

>> I'm always ready.

Nine minutes. Time was moving fast—I had to move faster.

"Let's go," I said, grabbing Cai's elbow and reaching for the door handle. She briefly adjusted her waistcoat and followed me out the door just as a very familiar song started playing.

"Is this . . . ?" Cairo started.

I let go of her arm and started spinning on the spot, craning my neck as I tried to find a blond head doing the same. And then I spotted him from across the room—head turning this way and that, spinning around almost frantically until he spotted me and shook his head, grinning widely. I smiled.

When we met in the middle of the dance floor, I raised my eyebrows. "'Ask Me Anything'?" I asked in a slightly amused tone. "Really?"

"I swear it's not me. I thought it was you!"

"Huh," I said. "Well, fancy that. Your favorite song in the world playing at the prom."

I extended my hand, and he looked at it for a second before taking it. He placed his other hand on my waist.

"You know," I started, "if this song were in a movie, it would play right at the moment where everything crumbled. Either that or right afterward, when the character is all stuck in their sadness, wandering around the streets and looking out of rain-stained windows."

Ryan laughed and shook his head. "It doesn't have to be a sad moment. It could play in a beautiful one too."

I looked into his hazel eyes, so big and filled with light and warmth, and I immediately hated myself for what I was about to do. This was it, the end of us. And all because of what? Things I couldn't express and didn't know how to handle? I couldn't tell the difference between what I wanted and what I didn't; how could I when they were the same thing?

"Ask me anything," I said suddenly, unexpectedly.

His eyebrows knitted together but his smile remained. "What?"

"I'm giving you one chance to ask me anything. Anything at all."

"Anything?"

I nodded, looking deep into his eyes, knowing that just as I was disposed to maintain eye contact in uncomfortable situations, he was disposed to look away.

"Um . . ." He looked down. I knew what he wanted to ask me. We both did.

"You know what?" I interrupted. "Hold that thought. You can ask me later. For now, let's just dance."

I lifted my hands and rested them behind his neck, and as we swayed, I watched the blue and purple circles swirling all across the walls and the ceiling and across Ryan's hair and his shoulders, and then I felt that feeling.

The one I'd been running from lately by distracting myself with fun dares and thrilling adventures: suddenly inexplicable hopelessness. The feeling that I was not quite as much in control as I thought I was. I knew I could either stunt it with something bigger and louder the way I usually did, or I could let it take me once and for all. I was not one for surrendering to stillness; X had said it himself.

I was going to have to go with louder and bigger.

I lowered my head against Ryan's chest and let the lights and circles blur without a care. I always thought there was something tragically beautiful about clumped lashes and wet mascara.

When the song ended, I pulled away, keeping my eyes down as I checked the time. Two minutes left. "I gotta go," I said without thinking.

"What? Go where?"

I looked up. "Uh. To the bathroom."

Ryan suddenly looked concerned. "Loli? Are you crying?"

I ignored his question and wiped my eyes as I started heading for the bathroom.

"Hey, wait! Are you okay?"

I could hear him calling my name as he followed me, and I picked up the pace as I neared the bathroom door.

"Hey, Lo!"

I grabbed the handle just as he reached me, and he grabbed my other hand. "What's wrong?"

"Nothing," I said, avoiding his eyes. "I just need to use the bathroom."

He waited for a second, his hand still on mine, trying to figure out what to say, before he finally let go.

As soon as he did, I pushed the door open and let it close behind me without looking back.

CHAPTER

36

TRACK:

SHORT CHANGE HERO
The Heavy

The window in the bathroom situation was slightly more difficult than anticipated. First I had to wait for the bathroom to clear (which probably would've been impossible if it hadn't been for the throwback Rihanna song that started playing), and then it took me a minute to realize that my method (climbing on top of the toilet in the nearest stall and attempting to haul my body over the wall and onto the wall ledge) was nearly impossible without a partner.

When the coast was finally clear, I climbed onto the sink and used the dryer as a stepping block onto the windowsill, which I did with tremendous effort. I grabbed the window ledge, slid out of the crack, and then I lowered myself safely onto the ground outside. Thank goodness for basement ballrooms—mission-sneak-out-of-locked-down-school-event was accomplished, now all I had to do was make it to Clay on time.

I placed the coordinates X had sent for our meetup into my GPS (something I hadn't even known was a thing on the maps app) and as I pressed start on my six-minute journey I plugged my headphones in and tapped on "Short Change Hero."

The walk was short and grime-filled. I trudged down trash-filled alleyways and turned down smelly streets. The streetlights became fewer and fewer as I went on my way, and so did the number of people.

Ryan called three times and Cairo called twice. I ignored them all.

I couldn't let them talk me out of it. I'd decided the last communication I would have with them would be a final text message saying goodbye and how much they meant to me, which I would send as soon as Clay and I were on our way. Now, as my phone pinged incessantly, it was occurring to me that I'd also have to either block their numbers or get a whole new phone entirely.

The music pumped through my ears and my steps fell in time to the beat even as the GPS interrupted to tell me to go straight, over the bridge, and down the hill onto an unlit street.

"The destination is on your left," it announced. I looked left. That couldn't be right. Left was just an alley leading toward what looked like a bunch of large metal trash cans.

The song looped and I took a deep breath. "Here goes," I said, and I turned down the alley.

"You have arrived at your destination."

I stepped out onto the other side and took in my surroundings. I was at some sort of abandoned train station that was littered with large rusty containers and immobile carriages. There was no platform, no people, and no working trains, only raw and exposed train track.

I stepped out and walked slowly toward the tracks, looking up and down until I spotted him.

X.

He was sitting between two railcars with his legs hanging off the edge, smoking his perennial cigarette. A soft streetlight glowed far above him, surrounding him in a hazy brown light. He pulled out his cigarette and smiled.

"Don't tell me you dressed like this for me?" he said, standing up.

"Nope," I said. "This"—I spread my shimmering skirt, exposing my leg through the slit—"is my runaway outfit."

He puffed and took me in. "You look beautiful."

"Of course," I replied. "It's not an option to not look beautiful on this night, of all the Woolridge nights of the year."

"Huh," he said. His mouth twitched into a smile. "So you did go to the prom."

"Of course I went to the prom," I said. "I had to leave the perfect last image in people's minds before I disappeared forever." I looked around. "Why are we here?"

"I thought this would make a cool meeting place before we go. What do you think?"

I looked around and before I could respond he interrupted me. "Wait, no. Hold on." He picked a metal bar up from the ground. "I can make it better."

Clay crossed in front of me and walked toward the side door of the last container. He shoved the metal bar under one of the clamps and it made a loud metallic clank as the lever lowered. After he unhooked the next one, he grabbed the handles with both hands and attempted to slide the door open.

I watched as he struggled by himself, and then I stepped forward and helped him by grabbing the inside of the door itself and pushing it backward. We stepped back, breathing heavily and dusting our hands.

"You know," I said, "we're not in competition anymore. We're a team. If you need help, just ask."

"Thanks," he said, tossing the bar to the ground. "I'll try to remember that."

He hauled a blue backpack I hadn't noticed before into the wagon and climbed up, then reached a hand down for me.

I paused, slipped my heels off, and hitched my dress as high as it could go, before I took his hand and allowed him to hoist me up. I tossed my shoes to the back of the container and then settled right next to him, hanging my legs over the edge.

"So what's in the bag?" I asked, nodding toward his backpack.

X looked back and grabbed it. "Mostly cash," he answered, picking it up and unzipping it. "Some water, some snacks, an ID, clothes . . . the usual."

He put his bag aside and looked at my clutch. "What's in the purse? Looks roomy."

"Hey, don't come at me for my clutch," I said in defense. "What was I supposed to do? Go to prom with a duffel bag? Your family might not mind you sneaking around with a bag but mine would've gotten suspicious."

He puffed out a short and bitter laugh. "My family. It's easy to sneak around with a bag when there's no one there to catch you."

"No one?" I asked, looking at him. "On a Friday night?"

"Yep," he said. He leaned back on his arms and looked straight ahead. "My mother works really late shifts at the hospital and—I think I already told you about my brothers. One's working at college for the summer and the other one is at boarding school."

Clay pulled himself to his feet and walked farther into the container. He turned back to face me, holding an arm out toward me as he dug his other hand into his coat pocket. "Come here."

I eyed him, confused, but I stood up and followed him in anyway. He looked down at me, eyes focused and intense as if he was waiting for something and bracing himself for it.

"You know," I started, "you forgot to do something the day we met."

"The climactic kiss?" he asked, stepping forward. "I didn't forget. Just wanted it for later."

He gently brushed his fingers down my cheek toward my chin, which he propped up between his thumb and fingers. My breath caught as he raised his other hand and slid his fingers into my hair. I closed my eyes, holding my breath as I felt him lean down to kiss me—which is something he probably would've done if the train hadn't suddenly and violently lurched forward.

My body jerked in the opposite direction. I gasped as I lost my footing and swayed right, smacking hard into Clay's outspread arms. I could've fallen right to the ground had he not so narrowly caught me. I blinked rapidly, trying to regulate both my breathing and my thoughts. We were moving. How were we moving?

Clay lowered me gently to the ground as the container moved along the tracks. Just as I was wrapping my head around the sudden change in circumstances, I looked down at the dozens of things that had scattered from our bags. As I zeroed in on one specific object, horror unfurled its fingers and gripped my entire being.

"Robyn . . ." X began.

I kept my eyes trained on the object on the ground.

Something was crackling. Voices? Instruments? Music. My phone had started that song up again. I ignored it, carelessly and desperately backing away from where X stood so that I could reach a leg out toward the shining piece of metal that lay amongst his things. When I did, I dragged the object up along with me until I was flat against the wall—then, I grabbed it and pointed it at him, my heart beating wildly beneath my frantic breaths.

We'd said no more lies. He'd promised me that.

"Hey," he said, raising an arm. "Take it easy."

He took a step forward, and I instinctively moved toward my clutch, intending to grab my phone, but it had slid across the floor along with Clay's backpack, now emptied of IDs, phones, clothes, water bottles, and the loaded gun, which was now in my hands.

Before he could move another inch, I released the magazine, letting it fall to the ground, and then locked the slide open, the way I'd seen in the firearm safety video I'd studied the day after our heist. Real or fake, I hadn't liked feeling unprepared around a gun. I made sure I'd never feel that way again. Clay quirked an eyebrow in surprise. I kept my eyes on him and kicked the magazine out the door. I knew there was the possibility of a bullet still being in the chamber so I held onto the weapon carefully and with two arms.

"Take . . . it easy?" I repeated, keeping my voice even and guarded. "You promised to always tell me the truth, Clay. Where the hell are we going?"

"I don't know," he replied just as evenly. "Wherever the train takes us."

"Hm," I breathed. "You're full of surprises. I can't tell whether I like that or not."

"Clearly you do like it," he answered. "I'd be willing to bet it's one of the only reasons you're here."

"Maybe," I said, heart still racing. "You got me to come along, sure. But at the end of the day, if you're going to face the world with someone, if you're going to fight together, tooth and nail, you need to know for a fact that they've got your back. You need trust. And right now, I don't trust you."

"Oh?" he remarked. "Why's that?"

I snorted. "Because you're deceitful, Clay. And dishonest."

"How exactly have I been dishonest with you?"

I looked at him in disbelief. And because I didn't have the patience to launch into the obvious round of questions concerning the matter of how his North Face bag haul had conveniently missed an entire gun, I opted for another route.

"Why don't we start with you telling me how you knew who I was before we even met?"

Not for the first time since it happened, I pictured the ace of spades flapping in the frame of my mirror and my stunned reflection as I picked it off. I'd been turning the question over in my mind ever since. It was a significantly large part of the reason I was there at all.

Clay leaned against the far wall, crossing one leg in front of the other.

The wind flapped my hair around, completely messing up my prom-perfect waves, and I propped my right leg up for balance. I didn't let go of the gun.

"Now," he said, "isn't that a little hypocritical?"

"Hypocritical?" I croaked and my chest tightened as it hit me.

He knew. He knew that I'd known who he was before we met. How had he known? My head started spinning, and it didn't help that the train seemed to be going even faster. I wondered if it was safe for people to ride in these.

The corner of his mouth twitched. "You know, it wasn't even my fault that I found out, it was completely yours."

"My fault?" I asked.

"Yes," he replied. "Your grave, thoughtless mistake. Don't get me wrong, you're a mastermind—the best I know. But it probably isn't a great idea to wear a one-of-a-kind necklace to a masquerade."

My arms wobbled in front of me. I couldn't tell if it was because of the bumpy train tracks or my nerves.

My necklace. How had I not thought of that sooner? "How long have you known?" I asked.

He shrugged. "Not long at all. You'd think I would've spotted it at least once out of all the times we encountered each other, but no. It was that day you came to our table—about a week ago. Remember? You were all chatty and curious, which I thought was a bit odd, especially since all of it was directed at me. But like I said before, I didn't much care for Loli Crawford, so I got up with some excuse to leave, and as I did, I noticed something glint at your neck. I got the shock of my life when I saw it was the necklace."

I sniffed and lowered my arms, keeping a firm grip on the gun as I held it against my side.

"After that," Clay continued, "I couldn't stop thinking about you. And I couldn't help but replay that moment in my head; the unexpected drop by of your own volition when previously you looked like you'd rather be anywhere else but at our table. Your choice of seating—away from your friends who are practically glued to your hips at all times. And your inexplicable sudden interest in me—someone you hadn't cared to speak to before."

Somehow, while he had been speaking, he had managed to light a cigarette, and he was now drawing from it between phrases. I scrunched my face. It didn't matter that a whole side of the container was flung wide open—I hated cigarette smoke.

Clay blew out a plume of gray. "I don't know how you figured it out," he said. "And you don't have to tell me. But as soon as I realized you did, I was gone. Fallen into your web. How do you manage to do it?" he asked. "How are you always one step ahead of me?"

I stayed silent, watching him carefully. There was something about the way he spoke and the words he chose to say. If he thought I was always one step ahead of him, why did I feel as though he was always one step ahead of me?

Clay pushed off the wall and took a few slow, careful steps toward where I sat on the ground looking up at him. He stopped at my side and lowered a hand for me to grab. "I'm sorry," he said. "About the gun. Come on."

I froze, trying to decide what to do next, when the most surprising thing happened: the last thing in the world I ever would've expected. Someone called my name.

"Loli!"

It was coming from outside. I turned my head toward the blurry lights and the dark passing shapes.

"Lo?"

I was on my knees before I knew it, twisting and crawling forward.

"Ryan?" I called out. "Cai?"

I inched toward the edge of the container, and that's when I spotted them inching up the side of the train on a motorbike.

"Guys!" I yelled in disbelief. "What the hell are you doing?"

They sped forward until they had caught up with our carriage and were riding right alongside us.

"What are *you* doing?" Cairo shouted. She was wearing a helmet, but I knew it was her from her long arms and the way she arched over the handles to steer the bike. Ryan sat behind her, grabbing her waist.

"Go home!" I shouted, cupping my hands around my mouth. "Turn around!"

I couldn't see how this could possibly end well. What did they expect? The train wasn't going to stop, and I sure as hell wasn't about to jump off a moving train and plummet to my death on prom night.

Ryan signaled toward the train with his arm, and Cairo's bike leaned closer to the tracks. Dangerously close.

"Stop!" I shouted. "Guys! Stop. It's not safe!"

Cairo didn't listen. She inched closer and closer, and I watched as Ryan moved his right leg around to the same side as his left, still holding onto Cairo, and then he raised himself up from his seat in a way that I'd only seen done in James Bond movies. He reached a shaky arm out toward the train and I yelped.

"Ryan!" I screamed. "Stop!"

He leaned forward and grabbed onto the handle. As he did, Cairo lagged slightly, causing him to wobble midair.

"Stop! Please!"

It was too late. Ryan wobbled and jumped off the bike, his lower half falling dangerously against the side of the train. Then he inched right and threw himself inside onto the hard floor.

I watched him in shock and fell toward him, placing the gun beside us. "Ry? Ryan? Are you okay?"

He winced, holding onto his side. "I'll be okay," he said, wheezing. "That's not the biggest issue right now." He sat up slowly and leaned against the wall. "What the hell is going on, Lo? What are you doing?"

I looked back at Clay, who was watching us silently, and then turned to Ryan. "We were going away," I said.

"Where to?" he asked. "And why didn't you tell me?"

"Because." I replied. "We weren't planning on coming back."

I heard the violins swell from my phone's speaker as Ryan sat up and stared at me. I hated that look. It was the same one he'd given me at Babble.

"You were going to leave me?" he asked. "Without saying goodbye?"

"I—" The one time I needed to say something, and I couldn't find anything to say.

"And with this guy?" he asked, motioning toward Clay. "Loli . . . you can't do this."

"Well, I am," I said, glancing at Clay. "We are."

"You don't understand. He's—"

Suddenly, Ryan's eyes grew wide. He lunged at Clay so quickly, I barely registered what was happening. I rolled aside and looked back in bewilderment as he tackled Clay to the ground and pressed a knee into his chest.

"Do you see this?" Ryan asked, turning around with the gun

in his hand. "He just picked this up from the ground behind you. He's dangerous, Lo."

Clay groaned. "You two are so dramatic. Can I sit up?"

"No," Ryan said. "I don't trust you."

Clay stared at Ryan, and Ryan stared right back.

"Okay," I said. "Maybe you can get off him and give me the gun?"

"I'm not getting off him," Ryan said. "If you'd heard some of the stories Wolf told us about this guy, you wouldn't either."

Clay scoffed. "Like you two don't have stories that would be equally as shocking."

"Not like yours, man. Nothing we've ever done has gotten anyone hurt."

"Guys!" The train rocked me steadily as I tried to stand up. "Let's just relax and put the—"

There was a flurry of movement, and suddenly Clay was on his knees wrestling Ryan for the gun. He twisted Ryan's arm around, and Ryan immediately let go. He knew better than to fight over a firearm.

Clay stretched his neck and rolled his shoulders, raising an arm in Ryan's direction. "Back off," he commanded. Ryan backed away from him with his hands up and Clay pointed the gun at him.

"Clay . . ." I said, slowly.

He kept his eyes fixed on Ryan, and despite the jolting movement of the train and the frantic flapping of the wing of his jacket, his arm remained steady.

"If you try to take my gun again," he started, "I will get it back again. And I swear I will shoot you."

I stepped forward, anger coursing through my body. "Don't threaten him."

"Okay," Ryan said, holding his hands higher. "Okay, that's fine. You don't have to worry about us taking your gun—we're leaving."

"Leaving?" I asked. "Leaving how? By jumping out of a moving train?"

Clay lowered his gun as Ryan reached my side. He clicked it and shoved it into a holster before putting it back in his backpack.

Ryan dropped his arms and turned his attention to the blurred moving screen on his left, as if he'd only just noticed it. "Well then," he said, tucking his hands into his pockets. "I guess I'm traveling with you."

"Great." Clay smiled sarcastically. "The more the merrier."

The atmosphere in the carriage shifted from one of danger to one of wariness. I didn't feel safe knowing Clay had the gun, even if it was temporarily out of sight.

"So . . ." Ryan began, tentatively. "Where the hell is this thing headed anyway?"

"We don't know," I said.

He snorted and threw his hands up. "Of course you don't. Typical."

Somehow, despite the circumstances, I was able to laugh. It was only a short, brief puff of air, but it was a laugh just the same. Ryan turned to look at me, and I half expected him to laugh too, but he only narrowed his eyes. He straightened his back and my smile disintegrated as he sternly and wordlessly walked toward me.

I blinked. Was he mad? Of course he was mad. There was no way he wasn't. I had promised him forever a million times and then broken it at the first sign of turbulence.

"Ryan," I started. "I—"

"Shh."

I looked at him and realized he wasn't staring at me, he was staring behind me.

"What?" I asked. I followed his eyes to the wide black square behind us and rested my own eyes upon a tall, familiar monument with flashing red, white, and blue lights.

"Dam," he whispered. I nodded. I knew exactly where we were—just a couple miles out of Woolridge, directly right over Melrose Dam.

"We don't have time to think about it," he whispered. "Yes or no?"

I glanced behind him and watched Clay scratch around the scattered things on the floor, trying to find the singing phone, and then I looked back at Ryan, heart racing. "Yes," I said, grabbing his hand. It was ride or die after all, wasn't it?

He stepped forward so that he was next to me. We didn't allow ourselves time to think twice about what we were doing.

"One," I whispered.

"Two . . ." he said.

And we leapt.

CHAPTER 37

TRACK:

TAKE MY TIME

Skinshape

I had thought the car incident was impressive, but that was because I'd never jumped out of a moving train. The feeling was horrific. My stomach lurched as we hurtled through the air, and my arms and legs scrambled for something to stand on, grip or hold onto, but they found nothing. Everything was black. I couldn't tell whether the dark expanse beneath us was water or land, and it made the chances of us living or dying pretty much equal in my mind. Hitting the water came as an unexpected but pleasant surprise, and the force of our fall pulled us deep, fast.

I pushed against the water with my arms and legs, pulling it all back hard and fast so I could find the surface again. When I did, I took several deep, gulping breaths before realizing I wasn't holding Ryan's hand anymore.

I splashed frantically, twisting and turning. "Ryan!"

Silence.

"Ryan!" I screamed again, panicked.

A tsunami-sized splash of water hit me from behind.

"Wow!" Ryan coughed and sputtered. "I can't believe we just did that."

I paddled toward him, and we floated for a while, lying in the water and drifting onto our backs as we caught our breaths and registered the fact that we were still alive. When we had and we were sure, we turned around and swam to shore, following the direction of the flashing lights above.

When we reached dry land, Ryan called Cairo, and I thanked God a million times for his waterproof phone.

Cai pulled up about fifteen minutes later (sans motorbike and in Ryan's car, thank goodness) with Wolf and Tyler in tow.

"Geez," she said, rolling the window down. An easy, lax song played on the radio—totally a different vibe from ours. "You two look like you've had a night."

"We have," Ryan said. He opened his trunk and pulled two beach towels out, then chucked one at me before slamming the trunk closed.

Once we'd assured the three of them that we were all right, Wolf told us about a post-prom bonfire at Waban. A warm fire sounded luxurious, after my impromptu swim. The one thing that could make it better was takeout from Dizzy's.

"Isn't Dizzy's closing round about now?" Tyler asked, when I voiced my thoughts.

"Oh, don't worry," I said. "Eugene always sneaks us in for drinks and curly fries when they're closing up."

"That's because when we get there you bat your eyes at him and laugh at all his jokes," Cairo said, flashing me a wry smile in the rearview mirror.

Ryan made a sound that sounded like a cough. "Pretty privilege. Told you."

I looked over at him. He had his head wrapped up like a babushka doll, and his knees pressed up against the driver's seat. There was so much I wanted to say but couldn't.

Everything with X had happened in a dizzying whirlwind. I felt like I had only just come up for air. Like I'd only taken the chance to survey my surroundings with clarity when I came up out of the water.

X and the train simultaneously felt so close and far away. "Hey," I said, burying my thoughts for later. "I'm a Black girl. I'll take whatever privilege I can get."

CHAPTER

38

TRACK:

LOLITA

Lana Del Rey

As predicted, Eugene welcomed us in with wide arms, supplying us with drinks, a box of large fries, mozzarella sticks, and chicken tenders—all of which we ate on Ryan's car in the Waban Trail parking lot.

We lay the food on the hood and ate, surrounding our makeshift picnic: Wolf and Cairo stood on either side of the car, Tyler right at the nose, and Ryan and I sat on top, just beneath the windshield with our legs folded so we didn't kick all the food off.

In the distance, we could hear the faint sound of music and sporadic shouts of people enjoying themselves. I smiled, knowing Raycher had probably brought his paintball guns and set one especially aside for me. I took a long sip from my to-go Shirley Temple and watched Cairo split the last mozzarella stick with Wolf, who had been eyeing it even as he chewed on one of his own.

"Okay, pack," Wolf said, tossing the last piece into his already stuffed mouth. "You guys ready?"

I looked at Ryan. Ryan looked at me. We'd never had our talk in the end, and after the events of tonight, there was a lot I needed to say. "I think Ryan and I are going to hang back," I said. "We need to talk."

Wolf's eyes lingered on Ryan. "Okay," he said. "And you two?" He turned to Tyler and Cairo.

Cairo clapped her hands together and pushed off the car. "Heck yeah! Let's go."

The two boys started for the forest; Wolf turned back to give us a sloppy salute, Tyler a little half wave. Cairo waited for them to disappear and then faced us. "Hey," she said, looking at me. "I'm glad you're okay."

"Thanks," I said, looking at the ground. "I—" The words *I'm sorry* hovered somewhere in the back of my throat. Cairo reached out a long arm, softly touching my shoulder, and I looked up to see her smiling.

"I know," she said, as if reading my mind. "Don't worry about it."

I smiled, grateful to have someone who both loved me and knew me so well. I promised myself I'd give her a real apology another day when I had enough energy and wasn't so fresh from a near-death experience.

Cairo dropped her hand and backed away, slowly. "If you guys decide to leave, don't worry about us," she said. "We'll catch a ride with Raycher or Sullivan." And then she ran off after Wolf and Tyler, disappearing behind the leaves.

When she left, I stole a secret side-glance at Ryan. He was as still as a statue.

"Did . . . did Wolf just call us his pack?" he asked, staring at the space where they had all disappeared.

"I think he did." I laughed nervously.

"Wow," Ryan said, stunned. "I thought he hated my jokes. Turns out they've just gone straight to his head."

I snorted, picking the greasy food boxes off the hood and placing them in the big Dizzy paper bag. Neither of us said a word, and there was no music as the wind stirred the trees. It was quiet. I let my legs hang off the nose of his car, swinging them gently as I gathered my strength.

"Ryan," I started tentatively, "I'm sorry about tonight."

He didn't say anything. Just looked down at his hands.

"Are you . . . are you mad at me?"

He looked up from his hands and gazed at something far off in the distance. "I don't know," he said, breathing out. "The events of tonight haven't really . . . sunk in." The wind blew, and there was a popping sound in the distance. "Were you really going to run away? Like, forever?"

I thought about it for a while. Why lie? "Yes," I admitted. "I was."

Ryan nodded slowly. "Right."

He turned his head completely away from me, and I opened my mouth to try to explain. But how could I possibly explain what was going on in my head when I couldn't even put it into words for myself? "Look," I said, "it's complicated."

"It's not that complicated," he replied. "You were going to leave without telling me." I could see only the smallest sliver of his face. "After everything we've been through. After all the stuff you just put me through."

"Ry—it's not like that . . ."

"Well then what else could it be like?" he asked, and finally, finally he turned to face me. "Because it sounds to me like you got bored of playing it safe and jumped up at the first sign of real danger." He shook his head. "Why am I surprised? It's what you do. You always want more, and you drop everything you already have to get it. Only this time it was us you dropped. The people who love you the most in life."

I watched him as he spoke and my heart broke. "Is that who you think I am?" I asked, but of course it was. What else had I given him to go on?

Ryan shrugged. "You saw something better and didn't even blink an eye before leaving us in the dust."

"No," I said adamantly. "No. I didn't want to leave, Ryan. I left because I thought I had to."

"Yeah, right," Ryan scoffed. "You expect me to believe Clay forced you? When have you ever done anything you didn't want to do? Ever?"

"No," I said. "No, Clay didn't force me. It was all me."

"So . . ." Ryan drifted off. "So what?" His eyes searched mine.

"So . . ." I said. I hadn't realized I was holding onto his arm. "I missed you."

A warmth found its way to my nose, behind my eyes, and before I knew it, everything I'd been holding back for so long finally came spilling out.

"You were only gone for one week, but I missed you more than I thought possible to ever miss someone. And I always thought I was strong and that I didn't need anyone, and that's probably what it looks like to everyone but it's all a lie because all these years there's been you propping me up. Over hedges, onto ladders, into trees, and in life really. I help you, you help me, we move together without talking or even thinking about it—there's no Loli without Ryan. And I've always known that—well, I always thought that . . ." I trailed off.

"Thought what?" Ryan asked.

"I always thought . . . no, I always *knew* what would happen one day, but that one day was always so far in the future, and I thought it was obvious and that it didn't need to be discussed because we both knew, but I think I also didn't want it to be true because I mean come on, it's so cliché, Ryan, it's the cliché of all clichés! And there's nothing I hate more than clichés. But not getting your stupid song recommendations? And your texts? Not being able to see your face, touch your hair or tell you that I was frightened to death of going into the abandoned house, not getting your reassuring smile or hug, or being able to turn around and give you the sign that everything was all right—it all made me realize that you're my summer's day, my partner in crime and it's the most predictable cliché thing in the world but I love you, Ryan. I always have. I always will."

I blinked and let the tears fall down my cheek, thanking God for waterproof mascara.

Ryan blinked rapidly, and even though his perfect prom 'do had become completely disheveled and fallen into his eyes I knew his eyebrows were knitted in the way he did when he was worried or concerned.

He swallowed and I sniffed. "It's like you said before." I wiped my eyes and laughed. "I should just . . . grow u—"

I'd kissed a lot of people before I kissed Ryan Pope, both the first and second time, but I'd never been kissed the way he kissed me right then and there on the hood of his brand-new car. I'd always imagined that kissing him would be sweet and timid, and meant to be, not like the unpredictable risky stint in his room or the wild pioneering that happened that night. He grabbed me by the waist, pulled me close and then he kissed me like our lives depended on it. No one's ever kissed me like that before—no one's ever been able to take charge, flip the balance of power.

But then, I guess Ryan had always been able to do that.

When we pulled apart, we looked at each other, and then Ryan leaned back and screamed out over the trees: "This is the best night of my life!"

"Shut up," I hissed, kicking him gently with my foot, and then I leaned in to kiss him again.

We decided not to join the rest of the group at the bonfire, opting for a much-needed walk and talk through the park instead. I didn't care that the slit in my dress had ripped dangerously high or that I was completely barefoot. The night was warm, and it felt nice to be able to hold Ryan's hand after I'd told myself never to do it again in the first grade.

I looked up at the trees and Ryan laughed to himself. "I can't believe," he started, "that an hour ago you were planning to run away, never to return, just because you didn't want to admit that you liked me."

I pulled a face that I realized he couldn't see and crossed my free arm over my waist.

"Of all the things you've done," he continued, "if anyone ever asks how dramatic you are, I think I'll start with that."

"Whatever," I said, looking carelessly over my shoulder. "The past is in the past, no need to harp on it."

"Yeah, sure." Ryan grinned and swung our hands as we walked

along the path. I watched our shadows dance before us in the passing light, and I remembered there was something else I had to put right. "Hey, um. Ry?"

"Yeah?"

"I'm sorry for that stupid thing I said during our fight. About you being confused about liking girls or boys. I was ignorant and angry, and I have since done my research on all things ace."

"'Ace'?" Ryan repeated, sounding surprised. "Look at you using the lingo."

"I'm serious. Quiz me."

Ryan looked at me and then up at the sky. "Let's see. Do you know the difference between being aromantic and asexual?"

"Oh please, I know about primary and secondary attraction, I know about gray asexuality and being demi . . ."

"Which is where I lie. Somewhere on that gray scale."

"Thought so."

"Yeah. No primary attraction at all. I've never had a celebrity crush, never understood the use of those pinup posters—do you know how many locker room conversations I've had to fake?"

"All of them I imagine."

"Well," he closed sheepishly. "Not all. There is . . . the secondary."

A gentle warm breeze cut through the trees. I leaned in closer into his side, clutching his arm with my free hand. "You ever wondered whether dating would ruin our friendship?" I asked, after a while. "I mean. What happens if we break up?"

Ryan scoffed. "Our friendship," he began, "is the most dangerously doomed friendship to ever exist. It's always been ruined, what difference would it make whether we're dating or not?"

I snickered. "This is what Clay was talking about when he called you dramatic."

For the first time since the game began, the thought of X—Clay—didn't make my heart race. In fact, I didn't feel anything but grateful that I wasn't still on that train.

"I think you're conveniently forgetting that he called us both dramatic," Ryan said. "Besides, if anything terrible broke us apart, I think our families would eventually force us back together. Do you really think our mothers would care to cancel dinner parties or make other arrangements for Christmas if we weren't talking anymore? We'd end up fixing things somehow."

I laughed. No truer words were ever spoken. "Hey, speaking of Clay . . ." I trailed off. We'd talked a lot so far, but we hadn't actually addressed the situation on the train as something real that had happened.

"What about him," Ryan said in a flat voice.

"Well, I was wondering . . . not so much about him but about the entire situation. Like for starters, how on earth did you find me in that train? I never said where I was going—and we were moving at, like, a hundred miles per hour."

Ryan took a deep breath in. "Well," he began, "soon after you left, Wolf told us he'd received an odd goodbye text from Clay. And when you didn't come out of the bathroom, we figured you two might be doing something together because what could possibly pull you away from a good time at a big event? Especially when you looked that good and had a line of guys waiting to dance with you—"

"A line of guys?" I asked, interrupting. "What line of guys?"

Ryan rolled his eyes. "Don't play dumb, Lo. There was Richard and Wolf, for starters."

"Wolf?" I asked, raising my eyebrows.

Ryan stopped walking. "You're detracting from my story," he said.

"Sorry. Continue."

"Anyway," Ryan said, starting his stroll again, "I remembered you still had your location on from the night you met Clay—"

"And how did you know that?" I asked, astonished.

Ryan cleared his throat, and I just knew that if it were brighter, I would've seen that his face was red. "You were keeping track of me?"

"Uh, well." He paused. "A little more than that. I followed you."

I stopped in my tracks, suddenly remembering that fleeting familiar scent in the first room upstairs. "Ryan Alexander Pope," I said with a growing smile. "I thought I smelled a rat!"

"I drove up to the house with my lights off at around the time I knew you'd be meeting, and when I saw you crawl into the house, I just went in after you. I didn't want to scare you, so I kept my distance. I climbed up the stairs when you made your way round the house, and then you followed right after, so I had to hide in that dusty old closet."

"Wow," I said, completely stunned. I shook my head and kept walking.

"Anyway," Ryan said. "Moving on. We left the prom—which was a feat in itself, honestly. They should make a movie out of the stunts we had to pull—and since Cairo's house was closer, we stopped there and got Kyle's bike. Imagine our shock when your location dot started moving faster as we got closer."

I smiled. "So naturally, you chased after it," I concluded. I couldn't help but beam. I loved my friends.

"Hold on," Ryan said, stopping to pull out his phone. "Phew. It's just a text from Cai. She says not to worry and that they found a ride home."

I looked back at the way we had walked. "We should probably do the same. I'm not trying to get your parents mad. Again."

"Good point," Ryan agreed.

We walked back to the car, and when we reached it Ryan walked around to the passenger side.

"You don't want to drive?" I asked, in disbelief.

"Look," Ryan said, dropping his hands to his sides. "I'm tired. I've just had the wildest night of my life. I can't tell what's real and what's not anymore . . ."

"Okay . . ." I said, walking around to the driver's side. I stopped before I got in, realizing that I'd left my clutch and my phone on the train. Of course, I had left X too, but I didn't really care about that. He was just a fun story I could tell people one day, and that was pretty much it.

"Hurry, Lo. I literally think I'm about to pass out."

I got into the car and backed out of the parking lot, pulling out onto the road. In the distance I could see the green shine of a traffic light, and I prayed for it to stay green as I headed toward it—Ryan was right. It had been a long day.

"You know," Ryan said, fiddling with his phone. "I found this song—hey! Don't groan. I found this song and it's just . . . perfect for you. It has these early demos that are really good too, and I couldn't help but think that if your life were a movie, this song would be your theme. Your movie would one hundred percent begin and end with it playing."

I glanced down at the title of the song just out of curiosity and groaned even louder as I read its name. "I hate it," I said. "I haven't even heard it, but I hate it already."

"Just listen," Ryan commanded.

We neared the traffic light just as it turned red, and I looked over at Ryan, a smile taking over my face as he pressed play. "Dare me to floor it all the way home?" I asked.

Ryan glanced over his shoulder and then leaned back in his seat, sighing as he propped his legs up on the dashboard. "Floor it," came his reply.

I looked at him, slightly surprised, and he just shrugged. "You know the consequences of your actions just as well as I do. If it heals you, if it helps you get over the past few weeks, I say go for it."

I turned my attention back to the road, barely able to contain my smile as I touched the pendant hanging at my neck.

Stupid of him to even ask. The answer was and always would be yes.

I revved the engine, glanced up and down the street, and as the violins wound down, I hit the pedal as hard as I could.

ACKNOWLEDGMENTS

It's surreal to be at the other end of writing this story. For years I've had Loli, Ryan, Cairo and X scattered in fragments across laptops and notebooks with varying names (Lola? Lolly? Lawley?), and it's so gratifying to finally have a finished product for other people to enjoy as well.

I'd always wanted a fun, teen-flick with a Black girl protagonist growing up. There weren't many movies, television shows, or young adult novels centered around characters of color at the time, and there were even fewer stories about Black girls just being girls and going on adventures and falling in love. I'm so glad that today's movie posters, streaming platforms and bookstore shelves look different and that I can be a small part of that change.

First, I'd like to thank my agent, Lauren Bieker, who has steadily encouraged me for years and whose continued faith in my writing propels me through uncertainty.

My wonderful editor, Alexa Wejko, who immediately understood both Loli and this book in a way not many people have, and challenged me with bright and brilliant ideas that brought the finer notes in this story out to full taste.

The entire team at Soho Teen, whose passion-filled work is so abundantly apparent in this book. From creative ideas for how best to integrate the playlist to wonderful artistic direction for the interior of the book—*Ride or Die* would not be the book it is today without your innovative minds.

My dear friends Kelly Young, Katie Pedersen and Lesego

Mtsolongo, who were fans of this story from the first manuscript and encouraged me every step of the way.

My parents, Gail and Tendai Musikavanhu, who have selflessly equipped me with everything I've ever needed, from Bryanston Pre-Primary to the publishing of this book. You have always encouraged me to follow God's calling and do what I love in life and supported me in getting there.

My sister, Michal, who knows everything about my characters before anyone else, and indulges me by talking about them like they're real people. My real-life ride or die; I wrote this book for me and then I wrote it for you.

Hannah Garrison, Mutsa Danha, Vimal Vallabh, Elizabeth Serunjogi and Cole Krasner, who continuously encourage me in my writing journey.

And of course, I'd like to thank the Lord for everything, every-thing, everything.

Mwari akanaka.